DIXIE WASN'T READY TO HAVE HIM GO

She touched his shoulder and reached to kiss him good-bye. It wasn't much for a man who'd risked his life to protect her property.

She aimed for his cheek. He turned and her mouth met his lips, cool as the marble on her pantry shelf. But as her lips caressed his, she knew only warmth and softness. He tasted of night and spice and excitement. Her mouth opened as his pressed on hers, but slowly, like a plant unfolding in spring warmth. Almost reluctantly, his hand smoothed up her neck and through her hair. She sighed and her tongue reached for his.

The heat of summer burst through her. She gasped, but not for breath; for more. And he gave it. Sweetness flooded her soul and need surged like a current through her brain. It was a mating of mouths, a coupling of spirits. Time stopped. Dixie knew nothing but spiraling warmth and an aching need for more.

Also by Rosemary Laurey

LOVE ME FOREVER
BE MINE FOREVER
KEEP ME FOREVER
MIDNIGHT LOVER

Rosemary is also featured in these anthologies

IMMORTAL BAD BOYS
TEXAS BAD BOYS
THE MORGUE THE MERRIER

Published by Kensington Publishing Corporation

KISS ME FOREVER

ROSEMARY LAUREY

ZEBRA BOOKS
KENSINGTON PUBLISHING CORP.
http://www.kensingtonbooks.com

ZEBRA BOOKS are published by

Kensington Publishing Corp.
119 West 40th Street
New York, NY 10018

All Kensington titles, imprints, and distributed lines are available at special quantity discounts for bulk purchases for sales promotion, premiums, fund-raising, educational, or institutional use.

Special book excerpts or customized printings can also be created to fit specific needs. For details, write or phone the office of the Kensington Special Sales Manager: Attn.: Special Sales Department. Kensington Publishing Corp., 119 West 40th Street, New York, NY 10018. Phone: 1-800-221-2647.

Zebra and the Z logo Reg. U.S. Pat. & TM Off.

ISBN-13: 978-1-4201-1495-9
ISBN-10: 1-4201-1495-6

First Printing: May 2010

10 9 8 7 6 5 4 3 2

Printed in the United States of America

For Sister Elizabeth Fitzgerald,
who many years ago piqued my imagination about
what happened in the Inn at Deptford.

Prologue

"You want me to give her an unwelcome?"

Sebastian Caughleigh almost smiled. His nephew caught on quickly. "We'll call it a . . . discouragement." With that laugh, James had definite possibilities.

"I can take care of one old lady."

"This is the granddaughter. The daughter died years ago and it seems the Misses Underwood's sister snuffed it a few weeks before old Miss Faith. This Dixie LePage is thirty and conveniently sent me her picture."

James peered at the photo on the desktop. An auburn-haired young woman with green eyes smiled at the camera. "Nice," James murmured. "Do I get to choose the inconvenience?"

"No! She's arriving on the twelfth and obligingly gave us the flight number. You find her at Gatwick. Lift her wallet. Without money or credit cards, she won't get far. With a bit of luck she'll run home in distress. A fainting female who can't take inconvenience."

A glint of appreciation lit James's pale eyes as he smiled

at the photograph. "Maybe I won't lift her wallet—first thing."

"You will. It's survival. For all of us. We can't have her poking around the house and finding stuff the Sunday supplements would kill for."

"What if losing a wallet doesn't delay her?"

"How far can she get without passport or money? She'll be stranded and run home—where she should have stayed. The damn woman could have had nice regular checks and no hassle, but she just had to come and see a 'real, quaint English village.'" Sebastian snorted. "I'll give her quaint."

James chuckled. "The wallet should work. Nice idea, Uncle. I salute you."

"It was Emily's. She lost her wallet and passport in Madeira last year and she's still talking about it."

A smirk played on James's pale lips. "Always knew you were attracted to the woman for her mind." He nodded. "I'm off then, Uncle. Got to work out the details of my 'welcome.'"

Sebastian frowned at the closed door. He hadn't told his nephew the half. If this wretched woman arrived and insisted on claiming her property, they'd have problems beyond measure. Once she was in the house . . . Sebastian pushed his chair from his desk. She couldn't get that far. James's little diversion had to work. If not, they'd have to get awkward, maybe even nasty. Others stood to lose along with him. Maybe it was time to call in favors.

Chapter One

Dixie LePage prayed for patience. A train strike! Just her luck! And all because she'd listened to her travel agent, who insisted the train was the best way to travel in England. "Fast, easy, and none of the problems of driving on the wrong side of the road." She'd tossed over a paying job and flown across the Atlantic on the strength of two letters and a phone call only to find herself stranded. She'd come out of curiosity, the promise of a sudden inheritance, and the prospect of being on a different continent from the man who'd made a fool of her, and was now stuck.

Dixie's plan B: to hire a car and drive the thirty or so miles, might have worked. But half the population of Southern England beat her to it. Her attempts to call Mr. Caughleigh, the lawyer, didn't go too well either. She lacked the necessary small change or a phone card. Resisting the temptation to smash the receiver into the wall, she muttered heavenward.

"Having trouble?" a smooth, very proper British voice asked.

Dixie turned and stared at the bluest eyes she'd seen since her ex-fiancé. "It's these stupid phones. There are no proper instructions!" This was unfair, she knew. Directions came in half-a-dozen languages.

"Oh!" Blue Eyes laughed. "American, are you?" What was so amusing about that? "Use your credit card. You do have one, don't you?" His long arm reached too close beside her and a manicured finger pointed at familiar logos. If she hadn't been so wound up, she'd have noticed them herself.

Mr. Caughleigh, or "Corly" as the secretary said it, wasn't in. "He'll be in about nine-thirty. I'll tell him you called, Miss LePage." So much for thinking he could help her.

"Need a ride?"

Blue eyes had lurked while she called. "No, thank you."

"I'm driving into Surrey, perhaps I could drop you somewhere?"

She remembered Gran's warnings about white slavers hovering around train stations. Airports made a good modern equivalent. "Thank you, I'm fine." She made to walk away.

"Don't trust me?" The idea seemed to amuse him.

"No." She'd never again trust a Norse god with moussed hair, a plastic smile and shallow blue eyes. She'd learned that much.

The smiling clerk at Travelers' Aid suggested she take a coach to a place with the improbable name of "Leatherhead," a short distance, he claimed, from Bringham. Dixie's image of something out of a Regency romance didn't last long. The coach proved to be nothing more exotic than a long distance bus. The so-called "express" bus made a dozen stops in a couple of hours. Dixie vowed to walk next time. Shoot, there wouldn't be a next time. She should have taken the lawyer's advice and let him sell the house and send her the proceeds. She settled back in the surprisingly comfortable seat and shut her eyes. Time to catch up on lost sleep.

"I'm sorry but I think you're in my seat." Dixie blinked. The reincarnation of Miss Marple half-smiled at her.

Dixie's neighbor settled with a flurry of packages and a gracious smile and chatted for the next hour. Or rather nattered on while Dixie listened to details of Miss Marple's married son, his wife's taste in kitchen decor and her grandsons' success in football. Dixie knew enough to know she meant soccer, however she did learn that Leatherhead was one word.

"Here's your stop, the same as mine," her neighbor announced and Dixie found herself and her suitcases on the sidewalk.

"Someone picking you up?" her companion asked.

"I thought I could get a taxi." Truth was, she hadn't thought beyond the bus ride and had no idea how far she still had to go. "I'm going to Bringham."

"Bring'em," she said and Dixie made a mental note to remember to swallow the 'h' like everyone else. She held out a wrinkled but surprisingly strong hand. "I'm Ida Collins. My son will give you a lift. He lives near Bringham. Stanley," she said to the man who'd appeared on the sidewalk with a young boy. "This young lady needs a ride to Bringham. No sense in her wasting money on a taxi."

Stanley took this in his stride. Maybe his mother foisted strangers on him all the time. "If it's not too much trouble. . . ." Dixie began. She figured she'd be safe. Rogues and abductors wouldn't have a small boy trailing behind them.

Stanley grinned. "Nah. We live in East Horsley, it's on the way."

"I've got luggage."

"We've plenty of space. I brought the Rolls. Mum likes it."

Stanley, with his blue jeans and zippered windbreaker didn't quite fit the Rolls-Royce image, but the coach hadn't matched her imagination either. "Thanks, I'm really grateful. My name's Dixie LePage." She held out her hand.

He took it. "How do you do? Stanley Collins. You've met my mum, Ida, and here's Joey."

Dixie smiled at a small boy, complete with freckles, Dallas Cowboys' sweatshirt, and a Chicago Bulls' cap. "Hello," he said through a wad of chewing gum.

Settled on the butter-soft leather upholstery, Dixie appreciated why Ida liked the Rolls. "Beautiful car," Dixie said, eying the rosewood dashboard and the soft carpet.

She'd said the right thing. Stanley beamed. "Best one we have. We keep it for weddings mostly—and picking up Mum," he added with a chuckle.

Dixie's jet-lagged mind clicked. "You rent it out?"

"Right you are! Collins Car Hire. That's me. If you ever need a car . . ."

"I do. Like now. You have regular cars?" She leaned over the high seat back, wide awake at the prospect of transportation.

Stanley grinned. "What's a regular car? I've a nice little Metro on the lot and a Fiesta due back in Saturday."

"I'll take whatever you have today." Dixie would have handed over her plastic money there and then.

Stanley chuckled. "You Americans make up your minds quickly."

"I made up my mind hours ago. The airport rental companies couldn't deliver."

Stanley grinned. "Cheers then! Let me drop Mum and I'll take you down to the shop."

The Metro turned out to be a small, red car—stick shift, but Dixie could handle that.

Stanley called Joey over to look at her license. South Carolina driver's licenses were an obvious novelty here. For her address, she gave the one Mr. Caughleigh had written, Orchard House, Bringham. "That's all I have. No street or number I'm afraid."

Stanley's eyebrows almost disappeared under his hair.

"You're living at Orchard House? You bought it or renting or something?"

"I've inherited it. It was my great-aunts'."

"Sheesh!" Stanley muttered between tight lips, his eyes not quite meeting hers. "You're an Underwood?" He made Underwoods sound like roaches.

"My grandmother was. She died just before Faith Underwood."

Stanley Collins sucked in his cheeks and looked Dixie up and down like a secondhand car of doubtful provenance. "I heard there was another sister who ran off with an American during the war."

Gran would laugh at that one. She and Charlie Reilly were married in the Grosvenor Chapel with his commanding officer's blessing, even if Gran's sisters had boycotted the ceremony. "That was my Gran."

Stanley rubbed at an invisible mark on the car hood. "Mentioned this to Mum, did you?"

"It never came up. Did she know my aunts?"

Stanley shrugged and looked away, intent on aligning the windshield wiper blades. "Everyone knew them. Interesting old ladies but you'd know that."

Dixie shook her head. "Never met them. And Gran never came back here after she married either."

He looked straight at her for twenty long seconds. "Good luck to you then. Now how long would you be wanting the car?"

They agreed on two weeks, or what Stanley called a *fortnight* and Dixie drove off with directions to Bringham scribbled on the back of an old envelope. She wondered about Stanley's words as she maneuvered the narrow lanes, remembering, most of the time, to stay on the left. A black sports car passed with about two inches to spare. Dixie gasped. Had renting a car been such a good idea with drivers like that on narrow roads?

Stanley's directions got her to Bringham in fifteen minutes. It took longer than that to find a parking place. The packed High Street stretched for fifty yards, a snarled mass of cars, pedestrians and baby carriages. At one point, it was blocked by a baker's van. Dixie looked around as she waited, fascinated by the narrow street and the old buildings. A wool shop and its neighboring florist had bow windows and paneled doors that hinted of hooped petticoats and reticules. On the opposite side of the street, a modern grocery store sat next to a Tudor tea shop. Definitely a street to explore on foot.

She parked in an impossibly narrow space in a crowded "car park" hidden behind the grocery store. Actually getting out of the car involved gymnastic feats, and she eased herself sideways between her car and the large BMW beside her.

Mr. Caughleigh's address was *Mayburn House, 29 High Street*. That shouldn't be too hard to find. A narrow alley led from the car park to High Street, and a sign on the fence asked, "Have you paid and displayed?"

"Paid and displayed what?" Dixie muttered to herself, a vaguely obscene image coming to mind.

"You're American," a cheery voice announced.

Dixie turned. A young woman pushing a stroller loaded with two toddlers and groceries stood at her elbow. "You were thinking aloud. Pay and Display. It's for parking." She slowed her voice as if talking to a child. "You did park in the car park didn't you?" Dixie nodded. "You have to pay." She led Dixie to a yellow machine. It needed £1 and 50p coins.

"I don't have change. I'll have to skip it and take my chances with the fine."

"You can't do that! The fine's fifty pounds."

Fifty pounds? She had to be kidding. Seventy or eighty dollars for a parking fine? What did you pay for speeding?

The smallest thing Dixie had was a ten-pound note. Minutes later, Dixie had a five pound note, five heavy coins, and had learned the intricacies of the parking system. A small round coin paid for an hour's parking. She received a large seven-sided coin for change and a ticket with small print giving precise directions for placing it on the inside of the driver's window.

Dixie squeezed between her car and the BMW, unlocked her door and set off the alarm. Silencing it took a good three minutes of searching for the manual and finding the right page. Why hadn't Stanley explained this instead of all the stuff about dipped headlights and windshield wipers?

To Dixie's surprise, the passersby ignored the siren. She wished she could and finally emerged, red-faced, after slapping the ticket on the window.

Mayburn House wasn't the gracious Georgian structure she'd expected, but a yellow-brick building housing a baker and an "off-licence." The latter looked like a liquor store. A brass plate by the front door announced "Woodrow, Hartscomb and Caughleigh. Solicitors and Commissioners for Oaths." *Oaths* fit Dixie's mood right now. At the top of the uncarpeted stairs, a glass paneled door stood ajar.

"I'd like to see Mr. Caughleigh," Dixie said as she pushed open the door.

A secretary glanced up from her typewriter, flicked her purple nails and asked, "Do you have an appointment?"

"Mr. Caughleigh's expecting me."

"You need an appointment," she repeated, tapping her artificial nails.

The click of her long nails snapped Dixie's nerves. Planting both hands on the desktop, she leaned over until they were nose to nose. "My name is Dixie LePage. I flew in this morning from the States. Mr. Caughleigh *is* expecting me. I wrote to him *and* left a message this morning. Tell him I'm here."

Secretary blinked her impossibly long eyelashes, pulled her shoulders back and pursed her mouth. "I'll see if he's in," she said and teetered across to the inner office.

Muffled voices sounded through the closed door. Dixie regretted her temper but gave Caughleigh five minutes before she pushed open the door herself. She took a deep breath and looked around the room. Battleship gray filing cabinets looked old enough to house secrets from World War I. Stacks of old deed boxes with faded names covered two walls and both chairs by the window appeared to have been quietly fading since the sixties.

"Miss LePage, I'm delighted to meet you at last." Dixie's images of a Dickensian lawyer were way off base. Manicured hand extended, Sebastian Caughleigh looked down at her, all six foot one of him, with bedroom eyes and a smile that could melt butter.

"You had a good flight, I trust," he said in a too-smooth voice.

"The flight was fine. Everything went downhill after I landed."

"Yes, yes, I got your message. These strikes!" He raised his eyes upward as if that would get the rails rolling. "Terrible. If you'd only left a number, I could have sent a car for you."

"It's hard to take return calls at a pay phone."

He showed pristine white teeth when he smiled. "Never mind. You're here now. That's what matters and we have a lot of business to discuss." He closed the door behind him. "You've met my secretary, Valerie Fortune." Valerie smiled graciously and Dixie decided anyone called Miss Fortune could be forgiven purple fingernails. "It's a bit late to ask Valerie to make coffee. Perhaps you'd rather a spot of lunch?"

She could use more than a "spot." The clock said two.

Her body was still at breakfast time with scant sleep. "Lunch would be very nice."

"We'll be at the Barley Mow," he told Valerie as he took Dixie's elbow.

"Uncle?" The inner door opened. Sebastian Caughleigh drew in his breath. Dixie felt her jaw drop. The Adonis from the airport stood in the doorway. "Hello," he said and smiled. Sebastian Caughleigh didn't.

"We're just going out, James. I'll talk to you when I get back." Then, as if remembering Dixie, he added, "My nephew, James Chadwick." Reluctance shadowed Sebastian's voice.

"We've met," Dixie replied. "James helped me out with a pay phone at the airport."

James's eyebrows rose, slowly. "I wish I could join you for lunch," he said with a sly smile.

"So do we, James, but I know you've got things to do. See you later." Caughleigh opened the outer door wide. Dixie stepped out and he slammed the door behind them.

"The Barley Mow is our local down on the village green. I thought, being American, you'd like lunch in a genuine old-English pub." She would, but she wasn't picky—anywhere that served food would be fine right now. "Just a short walk, not worth taking the car," he said as he went to cross the road.

"We might as well drive. I have to move my car. I only paid for an hour." A seventy-dollar fine would make an expensive lunch.

Sebastian Caughleigh stopped mid-stride. "You have a car?"

"A rental."

He jackknifed his long legs into the Metro's passenger seat. It took a good fifteen minutes to exit the car park, negotiate the traffic in High Street, turn right at a Norman church that invited exploration, and find a space in the Barley Mow's graveled car park. They could have walked it in ten.

The Barley Mow stood on the edge of the village green, just yards from a wide pond that edged onto the lane. Inside, it was an antique hunter's dream. Horse brasses hung on oak beams. A hammered copper hood decorated the chimney of an inglenook fireplace. Willow pattern plates, copper kettles, hunting prints and old maps decorated every niche and wall.

Sebastian led her through the pub. "Alf," he said to the dumpy man behind the polished bar, "this is Miss Dixie LePage, the Misses Underwood's great-niece. She's over from America to see about settling the estate."

"Hi, Alf."

"Afternoon." Alf looked up from counting money and smiled—at Dixie. "What can I get you?"

"Two ploughman's please, Alf." Sebastian turned to Dixie. "You'll like this. It's a pub specialty."

She would, would she? Irritation pricked down her spine. He hadn't bothered to ask before ordering. Were Englishmen still living in the Victorian age? And what the heck was he expecting her to eat? Meat, if the plates on the table she'd passed were anything to go by. "What's a ploughman's?" Dixie asked, pointedly looking at Alf.

His mouth twitched as he looked straight at her and gave her a little nod. "American, aren't you?" Alf paused, acknowledging her agreement with another smile. "It's a pub standard: bit of salad, pickle, a chunk of baguette, and Cheddar, Stilton, or ham depending on your choice."

That was something; she could have a good lunch without explaining or justifying her reluctance to eat meat.

"Two Cheddar ploughman's," Sebastian went on, sounding a little irritated at her interruption.

"I'd prefer Stilton, Alf," Dixie said.

Alf's smile broadened to a grin. "Right you are." He gave

Dixie a distinctly interested look as he turned to call the order through a hatch behind him.

Dixie rested a foot on the rail of the bar and leaned on her elbows. Jet lag sapped her energy. Chauvinistic Brit lawyers didn't help. Food might.

"A pint of bitter too, Alf." Sebastian turned to Dixie, "How about you? G and T? White wine?"

She shook her head. "Guinness, please."

"Right you are." Alf filled a heavy glass mug with great care, settling the head just right, rested the glass on a towel to take up the drips, then set it on a coaster advertising Merrydown Cider.

Dixie sipped, drinking through the foamy head. The taste took her back to evenings on her grandmother's lap, relishing the one sip Gran allowed. Something pinched deep in her chest at the thought. She took a deeper taste and met Alf's questioning eyes. "Great," she said. "Gran was right. It does taste better over here."

"That's because your people mess with it, changing the alcoholic content and I don't know what." Alf wiped a couple of drips from the bar top. "Staying long, are you?"

Caughleigh tapped her elbow. "We've got business to cover. Let's sit in the conservatory."

Irritated, Dixie followed him. Suppose she'd preferred to stay at the bar. Had he thought about that? She had a hard time not making a face at his broad, pinstripe-covered shoulders.

The conservatory looked out on green lawns, flowerbeds beginning to show bloom and a large jungle gym. Dixie sat down on the chintz-cushioned chair Sebastian held for her and set her drink on the wrought-iron table. They were alone except for a cat, curled up in sleep in a pool of sunshine. Dixie looked around at the faded roses on the upholstery, the polished tile floor, the geraniums on the windowsills and the mismatched wrought iron and mahogany furniture. Fashionable interior decorators would charge a small fortune to put together this look.

Dixie's arm brushed an immense, pink geranium as she turned in her seat. The sharp scent took her back to Gran's piazza overlooking the Battery. And her reason for being here. "Sebastian," she said, "I'd like to see my house after lunch."

He almost choked on a mouthful of bitter.

"I'm afraid that's not possible," he replied after he'd coughed into a linen handkerchief. "I only have one key. Mike Jenkins has it. I asked him to value the house. He's a local estate agent, very reputable. I'd recommend him to handle the sale."

"Can't you get it back?" Dixie looked across at his smooth, dark eyes. They didn't quite meet hers.

He took a slow sip from his beer. "How about in the morning? It gets dark early and the electricity's turned off."

Alf arrived with two plates overflowing with salad, a slab of cheese, pickles, relishes, and a small loaf. The sight and smell of food reminded Dixie how long ago she'd eaten her last real meal. Plastic food on an airplane didn't count.

"You didn't say how long you're staying."

Dixie looked up from buttering a hunk of bread. "I'm not sure." She hadn't really thought about it.

"I've booked you for bed and breakfast at Miss Reade's. She's here in the village. I'll take you there after lunch."

He had, had he? "I'd planned on staying in my house."

Sebastian's brows wrinkled. He smiled. He showed very white teeth. "Well, you could . . . but there's no electricity or gas and the water's turned off. I know how you Americans like your creature comforts."

"We do. But I've come quite a long way to see my property."

He put a lot of effort into his smile. His eyes weren't half bad either. "I wasn't sure what you'd want to do. The house isn't habitable right now. Your great-aunts were the local eccentrics, I'm afraid. I think you'll be more comfortable at Miss Reade's. If not, there's a good country hotel over in Bookham."

"I'll stay in Bringham." She hadn't come this far to end up miles down the road.

"Suppose I take you over to Miss Reade's after lunch? Leave you to get settled, unpacked and whatever you ladies do. In the morning, we can meet at my office and sign a few things that need taking care of. I'll have the key then. We can go over the house and find out what Mike Jenkins thinks."

Reasonable enough. Every muscle ached and her head throbbed. A whole pint on a jet-lagged stomach hadn't been a good idea.

Sebastian gave her a key for the front door of a tile-hung cottage by the Green. Miss Reade worked in Leatherhead and wouldn't be home until six. He carried Dixie's suitcase up to a floral-papered room in the eaves, explained the intricacies of the electric kettle in her room, and left after agreeing to meet her at ten in the morning.

Overcoming the odd sensation of inhabiting the house in its owner's absence, Dixie explored. This was her idea of an English country cottage: oak furniture, polished brass, open fireplaces, a spotless kitchen overlooking a neat back garden and a narrow, dark stairway hidden behind a door in the dining room. After hanging her clothes in the corner closet and placing the rest in the carved oak dresser, Dixie showered off the grime of travel and made a cup of coffee using the kettle and rose-decorated china in her room. Too weary to finish it, she crawled between the lavender scented sheets and slept the afternoon away.

"What the Hades were you trying? I *told* you to stay out of my office!" Sebastian Caughleigh stormed through the door.

James raised an eyebrow. "I wanted an eyeful of the American heiress."

"You already had one."

"No harm done then." James lounged in the wingback chair.

"No?" Sebastian sneered down at his nephew. "If you'd taken her wallet as you were supposed to, she'd have been delayed, maybe even gone home in disgust. Instead, she's here and oh so very anxious to look over her property. I've stalled her until the morning. You'd better find what we need tonight. There must be enough of it to fill a van."

"I'll find it. Trust me, Uncle."

"Trust you? I'm not that stupid!"

James ignored that. He stretched his thin legs out towards the empty fireplace. "Where is our eager American now?"

"Safely ensconced at Emily's."

"How nice. Tuck away your newest opportunity in your inamorata's cottage."

Sebastian sat in the opposite chair, rested his forearms on his thighs and snarled towards James, "A word of advice. Don't fail. It could get difficult for you if you don't succeed tonight. Remember whom you're letting down."

"Such unkind words, Uncle. Threats even. You hurt my feelings. Maybe I won't tell you what I took from Miss LePage."

"You will."

James reached into his pocket and hefted a small brown leather book. He made as if to toss it to his uncle, then pulled back his arm. "Interested?" He smiled at Sebastian's outstretched hand.

The hand stayed open. "Give," Sebastian hissed. James tossed the book at him. Sebastian caught it and flicked the thin pages. "Her diary. Wonderful. Now we know when she plays bridge."

"More than that, Uncle. I had a good read while you were out courting her. It's one of those 'everything' books—phone numbers, addresses, bank account numbers and every lunch date and dentist appointment since January. Without it she won't be doing much telephoning or sending postcards to her pals back home."

Sebastian wrapped his fingers around the soft leather. It might make interesting reading but its loss was hardly enough to make her leave. He glanced at the marble clock on the mantelpiece. "It's almost four. I'm taking her over to the house at eleven. That gives you eighteen hours. Find everything."

James tilted his chin. "Or else? What?"

"You may have to get an honest job."

James paused in the doorway. "Don't worry, Uncle. It won't happen. Who'd hire me?"

Sebastian frowned at the empty grate. Hadn't James understood anything? They couldn't risk those papers falling into anyone else's hands. Too many reputations were at stake and too much money. If only the wretched woman had stayed on the other side of the Atlantic. She could have had a comfortable three-quarters of a million. He would have settled some old scores, and been set up for life. Now—who knew?

She had to be gotten rid of. No, a better idea. Woo her? Why not? Court her a little. Break her heart and she'd go running back home.

A knock on the door woke Dixie. She stared at the unfamiliar pitched ceiling, and remembered. The door opened; she'd noticed earlier there wasn't a lock, only a wrought iron latch.

A pleasantly plump face smiled around the door. "Sorry

to disturb you. I'm Emily Reade. I'm about to put the kettle on. Would you like to come down in a minute and have a cup and I can explain things?"

Miss Reade liked to chat. She also wanted to be called Emily, took three sugars in her tea, and worked in a bank in Leatherhead. "Such a lovely house you have, beautiful. Worth a small fortune at today's prices. Of course, whoever buys it will have to spend a pretty penny on it."

Why did everyone assume she was selling? "Where exactly is it? I haven't seen it yet."

Emily's pudgy eyes widened. "Orchard House? It's just across the Green."

Why hadn't Mr. Caughleigh pointed it out? They must have passed it driving here. She'd look for it later.

Her arrangement with Emily involved bed and breakfast and unlimited cups of tea. Other meals Dixie fended for herself. She planned on exploring neighboring villages and the "Leatherhead" everyone referred to as the local metropolis, but tonight she'd content herself with the Barley Mow.

She'd walk. She needed the exercise. She'd barely moved her muscles the past twenty-four hours, except to sit or sleep. The evening was colder than she expected so she doubled back to the house and slipped upstairs.

Pulling a sweatshirt over her head, she heard a voice from the bedroom next door, ". . . . Out to get dinner. . . . I don't know. . . . An hour or so I expect. . . . No, of course I didn't. . . . I'm leaving all that to you. . . . When can I see you? . . . . Alright." Uncomfortable at overhearing a private conversation, she tiptoed downstairs and closed the door quietly behind her.

The Barley Mow packed a fair crowd in the evenings. Alf had a helper, a young man with a Mohawk and a large ring in one ear.

"Evening, Miss LePage. Guinness wasn't it?"

"A small one."

"Half pint it is then." Alf called to his helper, "Vernon, half of Guinness and watch the head. Anything else?" he asked Dixie.

"I need dinner. Do you have a menu?"

"Up there." Alf nodded towards a chalkboard on the wall.

Dixie scanned the scratchy writing: shepherd's pie, lamb curry, Cornish pasty, steak and kidney, scampi, bangers and mash, Dover sole and an assortment of salads. "I don't eat meat. What do you recommend?"

"Vegetarian, eh? If you eat fish, I'd go for the sole or the scampi."

"Scampi then, Alf." In the spirit of adventure she added a jacket potato. Whatever that was.

Dixie settled in an empty table near the window, took out a paperback mystery, and settled into reading as she sipped her Guinness.

"Why, hello there!"

Dixie glanced up from Stephanie Plum to meet James Chadwick's pale blue eyes. His smile implied she was just so lucky he'd found her. "Hi," she said and purposely went on reading.

He pulled out the opposite chair. "Ever so glad to bump into you again."

She wouldn't return his smile at any price. No way was she encouraging him. She didn't need to. He set his glass on the table. The nerve of the man! Three times in one day was beyond chance. Dixie debated emptying her glass into his lap. It would get rid of him, but it seemed a dreadful waste of good Guinness.

Kit Marlowe braced himself for the scent of human blood that waited on the other side of the closed door. He seldom came to the Barley Mow, but it was the best place for local gossip. He grasped the knob, remembering to hold it gently—no point in mangling doorknobs and getting unwanted attention. He stepped into the crowded bar, every nerve and sense alert and watchful. He froze. She was in here. He knew it. Nonsense! His senses hadn't developed *that* well. He might sense a known quarry when he hunted, but not this unknown Miss LePage. Besides, he wasn't *hunting* her. His only interest in her was an invitation into her house. The village telegraph claimed she'd arrived but the house was as deserted as ever.

Why did he sense her so keenly? Was she one of them? A member of another colony? Maybe. If Justin was to be believed, Vlad Tepes had half-populated the States with his offspring, but only mortals filled the crowded bar. He'd have scented one of his own kind immediately. He glanced around, nodding at familiar faces, noting the visitors, and found her almost at once.

Why? He just knew her the minute he saw her, sitting alone with a book. Auburn curls fell across her face as she read. He had a glimpse of smooth skin and a creamy hollow at the base of her neck. He sensed, scented the richness of her and forced himself to concentrate on the task in hand. He couldn't afford distractions. No matter how desirable.

A man walked across the bar to her table. Eyes green as church window glass looked up from beneath silky lashes. Angry eyes in a calm, cold face. Given the man standing over her, he didn't blame her. Caughleigh's nephew! She had brains equal to her looks if she already disliked Chadwick. She wrinkled her nose as if assailed by an unsavory smell. Kit smiled to himself, noted the glass she clutched like a weapon, and crossed to Vernon at the bar.

Close up, her skin had the bloom of early roses. The pulse at the base of her neck beat in perfect rhythm beneath flawless skin. She smelled of night air, lavender soap, and human blood. She never even noticed him. Her attention was focused on Chadwick. Her *irritation* was focused on Chadwick. The quiet thud of heavy glass on wood broke the tension as Kit put a new Guinness in front of her.

"Here you are, sorry it took so long."

She looked up. "River emeralds" was a better description for her eyes. Such sensuality didn't belong in any church window. She gaped when he put the second glass on the table. He let her gape and turned his will on Chadwick. He wasn't hard to bend.

"Marlowe? You're with her? I . . . I never . . . I didn't . . . didn't realize." His pale eyes popped like a demented Pekingese.

"Really?" One word. That was all it took.

"Didn't know you were with Dixie. See you later." James grabbed his tankard and disappeared into the crush.

Kit took the empty seat. "May I join you?"

She looked straight at him, chin up, her brows creased, studying him like a specimen. She met him eye to eye without faltering, a flicker of amusement twitching the corner of her mouth. Was she mere mortal? With a presence like this? With her ancestry, who knew?

"Suppose I say no?"

"Suppose I retire and give Chadwick another chance?"

"Too late, he just left."

"I'm desolate."

"I'll bet you are! You chased him off deliberately. What if you've destroyed a great romance?"

He liked her sense of humor. "I didn't."

The corner of her mouth tightened. He'd infuriated her. Women hadn't changed no matter how much the world had. "What makes you so sure?"

Elbows on table, he rested his chin on his hand. "I could *smell* the antagonism between you."

She opened her mouth to complain. Then shook her head and smiled as their eyes met. "Could you also smell too much beer?"

"Any amount is too much for Chadwick." He leaned back in the chair and watched her, willing himself to ignore the warm blood singing through her veins. "You despise him."

She shook her head. "I wouldn't go that far. He irked me the first time I met him. He isn't my type. You can't despise someone you've only known one day."

"It's possible. Trust your instincts."

"Yes, much safer than trusting a stranger who tries to pick me up in a pub." She looked around as Vernon thumped a plate down in front of her.

Her dinner. Good. A nice distraction. Dixie stared at the plate in front of her. A jacket potato was baked, without sour cream. She wanted to eat and read in peace. Fat chance. Man number two was a distinct improvement over James but anything would be. Dixie mashed butter into her potato as she thought about the tall man sitting opposite. He wasn't *that* tall. He just blocked out the rest of the room with his broad shoulders, black turtleneck and black slacks. All he lacked was the black hat to complete the villain outfit. But he had disposed of James Chadwick for her. That was a definite recommendation. Even if he looked like Long John Silver with his eye patch.

"Bon appetit," he said.

She looked him straight in the eye. Straight in his one eye, dark and warm as velvet. "You're going to sit there and watch me eat?"

The corner of his eye wrinkled. Was he smiling? "You'd rather I left?" Placing his hands flat on the polished tabletop, he made to stand.

"No!" She grabbed his wrist. Stunned at her action, she met his eye again. This time the smile was unmistakable.

He looked down at the hand circling his wrist. "I'll stay, if you insist. Why don't you eat before it gets cold?"

Dixie didn't think she'd ever be cold again. But he was.

His wrist felt cold and dry. Hardly surprising, the night was cool. Hadn't she gone back for a sweatshirt? She took her hand off his wrist. "I've no idea who you are."

"The name's Marlowe, Christopher Marlowe." Dixie noticed a silver signet ring with a black stone on his offered hand.

Long, cold fingers met hers. Strong, cold fingers. "Here to meet Will Shakespeare?" His fingers stiffened in her hand. His brow wrinkled. "Sorry. It just slipped out. I bet everyone you meet makes that crack."

"You're not the first." He smiled. He had a very nice smile. She wasn't about to think about his smile. Or the goose bumps on her arm. Holding his hand was quite enough. More than enough. She shook it and then let go.

"I'm Dixie LePage."

"Great-niece and heiress of the renowned Misses Underwood. Just arrived from America in one of Stanley Collins's vehicles. Staying with Emily Reade for the nonce."

He had her gaping for the second time. "How did you . . . ?" She gave up. Maybe jet lag caused terminal confusion.

"Village telegraph. It's chronicled your progress since you drove into town. Someone, somewhere already knows your shoe size, the color of your toothbrush, and how many sugars you take in your tea."

"Just like small towns everywhere."

He nodded. Slim fingers stroked the stem of his glass. "You may find Bringham . . . unusual."

"May? I have already. Total strangers accost you in pubs."

"I did offer to leave."

He had and she'd grabbed him. Maybe wrist-grabbing was a come-on in England. She hoped not. . . . "You don't have to. I'm going as soon as I finish eating."

"Stay and finish your drink." He nudged the second Guinness towards her. "I won't proposition you on the strength of one drink."

"How many does it take?" Dixie almost choked. She must be getting drunk. She never said things like that.

"I'm interested in your library. Not you." Reassurances like that shouldn't be disappointing.

"My library?"

"The one you inherited in your house."

It took her a couple of seconds to realize he meant Orchard House. "You want to buy my library? I'm not sure it's for sale."

"Just a few books. I'm interested in the paranormal. Your aunts had quite a collection. I'd like to buy some of them. I'll pay market price. I'm not bargain hunting."

A reasonable business proposal; it shouldn't leave her breathless. "I haven't even seen them yet. If I think of selling them . . ."

"You'll give me first refusal?" He leaned forward, waiting on her reply.

She nodded. "Yes, *if* I sell." She stood up to go. "Where can I find you, Christopher?"

"I drop by here every so often." He would from now on. "If not, I live in Dial Cottage, up from the station." Goose bumps again. It definitely was his smile. He stood with her. "Shall I walk you home?"

This was like something out of Jane Austen. "Thanks, but I'm fine."

Dixie was out the door before she wondered how he knew she'd walked. Lights from the pub windows lit the lane in each direction; they also showed the beginning of a dirt foot-path across the green. Looking up at the stars in unfamiliar positions in the cloudless sky, Dixie realized she wasn't the least bit ready for bed. Emily had said Orchard House was on the other side of the green. It couldn't be that far, and Dixie wanted a glimpse of the house she'd come to claim.

Chapter Two

The lights from the Barley Mow, and the moon shimmering on the pond gave Dixie a clear view. It would be an easy walk to cross the Green and circle back to Miss Reade's. The dry, well-trodden path skirted around the water's edge and joined the lane near three tile-hung cottages with neat hedges and lighted front doors. Turning right, Dixie followed the curve of the lane.

Five modern, brightly lit houses caught her attention with glimpses of flickering TV screens and a woman filling a kettle at the sink. The path ended and the road narrowed past a clump of trees that cast ragged shadows over the lane. Something fast and warm scuttled inches from Dixie's feet. Tempted to abandon what now seemed like a crazy moonlight hike, Dixie glanced back across the Green and realized the Barley Mow was a good hundred yards away. She had to be near Orchard House. She'd tramped this far. She wasn't going back. If she walked in the middle of the lane, she'd avoid four-footed nocturnals and tree roots.

Then she heard the owls. Two of them, calling back and forth like a pair of feathered Harpies. Nothing like it to add a bit of atmosphere. She was alone, in the dark, on a deserted country lane, in a foreign country, looking for a house she'd never seen. Dixie willed courage, marched round the next curve, and stopped.

This was her house. She knew it.

She peered through high wrought-iron gates. A gravel path led past shadows of overgrown shrubs to a square brick house where moonlight flickered on long sash windows. Paint and rust flaked in her hands as she shook the gate. The chain clanked like Marley's ghost, rattled and fell to the ground. Budging the gate took more effort. Either the gate had sunk or the drive risen in the past months. The hinges complained, but a few hard shoves opened it enough to slip in sideways.

Dixie stood on the gravel driveway and surveyed her property. Even in the dark, she could see she owned an elegant house. Eight double-hung windows were set in a beautifully proportioned façade, and four dormers rose from the roof. A dark shadow of a front door stood at the end of the uneven path ahead and the gravel drive circled behind the house. It could have been the set for *Sense and Sensibility*. And it was hers. Complete with moonlight.

In an upstairs window, on the far right a light flickered. It wasn't moonlight.

A burglar.

And in her house.

Fired by righteous indignation, Dixie raced up the steps to the front door and tugged the iron loop of the bell pull. Loud chimes echoed through the silent house. Standing on the step, Dixie watched the light disappear and then . . . nothing. What did she expect? The burglar to answer the doorbell?

Even the owls had gone quiet. Nothing moved in the night. Dixie half-convinced herself she'd imagined the light when a door banged. Twice. A loud cussword echoed through the night quiet.

Cautious now, keeping to the overgrown grass, Dixie crept round the side of the house. It was a whole lot bigger than it looked from the front. Odd corners and shapes jutted out behind. A cluster of outbuildings huddled over by a high brick wall. Deep shadows hid everything except rough outlines and shapes, and patches of moonlight made an eerie checkerboard of the backyard. Dixie waited by the corner, watched and listened. A dark shape slunk across the yard.

The intruder continued his path between a clump of overgrown bushes. Fury burned away all her caution. "What are you doing in my house?" she called. The intruder didn't stop to answer. One look behind and he fled across the grass and out through a side gate.

Dixie chased, racing through the gate, out into the lane and careened into a dark figure.

"What are you doing?" she demanded, too angry to consider fear.

"Dixie?" She knew that voice.

"Christopher? Christopher Marlowe? What are you doing here?" This was a bit much, first intruding on her dinner, then her property.

"Walking home. Are you alright? You're shaking." Strong hands gripped her shoulders.

That last bit was true. She shook from her knees to the shoulders he held. Dixie stepped back from his hands and looked sideways. They stood in a narrow, unpaved lane. Behind her loomed the high brick wall and ahead, distant lights from the new houses glimmered through the trees.

He stepped closer. "Something scared you. What are you doing here at this time of night?"

"Looking at my house." Had he been the intruder? He'd been suspiciously close but he wasn't breathing heavily.

After that sprint across the garden, a marathoner would be wheezing. "You really live out this way? You said you lived by the station."

"It's a shortcut." One hand went back to her shoulders. "You shouldn't be wandering around here after dark. It's not safe for a woman."

She'd ignore that. "Someone was there, in the house. I saw a light. He ran out this way."

"And you thought it was me?"

How did she answer that one? She still did—halfway. "There's no one else."

"I promise it wasn't me. I don't wander around empty houses by torchlight."

"You think I imagined it?" Let him dare answer yes.

"No. It's probably some teenager braving out a dare. The house is supposed to be haunted. You likely interrupted some lad's attempt at machismo. This time I *am* walking you home. You're scared and it's not wise to wander around after dark."

She let him walk her back to Emily's. Familiar with the path, he warned about roots and hazards hidden by the shadows. Crossing the edge of the Green, he took her elbow. "There's a dip here, watch out," he said. She stopped and explore with her foot. There was a hollow, deep enough to trip on but hidden by the grass.

"How did you know?" she asked, looking up at his pale face in the moonlight.

"I walk here all the time."

Ten minutes later they stood by Emily Reade's front gate. He waited. Surely he didn't expect her to invite him in? He *was* going to be disappointed.

"Thanks for the escort. I think I can find the way next time." She held out her hand.

A strong, cold hand grasped hers. "Take care, Dixie. I'll be seeing you around."

He waited at the gate as she walked up the path. Dixie turned and waved as she reached into her jeans pocket for the key. It felt warm after his fingers.

Without turning on her light, Dixie watched from her bedroom window as Christopher retraced his steps across the Green. Had he spoken the truth? Was that path by her house a shortcut to his? A few questions or a check on a map could answer that. She watched him halfway across the Green until his silhouette faded in the dark.

Christopher Marlowe paused in front of Orchard House and willed himself to think about the library inside. He wouldn't think about its new guardian, her copper curls, her skin smooth as clotted cream, or the warm green eyes that glittered with intelligence.

Most of all he'd ignore the warm rich blood that coursed though her veins. Temptations like that could ruin everything. With her ancestry, she was more likely adversary than ally. He wouldn't forget that. He'd learned that much in four hundred years.

"You're an incompetent idiot! What this time? Scaredy cat frightened by a ghost? Give me strength!" Sebastian felt the blood rise up his neck as he snarled at James.

Pale eyes glowered back. "You try it! Nothing's there. I've gone through that room twice."

"Make it three times!"

"You try poking round that mausoleum in the dark. I'm not going back."

A nasty chuckle vibrated in Caughleigh's chest. "You will. I'm taking LePage round the property in the morning. It'll be on the market by tomorrow afternoon. You've got one more night to find everything."

"Or, dear Uncle?"

"Or you'll find we're not as benign as you thought. We can be quite nasty when roused and crossed. As the old ladies found out."

That hit home. Sebastian smiled. He had James where he needed him.

"It's beautiful." Dixie ignored Caughleigh's benevolent amusement. She'd need more than a morning to grasp the reality of owning such a house. Mysterious and eerie last night, the red brick glowed a welcoming warmth in the mid-morning sun. The cracked paving stones were worn, not hazardous, and the garden looked neglected, not sinister. But the elegance of the house remained, like a weary dowager resting her tired bones in the sun. "How old is it?"

Sebastian shrugged. "Hard to say exactly. Too heavy to be Georgian. Maybe Queen Anne. The local historical society might know something. I think it's listed. The back is much older of course."

Dixie held out her hand for the key; it was four inches long and weighed several ounces. The lock turned slowly but it clicked. Dixie grasped the dulled brass knob and pushed open the heavy black door.

A musty smell and cold, damp air hung about the wide shabby hallway. Dustcovers protected the heavy furniture but a film of dust covered the marble fireplace and obscured the windows. Cobwebs decorated the crystal chandelier and the banister rails. It didn't take much to imagine mice nesting in the rolled up carpet by the wall. "Miss Haversham would feel quite at home here."

Sebastian Caughleigh smiled. "Your aunts had a reputation for eccentricity."

"Surely they didn't live like this?" She remembered Gran's obsessive spring cleaning and her insistence on linen napkins and polished glassware.

"Miss Faith died almost two years ago, she tended to be the organizer. I'm afraid Miss Hope didn't manage too well and the house has been empty since October."

Sebastian strode from room to room like a zealous realtor. Dixie followed, collecting impressions: a wide, airy drawing room with faded pastel curtains, a dining room with a heavy, black oak table and exquisite pale wood paneling with a carved fireplace to match. The breakfast room looked out on an overgrown flower garden. A small parlor with worn modern furniture and an ancient TV looked like the Misses Underwood's everyday room.

The kitchen was dark, low-ceilinged and several steps down from the rest of the house. "Much older," Sebastian said. "They built the new house onto an old farmhouse."

Upstairs were four bedrooms and another room filled with books from floor to ceiling. Dixie figured that must be the collection Christopher had referred to. A sixth room held an immense claw-footed tub, a pedestal washbasin large enough to bathe a small Doberman, and twin toilets with a double mahogany seat.

Dixie stared. "Why double toilets?"

Sebastian coughed. "Old-fashioned. You'd never see it nowadays. Whoever buys the house will have to modernize."

"But worth it. With some money spent on it, this would be a beautiful house."

"We need to get back. I promised the key to Mike Jenkins before lunch."

Dixie wasn't about to be hustled out of her own house. "I'm staying. He can meet me here."

Those dark eyes almost popped. "Staying? There's no water or electricity."

"I can manage for a couple of hours."

He frowned. "Fine. Drop the key by the office later."

The house settled back into quiet as the noise of his engine faded. An hour of signing papers in his office had set-

tled her possession of her property. She wanted time to herself to enjoy owning this wonderful house before she did the
practical thing and put it on the market. How much would a
house like this fetch? More than enough to buy and furnish a
nice, sensible house back in South Carolina. She'd ask Mike
whatever-his-name when he arrived.

He never turned up. But James did.

Busy removing dustcovers in the breakfast room, Dixie
heard the front door open and footsteps cross the hall and
start up the stairs. "Hi, I'm back here," she called, assuming
it was the realtor. She opened the door into the hall and
James stared at her from the third step.

"You're here?" he asked, gaping. Why shouldn't she be?
Hadn't he heard of knocking on doors? "Don't let me disturb
you if you're busy." He took another step up.

"I won't." A half-dozen strides took her to the foot of the
stairs. "Going somewhere?" she asked, one hand on her hip.

He squeezed out a laugh. "Sorry, I thought Uncle told
you. I'm looking at the furniture. A friend of mine is interested in making you an offer."

"I'm not interested in selling." At least not to any friend
of his.

That slowed him down. "Well . . . surely . . . I mean . . ."

"My furniture isn't for sale."

He stepped down. "If you change your mind, let me
know." He stood far too close to be polite in any language.

"It's not for sale, and not likely to be in the near future."
Dixie held open the front door.

Even James couldn't miss the heavy hint.

He held out his hand. Dixie took it out of common courtesy and wished she hadn't when he squeezed. "See you at
the Barley Mow tonight?"

Dixie grunted as she shut the door. Why had James just
walked in? He'd seemed right at home. Was he used to coming and going? She shrugged and went upstairs. The bed-

rooms could wait, but she did want to look at her books. If Christopher was to be believed, her aunts had an interesting collection.

The book room proved too much for one afternoon. She'd come back tomorrow with a flashlight if she couldn't get the electricity turned on. She looked around at the packed shelves, the stacks of books on the center table and the scattered footprints in the dust. Someone had been in here. Who? The person she'd seen, or imagined last night?

She looked at her watch. Her two hours had become four and no sign of Mike the realtor. She'd go back to Emily Reade's and get a much needed shower and find somewhere other than the Barley Mow for dinner.

She walked around the backyard before she left. Tool sheds, half-collapsed coal stores, and an old washhouse spanned one side of the kitchen garden. The gate she'd run through last night stood open but she couldn't close it. The wood at the bottom jammed on something. She hadn't imagined those lights last night. A heavy, black flashlight lay in the ankle-deep grass.

"I think that's everything for now, Miss LePage."

Dixie smiled at the bank manager and the chief cashier. Her breath didn't come clear enough to speak. With a couple of signatures, she'd just received ten times as much money as she'd earned since grad school. And that was only a beginning. "This is rather a surprise." *Rather a surprise!* She *was* getting British. They were lucky she wasn't dancing around like the sweepstake winners on TV.

"You'll need to make some investment decisions."

Dixie nodded. "I know. It's just this will take some getting used to."

"Of course." The manager smiled, delighted to have her as a customer, no doubt. "Contact us when you're ready. You have several options. With your non-resident status, there are some very attractive offshore opportunities."

"How about I get back with you next week? Same time next Friday?" Dixie shuffled through her bag for her appointment book but she couldn't find it. She took the business card he offered and scribbled a note on the back before tucking it in her pocket. She needed to get out of here and think.

Two buildings down High Street stood the Copper Kettle. Dixie chose a wheelback chair by the window, searched in vain for the elusive appointment book, decided she'd left it at Emily's, ordered a pot of tea, and contemplated her future.

She had a small fortune in the bank and more to come after the sale of securities and the maturity of some bonds. More money than she'd imagined saving after a lifetime of work, and still more if she decided to sell the house.

It didn't make sense. Gran had struggled with Social Security and the little bit Grandpa had left, while her sisters had sat on a stash. True, they hadn't lived high on the hog; the house showed years of neglect. A couple of old scrooges. What else was new? Gran had despised them. "A pair of old witches!" she'd once replied to a teenaged Dixie's questions about her English relatives.

A smart person would sell the house to the highest bidder, grab the money and take the first plane home. But where was home? She'd as good as blown her job. The man she'd loved had thrown her over for a richer (okay, not richer now!) woman with social connections. Her worldly belongings filled her neighbor's garage and still left room for his lawn mower and workbench. And she didn't possess a living relative on either side of the Atlantic. She'd give herself a month's holiday. She had the money and a roof over her head. Why not stay awhile?

Sebastian Caughleigh's face appeared distorted through the old bottle glass of the bow window. He took Dixie's answering wave as an invitation. As he sat down on the chair he'd pulled out, Dixie suppressed a wave of irritation. She didn't want to talk house, or money, or furniture. She wanted to luxuriate in financial independence.

"Fixed up things at the bank?" He signaled for the white-haired waitress. "Good to get it settled before you leave."

"Pretty much. I'm going to take my time. Thought I'd stay a few weeks. Maybe a month or so."

"Oh?" He frowned. Then smiled that smile. Did he practice in front of a mirror? "That will be nice," he said. "Since you're staying, would you like to meet some people this weekend? A couple I know, Janet and Larry Whyte—he's in insurance—are having people over tomorrow. How about I pick you up round seven? We can go over for drinks, you'd meet some of the locals and have dinner."

Why not? If she was staying awhile, it would be smart to get to know someone other than Emily and Smarmy James. "Sounds nice. I'd love to come. What does Janet do?"

"Janet?" Sebastian frowned.

"Janet Whyte, is she in insurance like Larry?"

"Oh no, she does something in one of the hospitals in Guildford." He made her sound like a candy striper. He stretched out his long legs under the table and sipped his coffee. "Do you have plans for this afternoon?"

"Just exploring my house." His legs shifted against hers. Dixie stood up. "Sorry to run but I've got things to do."

The house was as cold as a damp towel and this was early May. What would it be like in November? Or February? But the hour she spent in the phone booth on the corner paid off. By four o'clock Dixie had electricity and water reconnected and a promise of telephone service in the next week or so. She'd also discovered the impossibility of cleaning house with cold water.

"Could you make sure the water heater's working?" Dixie asked the service man from the electric board.

"You don't have one," he replied in the sort of voice used on a slow-witted child—or a foreigner. "That Aga of yours does the water."

"That thing?" Dixie asked, looking at the cream-colored behemoth that filled the kitchen fireplace.

"Yup," he replied, shifting his tool belt. "One of the originals, that is. Looks like a prewar one to me." Which war? The one with the colonies? "'Course, you could get it converted. Be a lot easier if it ran on gas or oil." He showed her the location of the meter at the back of the cupboard under the stairs, behind mops, brooms, an antique vacuum cleaner and a pair of wooden skis, and the location of the fuse box in the basement. "Need to get the place rewired," he warned her as he left.

Dixie stared at the Aga in the empty kitchen. She'd barely come to terms with the china sinks and wooden draining boards, to say nothing of the open fireplaces in every room and the absence of any form of furnace. Now it seemed she heated water on a stove. Would she have to chop down trees to get a decent shower? Her great-aunts had a fortune in the bank and lived like pioneers. If she had a phone, she'd call Sebastian Caughleigh and insist on selling the house before Monday.

"Hello. Mind if we come in?"

Dixie opened the door to her acquaintance from the car park.

"Oh, it is you," she said. "I knew it had to be. I'm Emma Gordon, your neighbor, just across the way." Her head nodded towards the new houses on the other side of the lane. "And this is Sally Smith."

The second woman smiled. "Welcome to Bringham. Thought we'd pop over and see if there's anything we can do."

"Have you any idea how to get that thing going?" Dixie pointed to the lurking Aga.

They had.

A search through the outbuildings discovered a shed of what looked like coal but which the others called "anthracite." Emma ran home for charcoal and a box of three-inch-long matches. "Swan Vestas," she explained. "They're easier for things like this."

Dixie took her word for it.

Lifting what Dixie imagined must be a cooking surface, they tipped in a bucket of anthracite, a good couple of handfuls of charcoal and a few twists of paper. Satisfied the fuel had caught, Emma dropped the lid back and smiled. "Give it a couple of hours and you'll have it going. My mum had one. Just top it up twice a day. It'll be brilliant in the winter."

Dixie decided not to stay long enough to find out.

Emma went home a second time and returned with a large, brown teapot, a bottle of milk and a tin of gingerbread. "You look as if you need it," she said, setting everything on the kitchen table.

Dixie didn't argue, but felt a stiff gin might do even better.

"Staying to sell the house?" Sally asked.

"I don't know. I thought I'd take a month or so to decide."

"It'll be nice to have someone living here," Emma said. "Ian and I worried about vandalism or squatters."

"Vandals?" Dixie asked, remembering Wednesday night. "Have you seen anything odd?"

Emma shrugged. "Lights sometimes. The villagers say the old ladies haunt it. More likely local yobs out on a lark."

"I thought I saw a light, the night before last."

"You were here after dark?" Emma seemed either impressed or horrified.

"Just strolled by. Admiring my property, I suppose."

"It is a beautiful house," said Sally, "or will be after a lot of work. It's a shame they let it go so, but it must have been hard for two old ladies on a fixed income."

Dixie wasn't about to tell the level the income had been "fixed" at. It still gave her shivers when she thought about it.

"I'd be careful around here at night. It's a bit lonely. Get good locks if you're staying." Emma sounded like Gran. "And let Sergeant Grace know. He'll keep an eye on things. The police house is on the left, past the church."

Between the two of them, they'd have her life organized— but it didn't feel like an intrusion. They were two women concerned about a third being alone. They knew the neighborhood and Dixie sensed she'd need friends if she stayed.

After they left, Dixie ran the geriatric vacuum over the ground floor and took down all the drapes and heaped them on the backseat of her car. She'd find a cleaner in the morning and get in touch with the locksmith, and Stan Collins. She'd need the car for at least another month.

With the windows clear, the house seemed lighter and airier. Tomorrow she'd open all the windows and let out the mustiness of the years. She found herself back in the low-ceilinged kitchen. The room fascinated her. With small windows overlooking the kitchen garden, it seemed another world from the spacious drawing room and paneled dining room. The world of servant and mistress perhaps? Except her great-aunts had lived alone. Before, when Gran and her sisters had been girls, things must have been different. Dixie imagined rosy-cheeked parlor maids and a plump cook seated around the scrubbed pine table.

Not for the first time, Dixie wished Gran had talked about her youth. She'd always evaded any questions and discouraged Dixie's curiosity. "Life's good here," she'd say. "Don't shovel up history." When a teenaged Dixie wanted to visit Gran's sisters on a much discussed, but never accomplished, backpacking tour of Europe, Gran shook her head. "A pair of nasty, spiteful old hags. You don't even want to know about them."

"Is that book intended to repulse the world in general or just Chadwick?" Christopher smiled down at her. He could melt glass marbles with that smile.

"It didn't work with you, did it?"

"Did you intend it to?"

A tougher woman wouldn't have smiled back or felt a flush of warm pleasure when he rested his hand on the back of the chair opposite and said, "May I?"

At least he asked this time. She nodded, trying not to grin.

"Don't let me interrupt your supper," he said. "How is it?"

Dixie looked down at the cauliflower cheese she'd ordered in a spirit of adventure. "Surprisingly good." She picked up her fork. She hadn't been aware of putting it down.

"How are things with the house?" He leaned one arm over the back of his chair and stretched out his legs. He didn't nudge knees like Sebastian had, but his feet posed a hazard to passersby.

"Fine. I've got water and electricity connected, and a promise of a phone. I've learned how to light an Aga, and met two neighbors. Quite a day, in fact." And so different from any other day in her life so far.

"You've moved in?"

"Not yet. But I plan to. Maybe next week."

"Are you sure it's a good idea?"

"Why pay for bed and breakfast when I own a whole house? Plus, if I'm in the house, it might discourage nocturnal visitors. Remember Wednesday."

"You're certain someone was there? It could have been moonlight on the windows. Or shadows."

"The man in the moon doesn't drop a flashlight heavy enough to figure as a murder weapon." She looked straight at him. Did having only one good eye double the emotion he showed? Dark brows creased almost to touching. They even caused his eye patch to shift. Was he angry? Worried?

"If you're sure about finding the torch, you'd better tell the police."

"That's what Emma said but it seems a lot of fuss."

He shook his head. "Fuss or not, report it."

He'd gone from suggesting to ordering in ten seconds. What next? "I will in the morning. If I get around to it."

"What's wrong with now? Sergeant Grace is right over there."

Dixie turned. A gray-haired uniformed policeman leaned against the bar.

"I'll get him." Christopher was halfway back before she thought to object.

"Evening, madam. I'm Sergeant Grace. Mr. Marlowe here says you've had a spot of bother." He pulled a chair up to the table, flipped open a notepad and took her name and address. "Orchard House, eh? Well, well, what's been going on?"

Dixie resigned herself to recounting the whole story. In the retelling, it sounded like the fevered exaggerations of jet lag.

Sergeant Grace didn't think so. He listened, nodded, and asked when she planned on moving in. "Well, well," he flipped the notebook shut. "Seems to me you'd best get good locks if you plan on staying. Probably some yobs with nothing better to do, but it never hurts to be careful. Miss Hope, she claimed someone was trying to break in. Of course, she was getting frail at the end." He stood up. "I'll ask the patrol cars to drive by once in a while. Just to keep an eye on things. Give us a ring if anything else happens."

She would, if she ever got a phone.

Sergeant Grace left. Christopher didn't. He seemed settled until closing time. "Feel safer with the law on the alert?"

"I like the idea of a car driving by. Discourages unwelcome visitors."

A slim, white finger circled the rim of his glass. "Would I be included in that description? I'm serious about looking over the library."

Smiles like his should be illegal. "No harm in looking."

"I'll be over in a couple of days. Can I get you another drink?"

"Thanks, but I'm driving home."

When she stood up, he followed her out. "Scared I'll get lost?" One hand rested on the roof of her car, the other closed the door for her and curled round the open window edge. Immaculately manicured nails appeared chalk white against the dark paintwork. It had to be a trick of the moonlight.

"Dixie," he said, his face a pale oval in the night, "don't explore anymore at night. This may not be New York or Atlanta, but things happen. That house has been empty for months. If you do move in, change the locks." A half-smile quivered around his mouth. "I suppose I sound like Uncle Christopher?"

No. He wasn't the least avuncular. "It's not that, but you're the third person today to suggest I change the locks."

"Might be good advice." She couldn't argue. She agreed.

Christopher watched the taillights disappear down the lane. So, she planned on moving in, claiming her property, and discouraging unwelcome visitors. She had guts to match her beauty, but no notion what she was taking on. He'd have his work cut out.

If he had any sense he'd leave. Now. But he couldn't. He had to see that library and Dixie would invite him in.

Dixie! Dixie LePage could be his downfall—if he let her. He wouldn't. He was stronger than any mortal, even one with auburn hair, green eyes like polished glass, a smile that scrambled his senses, and warm, sweet blood coursing through her veins.

But he wanted her and he'd never dare have her.

"Staying then?" Stan Collins asked.

"Just a month or so. Until I get things straight." She'd taken an hour off from scrubbing to drive over to Horsley and extend her rental agreement.

"It's booked for a weekend in June. If you're still here then, I'll give you another one. Just a weekend switch, okay?"

Dixie agreed and scribbled a reminder on a notepad she'd bought in the village. A search through her belongings hadn't turned up her organizer. They agreed on a special rate for a long rental.

"Just don't start driving to Scotland on weekends," Stan warned.

She promised not to, and drove home to her mops and scrub brushes.

Sebastian's Jag purred to a halt outside Emily's front gate. Glancing from her bedroom window, Dixie smoothed the linen skirt of her business suit. The loan of Emily's iron had improved its appearance, and an electric blue silk blouse she'd found at Maude's in the village completed her outfit. After a day of scrubbing in jeans, it felt great to be dressed up.

Downstairs, Emily and Sebastian faced each other like a pair of bristling porcupines. Dixie wondered if she'd need body armor to walk between them. Emily stood back and grunted some comment that could have been a wish for a pleasant evening. As the front door closed behind them,

Dixie felt a warm hand on the small of her back, propelling her towards the car.

"That color really suits you," Sebastian said. "It really looks wonderful. Not everyone can wear it, but you have just the right hair and skin." His breath on her neck felt even warmer than his fingers. Dixie hoped he'd keep both hands on the steering wheel.

The Whytes lived in a converted barn six or seven miles towards Guildford. Forty-odd people filled the high-ceilinged living room—not exactly the "drinks with some of the locals" she'd expected.

"How do you do?" A beaming, red-faced man clasped her hand in his enormous paw. "Glad you came."

In a whirl of introductions, Dixie heard and forgot a dozen names. With a gin and tonic plus extra ice—two cubes just wasn't enough—in hand, she looked around the Whytes' living room at the wrought iron chandeliers, the polished floor with hand-woven rugs, the stone chimney that rose two stories and what had to be an original Warhol soup can over the sofa. Insurance must pay well.

Glancing around the room, Dixie looked at all the people she didn't know and felt terribly alone. Why in the name of heaven had she left Charleston, home and security? She longed for a familiar face. As if in answer to prayer, she glimpsed her neighbor, Emma, through the crowd. Sebastian was deep in conversation about some plan to widen a road. Dixie crossed the room to Emma.

Christopher smelled her, sweeter and fresher than any other mortal here, the minute she entered the house. He hadn't expected her, and seeing her with Caughleigh puzzled him. Until now, he'd known what Caughleigh wanted. How did Dixie fit in? Was she pawn or partner? Christopher rattled the ice cubes in his glass and watched Dixie stroll across the room to Ian Gordon's wife.

At least the beautiful American had sense to distance herself from Caughleigh. Did she know what he was? He stifled the urge to cross the room, grab her and warn her of the risks Sebastian Caughleigh spread around. He'd let a pretty face drag him into trouble once before. Never again. He'd learned something in four centuries. He didn't need, want nor care for any mortal woman, no matter how warm her smile or sweet the murmur of blood under her creamy skin. She'd bring him nothing but trouble and he carried a miasma of disaster. The only person worse for her was Sebastian Caughleigh—or Chadwick.

Christopher leaned against the chimney breast, watched Emma pull Dixie into a group of young women and imagined the conversation about babysitters, window cleaners and the best place to get a manicure this side of Guildford.

"Admiring the rich American heiress?" Larry Whyte sipped from the inevitable Scotch as he smiled at Christopher. "Watch out! I think Sebastian Caughleigh has set his sights on her."

"Really?" That thought alone made him want to join the fray. "What about professional detachment and ethics?"

"We're talking about Sebastian Caughleigh." Larry chuckled. Christopher wasn't amused. "There's something about Americans," Larry went on. "They've got so much energy. All bounce and bubbles. She'd be a nice toss in the sack. I rather envy Sebastian, but don't tell Janet."

Christopher wanted to force Larry's bulbous nose into his Scotch until *he* bubbled. He wanted to pin him against the chimney and bash his face into the rough-cut stone. He wanted to wipe the complacency off his shiny face. But that sort of behavior raised eyebrows in the stockbroker belt, so he drew in his breath and his fury. His fist closed. Tight. He felt cold and wet on his cuff and realized he'd snapped the stem of his glass.

"You run a cleaning business?" Dixie asked, catching a comment in the conversation.

Sally nodded. "Want an estimate?"

"As soon as you can."

"How about Monday morning?"

Dixie couldn't wait. Today had shown the ineffectiveness of one woman, one mop to clean the grime of years. Sally had a cleaning business. Dixie definitely needed it.

"Let's try the goodies," Emma suggested and Dixie followed her to the buffet. A plate of vegetables and a bowl of hummus caught Dixie's eye. She dipped a square of pita bread into the creamy paste. Delicious! She took a second piece, reached into the bowl, and brushed another hand, a pale hand with long, manicured nails buffed to milky whiteness. She knew those fingers. Her hand froze but her eyes gazed up at a leather eye patch.

He smiled and her stomach slipped halfway to her knees. His eyes shone and her stomach went the rest of the way. Heart racing, she straightened, left the bread in the dish and held out her hand. "Hello, this is a surprise."

"That's a village for you. Always meeting the same people."

"Is that a disadvantage?"

His full lips quivered at the corners. "Not this time."

"This time you can enjoy the evening. You don't have to rescue me from James."

"Not from James," he replied and glanced over at Sebastian, who was still talking road widening. "You came with Caughleigh?"

"Yes, I did."

"You could always leave with me and set the village talking."

"Better not add any more to the gossip mill. I never realized how fascinating Americans are until I came here."

"There's not been much to talk about since your aunts died."

"Great-aunts."

They'd wandered from the table to the fireplace. Dixie

leaned back against the stone but Christopher grabbed her upper arm. "Careful," he warned.

Dixie barely heard him, between goose bumps from the cool touch of his hand and shock at the pile of broken glass she'd almost impaled her elbow on. "What ratbrain left that there?"

"Guilty," he replied. "I hoped to hide the destruction. It could get me blacklisted from the dinner party circuit."

"I won' tell." She couldn't help it. Eyes like his had to be smiled at. And his mouth—that didn't bear thinking about. He was a man she'd met in a pub, for goodness sake. She knew nothing about him. She wasn't going to fantasize about him. She'd be sensible. "Did you drop it?"

"What?"

"The glass you tried to conceal."

"Just squeezed it too tight."

That was crazy. Dixie took both his hands in hers and turned them over. "You didn't even cut yourself and that glass broke in a dozen pieces."

"I'm Superman," he said, stepping closer and closing her hands inside his cool grasp.

Dixie looked up at smooth, pale skin and parted lips and a smile that sent her stomach south.

"There you are. I thought you'd disappeared on me."

Dixie jumped at Sebastian's voice and dropped Christopher's hands. She heard a sharp hiss that wasn't Sebastian's.

"Three minutes longer, she would have," Christopher said.

Chapter Three

"I don't think Miss LePage will fall for your conjuring tricks." Sebastian sneered nastily enough for a melodrama villain.

Christopher leaned a cashmere-covered elbow on the chimney, just missing the heap of broken glass, straightened his neck, relaxed his shoulders—and smiled. "Come now, Caughleigh. What makes you so sure you know what Dixie falls for?"

"I'm not falling for this, that's certain," Dixie muttered. At least, she'd *meant* it to be a mutter. They both seemed to hear. Christopher positively grinned. Sebastian clenched his fists. He was as unamused as Queen Victoria.

He tapped her arm. "Maybe we should be going. The reservation's at eight."

What reservation?

"Tomorrow, then?" Christopher said. "Take care of her, Caughleigh. Or I'll have your blood!"

Somehow, she didn't think he was joking. This was positively Neanderthal. Better get out of here before the pair of them came to blows. "Tomorrow. But not too early."

"Perhaps afternoon? I'd call first if I could."

"I'll be there all day."

Sebastian had chosen an elegant country restaurant with oak paneling, pitched ceilings and mullioned windows. Another time, and in different company, the atmosphere, the starched linen on the tables and beeswax candles in the silver candlesticks might have charmed, instead Dixie felt shanghaied.

"Do you bring all your clients here?" The devil made her ask that.

He looked up from his sweetbreads in sherry. "No." In the silence that followed, his fork scraped his plate three times.

Two waiters appeared with their main courses. Dixie tried to concentrate on the chartreuse of vegetables in front of her and ignore the steak Diane sizzling inches from her elbow. She should be gracious and enjoy the meal but couldn't squelch the suspicion that *she* was paying even though Sebastian might sign the check.

Their knees banged again, just as the waiter slid the steaming meat onto a warmed plate. "Aren't you concerned about Mad Cow disease?" she asked.

Sebastian's hand froze, poised over his knife. "They only use Charolais beef, imported from France." Yes, she was paying for it. "More champagne?"

At his signal, a waiter refilled her glass before she could refuse. "You're not having any?" Sebastian had covered his glass.

"I'm driving." He expected her to finish the bottle? Gran warned her about men like him. She refused his suggestion of dessert wine with her flan and liqueur with her coffee.

As they crossed the parking lot, his palm warmed the small of her back. His fingers slid over the silk and up to her neck. She'd had enough. More than enough. "Thanks for dinner and the evening out. I did enjoy meeting so many new people."

"The evening isn't over. How about coming back for coffee?"

Coffee? "No, thanks. It's late. I've got a lot to do tomorrow."

He had one last try as they pulled up at Emily's gate. "I can't change your mind?" His sweaty hand cupped her knee.

She opened the door and got out. Fast. And spoke from the safety of the sidewalk. "Sebastian, I need a good lawyer more than I need a romance." He finally got the message. After she practically hit him over the head with it.

Upstairs, she kicked off her shoes and took out her earrings. The phone rang, echoing in the silent house. After a few minutes, Emily ran downstairs. The front door opened. Dixie couldn't help herself; she peered from behind the curtain, just in time to see Emily get in the car before Sebastian drove away. What next!

The night quiet settled on the house. Dixie felt tempted to wait up and ask Emily if she'd enjoyed her "coffee." This village was better than a soap opera. She would stay her month and then return to the normalcy of the good old U. S. of A.

Dixie opened the window and leaned out sideways, recognizing the dark outline of her house across the Green. That light again! Someone *was* in her house!

It took just minutes to pull on tennis shoes and a sweatshirt. She took the Metro. Ten minutes' walk took three by car. She turned off her lights and crept the last thirty yards in low gear. Stopping in the narrow lane beside the house, she grabbed the black flashlight. She'd use it against whoever had dropped it.

The house was dark now. Had she been a fool to come? A call to Sergeant Grace would have made better sense. Her hand tightened over the flashlight. Two steps inside the gate she saw a dark silhouette ahead of her. "Got you, buster!" Dixie shouted and shone her flashlight full beam ahead. The beam lit up a pale face and a dark leather eye patch. Christopher! So all that talk about wanting to buy books was a front.

"Dixie, turn out the damn light!" He sounded more irritated than guilty. The nerve of the man!

"No way. Get off my land and don't ever come back," she yelled, feeling like a heroine in a Western romance, waving a flashlight instead of a six-shooter.

He stared straight at her, unblinded by the light. "Hush, Dixie," he said and took a step forward.

"No way. Go now, or I'll scream."

"And alert whomever's in your house?"

He'd whispered but she heard him as clearly as the night. One glance confirmed the light still moved upstairs. As she watched, confused, his hand closed over hers and switched off her flashlight as he pulled her between two scratchy shrubs. She tried the evasion techniques she'd learned in self-defense. They didn't work. Something scraped her ankle and a twig grazed her cheek. His arm closed round her shoulders and held her tight against his hard chest. She flattened her hand and tried to push away. His chest felt like steel and his arm tightened like a vice. "Let me go."

"I will."

Not a muscle moved.

"When? Next week? Someone's in my house and I'm finding out who."

"This Englishman's-home-is-his-castle act is impressive, but foolish."

That did it. "I'm female and American. If you haven't noticed."

"Oh, I've noticed." She didn't doubt it. Her breasts were half-flattened against his chest.

"You'll let me go this week or next?"

"Now, if you promise not to go rushing out to protect your property."

"That's my house getting broken into."

"Yes, and burglars today carry guns, knives, tear gas and bicycle chains. Stay here," he whispered, "trust me."

"Give me one good reason."

"I'm not the one thieving your great-grandfather's first editions." He had a point. The light moved again, disappeared, then appeared lower.

"He's having a good look," Christopher whispered in her ear and pulled her beside him against the wall, his arms loosely circling her shoulders.

"Who?"

"You know it's not me. Who else could get in?"

"Sebastian, but he's giving Emily a cup of coffee."

She heard his chuckle but his chest never moved. "You resisted his blandishments then?"

"It wasn't hard." Even laughter didn't ripple a muscle in his chest. Where did he work out? "Enough of that." She'd come to waylay an intruder not discuss Sebastian's advances.

"Whoever it is, they're not afraid of being in a haunted house at night."

"Oh, please!"

"The villagers believe your aunts haunt the house."

"Well, I don't. I don't believe in ghosts. Especially ones that carry flashlights."

"They also believed they were witches."

"I don't believe in witches either."

"What a woman. You scoff at witches and ghosts. What about fairies, pixies and elves?"

"Not hobbits, either."

"What about . . ." He hesitated, then whispered, "Vampires?" As he spoke, his fingers trailed cool down the side of her neck.

At that, her foot slammed down on his instep. He didn't flinch or move away, just looked into her face.

"Only in Anne Rice. Quit fooling! I'm not here to play games. Anyway, what are you doing here?"

"Same thing as you. I was walking along the lane and saw a light." He almost hissed the words as he pushed her away. The night chill settled on her shoulders. He watched the window a minute. "I'll take care of this. Go back to your car and lock the doors. Better still, drive away."

"I'm not leaving as long as that intruder's there!"

He paused as if to take a breath, but Dixie never heard him inhale. "We could try scaring him out. Get rid of him before he nicks something. Are you game?"

Why not? It was her property at stake. "What shall I do?"

"Slip back out the gate, get in your car and lock the door." He spoke lightly but stared at her with an intensity that made her shiver. This close, his one eye seemed to warm as it met hers. For a minute she felt weak, giddy. Then she shook herself out of it. The tension was getting to her.

"You've got to be kidding!" Sit in the car while he confronted a possibly armed intruder?

He frowned. "Don't get so riled up. I want you ready for a quick getaway if things get nasty."

It sounded more like antiquated notions of chivalry. "Why lock it then?"

He pulled her closer and whispered, "Are you trying to be difficult?"

Again the giddiness, the feeling of warmth, of weakness. She *had* drunk too much this evening. "No. Sensible. You mentioned weapons. Why are you barging in unarmed?"

He chuckled. "I'm Superman, remember?" He took her hesitation as consent. "Trust me. I know what I'm doing. Wait in the car. I may need your help later."

Grudgingly, Dixie agreed and went out the side gate but didn't go straight to her car. A car parked up the side lane caught her attention. Christopher's? She imagined him driving something more stylish than a battered compact. Bennie the

Burglar's? Why not? With the help of her flashlight, she memorized the number.

So much for country quiet. Rustles, creaks and whines filled the night. Talk about spooky! She decided to ignore them *and* her body's reaction to being held close by Christopher. Impatience tugged at Dixie. This was crazy. She was going back.

A shriek cut through the night quiet. A door slammed and Dixie ran round the corner just in time to see a dark figure running for the parked car. The engine started, but as the car pulled away down the road, a second figure ran after it. Christopher? The car swerved just as he came alongside. Dixie's heart stilled as Christopher's body arched through the air, frozen in the headlights. She raced up the lane as he staggered out of the ditch.

"You were supposed to be in your car."

"You're hurt?" He had to be.

"Just shaken."

Shaken? He had to be injured after that fall. She imagined broken bones, internal injuries—but he was standing. "I'll get the car. You need a doctor." Without waiting for a reply, she tore down the lane. When she got back, he was leaning against a tree. As she stopped, he opened the passenger door.

"May I get in?"

He stood there, holding on to the door. Was this British or something? "Of course! Get in!" He got in, his legs a little too long for a compact car. Dixie flicked on the interior light. "That was a homicidal maniac, not a burglar."

"I'm okay. I just wish you'd seen the car number."

That did it. "Let's have a reality check here. You're half dead and you're worrying about a registration number. Anyway, I have it." She recited the memorized numbers, amazed that she remembered them after all this panic. "Now, let me look at you."

He didn't appear to be bleeding, but he had mud on his

face and clothes, grass in his hair and his cashmere sweater wouldn't see any more cocktail parties. One shoulder showed white where his shirt and sweater were both ripped open. She reached out to touch him. He had to be bleeding from a gash like that.

His hand closed on her wrist. "Go easy, my dear."

"You might be bleeding." He had some grip for a man who'd barely escaped death.

"I'm not."

"Let me check."

He put her hand on the steering wheel. "If you fancy tearing the clothes off a man, you had your chance with Caughleigh. Spare me. Your house is safe for the night."

"Forget the house! What about you? You're seeing a doctor."

His fingers closed over her hand as she clutched the gear stick. "Get this straight. I am not seeing a doctor and you are going home. I am not hurt."

"You have to be. I saw you tossed through the air."

"Ever heard of Jujitsu, Dixie? I know how to fall."

He couldn't sit that straight, grip like a maniac and argue if he were hurting, and his chest would heave if he'd had some injury.

"You *are* Superman, aren't you?"

"You believe in him, do you?"

She gave up—almost. She insisted on driving him home. He acquiesced, but refused to let her even come up his path. "I've a reputation to consider even if you haven't," he said. "Imagine the talk—you refuse Sebastian and then hotfoot it over to my house. We'd have to fight a duel for certain."

"I thought they became illegal in the last century."

"I'm a man with roots in the past." He squeezed her hand, as if in farewell. Dixie wasn't ready to have him go. She touched his shoulder and reached to kiss him good-bye. It wasn't much for a man who'd risked his life to protect her property.

She aimed for his cheek. He turned and her mouth met his lips, cool as the marble on her pantry shelf. But as her lips caressed his, she knew only warmth and softness. He tasted of night and spice and excitement. Her mouth opened as his pressed on hers, but slowly, like a plant unfolding in spring warmth. Almost reluctantly, his hand smoothed up her neck and through her hair. She sighed and her tongue reached for his.

The heat of summer burst through her. She gasped, but not for breath; for more. And he gave it. Sweetness flooded her soul and need surged like a current through her brain. It was a mating of mouths, a coupling of spirits. Time stopped. Dixie knew nothing but spiraling warmth and an aching need for more.

"Christopher," she murmured as he pulled away.

"Remember my reputation," he teased. She leaned into his strong shoulder. His fingers smoothed her neck from her ear to her throat. His touch promised heaven. She prayed he'd never stop. That he'd ask her to stay. Anything to feel this way forever. Her hand reached for his chest, searching for shirt buttons, questing warm, male flesh.

His hand closed over hers. "Dixie, we have to stop. I need time to rest." She sat up. How thoughtless of her! He was injured, bruised at the very least and here she was, jumping his bones. "Go back to Emily's and stay there. Don't try any heroics over the house. It's safe for tonight. Promise?"

She agreed but waited until the door closed behind him. She would have stopped by her house but she'd given her word. She couldn't break a promise made after a kiss like that.

Undressing in the room under the eaves, Dixie glanced at her watch. The whole incident with Christopher, her house and the maniac intruder had lasted less than a half-hour. She stifled a shiver. It was over. She didn't need to worry. She was too worn to worry. Repulsing amorous swains, chasing robbers and aiding the wounded had worn her out. She tossed her clothes on the chair and fell into bed without even brushing her teeth. Emily's linen sheets felt like cool, soothing balm to her worn body but nothing eased the turmoil in her brain. What had she done? Acted like a crazy wanton. Thrown herself on a man, an injured man at that, just because her hormones went into overdrive through a bit of stress. She still tasted his lips on hers, felt his tongue in her mouth and what the rest of her body was doing didn't bear examining. Tomorrow he was coming to go through her books. What had she started?

Sebastian ignored six rings, shrill above Emily's sighs. He slipped his hand over her breast as the answering machine clicked on. "Uncle, you have to be there. Talk to me!"

Sebastian wanted to spit. Couldn't James manage anything? He'd had all evening with that troublesome woman out of the way. He'd better be calling to announce success. Sebastian leaned over Emily and picked up the phone. "You found everything, I hope."

"No way. This makes three times I've scoured that room. Nothing's there."

"You'll find it on the fourth. Go back and don't come home without it."

"Not on your Nellie! You can't make me go back. That place is haunted. Not just noises. Tonight I saw a white face at the window. You're not telling me that was a local yokel."

"Get back there!"

"Never!"

Sebastian cussed as James hung up. He turned back to Emily.

She sat up on the desk, slowly pulled her skirts down and tucked in her blouse. "If he didn't find their records, we're in trouble."

"Not yet. We'll find them. If they're that well hidden, Miss LePage isn't likely to stumble across them. They have to be in that book room. I've gone through every other paper with a fine-tooth comb. Nothing's in the bank. I checked. Being executor has its advantages." He tucked in his shirt and zipped his pants.

Emily stood up. "What do we do if we can't find them?"

"Win time. Delay things. Inconvenience our Miss LePage. Maybe James needs a helper."

"Who?" Emily stopped. Her eyes widened as they met his. She shook her head. "Not me. Not in a million years."

"You have a lot to lose if the truth comes out. The bank wouldn't be too happy at the idea of a witch among their staff. Rather spoils the image."

"It's not illegal anymore. I don't have to worry."

"No?" One hand grasped her neck as the other stroked her chin. He kissed her, pressing his mouth down to part her lips. He kissed her long enough to release a sigh then drew back, his hand still firm on her neck. "You'll do what I ask, Emily. Because I want it."

"What shall I do?" What a mess she looked with her rumpled hair, smudged lipstick and creased skirt.

"Give me two days. Fix a nice Sunday breakfast for our Dixie and make sure it keeps her in bed for a couple of days."

Her eyes widened as his meaning dawned. "I can't do that!"

His hand trailed around her neck to her breast. "You will. Why be a skilled herbalist if you deny your skills to the coven?"

"This isn't for the coven. It's for you."

"It's the same thing. The old women are gone. I'm not letting an inconvenient American ruin everything. All you have to do is give her the collywobbles for a couple of days. She's a healthy young woman. Nothing can go wrong. Marlowe is poking into things. We're all set to take care of him. You get our Dixie out of action."

Color drained from her face. "Sebby, that's going too far."

Sebastian turned her face up to his again. "I'm counting on you, Emily." She nodded and he let her kiss him again. He watched her find her shoes, gather up her handbag and let herself out.

He needed her to come through.

He wondered what she'd use. Bryony root? Rhubarb leaf? He didn't want to know. If it went wrong, he preferred ignorance. He hoped it wouldn't. He still fancied a go at Dixie.

Dixie looked up at the uneven ceiling beams over her bed. It took a couple of sleep-muddled minutes to place the sound—rain drumming on the pitched roof. Pulling herself from under the duvet, she padded over to open the chintz curtains. Rain wasn't the word. A steady downpour beat a tattoo on the roof, gutters and street. Orchard House was half-obscured and a lone car drove down the lane, spraying water from every puddle. She'd heard about English rain and this was it. So much for a nice stroll up to church and a morning reading the paper on the Green.

Change in weather, change in plans. She'd spend the day going through her book room. She had all the time in the world. She only hoped that Aga-thing hadn't burned the house down.

Coming out of the shower, she smelled cooking.

"Good morning." Emily's round cheeks spread in a wide smile. "I thought I heard you up. I thought we could have a nice chat over breakfast. Sunday is such a nice, leisurely day, isn't it?"

"Perhaps a cup of coffee . . ." Dixie began. She tried to place the smell. It wasn't sausage or bacon.

Emily pressed down the toaster, turning on another smile for Dixie. "No, I insist you must have something to eat. I fixed something special: veal kidneys."

Kidneys! Dixie felt the bile rise from the lowest point in her innards. She could drink coffee while the woman munched on bacon but watch while she chewed kidneys? Never!

"Thanks, but I've got to go out early." She squelched her guilt at Emily's disappointment. She didn't stay for toast or cereal either. She had instant coffee in her kitchen and a packet of cookies. She'd make do with that.

The Aga hadn't gone out. In fact, the kitchen offered a warm welcome after the damp outside. Nothing like breakfast in her own house—but the milk had gone sour in the pantry. Mug of black coffee in hand, Dixie added "refrigerator" to her shopping list. Her handwriting jumped back at her. She was crazy. A refrigerator wasn't a purchase for a month's stay. How about staying longer? No way. Not with traffic on the wrong side of the road, unfamiliar currency, and no telephone.

She made another cup of coffee and carried it upstairs.

The repeated ringing of the doorbell broke Dixie's concentration. For over three hours, she'd lost herself among the books. Resisting the temptation to ignore the bell, she pushed the dusty volumes aside. Halfway downstairs, she paused. Who was it? Christopher? Comments about vandals and teenage intruders flashed through her mind.

The mahogany mirror in the hall showed the angle of the front door. Dixie paused to glimpse the reflection—nothing but steady rain. Pranksters ringing and running away? *Yobs*, as Emma called them. Dixie was ready. She'd dealt with teenagers for a living.

Hand on the brass knob, Dixie waited for another ring and peered through the window beside the door. Christopher! "Come on in, you're getting soaked!" She flung the door open.

Better than he'd ever imagined, she didn't just invite him in, she grasped his hand and pulled him over the threshold. After all these months, he was inside the house. Now he could come and go as he pleased, but Dixie's welcome triggered misgivings in the heart he didn't possess. "I got Alf to pack us lunch. A fair exchange for a look at your library."

Her warm hand brushed his as she took the basket. "For lunch you can have more than a look. All I have in the house is a pack of cookies. . . . Sorry, biscuits. I'm famished for something more."

So was he. A smile as warm as her skin could lead them both to disaster.

Dixie unpacked asparagus quiche, a Greek salad with olives and Feta cheese, something that looked like meatballs but Alf had promised wasn't, and a tub of fresh fruit.

"This is enough to feed a family," Dixie said, taking plates and knives from the oak dresser.

"You eat, I'll skip. I have severe food allergies and have to be careful what I eat." The practiced lie slid out. For the first time in his long life, it stung.

"I feel guilty pigging out while you watch. Could I at least make you coffee?"

She felt guilty? What was he supposed to feel after she'd rushed to his rescue last night? He'd better stop feeling at all if this was going to work. "Coffee would be great." His metabolism could handle liquids. "Sit down and eat." The sooner she ate, the sooner he could go through that room.

She insisted on making his coffee first. "Sure I can't tempt you?" she asked, looking at the food on the table.

Temptation? Sweet Abel! For over three years, he'd had

no desire to feed from humans. Now it came in great smashing waves and he had a whole afternoon to survive.

"Wonderful." She closed her eyes as she bit into a "meatball." "These are fantastic, I'm sorry I can't share with you."

"What are they?"

"Falafel—chick pea flour, garlic, herbs and something extra I can't place." She smiled up at him. "I can see vegetarianism isn't your choice."

No. He fed on smooth flesh and warm pulsing blood. He wanted hers and he'd never take it. Need like this made him vulnerable and he couldn't afford any risks. Not here. Not now. Not after her embrace last night. To business. "Let's take the coffee upstairs."

"You want to see the books? Fair enough."

She packed the leftover food into the walk-in pantry. "Hope it keeps. I was thinking about buying a fridge, but wonder whether it's worth it. I won't be here more than a month."

A month! Could he really be that lucky? "Didn't realize you were staying that long. Caughleigh said something about your leaving next week."

"Sebastian doesn't make my decisions for me. I need a holiday and this is as good a place as any—and rent free."

"I'm very glad you're staying."

The blood rose up her neck. Her eyes flickered and looked away. "Upstairs," she said, "I've something to show you."

She'd pulled back the shutters and turned on the lights. It did little for the decor. Ninety years' accumulation of books was stacked on shelves, heaped in corners and piled on the tables and chairs. "Someone went through everything," she said through a clenched jaw. "There's dust all over the floor and shelves but the books have been moved."

"You knew that already." Had she forgotten last night?

"Yes." Her dark eyebrows curled together. "I was pretty sure that first night and certain yesterday, but I'd only glanced in here before this morning. I thought they might have been going through the whole house."

"They haven't?"

"The other upstairs rooms haven't been touched since Sebastian closed the house. This one had footsteps in the dust and the books had been moved. Why?"

He let the question stay rhetorical. Answering it would trigger a dozen more. The less she knew, the safer.

"Anything missing?"

She chuckled, a warm sound from deep in her belly. "How would I know? It'll take me ages to check and then I'll never be sure if it wasn't gone before. I'll just make sure our visitor never gets in again. Tonight I'll leave the blinds and drapes open and every light on. Tomorrow I'm putting on dead-bolt locks, and a security system and after then, I'll be here."

"You're moving in?" This was wonderful, or terrible. She'd be closer but in danger. Why did he care? All he wanted was a few books. Mortals didn't concern him unless they got in his way.

"Don't look so shocked. It is my house after all. I'd rather be here than in Emily Reade's spare room."

"You're not worried about being here alone?"

"I've gotten used to being alone."

The words cut deep where he never felt. How could she be so beautiful and alive and alone? "Should you be here alone?"

She ran her hand over her forehead and through her auburn hair as if brushing away a hard memory or an old hurt. "I can look after myself. There's Emma just a few yards away, and I'll have good locks to keep intruders out."

They wouldn't keep him out. Not now she'd invited him in. What about the others?

"Look what I found this morning." She crossed to the shelves and reached for a book. When she turned back to him, her eyes glowed with excitement. "I'm sure you get cracks about this all the time but I can't help that." She pressed the book against her chest, holding it close. "You must see this." She held out the worn calfskin bound volume.

He took it with both hands, his thumb feeling the warmth where her breasts had pressed against the leather. He opened the book with care—rough handling could split the old binding apart—and stared at the title page. Had she guessed? How?

"*The Jew of Malta*. I found it an hour or so ago." He nodded, his cool fingertips smoothing the musty pages. Then he read the date, but he hadn't the heart to tell her. He looked up from the worn pages to her bright eyes. "It's old," she went on. "Probably a nineteenth-century forgery and worth something because of that, but the date says 1587 and I think that's wrong."

"It is. It came out in 1589." He should have bitten off his own tongue.

Her eyes widened. "You have studied him then?"

"My namesake? Why not? Yes, I know all about Kit Marlowe." He sighed. The past hovered like a crouching animal. He knew everything.

She perched on the edge of the oak table, watching him. "I read him some in college. I majored in English before I went on to train as a librarian. Marlowe fascinated me. So talented and mysterious. Who was he? Did he write Shakespeare? What really happened in the tavern at Deptford? It's as good as a soap opera."

"Will Shakespeare wrote Shakespeare. Kit Marlowe wrote Marlowe. And there's nothing fine about betrayal and treachery."

She started at his sharp words. "You *have* studied him then."

He forced his shoulders into a shrug. "You could say so."

She wasn't finished. "It just seems like a mystery novel. So young and talented and dying in a brawl and such an odd injury. . . ." She chopped her sentence off and bit her lip, looking at his face, then turning scarlet. "I'm sorry that was tactless."

He laid the book on the dusty tabletop and took her shoulders in his hands. "Dixie," he whispered, "it doesn't matter. It was a long time ago."

Her teeth worried her lower lip. "I didn't think. I was just running on. It's such a coincidence." She paused, her face tight with remorse. "I'm so tactless. I just . . ."

"Forget it. People have called me a lot worse. The kids in the village call me 'Pirate' behind my back. It doesn't matter."

"What happened?"

She wasn't asking about the inn at Deptford. But she was. And she'd never believe the truth. "It happened a long time ago—when I was young and playing dangerously. With one good eye, I have eighty percent of my vision. It's little more than an inconvenience."

Her white teeth still pulled at her soft lip. In a minute she'd draw blood. He couldn't let her. The scent of her blood would drive him crazy. He traced a finger over each curved eyebrow, smoothed her cheeks, tilted her chin, bent his mouth to hers and eased her lips away from her teeth.

Warmth and sweetness. She tasted like honeysuckle nectar on a June night. She curved warm into him like sunshine on marble. Her tongue met his and she moaned like aspen trees sighing in an afternoon breeze. She was everything that life had to offer and he was four hundred years dead. He pulled away gently, brushing his lips on her heated forehead. With her, he almost felt like a man again, and that would be dangerous for both of them.

"If we're not careful, we'll forget why we're here," he said, stepping back, just a half step.

"Why are we here?" she asked, her eyes glinting as her mouth twitched, her lips still swollen from his kisses.

"Flirt!" he said, still holding one hand but stepping back to arms' length. "The men in America must be desolate without you."

She laughed without a trace of amusement. "It wasn't quite like that." She pulled back her hand, as if a memory hurt. "Now, what did you want to look for?"

She was right. Keep it casual. He only hoped he could.

"I'm interested in paranormal and magic." He ignored her rising eyebrows, although his thumbs itched to smooth them. "Anything on witchcraft, magic, sightings, vampires." He tucked the last in as an afterthought.

"You believe in all that stuff? I thought you were kidding last night."

"I'm prepared to believe anything I haven't disproved."

"Oh, please." She rolled her eyes. "I'll look. If you really want me to." She made no attempt to hide her surprise. But then she never seemed to hide anything. She was open as a rose in summer and just as fragile.

Together they searched the stacks and assembled a small mountain of books on the wide library table. "Quite a collection," Dixie said, giving the heap an uncertain eye. "You won't get through it all today."

"May I presume on your hospitality some other day?"

She shrugged. "Whenever. I'll be here, or at least in and out. You can't phone I'm afraid, but the books are yours if you want them. I'm not into that stuff. I'll get them valued."

He held out his hand. "Agreed."

"Shall we settle the deal with a cup of tea?"

He shook his head. He'd only just absorbed the coffee. His body couldn't handle any more. Not in daylight. "I'll skip it."

She left to fix tea, and he found a corner away from the last afternoon sun. In a couple of hours it would be dusk.

"See you tomorrow," he said as he waved good-bye, a tall lean silhouette in the dusk. Dixie left shortly afterwards, leaving all the lights on and the shutters open. The house shone like a beacon across the village green, but it should keep unwanted visitors away. She planned a long shower to clear the grime and dust away, and then a nice quiet supper at the Barley Mow. And she'd make a point of not thinking about how Christopher kissed.

Chapter Four

On her way upstairs, Emily called to her, "Dixie, come in a minute, dear. I have a visitor."

It was a toss-up who won the prize for most uncomfortable: Emily seated by the silver teapot with a lace napkin on her lap; Dixie all too conscious of the cobwebs on her clothes and the dirt on her face; Ida Collins with her knitting on her lap and a plate of sandwiches at her elbow.

Dixie invaded their dainty tea, feeling like an unwashed coal miner. "I'm sorry," she said. "I'm in no state to sit down." She hesitated to even offer a hand to Ida.

Emily obviously didn't want Dixie on her upholstery. "Oh dear," she fussed, "and we were planning on a nice cup of tea and a cake with you. Ida brought some jam buns, they're raspberry."

"I think I'd better take a rain check," Dixie said and took a step towards the stairs.

"No," said Ida, quiet as a lady yet as insistent as a drill sergeant. "That isn't necessary. Emily can give you a cup to take upstairs and you must have one of my raspberry buns."

There was no gracious way to refuse. Dixie took the cup

and saucer in one hand, balanced the plate in the other and made it upstairs. She left the tea and bun in her room while she showered off the dirt of Orchard House. By the time she dried her hair, the tea was cold. She tipped it down the wash-basin. She wasn't hungry for the bun, not after the lunch she'd had. Not wanting to hurt Ida's feelings, Dixie wrapped it in a wad of Kleenex and tucked it inside a paper bag in her trashcan.

Weary, she stretched out on the bed. An evening reading appealed more than a night at the Barley Mow. By nine, she was asleep. At ten, Emily tapped on the door. Hearing no an-swer, she peered inside. Three quiet steps, and she removed the empty cup and plate.

Ida waited downstairs. "Asleep?" she asked.

Emily nodded.

"That's the poppy in the tea. She'll be out for about six hours, then the aconite in the buns will start working."

Emily frowned. "Are you sure it's safe? If something goes wrong—she's in my house."

"I know what I'm doing and it isn't kidneys in betony sauce for a vegetarian."

"I did my best."

"It wasn't good enough. This will work." She looked at her watch. "About four in the morning she'll start vomiting. Wait until eight or nine to be sure she gets it all out. Then call the doctor. She'll be weak but unhurt." She paused. "Be sure to flush and clean the loos. You don't want anything left."

"But you said it was safe." Emily felt the sweat pooling in her armpits. Sebastian had gone too far this time.

"It is." Ida didn't hide her impatience. "Now call Stanley to pick me up. I don't like being out late."

"How are you?" Emily's plump face peered out from the kitchen door.

At least no kidney's frying this morning—just coffee. "Fine. Just got up early. I've lots I want to do today."

"Feeling alright?" Emily looked unbelievably worried.

"You bet! Living here seems to agree with me." Her life had certainly taken a turn for the better this past week. Some week! She'd left Charleston, a newly unemployed school librarian, recently spectacularly dumped by the love of her life. Today she owned property in England and enough money to consider herself a woman of independent means. These things happened in the romance novels Gran used to read, not to Dixie LePage.

Dixie thought more about it as she drove into the village. Talk about life changes! She'd even found new men— Sebastian, polished, as good looking as hope and as worrying as a sore tooth; Christopher, strange as they come and faster than a speeding bullet; James, the obvious villain of the piece—the sleazy nephew.

She bought still-warm croissants from the baker on High Street and fresh coffee, ground to order in the small grocery store next door.

"Fine grind, I'll remember that," said the round and cheerful woman behind the counter. "You're the American who's moved into Orchard House, aren't you? We deliver on Tuesdays and Fridays. Call us and we'll send up whatever you need. I'm Kim, just ask for me."

"I will," Dixie replied, taking the business card from Kim, "but I'm still waiting for a phone."

"You are? Did you call British Telecom?" Dixie nodded. Sarah went on, "I'll have a word with my son. He works for them. I'll see what he can do." Dixie thanked her and left with her coffee and a plastic bag of milk that threatened to leak.

The Aga had gone out in the night, but Dixie managed to relight it on the third try and felt she'd scaled some new domestic height. On the back door she found a note from the milkman asking when she wanted delivery started, and how much. Someone had tucked a parish newsletter into the mail slot in the front door. It was as if the village suddenly decided to acknowledge her presence.

Sipping her coffee, Dixie wondered where she could buy more of the solid fuel to replenish the dwindling supply. She took a deep breath. Yesterday she contemplated purchasing a new refrigerator. Today, it was milk delivery and fuel. What next?

What next was Sally rapping on the back door to give an estimate for cleaning.

As they walked through the house, looking over the peeling wallpaper, yellowed paint and damp patches over the front door, a quick sale seemed the best idea. But a few minutes surrounded by the pear wood paneling in the dining room and imagining a good log fire in the marble fireplace in the drawing room, and Dixie knew she was here to stay. Maybe for more than a month—or two.

The front doorbell rang as they were halfway upstairs. It was the locksmith.

Sally called from the stairs, "I'll check out the upstairs."

Dixie hesitated. Why? She couldn't be in two places at once. Sally could easily look over the bedrooms by herself. The locksmith set his tool bag down with a clank. "Let's look at these locks of yours."

"Tell you what," he said after inspecting the doors. "I can give you a nice set of Chubb locks. Front, back and French windows, and that side door by the breakfast room. No sense in just doing the front door."

Dixie agreed, even though the price suggested gold-plated locks. She intended to prevent uninvited visitors, whatever the cost—and heck, she didn't need to pinch pennies now.

He busied himself drilling a perfect circle in the oak front door, and commenting on the antique lock. "Wonderful they are. All made by hand back then. Beautiful to use and work with, but they'll never keep out anyone who knows what they're doing."

They hadn't.

As he moved on to the French windows, another man arrived at the front door. "Cheers. Mum said you needed phones."

A couple of hours later, Dixie had phones in the kitchen, the front hall and the big bedroom overlooking the back garden that she'd earmarked for her own.

She closed the door on British Telecom just as the locksmith came in from the kitchen.

"You're all set up. They won't get in here easily." He handed her a set of bright keys and left her in a quiet house. No bustle of workmen, no toneless singing, no burr of automatic tools. Alone in her own house.

Except for Sally! The upstairs was deserted, but open doors and closets ajar showed where Sally had gone through the rooms. In the book room, someone had rifled through Christopher's stack of books. No doubt about it. The copy of *The Jew* had been at the top of the pile. Now it lay open, a few inches from the rest of them. Why worry? Sally had been curious, that was all.

Sally had left a note and estimate on the kitchen table. She'd slipped out, she said, because Dixie was busy. She could send in a crew on Wednesday if Dixie would call. The charges seemed reasonable enough, given a major spring clean was needed. Dixie went around and locked every door. It was getting late and she had to get back to Emily's and tell her about moving out in the morning.

"What the hell do you mean, moved out?" Sebastian barked at Emily. He imagined her holding the receiver from her ear and then covering it to block the sounds of his tirade from the nice, respectable bank employees.

"Sorry, Sebby. She just moved into her house. I could hardly prevent it, now could I?"

She could have if she'd done the job properly on Sunday. She'd made a pig's ear out of the whole business and Ida hadn't done any better. That's what happened when he left things to women. "You've made a mess of everything."

"I tried," she whined. "So did Ida. She said it was foolproof."

If he slammed down the receiver, she might put on a pout and stay away this evening. Sebastian sensed he'd need her by then. "We've got to get this sorted out."

"Oh, Sebby, never mind. I'll be over tonight and make you feel better, lovey. Between us, we'll fix things."

Sebastian thumped the receiver back on its cradle. He couldn't rely on the women in the coven. Emily had been plain stupid and Ida was getting on and must have mistaken the dose—or Miss LePage possessed extraordinary strengths. Sebastian's stomach clenched at the thought. Was it possible? He knew interest in Wicca had grown in recent years in the States and Miss LePage certainly had the ancestry for it. Was that why she'd come? To assume the mantle of her dead aunts? Impossible! He'd never relinquish power. He'd fight her to the last. Whatever it took.

He was sitting silently, considering his options, when someone knocked on the door. Emily? Too early. Who?

"You!" Sebastian almost spat.

"Me." Christopher agreed. "I need ten minutes. May I come in, or would you rather talk on the landing?" Sebastian might well snarl. Christopher had deliberately waited until Miss Fortune left.

Sebastian opened the door and jerked his head, hardly gracious, but an invitation nonetheless. "Gone casual have you?" Christopher asked, eying his rolled up shirtsleeves.

Sebastian ignored the comment. "I won't offer you a

drink, since you can't stay." He leaned against his desk, arms folded.

Christopher smiled. "Don't trouble yourself, Caughleigh. Just dropped by to mention something."

"What? Decided you want to make a will?"

Christopher chuckled. "Not yet, Caughleigh, not yet. I came about a far more immediate matter. Miss LePage."

"Yes, I noticed your concern. She'd be interested in your history."

"You'd have a hard time convincing her. She doesn't believe in me—or you. I just came to give a friendly, gentlemanly warning. If any harm ever befell Miss LePage, it would anger me."

"And you alone would take me on?"

"I wouldn't be alone."

"We have a full coven."

"Not yet. The new initiates have nothing but curiosity and a smattering of knowledge."

Amusement lit Sebastian's dark eyes. "Marlowe, you've lost your heart to her."

Caughleigh would never know how close that jibe hit. Ever. "We both know I don't have one. No, she's innocent and uninvolved and it will stay that way. Keep your delinquent nephew away from her. Leave her and that house alone."

"And if I don't?"

Christopher picked up the telephone receiver and clenched it in his left hand. There was a loud snap and another. Slowly the plastic crumbled under his fist. The muscles in Sebastian's face tensed and his complexion paled. He shivered. Christopher opened his fingers and let a handful of fragments fall over the leather desktop. "You will."

He took a step as if towards the door but instead took Sebastian's jacket from the hook. "You look chilled, Caughleigh," he said. "You need your jacket."

Quicker than lightening, Christopher threw the jacket on Sebastian's shoulders and pulled the sleeves tight around his neck. "Remember what I said," he whispered in his ear. Sebastian's hands clutched at air as his arms flailed. Christopher tightened his grip. Sebastian nodded. Christopher whispered, "I knew you'd understand." He held the sleeves until the seams made ripping noises.

Caughleigh slumped on the desk, the jacket still around his neck. He coughed and choked and managed a couple of profanities.

A wallet, keys, and date book fell from the jacket. Christopher pushed them aside until he saw the initials on the brown leather book: "D. LeP." He palmed it. Maybe he had no right to it, but neither did Caughleigh.

"Pleasant evening," Christopher said to the still-gasping Caughleigh and carefully shut the door. The evenings were still a trifle chilly.

He had his back to her, but there was no mistaking those wide shoulders and blue-black hair. After an afternoon watching him among the books, Dixie could pick Christopher out of a Super Bowl crowd. He turned before she closed the door. His smile broke through the smoky haze. Shivering wasn't enough. She ached at the sight of him.

She'd lost her senses. She didn't need them. She'd been crazy to come. What sort of woman came looking for a man in a bar? But this was the Barley Mow, with Vernon limping around, wiping tables and gathering up used glasses and Alf at the bar. Christopher and Alf exchanged words.

Alf took down a glass. By the time she crossed to the bar, a half of Guinness waited for her. "Your usual, Miss LePage." She reached into her pocket but he shook his head. "It's taken care of." He nodded up at Christopher.

A pale hand rested inches from hers. Dixie stared at the

white, perfectly manicured nails, slender fingers, narrow wrist and muscular forearm. "This one's on me," Christopher said.

She jerked her head up and saw his smile. Had he noticed her ogling his hands? Please, no. "Thanks." She took a sip from the heavy glass mug. Swallowing wasn't easy.

"What's going to tempt you tonight?" he asked.

"What?" And what did that grin mean?

"What gustatory delight on Alf's menu?"

"Oh." She stared up at the chalkboard menu and took three deep breaths. "I'll have a jacket potato with a shrimp cocktail, Alf."

"We'll be over in the conservatory," Christopher told Alf.

"We will, will we?"

"I want to talk business. If we do it here, we might as well publish it in the local paper."

That made sense. She took her Guinness and followed him until they found an empty table. He raised his wine glass to his lips and sipped, pursing his lips together as he swallowed, then a bright red tongue smoothed over his full lips. Dixie felt herself mirroring the gesture as her stomach did a flip. This was ridiculous! They'd come here to discuss first editions, hadn't they?

"Here you are, one jacket potato with a shrimp cocktail." Dixie stared at the plate Vernon placed in front of her. She hadn't realized the shrimp cocktail would already be sauced, and she'd never expected to get it on top of the potato.

"Looks tasty," Christopher said.

Dixie nodded. Once over the initial surprise, it did look appetizing. But when she met Christopher's eye, she wondered if he'd meant the spud.

She tasted a shrimp, the tang of cocktail sauce was sharper than she'd expected, a strange mix of vinegar and something she couldn't recognize. She let it sit on her tongue, trying to identify the elusive taste and hoping to calm her racing pulse. If her stomach didn't settle soon, she'd never be able to swallow. She managed one shrimp. It was small enough that she swallowed it whole. The taste lingered on her tongue, strange and unexpected as the combination on the plate in front of her, as alien as the one-eyed man watching her.

"I wanted to talk to you," she said, sipping from her glass to wet her dry throat.

"I know."

"About the books you wanted."

"Yes." He smiled. His wide mouth spread to reveal teeth white as alabaster. He laughed, a warm chuckle that came from deep in his belly, and his eye twinkled. His lips closed, but he still smiled as he leaned back and tilted his chair. "I know why you came, Dixie."

He whispered but it felt as if he'd shouted. The words echoed like a siren in her mind. Did he? How could he? Please, she wasn't that obvious, was she?

This time it took three deep breaths and a couple of mouthfuls of jacket potato, but at least she could still swallow. "The books you wanted. I found an antiquarian bookshop in Guildford in the yellow pages. I plan to get them valued."

"Name your price, I'll pay it."

"What about the first-edition forgery? You want that too?"

He nodded. "Especially that. Couldn't let my namesake get away, could I?" Broad shouldered and handsome as sin, one arm draped over the back of his chair, he could probably get away with anything. But not with her. She'd come here to get over men, not tangle with them. She'd successfully evaded James and Sebastian; she wasn't falling for one-eyed Christopher, no matter how wide his smile or inviting his lips.

"I'll get back with you as soon as I have a price."

"I'll be waiting." He rested an elbow on the back of his chair. Slim fingers rubbed his chin. He watched her the way a gambler might study his cards, assessing his hand and planning a finesse. His lips parted slightly, the pad of his index finger traced the fullness of his lips. Shivers raced like cold mercury up and down Dixie's spine. Who was she fooling? He wasn't talking first editions here. He wanted more than a look at her books. And so did she. Her body hadn't reacted this way for months. In the silence between them, a strange clarity hit her. This man could give her incredible joy and pleasure and heartbreak. And she'd had enough of the latter to last two lifetimes.

Now was the time for a quick exit.

She stood up. "I'll get back in touch with you."

Like one of the slow motion scenes in a movie, he reached over and wrapped his cold fingers round her wrist. She could have moved. She didn't want to. "Don't go, Dixie. Besides, you haven't eaten your dinner." She'd swallowed three mouthfuls, if that. "Alf put that on the menu just for you; don't hurt his feelings."

Alf's feelings would survive. Would hers? She sat back down to find out. And maybe find out something else. "Tell me about my great-aunts," she said. If he got talking, maybe he wouldn't look at her in quite the same way.

"What about them?"

"Anything. I'm living in their house, sleeping on their bed, making coffee in their kitchen and they're strangers. I know nothing about them. Except Gran didn't like them."

His frown eased a little. "What did your Gran tell you?"

"She broke with them when she married Grandpa. They never wrote or phoned or anything. It's so odd they left the house to her."

"Their father left it to the three of them for life, and then to their heirs. It came to you as the only survivor."

How did he know? "You're up on village gossip?"

"Not gossip. Fact. Ask your friend Sebastian."

"He's hardly my friend."

"I'm relieved to hear it."

Was he flirting? Smiling like that, who knew? "Get serious. Tell me about them. Gran called them witches. Were they?"

"I thought you didn't believe in witches and vampires and things that go bump in the night."

"I don't, but I spent a couple of hours looking at your books and the others in that section. Not everyone shares my skepticism."

His mouth twitched at the corners. "And what a beautiful skeptic you are."

"Yeah, right." But she didn't laugh it off—the snicker died as she met his eye. Flirting was one thing, this was—what?

"Right," he whispered. "Are you skeptical about compliments?"

"Not compliments. Men!" She wanted to choke herself. *That* wasn't supposed to jump out like that.

It didn't faze Christopher. His dry, deep chuckle emerged like a ripple of spring sunshine. "Don't worry. You'll be safe with me."

Meeting the warmth of his velvet-brown eye, she wondered about that. She gave her potato a lot of attention for the next few minutes. "Back to my aunts," she said. "Were they witches?"

"Black witches? No. They were a pair of eccentric old ladies who longed for the feudal ages when they'd have controlled the whole country."

"And all the books?"

"Bought by their father. A retired colonel from the Indian Army. An old martinet if ever there was one. He treated his daughters like unpaid servants, his servants like slaves, and ran the village. He was in charge of the local Home Guard during the war. One day a group came to discuss invasion defenses. One of them was a young captain from the United States Army. Your great-grandfather invited them to dinner.

"The rest, as they say, is history. They stayed around for a week or so. Six months later, three days after her twenty-first birthday, your grandmother got married in London. They say the old colonel never let a single man under sixty into the house after that."

That tallied with Gran's version. "Didn't they have a mother?"

"She died out in India."

"How do you know all this? It happened years before you were born."

He hesitated, just a beat. "This is a village. Gossip keeps a long time."

He'd given more information in five minutes that Gran had in a lifetime. She wanted to go home, and think about it. She drained the last mouthful of Guinness and set the glass on the table. The creamy rings of lather clung to the glass like stray thoughts, unclear and indistinct. Christopher watched her. She knew it even as she watched the slow beads of froth descend the inside of her empty glass. Her breath caught in her throat.

"You walked." It wasn't a question.

This time he didn't offer to walk her home. He didn't need to. There was no moon, but Christopher had no problem finding the path. She stumbled on a root, but he reached out and caught her. After that, it made sense to hold his hand and follow him across the green. It also made for distraction and wild imaginings. Her fingers felt warm against his, his handclasp firm and sure. How would his fingers feel on her neck, her shoulders, her. . . ? *Enough.* She didn't want *any* involvement. She'd come here to catch her breath and find peace of mind. Not lose it.

"No visitors tonight," he said as they stood on the gravel drive looking up at the house.

"With my new locks, they'd have to be desperate to keep trying."

"Maybe they are. . . ." He whispered it, as if talking to himself.

She walked up to the door, key in hand. He came with her. Did he expect to be asked in? He'd be disappointed. She wasn't ready for that. Wasn't likely to be, either.

His hand tightened around hers. Her heart tightened inside her chest. "Dixie, make sure you double check every lock and the windows."

"Worried about me?"

"Why wouldn't I be? Someone's up to no good."

"Offering to come in and protect me from ill wishers?"

"No." It came out a hoarse cry.

His hand closed on hers. She clenched back. She didn't want him to go. For two cents she would ask him in. No, she wouldn't! Why not? Because she wasn't stupid. Lightheaded from the Guinness and the night air, she turned to face him. "Christopher," she whispered, "I will be all right."

"I know. No one will bother you tonight."

"Good night, and thanks for the company." She kissed him.

Rather than the cheek she'd intended, she found his lips and stayed there. Warm, smooth and moist, his mouth opened and hers followed. She had to stand on tiptoe. She'd have climbed the wall for this. His lips tasted of wine and moonlight and his mouth offered passion and heat. She heard a groan like an echo in the night and reached around his neck as his hands framed her head.

His hands seared trails of sensation through her hair and his tongue half-scrambled her brain. She wanted more. She wanted everything he had. She wanted the night, the world, and the morning and she found them here among the overgrown roses and the ankle-deep grass. Her heart raced. Her breathing quickened as if trying to outrace her heart. She felt heat and need and want and satiation. When he pulled back, she gasped for air. The pulse in her neck throbbing and her body screaming for more.

"You don't know what you're doing," a hoarse, ragged whisper warned as his arms locked behind her back.

Why waste words? Kisses like his came once in a life-time. Her fingers locked behind his neck. She stretched up and met his welcoming mouth. His arms held her. Without them she'd be a wobbling heap on the front step. His hands smoothed her back, sending racing streaks of heat up and down her spine and then lower, until need sank deep into her belly. She leaned into him, wanting the feel of his hard body against hers. Needing his touch and his lips.

He pressed her against the doorjamb. His hands cupped her upturned face. "Oh Dixie," he whispered and gently covered her face with kisses hot as a thousand honeyed brands. Her knees shook. His legs felt like iron as she stood between them. She felt him hard against her belly. She had no breath to ask him in. All she knew were kisses that turned her mind to mush and her blood to fire. His lips brushed her forehead; they dusted her eyelids and caressed her cheeks. His tongue explored one ear and sent her nerve endings into orbit. A trail of kisses down her neck wrung a groan from her lips and a sigh from her constricted lungs. A shudder of delight whipped through every fiber in her body. His lips reached the base of her neck. He nipped, her body melted against his as stars and comets collided. He caught her as her legs gave way.

"Dixie!" Anguish sounded in Christopher's voice. She had to be grinning like a fool and she didn't care. Besides, it was dark and what was a grin after what they'd just shared? "Are you all right?" He sounded worried. He shouldn't be. That kiss alone made the whole trip worthwhile.

"I will be when I touch planet Earth."

"Look here . . . I didn't mean it to . . . I hadn't planned on that." He was embarrassed. He shouldn't be.

"If that's unplanned, your seduction routine must be something incredible."

"Don't joke, Dixie." He sounded hurt.

"I'm not. I meant it."

"Look here get in the house. I want you safe."

"And I'm not, with you?" The back of his hand brushed her cheek and then caressed her neck. She couldn't repress the sigh that rose as his hand brushed the base of her neck. "Get in the house, Dixie."

"Good night," she whispered.

He unlocked the door and handed her back the key. In the light of the hall, he looked drawn and wan.

"Sleep well," he said and closed the door with a dull thud.

She turned the lock and started up the wide, shallow stairs. The mahogany bed waited with its crocheted bedspread and down pillows. She was alone but not lonely. Not with the memory of a kiss like that. She'd thought stories about climaxing while kissing were wild imaginings. She'd been wrong.

A sudden weariness soaked her bones. The day had taken its toll on her. She dropped her clothes on the floor and stopped only to brush her teeth and wash her face. In the mirror, she noticed a mark on her neck. An insect bite? A mosquito maybe?

Lying between the cool linen sheets, she was all too aware of her body and the warmth between her legs. She caressed her neck, remembering. Her fingers traced the trail of his kisses. At the base of her neck, just above her shoulder, her fingers danced a memory, plucking chords of response. Without warning, her body leaped in reply and then her head sank into the soft pillows. The moon rose an hour later and Dixie slept a quiet dreamless sleep.

In the morning she saw it all differently.

Chapter Five

The click of Dixie's lock brought Christopher to his senses. Four hundred years of discipline and he'd fallen for shining green eyes and a smile that made him forget he was no longer a man. She was honest, open and giving, and he'd seized like a soulless vandal and violated every promise he'd made himself. With the taste of her blood, heady and sweet as aged mead, on his tongue, he knew one taste of her would never be enough. His body hungered and his mind yearned for more. Her richness and warmth acted like potent drugs.

Despising himself, he moved to the back of the house and watched as upstairs lights went on and then parted the curtains a few inches. She slept. A pale figure, her auburn hair spread like a warm halo on the pillow.

Lust roared through every fiber of his being as her blood sang to him. He fought the urge to cross the windowsill, beat back the desire to taste her again, and killed the need to feel her scented skin under his lips. She'd trusted him, offered him friendship, something he'd never expected except from his own kind.

His own kind. That was what he needed. There was his strength. With a last wrenching glance, he stepped from her window ledge and took himself thirty miles east.

"I wish you wouldn't do that, Kit," said a voice from the wingback chair. "I would like some warning. What if I were entertaining company?"

"Any company you entertain here would be friends of mine," Christopher replied, as he stepped from the open window and sank into the companion chair the other side of the marble fireplace.

"Who'd want to be your friend? You bury yourself in the wilds of the country and only come up to town when you want something. Not like the old days when you couldn't wait to come to London."

Christopher nodded, "You're right, Tom, as always. I need something now."

His old friend smiled. "And I thought you came to share a glass of port. I've got a nice vintage ruby in the decanter."

Christopher poured himself a glass, swirled the dark liquid and sipped. After Dixie it tasted like water. He sighed and leaned back in the chair, pressing his shoulders and hips into the upholstery. "I'm in trouble, Tom."

"The books?" Tom Kyd asked, raising his cigar to his mouth. He exhaled with deliberate slowness, watching Christopher through a haze of smoke.

"Not the books. I found what we expected and a few more. She's perfectly willing to sell. They're getting valued and I offered to pay market price. It's . . ." He looked across at Tom blowing smoke rings. "I wish you wouldn't smoke those things."

"Worried about my health? Who introduced me to Walter Raleigh?"

"Cut it out. I'm not in the mood for your humor." He stared

at the empty grate, angry at himself and his bad manners. "Tom," he said at last, "I'm falling apart."

"That, I doubt," Tom replied. "Seizing up seems more like it. If it's not the books, what is it?"

Christopher told him.

"You fed from an unsuspecting human and now you're riddled with angst. Why? Did you harm her? Did she resist? Does she feel violated?" Remembering the moonlit gleam in Dixie's eyes and the smile on her sleeping face, Christopher shook his head. "Stop worrying. You fed. Survival demands that. When did you last feed?"

"I didn't feed. I tasted her. I never intended to feed. It happened."

"When did you last feed?" Tom repeated.

Christopher leaned an elbow on the chair and dropped his forehead into his hand. "From a human—three years."

Tom's eyebrows rose. "How do you manage?"

A dry, unamused chuckle shook Christopher's shoulders. "I live in the country. Lots of cows and horses and nice plump pigs."

Ash fell from Tom's cigar as he shuddered. "And when did you last feed from one of your barnyard friends?"

"A couple of weeks."

Tom whistled through his teeth. "By Abel and all who went before us, you're a fool. You'll weaken yourself. No wonder you fed from this human. It was need pure and simple."

"I didn't feed," Christopher growled, "I tasted."

"And she was willing? She never resisted?"

His eyes stung as he shook his head, remembering her body molding against his in the dark and the warmth of her white neck, the scent of her skin, and the intoxicating richness of her lifeblood.

Tom leaned over and thumped him on the knee. "That's the answer, old man. Feed from her again. You need her strength. She's willing. Why not? No harm done. She'll go back to the States and tell her friends about this wonderful Englishman. Better be careful, though, or they'll be coming over in droves to find a legendary English lover."

He wasn't in the mood for Tom's wit. He ground his heel into the Turkish carpet. "No good, Tom. An eternity of feeding wouldn't satisfy my thirst." In the silence, Christopher heard the clock tick on the mantle piece, a conversation across the street as guests left, and a taxi change gear at the corner and drive down Curzon Street.

Tom's eyes widened; horror froze the muscles of his face. "You'd mate with her? A mortal?"

Christopher smiled, knowing the impossibility. "Mate? Mortals use another word."

"But you're not mortal. Mortals betrayed and killed you. Feed from her. Let her strengthen you. But for Abel's sake, Kit, never that!"

Christopher shook his head. "Don't fret so, Tom. I'll stretch naked in the sun first. She's safe. I've enough will-power for that." If he didn't walk with her in the dark and touch her in the moonlight.

"Keep away then. Stay here in town until she leaves."

"No. I must go back for the books. Too many curious and mischievous parties in that village for those volumes to remain there." He smiled at his friend. "You worry too much."

"Maybe. But the time of your revenance is close. Not two weeks away. That's when you're most vulnerable."

"As you have warned me every May for the last four hundred years and still I survive."

"More by luck than judgment."

"Luck has carried me this far."

Tom propped the stub of his cigar on a porcelain ashtray. "Dawn comes in two hours and the day is forecast to be sunny. Do you have strength to fly against the sun or will you stay?"

He'd stay. The flight had drained him. He needed rest. Dixie was safe for the night and if the day was sunny, he couldn't protect her even if he were in Bringham. "Your hospitality is always welcome, Tom."

The cleaners arrived as Dixie poured her second cup of coffee. Faced with a flurry of mops, moving furniture and warnings about wax on the floors, Dixie took her coffee outside into the sunshine. She found a perch on the crumbling wall that surrounded the flagstone terrace.

Before she finished the cup, the garden called her. She'd given the house all her attention since she'd arrived; the only time she'd really spent in the garden had been traipsing around, half-blind in the night, or dallying with Christopher. She blushed at the memory. She'd had to wear a turtleneck this morning to hide a monumental hickey.

She paced through ankle-deep lawns, grass-filled brick paths and rough gravel walks with creeping weeds. The dark shapes she'd hidden between with Christopher's arm round her shoulders proved to be lilacs in need of pruning. The odd hummocks the intruder tripped on that first evening were untrimmed topiary boxwoods. Weeds choked a rock garden, and green scum covered an ornamental pond with a silent fountain.

Dixie strolled down a rickety pergola overhung with wisteria and found her way through an arch in a yew hedge into a kitchen garden. A rickety tool shed leaned against the high brick wall, but what caught Dixie's attention was a door in the wall. The old hinges rasped as Dixie grabbed the rusty knob. She had to use her shoulder to push the door. Two old ladies could never have opened this. Half open, the door jammed—but it was enough. Dixie walked into her hidden garden.

And shivered.

The garden appeared a perfect square about thirty or forty feet each way. High brick walls on all four sides shaded everywhere but the center. Wide stone paths ran along all four sides and across to meet in the center. A mossy stone bench stood against one wall but it looked too high and too wide for comfort. Some garden designer's mistake, Dixie decided. Until she saw the crumbling pentagram carved in the wall above. What had she found?

The garden seemed desolate and unwelcoming. On the stone paths, Dixie noticed marks and carvings like strange hieroglyphics. Some looked like zodiac signs, others indistinct letters and runes. Dixie followed the paths to the center where they met at a square of green she'd first thought was grass but now, she realized, was some herb or other. Rubbing the leaves between her fingers, she tried to place the smell and remembered the chamomile tea Gran used to drink.

This must be centuries old. Didn't chamomile lawns date from Tudor times? Impressed but still uneasy, Dixie looked around. About eight feet square, the lawn stood at the center of the garden. The sun must have shone on this patch for hundreds of years, but the thought didn't give Dixie any thrill.

A moss and lichen encrusted obelisk stood at each corner of the lawn. Dixie took a few steps towards them for a closer inspection and froze. These weren't obelisks; they were stone phalluses. What had she discovered? Did she even want to know? She marched out and dragged the door shut behind her.

That was one place she would not serve tea in.

Among the musty damp and cobwebs in the shed, she found old tools, a wheelbarrow, and a near-antique lawn mower. Grabbing a wooden basket that fit comfortably over her arm, Dixie marched back to the flower garden and worked clearing the rose beds until the light started to fail. Tired and aching about the shoulders, she made it to the Barley Mow an hour before closing.

"Thought you weren't coming tonight," Vernon said as she came in. "Alf's got a nice veg curry."

Dixie agreed on the curry and sat by the window, disappointed Christopher wasn't there. Never mind. An evening alone would give her time to think.

Fat chance! Sleazy James sat himself in the chair opposite. "Well, hello. What have you been doing with yourself?"

Doing a bit of gardening and just happened to discover these eighteen-inch-high stone phalluses. Do you know what they're used for? wasn't a good opener. "Clearing the garden while the cleaners took care of the house," worked better.

"Don't ruin your hands," he said, running his fingers over hers.

Dixie pulled back her hand and clasped her glass with such determination that the table wobbled. She'd have walked out there and then but Vernon appeared with her curry.

"You've got a healthy appetite," James murmured, with a smirk that irritated more than the innuendo.

"I came in to get dinner," Dixie replied, fork poised.

"Nothing like a bit of company while you're eating." Dixie stopped mid-chew, hoping the knee contact was accidental. "How about dessert somewhere later?" James asked.

This time Dixie almost bit the fork. Accidental, her foot! The jerk was groping her knee. That did it! With both hands under the table, Dixie tipped the table away from her; curry, rice and the better part of her Guinness landed in James's lap.

"Oh! I'm so sorry," Dixie lied as James squawked for a cloth. "The table just wobbled."

"Here you are, Mr. Chadwick," said Alf, handing him a towel. "Let me get you another, Miss LePage," he went on, as Vernon picked up the unbroken glass.

"No thanks, I had most of it. Sorry about the mess."

"No problem. Not your fault. These tables! I should have seen it coming." He looked her straight in the eyes. "It's not the first time something like this has happened."

Dixie decided she really liked Alf. "Since I've managed to half-trash your pub, I'd better go home." She paused. "And maybe you should call me Dixie."

Alf smiled and held out his hand. "I'll be glad to, Dixie."

Eight members and two novices sat around the black oak table watching the burning ash twigs in the copper brazier. One of the black candles dripped wax on the polished table-top. Ida leaned forward to wipe the splatter.

Sebastian frowned. Couldn't the old woman wait? If she'd touched the brazier . . . The coven needed all the strength it could muster. Below numbers for years, the two novices were their most recent hope. Some hope! Maybe Sally held more promise than James. She could hardly have less.

Emily droned the incantation and stopped as the twigs crumbled to ash. In the silence she placed the gold ring on the ashes. After the prescribed pause, Sebastian stood and blew a long, deep note on a narrow pipe.

As the echoes faded, Ida asked, "What progress, James? What did you find?"

"Not a thing. I swear there's nothing there. I've been through that house three times and the old book room vol-ume by volume. What we're looking for isn't there."

"Really?" She didn't sound impressed. "Sally, what about you?"

She had none of James's bored confidence. She fairly bounced at the prospect of speaking. "I looked when I cleaned the house. I think James is right about the papers. I saw nothing. But . . ." She paused for effect. Sebastian despised cheap theatrics. "I did discover something. She refused to let me clean out the book room so I wondered if she was hiding something. I got as good a look as I could. No papers, but I found an interesting stack of books. A bunch of old books about magic and Wicca and spells."

"I wonder if she's as unschooled as we believe," Ida said. "Who knows what knowledge she inherited. Maybe her grandmother . . ."

No one seemed happy at the thought.

Ida placed her wrinkled hands on the table. Eyes turned to her. "We need to find out what she knows and then we can plan. Perhaps recruit her?"

Sebastian's mind raced in the ensuing silence. "I think not. The woman LePage is a problem and unreliable. First she seemed willing to let me handle the sale and send her the money. Then, out of the blue, she comes over to spend a week and see her property. Now she's moved in, started spring-cleaning and developed an interest in certain books. The next thing, she'll start exploring the grounds. . . ." He paused to let that fact sink in. "To make matters worse, the vampire is cultivating her friendship."

"The vampire we can take care of. We know the date of his creation. Let that be his destruction," Ida said.

"We can't kill him!" Sally's voice shuddered in the silence.

Emily, who'd been silent, placed her hands on the table. "My dear," she said, smiling at Sally, "one can only kill the living."

Sebastian looked across at Sally and James. Weak links, both of them. They needed forging to the coven. Dealing with Marlowe would tie them both up tight.

After dropping off the books to be valued and discovering a grocery store big enough to equal any at home, Dixie went home to bake. She planned on making brownies for Christopher as a "thank you" for lunch. It just seemed a neighborly thing to do.

Back home, unpacking groceries and stacking them in the closets along one wall, she found one door didn't open. It appeared painted shut. One more thing to get fixed. Later. Today, she had baking to do.

The brownies cooled on the window ledge; they smelled sweet and chocolatey as Dixie washed up and put everything away. By the time she washed, changed into a clean tee shirt and put on fresh lipstick, the brownies were cool. Dixie piled them onto a plate of rose-patterned china, covered them with plastic wrap and set out for Dial Cottage.

"Hi there!" Dixie called up at the open windows. Christopher had to be in. His car was parked behind the hawthorn hedge and the upstairs windows were open, but there was no answer. She strolled round the back, rapped on the back door and tried the knob and the door swung open. She stared into the darkness of the interior and called, "Christopher, it's Dixie." He wasn't there.

Uncomfortable at standing uninvited in his empty kitchen, Dixie decided to leave the brownies and go. She'd see Christopher later at the Barley Mow and explain. She scribbled a note on the memo pad from the phone, tore the leaf off and tucked it under the plate. As she replaced the pad by the phone, she nudged a pile of papers and they cascaded to the floor. She knelt and gathered them up and hoped to heaven no one came by. How would it look, her kneeling on the floor rummaging through Christopher's papers? She spotted a small leather book. With her initials.

What was Christopher doing with her appointment book? When had he taken it? In the pub that first evening? Too angry to think straight, she stuffed it in the pocket of her jeans, slammed the back door behind her and marched down the front path, giving the gate a shove as she left.

Dixie walked back through the village, across High Street and almost smacked into Sebastian.

"Going to the Barley Mow tonight?" He said it pleasantly enough, but she did wonder what he knew. Had James complained? She hoped so.

"Don't think so. I'm getting the hang of cooking on an Aga."

"Settling in nicely, I hear."

Dixie nodded. "Yes. Very."

"Must dash," he said. "But I know I can count on you for the Whist Drive next weekend."

"Whist Drive?" What was he talking about?

He smiled. He did have very white teeth. "Fund-raiser for the church roof fund. Everyone will be there."

She agreed before she had time to refuse, then shrugged. What the heck? What could happen at a parish fund-raiser? He could hardly hit on her in church. Besides, Sebastian might not be her sort, but at least he didn't take her property.

"I can't change your mind?" Tom asked.

Christopher didn't even shake his head. "I have business to transact. We all need those books."

Tom raised an eyebrow. "Don't get caught between the covers."

Christopher groaned. Tom hadn't changed in all these years. "You could wish me success."

"I'll wish you caution. You're stronger, but not strong enough."

"Tom, all I have to do is buy some books from a harmless young woman."

Tom's eyes shadowed as if seeing into the distance. "Remember the harmless young woman in Deptford."

"That young woman was a trollop."

"A well-paid trollop who played her part well."

Tom was right about *that*, but Dixie was different. Her transparency and honesty would impress even Tom. He twitched his mouth. "This isn't the same. Come down to Bringham, I'll introduce you to Miss LePage."

Tom shook his head. "No, my friend. I have too much sense of survival to consort with humans, if I don't have to."

Christopher! A slow shiver snaked down Dixie's spine at the knock on the door. She just knew he stood outside and she didn't want to see him. Her anger and confusion over finding her date book in his kitchen had gelled into a cold hurt. While she'd thought him a friend, he'd been prying into her life. Christopher wanted something from her. Fine. He could have the books they'd agreed on and nothing more.

"Hi," she said. Whatever else she'd planned to say stayed in her throat. He was beautiful. Hair dark as midnight shone in the light from the door. The same light that gleamed on the leather covering his shoulders and turned the pallor of his skin to nacre. He smiled. Dixie forbade her heart to thaw.

"Hello, Dixie," he said. It sounded like the opening bars of a sonata. Warmth caressed her skin. Hope and excitement wriggled in her belly. She dug her heels in the doormat and clenched every muscle in her back.

"Why, hello, Christopher." At this rate the conversation wouldn't go far enough to cause problems.

"I've been away for a couple of days."

That explained the deserted house but not the car parked in front. "Have a good trip?"

"Visited a friend in town."

This was ludicrous. Talking on the doorstep, as if he were a brush salesman. She had to get rid of him. She didn't want him in the house. She didn't trust herself near him. Just standing this close she could smell him and if she dared think about it, she'd imagine his touch again. "I ran into Guildford today and dropped off the books. I'll have a valuation by Friday."

"Wonderful. Just name your price." He took a fourth of a step forward. "Could I come in?"

"No!" It came out like a muffled shriek that tore the roots of her mind. "Not now." Ten minutes in the same room as him and her resolve would fade as surely as daylight. "It's not a good time." She gestured with her head to imply someone was in the house. The lie ripped deep within her. The look on Christopher's face made her want to cringe.

"Indeed," he said and stepped backwards out of the circle of light. A shadow seemed to slip over him. "Get back to me, Dixie. When it's a *good* time."

In the dark, she never even saw him reach the gate. Slamming and locking the front door, she leaned against it. Her heart raced like a Derby winner, her chest heaved so fast each breath hurt. Her blood seethed in her veins, pounded her temples and surged like a boiling flood ready to burst a dam. She wanted Christopher. She wanted his arms around her, his body against hers and his lips' warm caress. Forget it. Never. Not now.

Visceral pain tore through her. She pressed into the heavy oak door as if pulled by an outside force. She shook and wanted to cry out his name, but hurt gagged every sound but a moan. Her body slumped, her legs wobbled like a newborn foal's, and her lungs felt filled with concrete. Only her fingers clenched around the doorknob and her hip against the mail slot stopped her from crumpling on the doormat.

Her breathing normalized. Her heart rate calmed. Shaking her head as if stunned, she wobbled back to the kitchen. A half-eaten baked potato waited on the table. Dixie wasn't sure if she remembered how to chew. That did it! No man was tweaking her buttons. The minute they concluded their deal, she wanted nothing more to do with Christopher Marlowe.

Christopher leapt back from the stoop as if blasted. What conniving human was in there with Dixie? Sebastian, with his slick tongue and scheming heart? James, with his poisonous mind? Jealousy burned like acid, blocking Christopher's thoughts and shuttering his reason.

Transmogrifying in a blaze of fury, he shot through the night sky in an eastern trajectory until he reached the heart of the city. He found his safe haven high on St. Paul's dome. Strange, how often he came here to roost—but he'd loved the view ever since the new St. Paul's rose from the ashes of the Great Fire. He watched the quiet streets beneath his feet, deserted except for the stray taxi, and looked across the river to where the new Globe stood near the site of the old. He could trust London. A city wasn't fickle like mortals or perfidious like womankind.

Images racked his mind. Dixie was his. He'd tasted and marked her, but without her knowledge. The claim and need were his alone. And alone he'd forever endure his pain. Tom's warning had come too late. Socializing with mortals brought misery and danger, even death. A quest for knowledge and his own frailty for a pretty mortal had brought him to the rim of disaster but he'd pulled back in time. He'd close the deal then take Tom's advice and leave Bringham. With the coven strengthening, the village was too dangerous for his kind.

Christopher returned to his cottage less than half an hour before dawn. His body ached like the rotten tooth he'd once had pulled by the barber in Fleet Alley. Tom had been right about feeding; farm animals didn't offer enough nourishment to transmogrify twice in one day. His empty veins screamed for sustenance. The heart he didn't have called out for Dixie.

Dixie! She'd been here! He sensed her presence and smelled her sweetness. His mouth watered at the thought as fast as his mind seized with horror. Half-transmogrified hands grabbed the scrubbed pine table. He watched the return of human skin and nails with a wonder that never ceased. Nothing would alter the thrill he always felt at the power within his own body. He splayed his re-formed hands on the table, leaning into it on wobbly shoulders. He had to rest.

His head felt like a cannonball as he raised it and looked across the table. His eyebrows tightened as he noticed the plate on the table. Neatly encased in cling film, the even squares of chocolate appeared like pieces of a puzzle—the conundrum of Dixie LePage. The paper shook in his hand. He recognized a sheet from his own writing tablet. "Christopher," she had written in a hand as clear and open as her smile. "Forgive me for barging into your house but the door was unlocked. Here are some brownies, Gran's recipe, a thank you for the wonderful lunch. Went into Guildford this morning and left your books. He promised me a price by Friday so I'll get back to you. Take care and see you soon, Dixie."

The note crumpled in his grasp. Too weary to even consider the implications, Christopher dragged himself upstairs to his shuttered study and let sleep swallow his confusion.

Dixie drove back from Guildford in a daze. She had a small fortune in books on the backseat. Her throat tied itself into a dry knot at the prospect of actually asking for a check that large. Had Christopher any idea of their worth? Could he afford that much? She'd find out soon and demand an explanation about her appointment book. It had better be good.

He was in. She knew it as she turned the corner and saw the moss growing on the uneven roof tiles. Of course he was in. He was expecting her.

He was waiting, leaning against the open doorway of his cottage, watching for her from the shade of the front porch. He filled the doorway, with his long, slim legs stretching in front, one broad shoulder propped against the frame, and his head almost touching the lintel. Of course it *was* a cottage. He hadn't blocked her doorway quite the same way but he still had the smile that could melt permafrost.

As she opened the gate with one hand, balancing the box in the other, she sensed his excitement. He came towards her. Warm, rippling waves of anticipation came at her like a flowing tide. No one got this excited over a bunch of books. Well, he could want all he wanted. She had a deal to make and a bone to pick. He took the box of books from her. His arms shook as they hefted the weight. "Come on in and let me know the damage."

She followed him into the kitchen and noticed how his shoulders sagged with relief as he set the box on the scrubbed table. "I've got the valuation." She handed over the sheet of paper and waited for the shock to register.

He read every word and figure, his head moving from side to side as he scanned the paper. A slight crease of his brows and a little tightening of his mouth showed concentration, nothing more. He looked up and smiled, his eye gleaming with something like triumph. "Seems fair enough. I assume you're satisfied with the valuation?"

Dry-mouthed, Dixie nodded. Satisfied? This was more than she'd earned in six months as a school librarian. "Of course, I said you could have them."

He reached into the drawer in the table. "Check okay?" he asked, uncapping his fountain pen.

"Yes, I suppose." She'd never seen anyone write a check that large. He did it as easily as paying for a tank of gas.

"It won't bounce. I made sure I had enough to cover this."

"You knew how much it would be?" What sort of job did

he have to fling this sort of money around? Come to that, what *did* he do for a living?

"I had a rough idea. It was slightly more than I expected but inflation affects everything and collectibles particularly."

"Is this a hobby, buying old books? Or what you do for a living?" She'd been dying to ask. Having done so, she felt like a pushy American.

He didn't seem to mind. "It's a hobby. With some old friends, I'm assembling a library on the occult and the paranormal. I offered to buy from your Aunt Hope, but she wouldn't part with anything. I'm glad you agreed."

His shirt was open at the neck, showing a vee of fair skin and a few stay curls of dark hair. She forced her mind back to her question. "What do you do for a living, then?" Nothing that she'd noticed so far.

"Some years back, I made a few lucky investments. I'm a layabout. I write when the muse strikes me, drive too fast, ride when the weather's fine, and get on Caughleigh's nerves."

She couldn't hold back the chuckle. "I've noticed."

He shook his head. "Watch out for him, Dixie. The only person he's ever helped was Sebastian Caughleigh."

"I can take care of myself." Was he pursuing her just to get at Sebastian? "I came by yesterday to see you. The door was open."

His smile didn't quite become a laugh. "You left a plate of little chocolate cakes."

"They were brownies."

"Brownies." This time it was almost a chuckle. "You know the local meaning? Brownies are little people. They cause milk to sour, hens to stop laying and haystacks to self-ignite." His mouth twisted in a way that almost mocked her. "But of course, you wouldn't believe in them. You'd put them in the categories of witches and vampires."

"An interesting local myth." It came out sharper than

she'd intended but the hurt look on his face caused a twinge of guilt. "You don't share my skepticism. The occult interests you."

He smiled, but not at her. "That's why I'm building this library. Why not search for knowledge if it's there to find?" He tapped one of the books. "There's old lore here. Forgotten ideas. Old dreams and nightmares."

"I prefer to stick with realities."

"Everyone has different realities, my dear Dixie."

That did it! She certainly wasn't his "dear" anything. He had mentioned realities, she wanted one explained. She reached into her pocket book and closed her hand over her appointment book. "There's something I want to ask you." She pulled her hand out of her bag. "I noticed this when I brought the brownies and wondered if you'd explain."

She placed it on the tabletop and watched his knuckles whiten as they clenched the table edge. She swore she wouldn't speak first. He owed her the explanation.

"So, the kindly neighbor act was an excuse to come snooping." An icy cynicism crackled through his words.

"It was not!" Dixie felt the tabletop under her fist. "I tore a sheet off your message pad to write you a note, and the whole stack fell to the ground. I picked it up and just happened to find the agenda I've been missing since I arrived."

"And how did you get in?"

"I opened the back door. You left it unlocked."

"I did, did I? How remiss of me."

"Yes, you did, and you're lucky it was only me. It could have been a burglar. There are enough of them around here."

"I'm not worried about burglars."

He actually had the gall to grin. Dixie pressed her palms on the table and leaned forward, her face tensing in a frown. "You're avoiding my question, buster. Where did you get it and why was it sitting in your kitchen?"

"Isn't that two questions?" He raised his hands up, palms

out, as she leaned across the tale. "Alright, Dixie. You want to know where I got it?"

"Yup." She waited, determined to stand her ground until she got her answer.

"Caughleigh gave it to me. I offered to return it to you."

"But you didn't."

"I'm afraid I forgot about it."

She'd worked in schools long enough to know a lie when she heard one. "Why would Sebastian give it to you? I was in his office on Wednesday and I'm seeing him tomorrow night."

Christopher's mouth twisted as his eyebrows curled. "Enjoy yourself, my dear."

That did it! "I expect to."

"I hope you're not disappointed." It was almost a whisper but she heard it clear as day.

"Why should I be?"

"Because, my dear Dixie, Sebastian Caughleigh is not the man for you."

The laugh came from somewhere deep inside. She shook her head. "I'm thirty years old, Christopher. Old enough to decide these things for myself. Look, I didn't come here to fight. I just wanted a straight answer. Maybe I got it. I'll probably never know. Thanks for the check. Assuming it clears okay, our business is over."

"Maybe," he replied and walked her to the door. "Take care, Dixie. Make sure you choose the right company."

Just what did he mean by that?

What was the truth about her organizer? Had she dropped it in Sebastian's office? If so, why would he give it to Christopher? They acted more like adversaries that friends.

Christopher had to be lying. Why did she want to believe him? Did it matter? She'd see Sebastian tomorrow night. She'd ask him, And why believe *him*? Being a lawyer didn't guarantee integrity. She'd learned that the hard way.

Chapter Six

Perched high in the elm tree, Christopher watched Dixie lock her car and then go in the front door. He'd replayed their conversation a dozen times since she left. She didn't trust him now, just as well. He was nothing but bad news. But how he ached for her—his own fault. If he hadn't tasted that one time he'd never have known the warmth of her soul and the sweetness of her lifeblood, and now he'd spend eternity missing her.

He had no choice. He had to leave Bringham. Tom was right—it was getting too dangerous. If he stayed, it was only a matter of time before Caughleigh sussed the situation. And the thought of Caughleigh weaving Dixie into his machinations . . . Christopher's fists balled up at the idea. He'd take up Tom's invitation to stay in South Audley Street. Soon. He sagged against the tree trunk. By Abel! He was weaker than a fledgling. He shouldn't have gone out this afternoon. The sun sapped his strength and it would take more than a day's rest to restore him.

He had to feed. Sebastian's new hunter wouldn't match

Dixie's sweetness, but the prospect held a certain satisfaction.

Clicking her seat belt as Sebastian closed the door, Dixie wondered why she'd agreed to come.

He seemed to have no doubts at all. "I feel lucky tonight. I think we'll win." He flashed white teeth at her.

Win or *score*? She'd play Whist and that was all.

The same people she met at the Whytes' filled the village hall. Hardly surprising. This village made a small town seem like a metropolis, but there was a certain security in placing names on familiar faces—Emma with Ian, Sally, who looked very different with her hair cut short all over, Mark Flynn, the bank manager, and Emily Reade.

"Emily!" Sebastian almost hissed the name as she toddled towards them, a tin tray of sherry glasses in her hands.

She beamed at Sebastian. Dixie merited a polite nod. "Settled in your new place, are you? Have a sherry. We've sweet or dry. What do you prefer?"

Dixie chose dry. It suited her mood. She took two sips from the thick-rimmed glass and then almost gulped it all. Christopher was here! She scanned the hall but didn't see him.

"Looking for someone?" Sebastian smiled. He was at her elbow, close enough so she could smell his aftershave. She didn't care for his aftershave. "Anyone I know?"

Something told her he wouldn't appreciate the truth. "Just admiring the building." She looked up at the high ceiling and age-darkened rafters. "It looks like an old barn."

"It is." Emily was back. "An old tithe barn. They planned on demolishing it between the wars but the parish bought it."

By the look of the two of them, another war wasn't far off. Dixie remembered Emily's hurried exit to meet Sebastian after the Whytes. What was going on and how had she ended up in the middle? If Emily imagined some sort of duel for Sebastian, she could put her weapons away. Dixie wasn't interested.

"We're at the same table. Isn't that nice? I can talk to Dixie about her house. I've always wanted to see inside it. Your aunts were reclusive. They never invited anyone over."

"Drop by sometime." They reached the table and Sebastian held both their chairs. Dixie sat down, and again the certainty hit her—Christopher was very close. Was she going lightheaded from skipping lunch? Was sherry stronger than she thought?

"Got a partner, Emily? Or are we playing three-handed?"

Emily giggled. "We'll have four. Emma said there were several odd people."

"How unkind of her. She may call me eccentric, but I take exception at 'odd'."

At the familiar voice Sebastian hissed, Emily popped her eyes, and Dixie felt a warm glow inside. "Hello, Christopher. You never said you were coming."

"A last minute decision." He settled himself in the empty chair. "Well, Caughleigh, you look ready to cut."

Thank heavens they weren't playing Bridge. She'd never be able to concentrate in this company. Testosterone sparked between Sebastian and Christopher, and Emily smiled in a way that suggested Lucrezia Borgia. Come to think of it, the big opal on her finger suited the part.

Sebastian cut spades as trumps and dealt in silence. Dixie was fanning out her hand as Christopher asked, "Play to win and take no prisoners, right, Emily?"

He and Emily won the first three hands.

Dixie played carefully and remembered discards but her play couldn't match Christopher's. Even when she held four trumps in the last hand, she only managed to take two tricks.

"You're some card player," she said as Christopher trumped her last ace.

"I've been playing for years." He smiled.

"Make a living by it, do you?" Sebastian asked.

Christopher looked over his cards. He did look like a card shark in an old movie and every muscle showed he resented the insinuation. "I have, on occasion. We must play for high stakes one day, you and I." They both looked ready to stake each other.

"Are we playing Whist or War?" Dixie asked. It was like sitting between a pair of eighth graders.

"Peace, Dixie." The way Christopher smiled suggested they shared secrets. "I once fought over cards. Never again." With a smooth movement he played a king.

Silence fell over the table as Christopher's uncanny knack of winning tricks had Dixie pondering the truth behind Sebastian's insinuations. Emily made a couple of comments about play but silence seemed more cheerful than her twittering.

Dixie won the next trick by breaking trumps and decided to do her bit to keep the tension going. "Sebastian," she said, "thanks for giving Christopher my organizer. I was glad to get it back."

Sebastian stared, Emily gulped, and Christopher gave an innocent smile that wouldn't fool an infant. What was going on? Had Christopher lied, just as she'd suspected?

"I told Dixie you gave it to me, knowing I'd be seeing her." Christopher smirked. It was the only word for it. Sebastian gave him a look that could curdle milk. "You never did mention where you found it. Did you, Caughleigh?"

Sebastian hesitated, eying his cards before discarding a useless three. "James picked it up. I'm so glad it got back to you, Dixie."

Sleazy James? How did he come into this?

"That's right, your sister's dear son. He's not here tonight,

I noticed. Left the neighborhood has he?" Christopher seemed determined to niggle.

"He's in town for the weekend. If it's any of your business."

"None, really," Christopher replied and took the trick. He also won the hand. He stood up. "Let the winner get dessert."

"It isn't over yet." Fury seemed to seethe through Sebastian's teeth.

"You think not?" He pushed in the chair. The table wobbled.

Dixie stood up. "I'll help you carry them."

"Lovely. I'll stay and keep Sebastian company," Emily said.

The desserts were at the far end of the hall. Christopher seemed in no hurry. In fact, he walked as if worn out.

"You like to win, I noticed, almost as much as Sebastian hates to lose. It's only a game."

"Card games can be more dangerous than duels."

"Fight duels often, do you?"

He shook his head, his dark hair gleaming in the lamplight. "Not for a couple of hundred years." She chuckled and looked up at him. His eye seemed hard and cold. Then he smiled and her toes curled inside her leather pumps. "You're the only woman in years who's been willing to look me straight in the face. It doesn't bother you?"

"In a way. But not like that. I wish for your sake you had two."

"I don't miss it, except when it comes to looking at you."

"What happened?" Should she have asked? She didn't know him that well.

"I lost it in a fight. Years ago when I was young and foolish."

"Not the two-hundred-year-old duel?"

He shook his head and grinned, "Long before then."

"Trifle or cheesecake?" Emma asked, serving spoon in hand.

"You're not getting any?" Dixie asked as he placed three servings on the tray.

"I need to be careful what I eat—allergies, you know."

"Christopher *never* eats. That's how he stays so thin," Emma said.

Dixie felt inclined to believe her. Christopher's narrow wrists barely filled the cuffs of his linen shirt.

"Jealous, my dear Emma?" he asked, with a twinkle in his dark eye.

Emma grinned. "Watch it!"

Dixie filled the thick white coffee cups from the urn on a side table. "Enjoying your evening with Caughleigh?" Christopher asked, his voice too quiet to be conversational. "I bet he doesn't kiss like I do."

At that, her hand shook and she sloshed coffee into the saucer. "I wouldn't know," she replied, trying to sound very English and proper but knowing she missed it by a mile.

"I knew it! You shouldn't be wasting your time with him."

"Right now I seem to be wasting it with you."

"Nothing between us will ever be a waste."

Hair prickled around the nape of her neck. She felt heat rising between them. "Coffee's ready. Let's get back."

"Worried?" his voice teased. "You don't want to give Emily too much space. She might take advantage of poor old Sebby."

"I doubt anyone's ever taken advantage of Sebastian." The hum around them half-swallowed his chuckle but Dixie heard it all the same.

Christopher and Emily won the last hand. Sebastian appeared not to have enjoyed the evening very much. Emily almost bubbled with excitement as she claimed the centerpiece as her prize. The pink begonias matched her face.

"How was this as an evening of British culture?" Christopher asked Dixie.

"Come now, Marlowe," Sebastian said. "Don't put her on the spot."

Sebastian wouldn't answer for her. "Interesting. Like something out of an Agatha Christie. You know, cards in the village hall and someone found dead on the vicarage lawn in the morning."

"Now you're getting fanciful," Sebastian said, his mouth tightening.

"You're right," Christopher said, smiling at Dixie. "But for that scenario you need a vast twenties vicarage, not the three bedroom bungalow Reverend James lives in, plus a parlor maid to find the corpse before breakfast."

"Stop this, both of you!" Emily fussed. "There aren't murders in Bringham. Dixie was just joking. Americans do that all the time, I'm told."

Dixie wanted to ask who'd told her, but bit it back. All she needed was to get home. Alone. And she fancied Christopher planned to complicate that.

He leaned back in his chair, causing the thin metal legs to scrape the floor. "We had one recent death at the vicarage."

Sebastian hissed, and Emily paled before she flushed and snapped, "Oh, please! Not here!"

"What?" asked Dixie, looking from Sebastian's tight mouth to Emily's red face to Christopher's smirk.

"You hadn't heard?" Christopher asked.

"Heard what?" What did they all know that he wanted to tell?

"I thought Caughleigh would have mentioned it." Christopher smiled at Sebastian. "Your great-aunt, old Miss Faith, died on the front steps of the vicarage. The milkman found her. She'd had a stroke."

Something spun inside. No, Sebastian hadn't told her. Christopher knew that and he'd chosen this moment to tell. Why? She was heartily sick of being used to get at Sebastian.

"She was an eccentric old lady, given to wandering.

Probably felt herself taken ill and went there for help. I think your timing's disgraceful, Marlowe. You've upset Dixie."

"I'm fine, Sebastian." He was halfway around the table and Dixie didn't want his arm supporting her. Not at any price.

She offered to help Emma tidy up, glad of the chance to talk with her neighbor, and in the sneaky hope that Emily would convince Sebastian to take her home. She didn't. Emily and Sebastian stood in a corner talking to Sally, while Christopher stacked folding chairs with Ian. By the time they loaded the last dish in Emma's Range Rover, all Dixie wanted was her own bed. Alone.

"Ready?" Sebastian asked as Ian and Emma drove off.

"Yes, I enjoyed the evening, but I'll be glad to get home." She hoped the hint was heavy enough.

Emily stood beside Sebastian and Sally, looking from one to the other as if wondering what would happen next. "I need a ride. Could you drop me off, Sebby?"

Dixie grabbed the chance. "Of course. He can drop me off on the way." She half-hoped Christopher would offer to take her, but he just stood there enjoying the performance.

They were all halfway to their cars when Sally swore, "Blast! I've got a puncture. It would be tonight when Robert's away."

"I'll give you a hand," Christopher offered. "No point in everyone hanging about here." Dixie's last sight of Christopher was his broad shoulders as he walked towards Sally's Land Rover.

Christopher offered a ride home, but Sally insisted on a wheel change. "I need the car tomorrow and who'll change it on a Sunday?" she wailed.

So he agreed. He felt sure Dixie was safe tonight. He'd sensed Caughleigh's irritation but no spite. Besides, he could change the wheel in five minutes and stop by Orchard House on his way home. Sally helped, handing wheel brace and jack as he needed them, but her inane chatter got under his skin. If he heard one more, "I don't know how this happened, Robert promised me they were new tires," he'd be tempted to gag her with a wheel brace.

He hoisted the spare on the axle and felt the weakness in his muscles. He should be resting, not changing spare wheels for the local gentry. "All done," he said as he tapped the hubcap in place and reached for a rag to wipe his hands.

"At last," Sally whispered.

Christopher turned, something in her tone alerting him, too late. The moonlight showed something pale in her hand. A wrench she was packing away? He knew it wasn't when he felt the blade against his skin. Slowed by his exertions of the last week, his reactions failed him. Searing pain ripped between his ribs and tore through him like fire. His hands clutched at the air.

"Got you!" she half-yelled her excitement. Like an echo, the words swirled around the deepening fog in his brain. He tried to speak, but darkness followed the pain. He stumbled against the car, slipped, and the gravel came up to meet him.

"I wanted to see the house. She'd have asked us in if you hadn't insisted on leaving."

Emily was beginning to get on his nerves. "She had no intention of doing so," Sebastian said.

"Where are we going? Your office, Sebby?"

The woman was a fool. That's all she thought of. "No, my dear, it's time for you to do your duty by the coven."

Her voice rose. "No more doctored food. It didn't work. Ida's didn't work either. It's too risky."

"Forget your simples and mixtures. We're using more reliable methods."

"Sebby, no magic. None of that stuff. I won't do it."

"You will. Sally's met her commitment. We need yours. Tonight." He pulled back into the village hall car park. Emily had her uses. Several of them, in fact, but he had no time for her inane scruples. She'd help. She had no choice. She was in as deep as he was.

As he pulled up beside the building, Sally's face appeared at the car window. "I did what you said. It worked, but I need help to lift him. He's a dead weight."

"And soon he'll be permanently dead," Sebastian replied, stepping out beside her. He neither spoke nor looked at Emily. He pulled at Marlowe's shoulder, smiling as his opponent groaned. "The last trick's mine," Sebastian said. Getting no response, he ripped off the leather eye patch; Christopher's neck jerked as the elastic yielded and revealed the whorl of scar tissue that filled the spot that had once been an eye.

"You k-killed him," Emily's shaky voice stammered out.

"Not yet, my dear. Soon. When the time is propitious."

"What d-do you m-mean?"

"We'll let him keep until Monday. Let him enjoy a little misery before he goes to hell."

"Sebby." Her hand grasped his shoulder like a claw. "Why Monday?"

He didn't waste time looking at her. "May 30. The day he died. The day he's the weakest. He's been slowly losing strength the last week or so. Sally's well-placed blade just helps him along. He'll get weaker and weaker. By Monday he'll be unable to move a muscle but he'll feel and know everything. He won't enjoy the dawn but I will. And as he fries, we gain his strength. Think what we can do."

"This isn't what we stand for." Emily's voice rose in her panic. "Do no harm! That's what I was taught! We don't destroy. We use *our* power. We don't take others'."

"Yes, we do! With his strength, we have a chance of knowing and running everything, just like the old women did." Sebastian turned to Sally. "Open the back. We'll take him to a nice, undisturbed haven."

"I'm not coming with you."

Sebastian laughed at Emily's attempt at non-involvement. "I know. You're driving his car home for him."

"No!"

"Don't waste my time." He searched through Marlowe's pockets until he found the bunch of keys and tossed them to Emily, snorting with impatience when her fingers closed over air. Her hand shook as she picked the keys off the ground. "Park it on the side of his house the way he always does. Then meet me at my office." She'd never refuse that offer.

"Sebby . . ." The last mewling protest escaped her thin lips.

"For God's sake, don't crash it or get stopped. Banks don't care for car thieves on their staff. Now, shut up and help take his legs."

They heaved Christopher into the back of the Land Rover. A deep groan wrung from his pale lips as they dumped him on his face. Sebastian reached for a rug from the back of the seat and tossed it over him. "No point in risking anyone seeing him."

"What if he bleeds on it?" Sally asked. "They can match and trace everything these days."

He laughed at her anxiety. "I'd love to see how he does in a DNA match."

They dumped Marlowe in Sally's storeroom. He'd be safe, if very uncomfortable, among the mops and gallon cans of floor wax. By the time her employees arrived on Monday morning, Marlowe would be up in smoke. Sebastian wondered how literally that end would come. Pity he couldn't hang about to watch. But all that really mattered was the revenant would perish and the coven would absorb his power and strength. Now if they could only acquire the Underwoods' knowledge . . . They would. He could wait out Dixie LePage. She might linger for a summer, but how long would she last in that barn of a house without central heating? He just couldn't see her heaving buckets of coal and riddling grates.

Christopher felt the concrete damp under him and fought to stem his rising panic. He couldn't sweat, so what was the moisture on his body? Was his life force draining? The pain in his side radiated in great swamping waves. He knew the cause. He'd felt a knife before but not even the dagger thrust in Deptford had pained like this. As he clenched muscles, the blade shifted, raking forgotten nerve endings. Had he ever been this weak in his first life? Who remembered that far back?

He slept. Dozed. Passed out. He never knew which. Blackness receded after a while, and cold, damp and pain returned. He couldn't even sense light or warmth. Where was he? Underground? Inside a lead casket? Impossible! The space didn't embrace like a coffin. Willing strength into his right hand, he tried to dislodge the blade. His efforts succeeded in sending painful flashes down his leg and nerve shocks up his shoulder. The truth dawned. He was dying and this time he faced true death and judgment.

Behind him, a door opened. Outside this cold hell, sunlight beamed. The door closed. A mortal stood over him, breathing hard, and exuding hate. He knew that smell—Caughleigh.

"Sorry to disturb your Sunday afternoon nap. Just wanted to see how you're doing." A hand clutched his hair and pulled. Once, Christopher could have grasped that hand and crushed bones or willed Sebastian into silence. Now his neck stretched up in Sebastian's grasp and the movement shifted pain down to his hip. He felt his face contort as light shone in his eyes. "Feeling uncomfortable, old chap? Enjoy it while it lasts. It can only get worse."

"Why, Caughleigh?" Two words took more strength than climbing St. Paul's.

"Why?" A half-chuckle simmered behind the word. "Why should I tell you? Maybe I'll let you sweat it out. But, of course, you don't sweat do you? Don't eat. Don't drink. Don't piss. Don't fuck. Don't do anything like puny mortals. Right?"

The light hurt his eyes. Was that weakness or some vestige of humanity returning? His lids closed until Sebastian shook his head.

"Listen to me, and listen well, Marlowe. It's almost over. You won't see beyond tomorrow's dawn. The circle closes tomorrow."

"Why?" He had to know. Dislike and antipathy were one thing, but why this hate?

"Persistent devil, aren't you? I'll be gracious and satisfy you. I hate you. You are a blot on the village. The Surrey Vampire. You need to be eliminated and I'm the man to do it. I did my homework. Read some of the books in the Misses Underwood's library. Figured out the rest.

"And why do I hate you? Your kind was made to war with mine. Old magic and your power don't mix. You got between me and the old ladies. Your interference kept the LePage woman here when I could have run her off. I've wasted too long over her. You'll perish in the sunrise tomorrow. I'll absorb your power by midnight and then . . ."

"And then what?" Christopher fought for thoughts and words. "You or the coven? You don't know what you're dealing with!"

"Neither do you!"

He was right. What happened with a dead revenant's powers? Could they be absorbed? Tom might know, he'd studied lore. It was a bit late to ask. "You're a fool, Caugh-leigh."

"And you've lost. You challenged me and lost. When you're gone, I'll have your strength and the old ladies' knowledge. I'll lead this coven and every other one for miles around."

Christopher heard cartilage crunch as his nose hit the floor. Despair choked him. He believed every word of Sebastian's threat. The man was crazed with power. Caughleigh mustn't ever guess the way he felt about Dixie. Lord alone knew what form his revenge would take against her. Dixie! He remem-bered the warmth of her skin against his lips, smelled her sweetness, longed for her softness in his arms. The yearning shaped into a mind-racking torment. He needed to protect her, to save her from the taint and threats of Sebastian Caugh-leigh. Fat lot he could do immobile on his face on the con-crete.

"Enjoy your despair, it won't last much longer."

Christopher heard the door slam. Darkness enveloped him but he found scant comfort in it. He couldn't even rest. Caughleigh had covered every wicket.

Almost.

Christopher smiled in his pain. Maybe he would die, but he still possessed enough power to protect Dixie and ensure Caughleigh never laid his filthy mitts on her. Draining every last vestige of strength, Christopher focused on her. There was darkness and confusion but suddenly, like a sunny gap in a mist, he felt the link. Their minds joined. "Go home," he com-manded. "Go. Leave this place. Go back to where you be-long. Go. Leave."

He ignored the answering question. Couldn't she just lis-ten? But no, his Dixie wanted to know why. He blocked the question and sent one last urge. "Home. Safety." He pressed the thought through the boundaries of her mind. It took his last remaining strength but he felt her will hesitate under his.

He'd won. The effort drained his last consciousness. His mind shut down, depleted from the effort. His body shuddered and lay still.

Dixie looked back at the border she'd spent the last hour weeding. At least she could now see where the path ended and the border began, but she suspected she'd pulled a few plants among the grass and weeds she'd heaped in the wheelbarrow. It was a beautiful afternoon, perfect for gardening.

A black Jaguar pulled up at her gates. Damn! She'd be paying for weeks for her stupidity in accepting his invitation last night. "Hi, Sebastian," she said as she stood up. She *wasn't* conversing with him on her knees.

"Dixie." He came up the path smiling. And what a smile. Wolfish was the only word to describe it. Did that cast her as Red Riding Hood? No way! She reminded herself what happened to the wolf.

She rubbed a dirt-encrusted hand on her jeans and looked at it. "I'd shake hands but I don't think you'd want to."

"I see you've found a nice little hobby."

He made her sound like a debutante doing Junior League work. "Seems more like sweated labor to me."

He smiled. Maybe alligator suited him better than wolf. "I dropped by to ask you to dinner tomorrow. I'm planning a little celebration. Could I pick you up at seven?"

"Sorry. I'm busy tomorrow night. Thanks for asking."

His eyes flickered and froze. Temper? Disappointment? "Tuesday, then?"

"I'm not sure. . . ." That was a lie. She was as sure as her birthday came in November.

He nodded in acknowledgement. "Until later then, Dixie."

"Yeah, when I'm old and gray and desperate," she muttered to his back as he walked down the path. She heard the car door slam and refused to look up from the patch of ground elder she was attacking with her trowel. He'd taken the pleasure out of her afternoon.

"Go, home, Dixie!" a voice inside her head whispered. "Go home!" The voice echoed in her ears as a great wave of homesickness wafted over her. Why not? Home. Away from all this. The idea appealed, then faded.

Like hell she would! She wasn't running off. She had a toehold in security here, a roof over her head, land—well a little bit anyway—and enough money to cover this woman's dreams. Sebastian Caughleigh wasn't messing things up. If he tried anything more, she'd . . . she'd report him to the law society or whatever the British equivalent was. Pleased at her decision, Dixie shoved harder at the tangle of roots and pulled with her left hand. It came up with a sudden jerk, spraying dirt over her face and arms.

Owls slept more than Dixie did that night. Just before midnight, she sat bolt upright, wakened by something on the edge of a dream. Foreboding rippled through snatches of sleep. She tossed and turned and blamed the Bombay potatoes she'd eaten at the Barley Mow. A little after dawn, she woke for good.

Dixie shuffled on slippers and pulled her robe round her shoulders and felt a steady ache over her skin like poison ivy itch. Whatever it was, she felt awful. She needed air.

She pushed up the sash to its limit and leaned out. Then it hit her: a soundless scream of liquid pain. She tore downstairs almost tripping on her robe. Shaking hands fumbled and rattled the key. Endless seconds later, she threw open the door and ran. Dew drenched her thin slippers; she'd have ignored snow and ice. Torrential rain couldn't slow her.

She never thought, just followed her instinct, her heart, understanding that scream for help. She'd have run over anyone barring her way, but only birds and a frightened rabbit witnessed her frantic race, across the uncut lawn, through the yew hedges and the orchard, to the looming brick wall and the gate by the potting shed. She'd steadfastly avoided that walled garden, telling herself she'd have landscapers in to clear it one day. Now she rushed through the gate, almost wrenching the hinges open.

She'd been right, sensing evil between these high walls, and it wasn't just phallic garden ornaments. She imagined a tortured animal, or some dark, satanic rite. The stench of burning flesh hit her first, gagging and choking, dredging hideous memories of her parent's car accident. The worst horror movie couldn't depict this. A creature inside her skin screamed. Her voice rising higher than pain in the morning light, great rising curls of anguish reaching from her core and grating her throat like sandpaper and searing her soul like acid.

But she wasn't screaming. The sound out of her mouth came from the writhing white figure in the grass.

She raced towards the stench of burning flesh and flung herself on the writhing form. He calmed as her body blocked out the sun's rays. "Christopher," she wailed without even looking at the contorted face. A strangled sound came from his swollen lips. The heat of his skin burned through her cotton robe but as she lay panting on his burning flesh, she felt his body cool. He had to be moved. How? The sun shone with the warmth of a June sunrise. "Christopher, what should I do?"

Garbled, anguished syllables sputtered from his throat.

"Tell me, tell me," she wailed, but meaningless gurgles from his chest told her nothing except Christopher was dying.

Unless she did something.

Reaching across his supine body, she tugged at the knots that held his arms spread-eagled on the ground but the twisted knots in the plaited ropes refused to budge. They were anchored to the four stone phalluses. If they pulled out of the ground, she'd free him but they were cemented hard or buried deep. What now? Her frenzied mind raced at Mach speed. The sun burned him. She had to get him into shade, but first she had to free him.

The potting shed!

There had to be a knife there. She scrambled to her feet but as the sun touched his skin, he writhed and twisted from pain. Dixie pulled off her robe and threw it over him. The thin fabric wasn't enough. She yanked off her nightshirt. It still wasn't enough, but it was the best she could do.

She ran through the gate, ignoring the scratches and scrapes from bushes and twigs. She skinned her knee, forcing aside the wheelbarrow as she fumbled in the semi-darkness. Her hand closed over a pair of secateurs. If they pruned old wood on rose bushes they'd surely cut rope.

They hacked it. Rope this strong should be sold to mountaineers. Now she had his hands and feet free but it did no good. As she tried to pull him up, his legs crumpled under him and he fell, pulling her down with him. The soles of his feet were blistered and raw. He could never walk, but she had to get him out of the sun. Even these few minutes heated his skin until it burned red like scalded lobster.

The wheelbarrow!

Leaving him in a heap where he fell and stopping only to cover him again, she sped back and pulled the ancient wheelbarrow into the light. It looked old enough to have carried fuel for Armada beacons. Who cared? It had a wheel and she found a folded tarp under the dirt and dust. She shook out the tarp. Full of holes and thin places, it would still shade Christopher from the worst of the sun.

Getting him in the wheelbarrow almost defeated her. A dead weight, she couldn't lift him, but she finally tilted the wheelbarrow and half-scooped him up like a heap of prunings, then righted the barrow so he half-slumped in, half-dangled out. The tarp covered him. Just. After tucking in the edges so they didn't snare the wheel, she heaved with all her strength and ran through the orchard as if the furies followed.

She made it to the basement steps and the shady side of the house. As she wrenched open the heavy hatch, she noticed her scratched arms and her bare breasts, to say nothing of the rest of her. Thank heaven for high walls and thick hedges! She had to get Christopher out of sight before she gave the milkman a thrill. She did stop to pull her robe on, but by now it was so tattered it barely seemed worthwhile. Far better to use her time getting Christopher out of the light.

Getting him down the worn steps seemed a bigger challenge than loading him in the wheelbarrow. She could hardly tip him down like a load of coal. She spread the tarp on the ground, dumped him onto it and dragged the tarp down the stairs. She felt his pain as his head bounced and his limbs jerked down the steps. If only he'd moan or scream again, she'd know he was still alive. Alive? She bit her lip to stifle a hysterical giggle.

She'd just saved a vampire's life, and when she'd got out of bed this morning she hadn't believed they existed.

Chapter Seven

The stone floor rubbed her knees roughly through her tattered robe. She barely noticed. Her shaking fingers searched for a pulse until she laughed at the futility. If her guess was right, there'd be no pulse, no heartbeat, no breathing. What should she look for? She needed some signal that he wasn't dead. But he was. Very. Cooling sweat sent shivers across her skin. After racing through the garden, sitting in a chilly basement wasn't the smartest thing. For either of them.

It took three trips to carry pillows and blankets down to the basement. She tried reasoning through the fragments of vampire lore she remembered from Dracula movies. If Christopher slept through the day, would he recover by tonight? Would he turn into a bat? Darned if she knew. Red Cross First Aid hadn't covered vampires.

She couldn't rustle up a coffin, but she did manage a cocoon of blankets. She rolled him over, they way she'd learned, and tucked a thick pad of blankets under him. Resting his head on a pillow, she brushed the dark hair back from his eye. Her heart twisted at the sight of the gnarl of proud flesh that had once been an eye. What doctor left a scar like this? If this was British medicine, she'd get on a plane if she needed surgery.

His eye might have been butchered, but there was nothing wrong with the rest of him. The muscles on his arms and chest rippled under the sunburned skin. Her fingertips smoothed the springy pelt of dark hair that covered the curves of his chest and then trailed down to his navel. There they stopped, but her eyes didn't. This wasn't the behavior of a Southern lady. But how many Southern ladies found vampires in their gardens before breakfast? And Christopher was a feast for the eyes.

A flat stomach gave way to strong thighs and shapely legs and between them, nestled in the dark hair, everything a man needed. Her hand brushed his thigh; her breath caught as she watched the change there. He might lie as still as a stone crusader in the church, but he wasn't dead. Not yet.

"Didn't your mother tell you it's rude to stare?"

She almost choked, whirling round to meet his gaze, blood surging to her face. "Here," she said, "I brought you some blankets." She dumped the rest over him and made a pretense of tucking them in, not wanting to meet his eye but determined not to look where the blankets tented below his waist.

He didn't say a word. In the silence, she heard footsteps up the path and the clink of milk bottles. She hoped to heaven the trap door over the steps wasn't ajar.

Christopher tried to lean up on one elbow but collapsed back on the pillow. "Look all you want, Dixie. I owe you that much."

She wasn't about to discuss *that*. "Are you going to be okay?"

"Eventually." He paused as if exhausted. "I have to rest. Until dusk. Then feed." His chest heaved with the effort of speaking. "Don't let them find me, Dixie. Not until I've regained strength."

"No one's going to find you, but you'd better explain everything. Tonight." His eye closed. He looked terrible. The concrete floor had a healthier color than he did.

She was shaking, whether from cold or tension, she'd never know. She tucked the blankets around him, draped towels over the narrow windows to obscure any possible light and left him in the dark.

A soak in a hot bath should have relaxed her. It didn't. Her mind raced in crossed circles. She tried pinching herself in case she'd been dreaming. She wasn't. Reddened knees from scrambling about the cellar floor and a broken toenail, to say nothing of scratches all over her body, convinced her that, though this might be a nightmare, she sure wasn't sleeping through it. She had a dying vampire in her house. Was that possible? Wasn't he dead already? Or undead? Was he dying at all? He'd muttered something about being okay after he'd rested. He should know.

Someone had tried to kill him. Would they search for him? What if they came back to gloat over his charred remains and found nothing?

She jumped out of the tub, dripping water on the mat. She'd better cover Christopher's tracks. Before "they" came back.

She raked over the wheelbarrow tracks, which had flattened the grass. She could close up the garden door and hope the loosened ivy didn't look too disturbed, but what to do about the remnants of rope dangling from those hideous stone erections? She shuddered and chuckled at her unconscious choice of word. Looking closer, she noticed the grass brittle and yellowed where Christopher's shoulders and hips had pressed. The blades crumpled in her fingers. The heat of his body had dried the grass to hay. If she hadn't found him, would he have burned? Hell if she knew! But that was the myth and it was all she had to go on.

She had a garden broom handy and the hose connected in case the fire got out of control. With the Swan Vestas from the kitchen and the gas she'd bought for the lawn mower, she worked away. She poured trails of gasoline for each arm and leg, a blob for his head and a rough rectangle for his trunk. Some masterpiece. It resembled a pyromaniac toddler's stick man more than Christopher's manly shape but it would do. She hoped. As a last touch, she put a match to the remains of rope, and watched amazed as they flared to ashes.

She could keep him safe until sundown. What then? And what about whoever had tried to kill him?

She needed a second bath and a shampoo to rid herself of the smuts and smell. It was almost lunchtime before she sat down to coffee and the turmoil of confused thoughts. What if Christopher died despite her efforts? What if he didn't? What was she going to do with a vampire? He'd muttered something about "feeding." *That* she didn't want to think about. He wasn't snacking off *her,* but she couldn't stand by and let him die. He needed sustenance. That much was obvious. Since she'd no idea of the right way to revive a vampire, she might as well go on guesswork now and worry about it later. Time to shop for his supper.

The smell of blood sent her stomach heaving. Raw liver slid between her fingers and dropped in soft wet thups out of the plastic tub. This was why she never touched meat. Disgusting wasn't the word—but disgusting or not, she'd spent the afternoon defrosting the mammoth tubs of chicken livers from the freezer center in Leatherhead. She hoped it worked.

She drained the revolting mass in an antique jelly press. From the six tubs she had a pint and a half of blood. Pints were bigger here than at home but it didn't look enough to make a man's supper. But Christopher wasn't a man. Sheesh! She had a headache from thinking about it.

She shut the pantry door on the jug of blood and the pan of liver, and scrubbed the sink with bleach. Slathering her hands with cream, she looked at the clock. Only late afternoon. Hours before dusk. Why was she waiting? Hadn't Christopher come over that Sunday during the day? Maybe all that dusk and dawn business was a figment of Hollywood's imagination. Maybe this whole day was a figment of *her* imagination.

One look at the inert body in the basement told her it wasn't.

"Didn't I tell you not to call from work?" Sebastian resisted the urge to slam the receiver down. He'd talk to Emily briefly and then not see her for several days. She'd soon get the message. A week of enforced celibacy would bring her back to heel.

"It's urgent, Sebby. I'd never have called otherwise. I'm at work, too."

"It had better be good."

"It's terrible! You know how I random check journal entries?"

He didn't and didn't care to. "Go on."

"Just now, barely five minutes ago, I had an awful shock. I couldn't believe my eyes. I had to double-check to make sure, but there was no mistaking. It's not every day you see the name Dixie."

That caught his attention. "What the hell are you wittering about, Emily?"

The phone amplified the sucked-in breath. "I'm not wittering! At first it just surprised me. Then the full implications dawned. I had to sit down for a couple of minutes, my legs were shaking."

Her teeth would be, too, if he'd had her in the same room. "Emily, get to the point. I have an appointment waiting. If it's important, tell me. If not, get back to your Nescafe."

She sniffed. Over the phone it sounded like a seal lion honking. "Oh, Sebby, listen. You have to. It's terrible."

Now it was his turn to inhale. "What's so terrible?"

"I've been telling you! Dixie's deposit. A massive one."

"How much is massive?" Emily told him. "What? You're certain *she* made it?"

"Yes, Saturday afternoon. In the money machine."

Where was Dixie LePage getting extra money? Selling off furniture? Not that sort of amount. She had to have discovered the old ladies' hoard and started blackmailing. But who? "Cash?" he asked.

"No! That's what I've been trying to tell you." Emily was panting. He could picture the sweat beading on her upper lip. "She deposited a check. I couldn't believe it."

"Who wrote the frigging check?"

She squealed at the profanity but it got him what he wanted. "Mr. Marlowe. Mr. Christopher Marlowe." Cold sweat trickled down his spine and fear prickled the hairline on his neck. If she got that much from Marlowe, he'd never escape for less than six figures.

"What are we going to do?"

"I'm going to think, Emily, and I suggest you stop squealing and do the same!" Sebastian slammed down the receiver. He wanted to scream or smash furniture, but decided to save his energies. His survival depended on swift action. He rather enjoyed the irony of Marlowe making a desperate payment so close to his end. If only James had found those files. The old ladies had been content to take leadership in the coven as their price of silence but Dixie was an avaricious, grasping little bitch.

How he'd been fooled by her, all this while privy to her old aunts' files and planning on using them. That whole tale about never knowing her aunts had been a lie. Had they schooled her in the family business? The question was academic. Dixie would have to be taken care of. Professionally. It wouldn't be as satisfying as eliminating Marlowe but would pay dividends in savings, not power.

Dusk came at last. Only the day Gran died had dragged on this long. Dixie grabbed the sweatsuit and slippers she'd bought—he wasn't spending the night naked in her house—and went downstairs to face the monster in the basement.

He was sitting up, his chest pale as ivory in the gloom. But he smiled, and her stern resolutions sputtered out faster than a match in the wind. "Where am I?" he asked, his voice edged with weariness.

"In my basement. I found you in the backyard."

His chest moved in a silent chuckle. "I must have been a sight for sore eyes."

"You didn't smell too good, either."

"Tell me what happened."

"I was about to ask you that." She dumped the plastic shopping bag on his lap. "I bought you some clothes. May not be your usual style, but they're the best I could manage, not knowing your size. You can't sit around the way you are."

"No?"

She chose to ignore the velvet note of amusement in that syllable. "No way," she replied in her best librarian's voice. "I always insist men get dressed after I save their lives."

A shaky white hand closed over the bag. "I owe you for that, Dixie."

"Then get dressed, come upstairs. I've got you something to eat." She turned to walk up to the kitchen.

A groan and a thud turned her around before she'd gone three paces. Christopher lay on his face, one knee crumpled under him.

"Christopher!" Her shrill cry echoed in her own ears. He lay in a quivering heap, as a suppressed whimper slipped from his clenched lips. The red burn of his skin had faded but he seemed so weak and frail. She tucked the pillow under his head to protect his face from the stone floor, and reached for the blankets. Then she saw the wound.

"What happened?" She stifled her scream but it reverberated inside her skull as she gaped at the hideous scar. With his entire body sunburned, she hadn't notice it. Now that his skin had faded to pale it stood out, a raised welt of pain. A mass of livid flesh closed over a two-inch-long cut. Redness radiated outwards like an infection and his whole hip appeared swollen and tender. "You need to get to a hospital."

"No! They can't help me."

Maybe not, but basic first aid wasn't enough. "You need help, Christopher. You're weak."

"I've noticed." He lifted his head and half-turned on one shoulder to smile at her. He still had a smile to raise dreams. But right now he needed to get some clothes on.

"Can you get dressed?"

"Since I can't stand on two feet, I doubt it."

"You can't spend the rest of your life nude in my basement."

"Shame, it's a pleasant thought." He moved to sit up as he spoke and grimaced with pain.

"Still saying 'no' to a doctor?"

"My dear Dixie, haven't you worked it out yet? There's not a mortal doctor who could help me. I'm a revenant, a vampire. One of the mythical creatures you don't believe in."

That stung. "I worked that much out for myself. Now you tell me what happened."

His face twisted. "It seems I made some enemies." He pushed himself up on one arm and sagged back down on the pillow. He'd end up dying while they argued.

"Christopher," she said, brushing the dark hair from his face, "you've got to let me call someone." He'd gone from pale to gray and his skin felt loose as a chicken's.

"I'm fading, Dixie." A thin, wrinkled hand clutched at the air by her leg. "Help me." It came out like a mewl.

"How?"

In reply, he turned over and pushed the blankets off his back. Another time she might have admired his tight butt. Right now she wasn't in the mood.

"The wound. It's been festering since Saturday. There's a blade in it. Get it out. I beg of you."

"There's nothing in there. It's just a nasty gash. You need stitches." Nasty wasn't the word. It looked like raw meat.

"Look closely. It's closing over, but it's there. I can feel it. I broke off the handle but I couldn't budge the blade."

His skin burned under her hands. He had to be infected. Why were men so stubborn? Perhaps he was right about seeing a doctor, but what did he expect her to do? "I can't see anything but a very angry wound."

"Look closer. Open the cut."

The raised flesh felt as soft as the disgusting liver she'd handled earlier, but at least it wasn't bloody. Wasn't that odd? A cut this wide should have bled. Biting her lip, she rested her splayed fingers on either side of the cut and eased the wound open. Something like a giant splinter lay deep within the swollen flesh. "Let me get a pair of tweezers. I'll be right back."

"It's a six-inch blade, not a thorn from one of your rose bushes. Tweezers won't work."

"What am I supposed to use then?" She hated to snap but forgave herself. Stress wasn't the word for the past twelve hours.

"Pliers." He gasped the word. She felt the edge of the "splinter." It wasn't wood. Could he be right?

The toolbox on the dusty workbench belonged in a museum, but tools were tools—even if they had embossed handles and brass decorations. She found two pairs of antique pliers. She'd try the needle-nosed ones first. "I found a couple of pairs," she called. "I'm running upstairs to sterilize them."

"Don't be silly!"

That did it! Here she was, preparing for battlefield surgery in her basement, and he called her silly. "They're filthy, Christopher. I have to go upstairs. I'll be back."

"Sepsis is not a worry right now."

"It might be later. Give me a couple of minutes."

He had the nerve to frown at her. "I'm immune to human infection. I'm not immune to this blade. If you don't get it out, I'll extinguish and solve the problem."

Not while she lived and breathed! With the cold stone hard against her knees, she looked down at his wound. It did seem redder and larger than before. She had to use both hands to ease the flesh open. Doubts hit her like hailstones. Could she do this? Band-Aids and nosebleeds were one thing, but this . . . If she didn't, he'd—what was the word? Extinguish. A cold twist seized her heart. "I'm afraid I'll hurt you."

He half-turned on one shoulder, his eye pale in the gloom. "Dixie, my darling. Get it out. Please!"

She pried open the engorged flesh over the wound. Deep in the rent, the rough edge of the blade moved as she applied pressure. She closed the needle-nosed pliers over the edge, gripped tightly and pulled. The pliers slipped and he caught his breath as the sharp point scratched the soft, swollen flesh.

"Sorry. I'd better use the big ones."

"And you thought tweezers would work."

"Quit complaining! You insisted on an amateur! I wanted to take you to a hospital." The nose of the pliers dug into the flesh on either side of the cut but they locked and held as she pulled. The blade shifted. A tad. "It won't budge. Let me get you to a doctor." She heard panic in her voice.

"Dixie, it's okay." He might have been an adult calming a scared child. "You can do it. Pull with all your strength. Remember how you tipped the table and gave James a meal to remember? You were strong enough then."

"How did you know about that?"

"Village telegraph." His chuckle turned into a grimace of pain.

"Lie back down. I can't do anything with you staring at me like that." Or rather her body did plenty but not what she wanted. Pliers locked back in place, she tightened both hands on the ridged handle and pulled from her shoulders. "I think it moved." Had she imagined it?

"About an inch. Five more to go."

"You can tell?"

"Oh, yes. Give it another tug." She ground her teeth and pulled until she grunted. The knife moved but she stopped when she heard a grating sound like stone on metal. "Why stop? It was moving."

"I hit something. Perhaps a vital organ."

"I only have one vital organ and I'm lying on it." Only a male could make cracks like that. Her hands tightened again. She tugged until she felt sweat beading on her forehead but the blade yielded, grating again, and then stopped moving. "It's jammed between my ribs. You'll have to pull hard."

"I have been pulling hard." Sweat trickled under her arms

and down between her breasts. This was harder than lifting weights.

"Don't give up on me. It's like acid in my flesh. Dixie . . . please . . ."

His agonized whisper ripped her heart in half. Here she was, worrying about sore hands, and he had a knife blade lodged between his ribs. With every muscle in her hands, she clenched the now-warm pliers. Bracing one knee against his side, she pulled. Sweat ran down her nose. The sinews in her neck tightened and pressed against her skin. Her shoulders shook. She tasted blood as she bit her own lip, but the knife gave. Scrape by agonizing scrape she worked it between his ribs, hoping he was right about no internal injuries.

Just as the blade narrowed to a point it jammed tight as if unwilling to concede defeat. She swore, first under her breath, then aloud as she braced her knee and shoulders for a last effort. For one awful moment, she feared it was stuck tight in the fissure between his ribs, then it came clean and she fell backwards, legs sprawled as she yelled out, "Got it!" And the pliers and blade shot out of her hand to clatter on the stone floor.

Christopher leaped to his feet. Still a little wobbly on his legs, his strength seemed to return as she watched and his two-hundred-carat smile lacked nothing. She stared up at his face, refusing to look lower. Damn him! Here he was, as naked as the day he was born, grinning down at her. Taking the hand he offered, she scrambled to her feet, looking everywhere but at the most obvious part of him.

"Okay now?" she asked, looking up at his eye that gleamed as it met hers. He smiled. She felt the sweat pooling between her breasts as she read the desire in his eyes, smelled the need on his skin, and saw his thoughts.

"You have blood on your lip."

The words etched horror in her heart. She hadn't saved him so he could feed off her! She took two steps back. He didn't move. Could he? Would he? "You can't stand here naked! Get dressed!" She waved at the blue plastic bag on the floor, her chest heaving so fast she had to spit the words out.

"Your blood . . ." His eye flickered and faded as it fixed on her lip. Her heart raced. Surely even he could hear the thumping.

"I've got you some blood. Upstairs!" She turned and ran up the uncarpeted stairs.

The door slammed at the top of the stairs but nothing stilled the fear that hovered in the air around him. He'd acted like the monster she believed he was. She'd saved his life. Heaven only knew how. He'd been barely able to lift his head by the time Caughleigh and his cohorts arrived around midnight. The coming dawn he'd sensed through his fog of pain, and as the sun rose . . . He shuddered at the memory. Somehow Dixie had spirited him from the garden of hell.

She'd brought him here to rest until dusk, removed the witch blade from his side, and he'd frightened the dickens out of her by lusting after her blood. He stared down at his recovering body. Abel! No wonder she'd fled. She probably thought he was going to rape her. He owed her a dozen explanations, and he could only spare a couple at the most. But first he'd better dress. The blue plastic shopping bag lay on the floor where she'd dropped it.

She was right, it wasn't his style, but it beat nakedness. He took out the black sweatsuit. Reaching into the bag, he found underwear, socks and a pair of soft-soled cotton slippers. Bless her! She'd added a brush and toothpaste, a comb and a disposable razor, even travel miniatures of deodorant and shaving cream. The only one he needed was the comb. She had a lot to learn about vampires and the longer she stayed ignorant, the better for all of them.

"Dixie?" he called as he pushed open the door at the top of the stairs. He didn't want to scare her again.

"Hello." She looked up and smiled. Her shoulders relaxed as he stepped through the door. Had she expected him to burst through naked? Probably.

"Thanks."

She smiled, as if unsure of what to say next. "I got you some blood." She nodded at the glass jug in the center of the scrubbed pine table.

His feast beckoned, the aroma heady and intoxicating. Driven by instinct, he hefted the jug in both hands and chug-a-lugged. He savored the sweet taste on his tongue, as richness and nourishment flowed down his throat, warming his core. Renewed strength flooded to his extremities as he drained the last drops from the tilted jug, and his eye met Dixie's over the glass rim. "Sorry. Should have done that in private. We're not an elegant species when it comes to feeding."

She nodded, her face visibly paler than before. "Want a napkin?" She handed him a paper towel. He didn't doubt he needed it.

As he sat down and wiped his mouth, a hideous thought shook him. "Was that your blood?" He'd had over a pint. How could she have . . . ?

"Chickens."

"You never got that much from a chicken."

"No, I defrosted twenty-five pounds of chicken liver. I've done some odd things since I came here, but today's been positively surreal."

"It's not been an average day for me, either."

Her chuckle brought light and amusement to the tension that lay between them and reminded him of the gulf wider than humanity. "You look better. Your color's returning. You were so white . . ." She broke off and bit her lip as understanding clouded her eyes.

"I was pale because I needed to feed. Lack of nourishment combined with the torture nearly finished me." He reached across the table, his will urging her not to draw back. He closed her warm fingers between his cold hands. "I owe you my existence, Dixie. Anything you want, just ask." What else could he say? As if the rescue wasn't enough, she'd spent the afternoon defrosting liver to gather blood for him—and she couldn't bear the thought of eating a bacon sandwich.

"You could start by answering a few questions."

And he could end by putting her in danger when they discovered he wasn't dead. "You might be better off not knowing."

Eyebrows rose over those bright green eyes. Most mortals would flinch at the sight of his disfigurement. Not his Dixie. "I'll decide about that." She moved her hand from his. Cold filled his empty palms.

"Dixie . . ." he began.

"No. Listen. You're a vampire, right?"

He nodded. Safe enough question; he only confirmed what she'd undoubtedly worked out herself, hours ago.

"Who tried to kill you?"

"People who want me dead."

Her eyebrows almost met. "Smart-ass, how about a nice, stra . . ." She stopped mid-syllable as the doorbell rang. She turned to the doorway, then back to him, her eyes creased with worry. "I'll see who it is."

The front door closed and Dixie came back, balancing a stack of blue booklets. "It was Emma. I got rid of her by agreeing to deliver parish magazines." She dumped the stack on the edge of the kitchen dresser and sat back down. He wished to heaven she hadn't. His hunger was piqued rather than eased by the blood he'd swallowed, and now he smelled hers. He heard it coursing under her warm skin. He imagined it warm against his tongue. The thought of her lifeblood sent his mind into a spin. He wanted nothing more than to tip her head back, bury his fangs in her soft skin and drain her dry.

And probably kill her. He clutched the table edge, fighting back his physical need. He had to leave. Fast. Before Caughleigh and his cronies discovered the lack of vampire remains. Before someone knocked on the back door and found him in a tête-à-tête with Dixie. And before survival instinct overrode respect for Dixie's life. He'd flit right now, but he barely had the strength to stand, much less transmogrify—or even drive himself.

She reached across the table to him, her soft hand over his clenched fist. "You still look terrible, Christopher. Anything else you need?"

This was no moment for the whole truth. He paused. "I need your help. To get away. I can't stay here. For both our sakes."

Concentration replaced the worry in her eyes. "You want me to take you somewhere? You can hardly go back to your house."

"I need you to drive me up to town. To London." At Tom's he'd be safe. He'd worry later about Tom's reaction when he drove up to the front door with a mortal.

She didn't hesitate a second. "Right. I'll have to check the map Stanley gave me. Or perhaps you know the way."

"I know the way."

She drove carefully. Just as well. He slipped in and out of consciousness like a drifting leaf. "I'll owe you forever for this," he said.

"I'll collect when I need to."

"Tell me when we get to Hyde Park Corner," he said and slumped against the seat.

Dixie hoped they'd get that far. She was tempted to ignore his insistence and take him to the nearest hospital, but he was right. She couldn't drive up and say, "I need help for an injured vampire." They'd lock her up.

Cold panic hit her at a roundabout, but she negotiated it and would have patted herself on the back except she needed both hands to maneuver a lane change. The traffic got denser with every mile. Stuck in a jam somewhere near Wandsworth, she glanced over at Christopher. He looked gray as doom.

The streetlights cast odd shadows, highlighting the empty socket and his sunken cheeks. She drove on through the massed traffic. If this was evening, she didn't want to see rush hour.

"We're at Hyde Park Corner, Christopher."

He didn't open his eyes, but he'd heard her. "Go up Piccadilly." She had to concentrate to hear his voice above the noise of the traffic. "Now left here." She noticed the name, Half Moon Street. "Now left. . . . Second right. . . . To the end, then left." A narrow road turned abruptly by a pub at the corner, The Red Lion. "Through the gateway." There were high walls behind and houses in front, and at the end, another wall with a black garage door. "This is Tom's. You can park inside."

"How do I get in?" As she spoke, the door rose and closed behind her as she pulled to a halt in a small yard behind the tall, dark shape of a townhouse. A tall figure made a silhouette against the light in the open French windows.

"Kit?" The voice echoed with worry in the night air. He bounded across the yard and wrenched open her door. "Who the hell are you?" he asked as Dixie stepped out of the car

"I'm Dix . . ." She could have been Ivanna Trump for all he cared.

"Kit," he called, and then saw Christopher, slumped and unmoving in the passenger seat. "What have you done to him?" he demanded and vaulted over the car roof. Pulling the door open, he gathered Christopher in his arms. Fury sparked behind his eyes. "Be glad you're a woman. If you were a man, I'd tear you limb from limb for this."

"For what? For bringing him here? It's what he wanted. Do something, can't you? He called you his friend." Dixie yelled. She hadn't done all this to be griped at.

"Who are you?" The voice cut like a knife across the night as he strode towards the house, carrying Christopher as lightly as a plate of cookies.

"I'm Dixie LePage."

"Oh." He carried Christopher through the garden door. Taking that as an invitation, Dixie followed.

Christopher looked worse in the light. The color he'd gained earlier faded. He'd gone past pale to a green-gray color that suggested morgues and cold slabs. Her heart clenched cold in her chest. "Is he dying?" she asked Tom's fast-moving back.

"He's been dead four hundred years," he snapped without turning his head.

That did it! Half leaping, she caught up with him and grabbed the sleeve of his shirt and walked across the room beside him. "You know exactly what I mean, smart-ass! He said you'd help him!"

The man stopped mid-stride and turned a pair of onyx-hard eyes on her. Tears welled up behind her lashes. She forced them back. She wasn't crying in front of this bastard. Why had she ever come? If he did anything to Christopher, she'd clobber him. "He's safe with me. I'd as soon harm myself," he said, his voice strangely gentle, "but it may be too late."

"No!" The word screamed like a tempest in her brain. "He said he'd be safe if I got him here."

"Safe is not the same as sentient. You brought him here. I thank you for that. You'd best leave."

"No way, José! How do I know he's really safe with you?" She parked both hands on her hips, standing square in front of him to block his way. He never spoke. Just looked as if searching her soul. The burr of traffic and the scent of some night plant outside the open door hovered in the background as they fought for Christopher.

"You wouldn't have brought him if you really doubted." He angled his head to the open French windows. "I'm taking him upstairs. There's nowhere down here to lay him." She couldn't argue that one. Wall to ceiling bookshelves, a massive antique desk, a computer, and a pair of swivel chairs were the only furnishings. "Shut the door. I don't want the house full of mosquitoes or moths."

"He's dying and you're worried about mosquitoes?"

"And neighbors who might summon the law if you keep shrieking."

Was she shrieking? Probably. It was a wonder she wasn't screaming the house down. She took a deep breath. Before she exhaled, he spoke again, "Shut it, Miss LePage. Do you want me to waste energy that might save Kit?"

There was only one answer to that. But by the time she turned back from shoving the last bolt home, he'd disappeared. He wasn't getting away. She ran through the open door and up a wide, curving staircase. She ignored the three closed doors. In the fourth room, Tom bent over Christopher, two black shapes so close they seemed one through the blur of her tears.

Tom turned as Dixie approached. "Wait outside a couple of minutes. I'm getting him in bed."

"I'm staying." She closed the distance between them. Christopher looked worse, if it was possible. Moisture beaded on his face and neck. Sweat? "What's happening?"

Tom didn't even look up. "His life essence is evaporating. It won't be long now. He'll be gone before dawn."

Choking back tears, Dixie grabbed Christopher's shoulders; they felt like bits of chicken. Dead and lifeless. "Christopher, don't. Not after everything!"

His eye opened, like the shutter of a camera without film. "Dixie, thanks." He never spoke, but she heard him clear as bird song.

Her hands were shaking as Tom lifted them away. She half-noticed his fingers were bent and twisted. "Go outside a minute. Let me get him ready. I won't be long."

Dixie wanted to laugh. Or scream. It hardly mattered. "It's a bit late for modesty. I think I've seen everything." He just looked at her. She was tempted to scratch out those piercing eyes. "I found him. Naked. And got him out of the sun. I also yanked the knife blade out, among other things . . ."

"What blade?" His hand grabbed her wrist until it hurt. His hands might be deformed but his strength was—like Christopher's used to be.

"The one someone stuck in his ribs. And don't ask me who put it there. He didn't say."

"Where?" He pulled the sweatshirt from Christopher's waist.

"On the side, roll him over." He did that as easily as turning a page. Dixie pushed up the sweatshirt and stared. Now there was just a small knot and a shadow like a fading bruise. "There was a wound. A great gaping one. I didn't dream it. I swear."

His awkward fingers smoothed Christopher's side. "I believe you."

"What happened?"

"He healed and used up his last strength." If she opened her mouth, she'd bawl. Tom didn't comment as she helped pull the sweatshirt over Christopher's head and the pants down off his cold feet. If he had, she'd have swiped him, vampire or not. They pulled the covers up to his chin, the crisp-ironed linen making Christopher's face appear even grayer. Tom turned to her, his eyes softened. "There's a bed in the next room. This is your time to sleep. I'll watch and call you when the time comes."

"I'm not leaving him." To demonstrate the point, she sat down hard on the edge of the mattress. The bed sagged as he perched on the opposite side.

"It won't take long, he's fading fast." The choke in his

voice made her turn. She wasn't the only one heartbroken. "Tell me what happened."

She condensed the wildest day of her life into half a dozen short sentences. "I thought bringing him here would save him," she spat out the words with anger and frustration.

"You did save him—from slow death by torture. Wouldn't you rather pass away surrounded by friends than scorched slowly by the rising sun?"

She shuddered hot and cold at the idea. "I thought vampires were supposed to be immortal."

"Didn't Kit answer that one?"

"We never got the chance to talk about it."

He shook his head, as if to shake away tears. "No, I suppose not. It's quite simple. We're beyond life and death, but that doesn't mean we can't be extinguished. If someone's determined and knows the way . . . With Kit, they took no chances: sunlight and an incision."

"But I took out the knife, and he slept all day in the dark. Why didn't that cure him?" She'd given up trying to hold back her tears.

"He was already weakened when they took him."

"How?" Shaking fingers tried to dry her cheeks but tears came as if her heart were draining. Maybe it was. He pushed a folded handkerchief into her hand. Another time she'd have appreciated the luxury of wiping tears with silk. "How was he weakened?" she repeated.

"A combination. The immediate reason, it was the time of his borning, the anniversary of his transformation. We're always weakest then, and they knew that. They knew to pierce him and drain more strength that way. Also . . ."

"Also, what?"

The dark shape shrugged. "He'd transmogrified—changed shape—a couple of times the past week or so. That drained him. And he doesn't feed like a sensible revenant. His stupid scruples."

"What do you mean?" Christopher had no hesitation about draining that jug on the table and it had restored his color, for a short time. "Should I have given him more? I had no idea how much."

Tom reached over to steady her shoulder; she found the twisted fingers strangely comforting. His voice gentled as he looked across the bed, "It's nothing you did or didn't do. Just his stubbornness. He has an aversion to taking human blood. He's fed off animals for years."

"And that's a substitute?"

"From day to day, yes. I feed from animals myself, sometimes, but on a long term, no. Add that accumulated weakness to the torture he endured . . . No revenant could survive both."

Kit seemed to shrivel as they watched. Fear skittered up and down her spine. Dixie leaned over to kiss him. He felt as cold as Gran in the casket. She'd just met him and now she was losing him. Did everyone she loved have to die? Tears coursed down her cheeks. She didn't bother to wipe them anymore.

The mattress sagged behind her. Tom had moved to her side. His arm wrapped her shoulders. "He was my friend, too," he whispered, his tears wet and warm on her neck. "We were young together."

Night passed with only the buzz of endless traffic outside the curtained window and the tick of the marble clock on the mantel to mark the time.

"It's three. Dawn's not far off. He's lasting longer than I thought." Tom's voice shattered the quiet. Or was that her nerves? He'd barely whispered.

"No." She wasn't going to just sit here and watch Christopher die. She'd . . . Damn it, she knew what she'd do. "Listen! You said he was weakened because he won't take human blood." Tom nodded, his eyes heavy-lidded and red from crying. "Would human blood save him?"

Chapter Eight

Tom's eyes widened with understanding. "At this point?" He shook his head. "I don't honestly know."

"But it's worth a try, right? What have we got to lose?" Let him answer that one.

"Remember his aversion—"

"No! Use your sense! My blood might save him. I should have thought of it hours ago. Besides, I think he has fed from me. One night, weeks ago, I thought he'd given me a monumental hickey but on second thought . . ."

"Dixie, if he'd fed, you wouldn't 'think' he had. That time, he tasted in the heat of passion and dragged me through forty-eight hours of angst over it."

"He told you!" Her chest heaved with fury.

"He was consumed with remorse. He felt he'd abused you."

That was why he'd stayed away those days and when he came back, she'd suspected him of stealing her appointment book. "Well, I didn't feel abused. I felt abandoned when he disappeared, and I'm not standing here arguing. If he needs blood, I've got a body full."

"Dixie, do you know what you're suggesting?"

"I've been a blood donor since college."

"This isn't the same."

He was right there. A thought struck her. "If he feeds off me, will I become a vampire?"

Tom shook his head. "No. You'll feel the loss of blood. That's all. If feeding caused transformation, we'd outnumber you mortals."

"Then I can give my blood and not worry."

"Except about Kit's scruples. Forget it, Dixie."

"But it's doable. You feed from humans. How do you do it? A nip on the neck?" She spoke lightly to ignore the shudder that started between her shoulder blades and spread like an infection. His eyes questioned her sanity. She half-agreed. "I'm serious, Tom. Please tell me what to do."

"If it works, Kit will curse me."

"Then leave. I'll tell him you had to go to the bathroom."

His mouth twisted in a reluctant smile. "I'm a revenant. What use would I have for a bathroom?"

"Hell, I don't know. Oh, damn it! Help me. Look at him." Grayer than dust, Christopher's face showed lines and creases like an old man. He *was* old. Centuries old. Dixie choked back her horror as she saw it reflected in Tom's eyes.

"I'll tell you," Tom said. "It's simple. He has to feed from a vein or artery. The neck works but so does the wrist, thigh, anywhere."

"But he can't move. How can he bite? You do it!" She pulled down the neck of her tee shirt.

"No!" He backed away, hands raised as if to fend her off. "We never feed from another's bite. It's taboo."

This was no time to debate revenant ethics. "But how? We left it too late." Fear as cold as mercury slid through the marrow in her bones.

"Wait! There's a way." He disappeared, then reappeared before she had time to think. "Here." He handed her a surgeon's scalpel. "It's sterile."

Dixie stared up at him. "Where . . . ?" she began.

"An old friend of mine is a doctor. He leaves equipment here for when he's in town." She should ask something more, but her brain no longer formed sentences. The gleaming metal shone like a mirror. It looked deadly. The blade winked as her hand shook. "Open a vein. When he scents the blood, instinct will start him feeding. With willpower we can resist, but as weak as he is it'll work as a reflex."

"You're certain?"

"I'm certain you're brave enough to do it."

She might trade her life for that certainty but wasn't she gambling Christopher's? The blade felt colder than fear. She couldn't just slash her neck, blind. "I cant see what I'm doing. I need a mirror."

"Not in this house, Dixie."

She hesitated, then looked back at Christopher. Gray peppered his dark hair and the wrinkles stood like furrows in his cheeks. She couldn't dally any longer. Pulling back the sheets so she could sit close, she glanced down at his wasted arms and shrunken chest. "It's too late."

"No. Close, but not yet. I'd know."

"How?" Gran had looked better in her casket than Christopher did right now.

"He made me. I'll know when he extinguishes."

"Will you die, too?"

He shook his head. "I won't die but I'll feel his going."

"Not yet you won't." She poised the blade over her wrist. Which vein? Half a dozen showed blue under her skin. What if she got the wrong one? Her wrist just wouldn't work. She leaned close; her weight on the mattress caused Christopher's head to turn towards her, his cheek resting just inches from her breast. That might just be easier than slashing her own wrist. But . . . She looked over her shoulder to Tom. "You may not need to use the bathroom but would you mind making me a cup if tea or something? I'd much rather not have an audience."

He hesitated, then nodded and left. Dixie was alone with Christopher, clutching a scalpel that she had to find the courage to use.

She cradled Christopher's head and leaned over, bringing his mouth as close as she could. Her right hand clenched the now-warm scalpel. This wouldn't work. She needed a third hand to open her tee shirt. She laid his head back on the pillow as gently as she could, set the scalpel on the nightstand, and pulled her tee shirt over her head. She raised his head again. This was harder than she thought. She really did need two hands. What if she cut too deep? What if he faded while she hesitated?

As she pulled him close, he turned to her breast. Had he moved? She looked down at the worn face nestled in her bosom. That was it! She unsnapped her bra and slid under the covers until she was stretched out beside him. Propped on one elbow, she leaned over him until her breast rested by his lips. Gritting her teeth, she poised the scalpel over her skin, shut her eyes, and nicked. She winced at the pain but opening her eyes saw only a scratch. To draw blood she'd have to cut deep. Hesitation hit like a killing frost. Was she crazy? A glance at Christopher quickened her resolve.

Her wrist moved. She cried at the pain, but smiled at the gush of blood. She leaned into Christopher, caressing his mouth with her breast. He lay like a granite statue. She'd dithered too long.

Suddenly, his lips parted and a great surge of pleasure swept through her as his mouth closed over her breast. She melted into him, as sweet warmth washed and lapped at the fringes of her reason. She forgot the pain. Pain didn't exist, only joy. She rolled closer, wanting his touch on every inch, his closeness. Her arms cradled him as he suckled her strength and her mind floated in a cloud of light that carried her ever higher.

She sighed, she moaned, as his insistent mouth clamped and suckled. She cried out as his jaw slammed tight with returning strength, then pleasure mixed with the pain, as his arm closed round her. "Christopher!" Every worry and fright of the day evaporated at her cry as response coursed through every nerve. Her hips moved against him. Her thigh rocked against his arousal. She'd ceased to think, to breath, to reason. She wanted Christopher, today and forever.

He moaned. She sighed in reply. He bit. She buckled against him, urging him to drink harder, deeper, yearning for the sweet pleasure he took and gave. His arms now held like a vise. A sweet velvet vise that took her being into his. She'd never in her life known such closeness, such yearning, such joy.

"Dixie." He lifted his mouth as he spoke and blinked at her, his eye pale with passion. "What have I done?"

"You took what I gave and you needed." She smiled, wanting to giggle but she didn't have the energy. "And treated me to a new experience." She felt lightheaded and giddy. The room seemed to fade before her eyes.

"You shouldn't have, Dixie." She heard his worry through the mist of her consciousness.

"Why not? It saved you, right?"

"At what price, Dixie?"

She didn't answer that, as his face, the bed, and the room spun off into darkness.

"Do you have no sense? How could you let her?" Christopher yelled from the doorway.

Tom looked up from the document in his hand and leaned back in his swivel chair. "By 'her' I take it you refer to the young woman who brought you here last night and, by her intervention, assured your continued existence." He smiled. "You certainly look better than the last time I saw you. I feared our long friendship was over."

Christopher's hands splayed on the polished oak as he towered over his friend. "Maybe it is! You should have stopped her."

Tom lifted his eyebrows. "Maybe I, too, didn't want you to expire."

Christopher's elbows sagged as his head dropped. "You could have prevented her."

"You really believe that? Your young woman isn't the sort to be stopped. I willed her to turn around and leave and she marched past me and into my own house as if she owned it."

"But you told her what to do."

"I didn't *tell* her. She put me through a scrutiny that would have done credit to Francis Walsingham. She asked me point-blank if her blood could save you. Did you want me to lie?"

"Yes!" The room spun but he ground his nails into the desktop for support. "Tom, I abused her kindness. I took advantage of her generosity."

"No, you didn't." He stemmed Christopher's protests with a shake of the head and a raised hand. "Listen! She committed herself to you when she rescued you from the torture. She sheltered you from the sun and fed you and brought you here at your request. And, yes, she told me everything, even about the chicken livers. A woman of resource.

"We talked as we kept vigil and by then I decided you were right and I was wrong. She'd had no part in trapping you. All she wanted was to save you. She'd brought you this far, she'd earned the right to stay. She asked why you were so weak and if anything could save you. I told her. The truth shook her but she chose. And willingly. You're right, she is honest and kind, and, I suspect, loves you."

"That's what I feared. I fed, we're bonded."

"You fed once and tasted her some days ago. That's not an eternal bond."

"No? It's an eternal debt. I took so much blood. What if I'd taken too much? She's hurt. She has a great wound in her breast." He frowned up at Tom. "Don't try to tell me she brought that scalpel in her handbag!"

"I gave it to her. She was ready to bite herself if need be. I made the inevitable easier. Kit. You were fading, she offered the means to save you." His voice softened, "Once, you and Justin brought me back from death. I just repaid the debt."

"At Dixie's cost!"

Tom glanced at the ceiling. "She may well consider the price was reasonable. What's done is done. If you don't rest, what good will her efforts do? Don't let her gift be in vain."

"She's hurt. She's weak. What sort of repayment is that? She needs stitches. She can't go to a hospital. Imagine the report sheet. Cause of injury? Succoring a dying vampire. She'd end up in the psychiatric ward."

"Justin can stitch it and give her blood." He grinned as Christopher started forward. "Don't get me wrong. He'll use blood bags." Tom clasped his shoulder. "Kit, go rest. Dawn isn't far off and I doubt you'd live though another sunrise. When Dixie wakes, I want to be able to tell her you're safely resting, not charred to ash despite all her efforts. I wouldn't want to be on the receiving end of her anger."

"The last man who miffed her got a pub table in his chest and a plate of hot curry on his love life." He'd laughed the first time he'd heard that. It lost nothing in the retelling.

Tom stood up. "If you can laugh again, you'll last. Go rest. I'll wait up for Dixie. Anything else you need?"

Christopher steadied himself on the desk. He hadn't felt this weak in his mortal days. "Get Justin to take care of her."

*   *   *

Dixie felt the hand on her shoulder just before her eyes opened. She half sat up, then grabbed the sheets to cover her chest. She recognized the room, but not the man sitting on the edge of the bed. Where was Christopher?

"Don't be afraid. You're safe." He might sound reassuring but Dixie wasn't that easily convinced. She looked around, judging the distance from bed to door, wondering if Tom was within earshot, and if he'd help if he were. "I should introduce myself. I'm a doctor, Justin Corvus. Our mutual friend Kit Marlowe asked me to attend you. I believe you're injured."

She couldn't deny that. Her boob throbbed like a hang-over headache. But . . . "He did? He gave me the impression he didn't trust doctors."

The man nodded, his eyes crinkling a little at the corners. "Kit, like all of us revenants, avoids mortal doctors." He paused. "He called me in because I'm a member of the same colony. Your injury would be difficult to explain anywhere else."

He was right about that! She didn't fancy explaining her particular injury in an Emergency Room. "My hand slipped chopping onions" or "I caught it in the zipper of my parka" sounded as incredible as the truth. "You really are a physician?"

He inclined his head, "Yes, madam, I am and have been since I arrived on these islands."

"Which was when?"

Amusement quivered around his mouth. "I came as a surgeon to the Ninth Legion Hispania in 136 and stayed." She felt her mouth drop. His smile and reassuring hand on her shoulder were no doubt to ease her shock. "Don't be afraid. My skills have advanced considerably since then. Trust me," he said, "I wouldn't attempt heart surgery, but I can repair cuts. It was one of the first procedures I learned."

Trust him? Heck, why not? She half-expected to hear the

Twilight Zone theme. Minutes later, she sat propped on pillows while Justin Corvus donned surgical gloves and emptied his bag of instruments that looked very twenty-first century.

"You're still worried about Kit," he said as he checked her blood pressure and pulse.

"Yes." She looked up at the dark eyes. "Last night I thought I'd lose him."

"So did Tom. We both owe you a debt. One we will not soon forget. Few mortals have your courage."

"I'm not sure about the courage bit. I was terrified."

"That, I believe, is how one defines courage—persisting in the face of fear." Gently, he eased away the sheet she still clutched and looked at her wound. "You cut deep, but we can fix that." She shivered as he swabbed the wound with cold solution. "The scratch on top will heal, but this one I must stitch." She felt the sting of the hypodermic and spreading numbness.

"Why haven't I bled more?" It really didn't make sense, just a wide, red gash.

"We heal where we feed," he replied, "just as our own injuries heal fast. Kit's scar from the knife has almost vanished by now, but we cannot heal our own mortal injuries. Hence, Kit's eye or Tom's hands. I brought Kit back from death, but restoring his sight was another matter. Kit made Tom, but couldn't repair the ravages of the rack."

"You made Christopher into a vampire?" He was stitching now, she saw the movement of his hands and felt the tug on her flesh, but this conversation could distract her from amputation.

"I prefer the term revenant. Popular fiction and Hollywood have sensationalized 'vampire.' "

She winced as a thread pulled the tender edge of her flesh. "Let me get one thing straight. Kit, Christopher, is *the* Christopher Marlowe, who died in the tavern at Deptford."

She expected his answering nod. She didn't expect it to knock her for a loop. Suspecting was one thing. Actually having someone confirm it was another.

"You're still suffering shock. You probably have a hundred questions. If I can clear up your confusion, ask. I cannot tell you about Kit or Tom. Their histories are theirs alone to share. But about myself, or our kind in general . . ." Stitching finished, he applied a thick gauze pad with strips of adhesive. "Have those stitches out in a couple of weeks and all will be well. The scar will fade in a year or so."

"So I just knock on the door of my friendly neighborhood physician and say, 'A seventeen hundred year-old doctor put these in, please take them out'?"

He chuckled. "You're right, that won't work. They wouldn't have the right form for the National Health. I'll do it. Now, I'll go find some blood for you."

Dixie pulled her tee shirt back on as the door closed behind him, wondering where he "found" blood. He should know. It was his bread and butter after all. She grimaced at that thought. Justin returned just minutes later with two bags of blood. "Tom keeps a supply of blood?"

"Of course." Justin smiled. "Don't you keep spare food on hand for emergencies?"

As she digested that comment, Justin hooked the bag on the top of the brass bedstead and then fiddled with a valve in the tubing. "Any more questions?"

"Yeah, lots. Mirrors. Hollywood's right about the reflection bit." She remembered the time she hadn't seen Christopher in the hall mirror.

"Partly. Our bodies don't reflect but if we look in one long enough, we see our life reflected back." He smiled and inclined his head. "Imagine how you'd feel having all your mistakes thrown at you each time you looked in a mirror. Multiply that by the length of our existence. The experience is one we tend to avoid."

She understood. What if her years with her ex-fiancé were hurled back at her every time? "That makes sense, but I'm confused about the day-night issue. I've seen Christopher out in broad daylight but Tom said it was sunlight that nearly killed him. What gives?"

He unhooked and replaced the now-empty bag. "Right on both counts. We can go out in the day, but direct sunlight can be weakening. If we feed regularly, we can survive without a problem. In fact," he paused to readjust the valve and start the second bag of blood, "Hollywood's creation of the 'fatal daylight' myth has been a great gift to us. Almost everyone believes it, including many of our enemies. If the world were more literate, they'd never be so deceived. Bram Stoker knew the truth, at least in that area. But all that hocus pocus about crucifixes and churches and sacred hosts—nonsense!"

"But why did the dawn light burn Christopher? He was *burning*. You don't mistake *that* smell for anything else."

"He was naked. Clothing affords us protection. And they knew his weakest time. It was the day of his revenance, when he returns close to death. It happens each year."

"Wouldn't it have made sense to go off somewhere safe for a couple of days?"

"Yes."

He didn't say any more. He didn't need to. "He came back to see me."

"Yes. But of his own free will. Kit does what he wants. I noticed that trait several hundred years ago."

"That doesn't alter the fact that he nearly died because he came back to me."

"And that he survived because you were near and possessed the courage to act in the face of the unknown." He picked up the last bag. "Life happens and the end comes to us all, even revenants and vampires. This wasn't Kit's time."

"You sound like my Gran. She always believed things were meant to happen and that they always worked out."

"Wasn't she right? You inherited the house, which you never anticipated, came over to see it, which no one else expected, and let Kit have the books he wanted, which was more than we ever dreamed."

"Why are they so important?"

"Ancient lore we'd rather our enemies didn't master." He stopped to ease the needle out of her arm, placed a cotton swab over the bead of blood in the crook of her arm and bent her elbow. "All set," he said with a satisfied smile. "You need to rest. I suggest you sleep and give Tom a chance to get ready for a mortal visitor."

She thought she couldn't sleep, alone, injured, in a strange house full of vampires. She was wrong.

She woke to late afternoon sun, a thermos on a tray beside the bed, and a pile of shopping bags on the floor. She reached out for the white card propped against the thermos. "Dear Dixie," she read. "While Kit rests, accept my hospitality. Here's coffee, and Kit thought you might need clean clothes. There's a bathroom at the end of the hall. Help yourself. Call if you need anything. I'll be downstairs in my study. When you're ready, I'll take you out to eat, Tom Kyd."

She showered fast. The clothes fit pretty well, but she'd never have bought designer jeans or a silk blouse. She toweled her hair dry and decided she'd better go down and face the vampires.

She hadn't imagined the curving staircase last night. It was big enough to drive a compact car down. And the front hall wasn't exactly small either, with the wide marble floor and antique side tables. This was some house.

She found Tom in his study, frowning at his computer monitor and Justin sitting in a wing chair looking out on the garden where her car was still parked.

They both stood up as she opened the door. "Feeling all right?" Tom asked.

"I'm still a little light-headed, but other than that . . ."

He nodded, a hint of a smile behind his eyes. "It's been a few hours—for both of us. I'm not used to being in debt to a mortal. It's unnerving."

"*You're* unnerved! What about me? I feel I've slipped into the Twilight Zone. You at least knew about ordinary mortals."

The smile spread to his mouth. "Dixie, the fact we're having this conversation proves you're no 'ordinary' mortal."

She crossed the room and sat down, then realized she was alone, with two bloodsucking vampires between her and the door and not a single living creature knew where she was.

Her heart hammered so loud, she barely heard Justin's quiet voice. "Don't be so alarmed. You'll come to no harm. For all his suspicions, Tom owes you as big a debt as I do."

"Can you read my mind?" What chance did she have now?

"Not your mind, your face," Tom said. "Your thoughts are written all over it."

"Yeah, well, I used to be good at keeping a straight face when confronted with the outrageous. Must be losing my touch."

"No, just coming to grips with a new angle on reality."

"My biggest reality, right now, is hunger."

"I thought it might be. You've had shock and blood loss. We'll take you down the road for a steak."

She shook her head at Tom's offer. "Something else, please. I'm vegetarian."

No one commented on the strangeness of two vampires taking a vegetarian out for a late lunch. They shared a bottle of red wine, while Dixie ate a mushroom omelet, a large salad, and cheese and biscuits in an elegant, very expensive, coffee shop just doors down from Tom's house.

"Tell me as much as you can about how you found Kit and his injuries—if it's not too much to ask," Justin said as he refilled her glass.

She told him. He asked about the walled garden. She described it in detail, including the stone phalli. He wanted to know exact details of Christopher's wound. That, she had no trouble describing; the image had seared itself into her brain. "I couldn't believe how he healed once the knife was out."

"I'd give anything to see that knife," Justin murmured.

"But you can." She opened the pocket book she'd retrieved from her car, rummaged thought the mess, and pulled out the knife wrapped in a sandwich bag. "That's all that's left. Christopher broke the handle trying to pull it out."

"How did you get it out?" Tom asked as he passed it to Justin.

"Pliers and prayer."

Justin held the dark blade with two fingers. "As I thought, a Druid knife. I wonder how long they've had it."

"Who are 'they'?" Dixie asked. She didn't get an answer. "What's a Druid knife?" she tried again.

"The originals were made by the Druids for sacrifice and to gather sacred mistletoe. Others have been made by the ancient methods, and are imbued with the same powers." Justin placed it on the table between them. "I believe this is an original."

"A Druid knife?" What had she heard about Druids? Not much.

He nodded. "It's slaughtered quite a few victims, I shouldn't doubt, and we know of one failure." He slipped it back in the bag. "I'll take care of it, and make sure it won't find another victim, I promise you."

"Dixie," Tom said, "I owe an apology for my lousy welcome last night. You saved my oldest friend. Thank you."

"He's my friend, too," she replied, "even if you do have the advantage of years."

"About four hundred, give or take a few."

"Yes, I've wanted to ask about that." She paused, wondering if there was some vampire etiquette about these things.

"You're Tom, short for Thomas Kyd, Christopher's contemporary, right?"

"Right. Kit died fifteen months before me. Our deaths were linked—both victims of Tudor politics—but we'd been friends, even shared lodgings, and he changed me. We stayed friends ever after."

She turned to Justin. "And you turned Christopher into a vampire?"

"I transformed him after he was killed, just as Kit transformed Tom when he died."

"And you, how did you get to be a vampire?"

"A Druid priestess transformed me, after a Brigantine arrow got me through the throat. Nowadays, I wouldn't die from such an injury. Back then, I drowned in my own blood and Gwyltha found me. She'd never before transformed a Roman." He paused as he thought back over the centuries. "I was the only non-Druid revenant for many years."

"The Druids started it?" This wasn't the version of popular fiction.

He shook his head. "There are colonies much older than the Druids. Some date back to ancient Babylon." And she'd always thought it started in Transylvania.

She looked around the coffee shop; a couple leaned close in one corner, a group of women laughed and gossiped at a round table, a trio of men in pin-stripe suits talked closely and shuffled papers back and forth. Dixie would bet her house and bank balance they'd all collapse and croak at the thought of the conversation she'd just had. Heck, she barely believed it herself.

The sun was setting. They looked out on the long summer twilight that would last until late in the evening. They'd sat here all afternoon.

"Kit will be waiting," Tom said.

Dixie clenched her fists. She wanted more than anything to see him and the thought scared the daylights out of her.

Before, he'd just been a man who intrigued and attracted her. Now what? She was about to find out. The twenty yards to Tom's front door, with its twin bay trees, stretched like as many miles.

"Dixie," Justin said as he walked beside her, "few mortals know what you know." She'd figured that much out for herself. "And many, many fewer have done what you have done. In all of history, only a handful have shown your courage and faith. Within our colony—you are the first. That will never be forgotten."

"I'm not going to forget it in a hurry either." Why so flippant? Was it the thought of seeing Christopher again, of feeling his arms around her? Her breasts tingled at the thought. Her whole body tingled, come to that. Because he was close. And alive. She shook her head. Would she ever get the vocabulary right?

"Kit's waiting for you." Tom stopped at the steps leading up to his front door.

Justin stood beside him. "Go on in. He's expecting you."

And she had no idea what to expect. She turned the polished brass knob. The heavy door swung open on well-oiled hinges and she stepped inside, into the wide, square hall with its marble-tiled floor and the wide, sweeping staircase.

He stood in the doorway to her right.

"Christopher." She almost choked on his name. Her heart beat like a tom-tom under the still-tender stitches.

He stood there, like a living dream, just out of arm's reach. And smiled. "Hello, Dixie," he said. Warm ripples washed her like gentle waves on a summer beach. She wanted to answer, to say something, but the words jammed in her throat and caused her eyes to lose focus and her hand to shake.

"You look . . ." She struggled for the word, but her mind wouldn't cooperate. "You look a whole lot better than when I found you in the backyard," she said, then wanted to kick herself as he winced.

"Must have been quite a shock, given you didn't believe in me."

"It was. I've learned quite a bit the last twenty-four hours."

"I'm sorry, Dixie." It sounded like an apology for every discord between the sexes since Adam blamed Eve for the apple.

"For anything in particular, or life in general?"

"For the whole fucking mess."

The profanity hurt like a pistol-whipping. Catching her breath, she glanced at the warm, smooth face beside her. She'd seen every change possible in the last couple of days. Or thought she had. "I don't care for your choice of adjective." Okay, she sounded like a reproving school marm with an eighth-grader, but after all, the author of *Dr. Faustus* could manage better than your average thirteen-year-old.

An eye wide with remorse met hers. "That's what it was."

This time the blow came like a kick to the gut. "I see." She didn't.

Christopher rested a hand on her shoulder. Her confused body didn't know whether to flinch or lean into him, so she stared at him instead. His skin had lost its pallor and glowed with the warm bloom of life. The open neck of his black linen shirt showed a vee of stray hairs. A pulse throbbed at the base of his neck. With an emotion between awe and horror, she realized *her* blood flowed in his veins.

"You begin to understand," he said.

"No, I don't." In fact, the more she thought about it, the less she followed.

"I'm sorry, Dixie," he repeated.

"What for?"

"For dragging you into this mess. For abusing your kindness and presuming on your goodwill. For yanking you up here when you should have been safe in Bringham watching TV or drinking Guinness in the Barley Mow." He paused to run his fingers through his dark hair.

Dixie jumped in. "Now, wait a minute! Everything I've done since the moment I found you Monday, I chose to do! I decided! I could have left you there. I didn't. I got you out of the sun. I scoured Leatherhead for those hideous chicken livers. I agreed to drive you up here. So quit telling me you push all the buttons."

His closed mouth curled at the corners. His eye darkened. "Dixie, you could no more have walked away from a person in pain than you could stroll naked down High Street. It's not in you. You're out of your depth and you're not thinking straight."

"And you are?"

"I have a better memory and clearer understanding of the situation."

"Oh, yeah? How much do you remember? You were pretty far gone when we arrived."

"I remember. And you'd best forget. You need to go back to Bringham and forget you ever knew me."

"Just like that." Her body didn't know whether to sweat or shake, so it did both.

"Dixie, listen. I don't want to hurt you."

"For someone who's not trying, you're doing a darn good job!"

He ran both hands through his hair and then reached out as if to touch her, but pulled back. "I owe you my existence, Dixie. You gave me back life. No mortal has ever done that, and you did it without question, but we've got to get things straight."

"I've spent the last few hours completely rearranging my ideas of truth and fantasy and you tell me to get things straight. Maybe I can't."

"Then I will." His clenched fists brought up the muscles in his forearms. His forehead creased and his eyebrows almost met. "It's simple. You're mortal. I'm a vampire. There can't be anything between us. Go on back to Bringham and forget you ever knew me. Put Tom Kyd, Justin Corvus and Kit Marlowe back into the mist of history and get on with your life."

"That all?" His words still hammered against her ears and her heart pounded inside her ribs.

He sighed as if he'd climbed Everest in the last fifteen minutes. "Dixie, you have to understand. They tried to extinguish me. They'd have succeeded without you. As it is, that coven is just a group of minor magicians, dabbling in the dark. If they'd taken my power, who knows what might have happened. I have to stay hidden—for years maybe. It's the only way."

A cold empty hole opened up inside. She'd just found him and was losing him before she really knew him.

His arms went around her like warm bands of steel. She rubbed her cheek against the roughness of his linen shirt as his hand smoothed the top of her head. "If I had power or knowledge to do it differently, I would. It's the only way Dixie, for both of us."

She couldn't argue. Talking to Justin and Tom had more than convinced her they came from different worlds. But what of it? That couldn't ease the pain under her ribs. "I'll miss you. What am I going to do without you?"

He dropped a kiss on the top of her head. "Go back home, to South Carolina, meet a good, honorable mortal and live happily ever after." She didn't want to tell him she'd tried that route once—and got herself a rat. His arms tightened. "If you leave now, you'll get back before too late."

He really meant it. At least his words did, even if his arms said otherwise. She pulled back and looked up at him. She wanted to speak but the words just jammed up in her throat. Arm round her shoulders, Christopher led her through the hall, toward the sitting room and the French doors. "No one must ever know what happened Monday. Never mention it. Just leave Bringham as soon as you can. And don't let Caughleigh get close. The man's bad news."

Was he jealous? No. Sensible. "Don't worry about him. I'd rather have a toothache than another evening with him. I'll ask Vernon to come with me, if we have another Whist Drive."

He chuckled. He had a very sexy chuckle and she'd never hear it again.

"I'm going to miss you like hell."

"Who's swearing now?"

"It's justified." He was darn lucky she wasn't howling and clinging.

"Here." She looked down. A jeweler's box filled his hand. "Take it. I want you to remember me." She flicked open the velvet lid. A smooth black oval, set in silver, gleamed up at her from the white satin lining. "Whitby Jet. From the earth that gives us all life." She only half-heard him. "Here." He took it out of her hand and fixed it around her neck. The heavy silver chain was longer than she expected and the stone hung between her breasts. "Wear it and think of me."

Something caught inside her. "Is this really necessary, Christopher? Can't you stay here, and I'll come up and see you?"

She knew he'd shake his head. "I won't be here. This is the only way, my love. For both of us."

His arms pulled her close against the strong wall of his chest, and the hard lines of his body. She moaned as his mouth met hers and her moan turned to a sigh of delight as the warmth of his tongue met hers. Her heart ached at the prospect of loss and emptiness.

She was in the car. He'd shut her door. She turned the key in the ignition. The black garage door went up and she steered out into the street. As she drove away, a cold loneliness enveloped her like an arctic mist.

Chapter Nine

Christopher swallowed two glasses of port without tasting them and poured himself a third.

"It won't help. We don't intoxicate like mortals." He didn't need Justin pointing out what he already knew any more than he'd needed Tom reminding him he had to separate from Dixie—for *her* survival, if he cared nothing about his own. He tossed back the contents of his glass and reached for the decanter.

"Go easy, on it, Kit!" Tom said and reached out to reclaim his port, but he drew back his hand at a glance from Justin.

Justin shook his head at Tom. "Let him. Sometimes we remember enough of being mortal to let the alcohol ease the pain."

Justin knew. He'd recovered from a broken heart. But why had he never warned how much it burned and seared the remnants of your soul?

"You did the right thing, Kit. The *only* thing."

Kit ignored Tom and swirled the red liquid in his glass before swallowing it in one gulp. After Dixie's lifeblood, it tasted like straw.

"She took the jet?" Justin asked.

Kit nodded. "She's wearing it."

"The connection to the earth will protect her from the worst heartbreak, but it won't be easy for her."

Thanks, Justin! Rub it in! Kit refilled his glass and wondered why he bothered. "I know," he said, looking over the rim of his glass. "I did the right thing—the only thing. There's no reason for them to connect her with me. My disappearance will be a nine-days' wonder until someone gets pregnant or runs off with the curate's wife. Then Bringham will forget Kit Marlowe ever existed.

"She even covered my tracks with the blasted coven." He liked that touch. The coven thought him incinerated. He could rest for several years and then find a new place to call home. That way she'd be safe. Caughleigh and his cronies had no reason on earth to harm her, and if she left as soon as possible, she'd be secure.

"We'll watch over her." They would. When had Justin ever let him down?

"You couldn't have told her the whole truth."

Tom was right. If Dixie had any notion of Sebastian's involvement, she'd be pounding up the stairs to his office demanding retribution. Better to let her stay ignorant.

After getting lost twice and being stuck in seemingly endless traffic, it was almost ten by the time she reached Bringham. The lights of the Barley Mow gleamed like a homing beacon, a welcome stop before facing an empty house. Dixie wanted food, a cool Guinness, and human company, "human" being the operative word.

"Left it a bit late, didn't you, my dear?" Alf said as he handed her a half-pint. "Almost closing time."

"I've been in London." If she needed an alibi, here was as good a place as any to start it.

"Better off than staying here. It's been a rotten night."

"I was hoping to eat. Can I get something to go?"

Alf cocked his head on one side. "To go? You mean take-away? I'll see what I can do. It's been busy here without Vernon. I'll spiflicate him when he turns up."

"What happened to Vernon?"

"Lord knows. Never arrived for work Monday and he doesn't answer his phone. I'll advertise his job if he doesn't show up tomorrow."

As she drained her glass, a foil-wrapped package appeared. "One cheese and chutney 'to go,'" he said with a grin.

Dixie tucked the package under her arm and added a couple of bottles of Guinness for good measure. Sitting in the bar brought back too many memories of Christopher. Better go home.

She slid between the worn linen sheets, tented the covers over her knees and dropped crumbs on the crocheted cover as she munched down on her sandwich. Flipping the lid off her last Guinness, she questioned the wisdom of three in one night but swigged it down anyway.

She felt under her breast for the carefully-taped dressing. She'd have a scar there forever, and a worse one where it wouldn't show. But Christopher was safe.

Fuzzy headed from alcohol, heartache and fatigue, she snuggled down under the covers. As she drifted off into sleep, two thoughts struck her: she was in love with a vampire and she still had twenty-five pounds of ripening chicken liver in her pantry.

The next morning she buried the chicken livers between the gooseberry bushes and the raspberries. She was raking the earth smooth when Emma walked in the gate. "Just came to see how the delivering's going."

Dixie hadn't given it a thought. She'd been very definitely otherwise occupied. "I planned on doing them this afternoon."

Emma smiled. "Shouldn't take too long. It's just from here down to the station and the houses behind you. You won't have to walk up to Dial Cottage now. That's one saved."

"What do you mean?" How could she know?

"You don't know? How you slept through all those fire engines beats me."

"What fire engines?"

"Monday night, or maybe Tuesday morning."

"I was up in London. With a friend."

"Anyone I know?"

She'd have to be careful. Whatever she told Emma would be broadcast on the village telegraph by lunchtime. "A friend from college."

"Was he worth it?" Emma asked, eyes glinting with curiosity as heat rushed to Dixie's cheeks. "You're a quiet one. Here we were, thinking you did nothing but work in your house, and you've got a man up in town! When are you bringing him down to show him off?"

"He's leaving for the States soon." Gran had been right. One lie did lead to another. Time to change the subject. "What happened Monday night?"

"Oh, a proper knees-up, it was. Fire engines all over the place. Two of them came right past the lane here. We watched the fire from our bedroom. Dial cottage burned to the ground. They never got Christopher out. Seems he was smoking in bed and set the place on fire."

Christopher hadn't died in the fire Monday night. They'd soon find that out without her help. She couldn't tell the truth. She didn't know the whole truth.

* * *

Dixie headed out with Emma's list and a sheaf of St. Michael's Trumpets. She had a valid excuse to knock on total strangers' doors and tap the village fondness for gossip.

Taking the opportunity to chat at each house, she asked leading questions about the Dial Cottage fire and learned nothing new. Except that people disagreed about the exact number of fire engines.

Dixie walked up the lane towards Christopher's Cottage. The walls were still standing, but not a pane remained intact in a single window. The wide roof beams that had outlasted storm, winds and the Luftwaffe stood charred and naked against the blackened trees. Crisscrossed footprints marked the once-smooth lawn, and feet or hoses had flattened plants and broken shrubs. A line of blue and white police tape framed the desolation.

"Madam, you can't go in there. It's an investigation area." Dixie turned at the shout. Sergeant Grace stood at the corner of the ruin with two men. "Miss Page, isn't it?"

"LePage."

"Just the person we need."

"Miss LePage," the tallest man said, "I'm Detective-Inspector Jones and this is Detective-Sergeant Wyatt." The other man nodded but didn't smile. Jones looked at the sheaf of blue papers in her arms. "I wouldn't bother to leave one of those. He won't read it now."

"You're right." Her eyes strayed to the charred shell that had been Christopher's home.

"I gather you knew Mr. Marlowe. Perhaps you can help us," Jones said.

Dixie looked at Sergeant Grace and his two companions. They didn't carry guns. They didn't have badges. They looked like a pair of accountants. So why did cold apprehension settle like a lump of lead in her chest?

"You saw quite a bit of Mr. Marlowe I understand," Jones said. "Did you go out with him?"

What was this, the morals police? "I don't quite follow you." Heck, she was catching Britspeak.

"Don't take it the wrong way, Miss LePage," Wyatt said. "We just need to find someone who knew his habits and ways. Everyone seemed to know him, but no one knew anything about him, so to speak. We thought perhaps . . ." He left the rest unsaid.

"You think I know more than people who've known him for years?" She wanted to choke. She did know more, and there was no way she'd tell.

Jones nodded. "You wouldn't happen to know his doctor or dentist would you?" Dixie shook her head. They *were* on different wavelengths. "Pity. We need them to help identify the body."

How could there be a body? "I've no idea."

"Not to worry, Miss LePage," Grace assured her. "We'll find them. Can't be too many doctors who have one-legged patients."

"One-legged? What makes you think that?"

"From the body, Miss LePage."

Body? They had a body? "Impossible! Christopher lost an eye, not a leg."

"He'd lost a leg, too," Jones said. "Hard to tell these days. It's not like the old metal legs from the war days."

"He hadn't lost a leg." All three stared. She didn't much care. Whoever tried to kill Christopher had managed it with someone else. That thought stirred a rage for justice. "Christopher had both legs."

"Sure about that? Sure enough to swear in court?" Jones managed to sound interested and look bored at the same time.

"Yes!"

"Why would you be so certain?" Wyatt asked.

"I've seen both of them." She just hoped they wouldn't

ask when. Jones looked at her in a way that made her wonder if extramarital sex was a misdemeanor in Britain.

"You'd be willing to make a statement to that effect?"

"If necessary."

Jones nodded. "Get her name and phone number, Wyatt." Wyatt scribbled on his flip-top pad. "We'll be in contact about that statement in the next day or so, Miss LePage."

They turned back to the house. Or was it a crime scene? Had to be. Something was very rotten in Bringham and she was darn well going to find out what.

Dixie went back to her empty house, made a cup of tea and then watched the milk form a skin on the surface as it cooled. Under her lassitude, tension coiled like a tight spring. She had to do something, anything, to keep her mind off a million questions. She could work in the garden. There was enough there to keep her occupied until the first frost. But no, if she as much as looked at the wheelbarrow or the garden shed, she'd break down and wail.

She settled for polishing every piece of brass and silver in the house. She was halfway through the andirons and fender in the drawing room when the phone rang. It was Sally, insisting Dixie join her and Emma for lunch and shopping tomorrow. Why not? It might do her good to get out of Bringham for a while.

She glanced at her watch. Why not call it a day here and walk over to the Barley Mow?

Guinness in hand, Dixie took a table in the corner, away from the crowd at the bar. She did not feel social in any degree.

"Hey! Put a sock in it!" A heavy-set man at the bar called to his companions. "What about that? Who'd have thought it?"

Dixie looked up from the cauliflower cheese she hadn't been eating.

"Well, I'll be blowed!" His neighbor began, his eyes on the TV over the bar.

Dixie stared too. The pub went silent except for a few cheers from the people at the dartboard, but even they turned at the sudden quiet.

A sketch of Christopher's face stared from the TV screen. ". . . anxious to contact Mr. Christopher Marlowe. Anyone who knows his whereabouts or can give information is requested to contact the Surrey Constabulary. . . ."

Good thing she hadn't eaten much. She'd be lucky to keep it down. If the police were looking for Christopher, it could only be on account of her big mouth. Until she spoke to Inspector Jones, they'd believed him dead.

The pub broke into a buzz of speculation. "What's he done?"

"Quiet chap. Wouldn't have thought it of him."

"Anyway, I thought he was dead."

"Can't be if they're looking for him."

"Must be something about that fire."

"Maybe he set it off to get the insurance."

"He wouldn't have scampered then. Would he?"

"Maybe they figured it out and he off and run."

Alf grunted as he gathered glasses. "They were over here this afternoon, asking about Vernon. Monday, his mother reports him missing and they're too busy to bother. Now, all of a sudden they want to know if he and Marlowe were friends. and if they spent time together." He wiped up the beer spills on the polished bar top. "I told them they'd better find him. I can't handle this place at night without him. They suggested I advertise for a replacement. I don't like to think what that means."

Neither did Dixie. And she certainly didn't want to ask if Vernon had a prosthesis. Remembering his shuffling gait as he worked his way round the room clearing tables, and the awkward way he bent to clean up the mess the time she'd dished her dinner on James, she didn't need to.

Vernon was the dead man in Dial Cottage and the police thought Christopher had killed him.

"You have to leave, Kit, as soon as it's dark. It's the safest place."

He couldn't argue with Tom. But Christopher wasn't even sure he wanted to be safe. Not without Dixie. He owed his existence to a mortal. He'd lost his heart to an auburn-haired human, with sparkling green eyes and lips that sent his body into overdrive, and he could never see her again! Damn it!

"I'm going, Tom, back to our haven. Maybe I should have stayed there." Christopher glanced down at his feet and for a minute or two amused himself by untying and retying his shoelaces with his mind. Last night, he'd climbed St. Paul's. His physical and mental strengths were back in full, but what use were they without Dixie?

Tom treated his friend to a long, intent stare. He might have been reading his mind. He probably was. "Kit, you're hurt, inside, where even we can't heal ourselves. Time is what you need. Remember when we were lads? Smashed and broken hearts heal. Give yourself time."

He wasn't sure he wanted to. "What about Dixie? She can't snatch a vampire nap for a couple of decades to mend her heart. I didn't just break her heart, I smashed it to smithereens."

"Hurting her wasn't your choice. It happened."

Christopher turned at Justin's voice. "Came back to make sure I leave?"

"No, I came back to tell you she'll be safe. We'll watch her."

"For her sake, or ours?"

Justin shook his head. "You were always a cynical young man. For all our sakes, but mostly for hers. Few mortals have her courage or her faith. She almost deserves immortality."

A flare of hope surged in Christopher's aching heart. "You mean it?"

Justin raised a hand. "Kit, think! She's young and healthy. No sign of disease. You know the colony's rules. No killing. No transformation before death. Don't even think about it."

He should have known better than to nurture false hopes. Dixie was mortal. In this day and age, young women seldom died, and there was nothing he could do about that except sleep away the decades. Until she aged and died a natural death—and hadn't her great-aunts lived into their nineties? He had a long rest ahead of him.

Tom poured three glasses of velvet-colored port. Christopher inhaled the rich bouquet that triggered thoughts of warm sun on dusty vines—and the taste of Dixie's lips. "A new one?"

Tom smiled as he raised his glass. "An 1800 pre-phylloxera. In your honor."

Christopher nodded to acknowledge the compliment. "Must be one of the last bottles in London."

"The last but one. I'll save the other for your return."

His return! He'd sleep away the years while Dixie forgot him, aged, and died. But she'd never forget, any more than he could. He had to see her, just see her, one last time. He was strong enough to transmogrify, fly there and still reach the refuge in Whitby before dawn.

They drank in silence. The only sounds were the traffic outside, the pedestrians passing under the window, and the clock ticking on the mantel.

"Time, I think," Justin said quietly. Maybe he didn't even speak.

Christopher nodded and walked over to the window, throwing up the sash and looking down on the street below

and up at the hazy blueness of a city night. A knee on the
sill, he turned back to his friends. His oldest friends. "Soon,"
he said, perched himself on the window ledge, and, in a
flash, shot out into the murky sky.

Tom watched, long after mortal eyes could have seen the
dark speck in the azure sky. "He's going west, not north."

"Yes."

"Fool," Tom murmured.

Justin clapped him on the shoulder. "That's one thing we
still have in common with mortals."

She lay against the white sheets, like a beautiful dream.
The sweet truth of fair skin in the moonlight and auburn
curls against the pillow. Christopher willed himself to stay
on the window ledge. He could enter. He had an invitation.
She'd given him that, and life and blood, but if he came close
enough to touch, his resolve would melt in her warmth and
he'd never leave.

Now he understood Justin's unease with humans. A pair
of sparkling green eyes, a smile as sweet as springtime, and
a heart greater than the wide arc of the heavens had seduced
his soul. She'd given him life and blood, and he'd repaid with
heartbreak.

He was leaving her for eternity, but he'd make this last
contact as sweet and loving as her soul.

Reaching out to her mind, he sensed anxiety. *She worried
about him!* He'd half-drained her life and torn her heart from
its roots and *she* worried about *him*. What had he ever done
to merit this care? Giddy with the thought of her, he touched
her forehead with his mind. She stirred as he felt the warmth
of her brow from her eyebrows to her ear. A smile flicked on
her full lips as he thought down the pale column of her neck.

The scent of her skin came heady as a new vintage. He
longed to taste her, feel the heat of life against his lips, but

he anchored himself to the ledge and pictured his lips on her pulse. The low throbbing just beneath the pale skin set his teeth on edge. He stifled the sensation. He'd come to give, not take. His thoughts edged the sheet off her shoulders. Her lips parted as her tongue reached round to moisten them. She was aware. He vowed she'd remember each caress for the duration of her mortal life.

She shivered as the night air touched her. He breathed warmth on her and brought a relaxed smile to her moist lips. He yearned to devour those lips, to suck their sweetness until they swelled, took his satisfaction in watching them pout under his mind's touch, imagining their satin smoothness and the taste of her mouth.

Abel, how he wanted her!

How he ached to touch her breasts, mounds of nacre in the moonlight, and lying between them, the warm gleam of a silver chain and the oval of jet, dark as despair against the pale blue of her nightgown. He willed the taste of her breast into his mouth and felt the warm ridges of the rosy flesh against his tongue. She moaned as he imagined his lips closing on her hardening nipple. In the moonlight her hand rose like a silvery caress as she reached across the snowy pillow. "Christopher, I love you."

The whispered words tore across time and reverberated through space. This woman loved him, after all he'd done.

In less than one of her heartbeats, he sloughed his clothes and crossed to her bedside. Her eyes opened. She knelt up and stretched out her arms, her face radiant. "Christopher," she whispered as clear as church chimes across a frosty night. "I thought I was dreaming." He melted into the circle of her arms and held her close in his own eternal embrace. "You're real." Her eyes shone like gems in the moonlight. She tasted the curve of his shoulder and smiled. "I thought I'd never see you again. Tell me I'm not dreaming."

"This," he replied, drawing her close to him, "is a real dream."

"You're the most real person I've ever known," she said as she traced the contours of his face with a touch that scared him. How could a mere mortal leave him weak and longing and trembling in his soul? Her fingers moved slowly, as if memorizing each curve and hollow, across his face, down his neck. She snuggled against him as she smoothed the flat of her hand across his chest. "You're like a man, but more," she said, nestling her fingers amidst the thatch on his chest.

"How?" He chuckled as her fingers moved down his belly.

"You look like a man. Most places."

"The important ones I hope."

"Oh, yes."

He felt her shoulders shake under his circling arm. "Laughing at me are you?"

"On, no. Just thinking that you're very like a man about *that*!"

"And how am I different?"

Her chin nuzzled his neck. "Your face is smooth. You never have a five o'clock shadow. But you're very hairy on your chest and your legs." A warm foot snaked up his calf.

"Advantages of the vampire life . . . I never need to shave and my hair no longer grows. I did have a beard and moustache as a mortal, but I shaved them off in 1825 and they never grew back."

"Better not get a crew cut then," she replied, her hand ruffling his hair.

"Any other things?" he asked. "Beside the obvious ones of eternal longevity and ability to transmogrify?"

She looked him straight in the eye. She never wavered or stared, but just met him as an equal being. But this time her sweet mouth twisted in a moue of mischief, and her green eyes glimmered like sun through a church window. "Well, I suppose you could say that . . ." She paused as she reined in a grin. "You kiss in a rather splendid way."

"Just splendid?" His hand cupped her breast as he spoke, feeling the warmth and softness of her flesh under her satin nightgown.

"Perhaps tremendous, incredible, fantastic are better words," she offered.

"Made a study, have you?" he replied, feeling a sudden urge to annihilate every mortal who'd ever touched her.

"It hasn't all been from books," she replied, leaning up on one elbow and looking down at him. "Did you come here in the middle of the night to discuss my past sex life?"

No, and he didn't want to. He didn't want to even consider the thought that a mortal man might have desired, much less enjoyed her. "I came for just one glimpse, then I was going to fly away. But I couldn't. I promised myself one touch, no more. But it didn't work. I don't understand what you do to me. I've never before felt what I feel with you, and heaven alone knows no other creature, mortal or immortal, has done what you did."

She leaned over, her lips parted so he felt the warmth of her breath like the kiss of life. Lips sweet as honey met his, her mouth as open as her heart and as warm as her soul. If he had a heart, it would be pounding. Instead his mind and body burned with the need of her. She drew him in like a vortex, whirling him from reality into the passion of her soul. Her lips promising more than eternity as her warm arms locked behind his back. He levered himself up on his arms and looked down at her tousled head and glittering eyes. His body ached with need, but this time it would be slow. They'd spend all night loving.

She grinned up at him. "Definitely splendid."

"You're overdressed." His voice came dry as leaves in autumn. His fingers trembled untying the ribbon at her neck.

"Don't let it stop you." Her breasts shook as she chuckled, her nipples hard under the pale blue satin. Raising her shoulders with a protective arm, he eased her nightgown to her waist. He froze, the white splash of gauze on her left breast a stark reminder of the price she'd paid. For him. Her fingers tipped his chin to level his eye with hers. "You're not changing your mind, are you?"

"You're still healing. What if I hurt you more?"

"You won't. You couldn't."

"My dearest, I'm overwhelmed at what you did." With hesitating fingers, he traced the tops of her breasts. Wriggling her hips, she eased off the tangle of satin and kicked it away. Did she have any idea what she did to him? Oh, yes. She did. Her fingers trailed down his torso, lines of liquid fire that stopped just below his navel.

"I'd like to be overwhelmed, too," she said.

With something akin to awe, he cupped the underside of each breast and lowered his head. He wanted to suffocate in her warmth and drown in her loving. She smelled of soap, lavender, clean linen, and woman. He'd be happy to expire in her arms, but her hands kept him alive, teasing and searching while her body woke to his touch and she uttered sighs and cries of pleasure.

Were other mortal women like this? Not in his memory, long though it was. She was fire and peace, tease and balm for a lonely soul. To think he'd been content until he met her, and now he'd never know peace of mind again. The memory of Dixie LePage would last him for eternity and he owed it to her to make tonight her own.

He'd planned to make love to *her*. But she met him at every turn. He kissed. She stroked. He caressed. Her lips drove him crazy. He explored her body's secrets. Her fingers found nerve endings he never knew he possessed. Timeless equals, they loved as if they'd never part.

"Christopher, I want you," she whispered, her voice husky

with a desire that mirrored his turmoil. She smiled up at him, her eyes bright as moonbeams, her breasts proud and high, her legs pale as ivory, open and waiting.

"My love, I'm yours," he replied, seeking her silken warmth.

She came as he entered her, her hips bucking, her arms grasping and nails scraping his back. Her body wound in a convulsion of pleasure, she cried aloud her joy as she quivered and trembled with the aftershocks of passion.

Her sobs of pleasure snapped his control and he exploded in a paroxysm of emotion as he took her up to the heights again. Together they soared in an arc of ecstasy that carried them to the stars, circled the planets and rode the comets before returning in each other's arms to the tangle of bedsheets, the soft warm embrace of limbs, the sweet, salty taste of sweat, and the scent of love in the night air.

They lay in silence awhile, lost in thought, emotion and each other. While the night scent of roses wafted from the garden outside, somewhere in the night an owl hooted his courting ritual.

"I'm so glad you came," Dixie said, her voice half-muffled by his chest. "I thought I'd never see you again."

"I had to see you one last time. I never intended to stay. I thought I had hurt you too much to ever be welcome again."

She smiled up at him in the moonlight. "You'll always be welcome."

"I dread leaving you, Dixie. I'm not sure I can."

She leaned up on one elbow. A frown creased her forehead. The glint of a tear gathered in the corner of her eye. Had he hurt her that much? "You've got to go. Leave. Now," she said, her voice taut with emotion.

Chapter Ten

Christopher wiped the tear from her cheek. "I never meant to hurt you." What could he ever say or do to repay her?

"I'm fine. Or I will be," she amended. "It's *you* who's got to be careful, and not just of whoever tried to get you last time. It's the police. They think you killed Vernon."

Christopher grasped her bare shoulders. Her skin under his fingers was warm with the afterglow of loving. "What are you talking about? They think I killed Vernon? Why?"

She explained, biting her lip until it bled and he longed to taste. "I just lost my temper," she finished, shaking her head. "I thought how they'd tried to kill you and succeeded in killing someone. I didn't know it was Vernon then. I just knew they couldn't get away with it. So I told the police it couldn't be you. I thought they'd start looking for the killers. I never dreamt they'd look in your direction." She propped her chin in her linked thumbs and ran her hands over her nose and mouth as if praying. Maybe she was. Eyes heavy with worry met his. "I'm so sorry, Christopher, I never imagined . . ."

"Hush, love, don't worry." He wrapped his arms around her shaking shoulders. Of course she hadn't imagined. How could she? She was all honesty, openness and fairness. How could she think like that clutch of witches? "You weren't to know. It'll work out. They can look all they want, but they won't find me where I'm going."

"Where are you going?"

She would ask and he'd hurt her by seeming not to trust. "Somewhere safe." He shook his head as she started to open her mouth. "I can't tell you. It isn't my secret. I'll tell you anything else you want to know about me, but I can't speak for the others."

"That's Justin and Tom, right?"

"Among others. We have a safe haven for times of trouble."

"And you're in trouble now. Because of my big mouth."

"Dearest, I'm still in existence because of you. I'm threatened because I'm caught in a coil of evil. If they found out I wasn't extinguished and realized who'd foiled their plans . . ." He let the unsaid words hover between them. "I can't, won't risk your safety. I'm disappearing for several years and you've got to promise me to go back to the States."

"I will." He almost gaped at her acquiescence. He'd half-expected outright refusal. "Soon, but not tomorrow. I've got some things I have to do."

"What? Isn't saving a vampire enough for one summer?"

She elbowed him in the ribs. Gently. "You're not the only person in the world. I've got to decide whether to sell or rent out the house. I've got money things to settle. I have to if I'm going back. I'm not leaving that to Sebastian. I don't altogether trust him."

He wouldn't disagree on that point. "Promise me you'll leave as soon as possible. Go back to South Carolina."

"I will." She looked up at him, eyes dark with worry. "Quit worrying about me. Shouldn't you be going? There's a police warning about you."

"The way I travel, no one will ever see me. I'm safe. You have to make sure *you* are."

"What do you mean?"

"There are killers in this village, Dixie. They think I'm dead, but if they ever realize I'm not, and if they suspect your involvement . . ."

"Why would they?" She smiled as if dawn would never come. "I'll never tell."

She was his every dream come to life. He had to touch her again. He traced from the pulse at the base of her neck up to the warm curve of her chin. She moved and caught his finger between her moist lips. Her tongue teased his fingertip, pulling him in deeper to the warmth within. "I want to make love to you," she said. "Do we have time?"

"What else is time for?"

Her smile promised joy beyond belief. The fragrance of her skin sent his head reeling. Once again, he was a crazed youth in the meadows by the Medway exploring the promises of love before the years at Cambridge and London taught him the cynicism of sex. He bent to kiss her warm breast and nipped at her hard nipple until she squealed with pleasure as his teeth pulled at the sweet flesh.

"Stop that," she giggled, wriggling under his hands.

"Why?" he asked through his lips, never moving his mouth from her breast.

"Because *I* want to make love to *you*."

How could he refuse such an offer? She leaned close, pressing herself against him with a need that stirred the marrow of his bones to lust. He wanted to sate his need in her sweet warmth but that would deny him the pleasure she'd just promised, and more than eternity itself, he wanted Dixie LePage to make love to him.

She grinned. It was the only word for it. A grin of mischief, promise, and anticipation. Having realized her power, she reveled in it, relishing the prospect of reducing him to helplessness. Just as he welcomed the thought of becoming vulnerable in her arms.

"I want you," she said. It was a declaration of need, loud and clear. "I want you in every way I can imagine and a few more for luck. You're going before morning, and this is what I'll remember you by."

A tear glistened in the corner of her eye. He wiped it away with the pad of his thumb. "We'll remember each other. How could we forget?" He had eternity to miss her. He'd weep too, if he could.

Her lips swept him up in a maelstrom of need as her tongue slipped between his lips, teasing and exploring every recess of his mouth, dancing over his teeth, curving, stretching and provoking, testing her own strength within his and uttering little moans of delight at her success. "Trying to drive me crazy?" he asked as she came up for breath.

"Oh, yes," she replied, "but that was just an appetizer."

She slid to her knees, locking her arms around his hips and pulling him to her until his erection pressed against her face.

"Dixie," he groaned, "do you know what you're doing?"

"Of course."

She knew what she was doing, alright. Hot thrills of anticipation snaked a burning trail through every nerve in his body. How could a mere mortal do this to him? But she was no mere mortal. She was his woman, his soul mate, his reason to exist. He reveled in her touch and basked in her loving, and blocked out all thought of morning.

"Christopher." His mind still spiraling somewhere in the outer galaxy, he opened his eyes at her whisper, his fingers tangled in her auburn curls. She smiled up at him.

"My love." She shouldn't be on her knees. He reached down for her arms and pulled her up. He moved his head and tasted warmth, sweetness, and himself on her lips. "Let's love the hours away 'til morning." Her eyes answered him.

"My heart," he whispered as she pressed him down. Her fervor sent this body and mind into overdrive. This time she led. She loved. She brought him to new heights. No woman had ever loved him this way. How could she? In all creation, there had only been, would only be, one Dixie. She teased and promised as his mind soared and his body raced through the heavens until she rode him to triumph, her warm thighs astride his hips as he climaxed, buried deep in her warmth.

She was mortality, glorious mortality that he'd lost centuries ago and had never regretted or missed. Until now.

He eased her off him and tipped her on her back. Panting, flushed and worn, she smiled up at him, exhilaration lighting her eyes until they flickered like stars in an evening sky. Her hair shone like copper in firelight. Her skin was warm as the summer sunlight he shunned and soft as the grass in new spring meadows. The flush of love bloomed on her face.

And he had to leave her. Forever.

But first, they'd both remember this night.

He leaned over her gently, remembering the stitches in her breast, the mark of her love. He brushed back the curls that clung damply to her forehead, and tasted the sweet saltiness of her skin. Then, with all eternity before him, he trailed soft kisses over her face, brushing her cheeks and dropping sweet butterfly kisses on her eyelids. The sound of her blood echoed like a waterfall in his ears. He could smell it under her skin, sense the pulse that beat a little faster with each kiss. As his lips moved down her neck, she arched and moaned, stretching and curving her neck until she lay tilted and ready. Her chest heaved as she panted, waiting, wanting and needing.

She stretched her neck back against the pillows. His lips tasted life. The scent of her blood caused a whirl of emotion scrambling through his consciousness and the sound of her heart pounded his ears like a rushing flood. His fangs emerged, then pierced her neck. He tasted heat, passion and richness and felt her body convulse with ecstasy. Still one with her, he felt her joy, the white-bright pleasure that coursed through her as her body tensed and jerked, then melted into warmth as her arms wrapped around him.

Her eyes met his. She smiled, a satisfied woman's smile that knew his secrets and gloried in them. The heat of her body warmed the tattered remnants of his soul. He'd gladly trade eternity for an endless now, but even vampires couldn't stop time. Morning brought danger. Protecting her was his first concern.

He cupped her breasts in his hands, the gauze pad and tape a poignant reminder of her commitment. "Dixie, I want you safe. Please leave. Go home as soon as you can. How about in the morning?"

She looked up at him, the flush of love still a bloom on her skin. "Not that soon. If it'll keep you from worrying, I'll call the airline in the morning, I promise that much. I can't even think about it now. You wore me out." As if to prove her point, she nestled against his chest and closed her eyes, lying close until her breathing changed and she slept.

He could have watched forever, her breath shallow and warm against his chest and her soft hair brushing his chin. Pain, sharper than the knife stab in Deptford, ripped through him at the thought of parting. For the first time in four hundred years, he cursed his vampire state. She was a woman to grow old with. But he couldn't. If Justin hadn't followed him to Eleanor Bull's, he'd be a heap of mouldered bones and never known the life and loving of Dixie LePage. Far better this crumb than oblivion and the cold tomb. He'd have a glimmer of her light to carry forward to eternity. He'd have more than most immortals.

He'd stretched custom a bit. A bit? He'd stretched it beyond the limits, but custom was settled long before Dixie LePage burst into their world. She'd even flummoxed Justin, and Tom would never get over her refusal to cooperate when he tried to throw her out.

He could smell the approaching dawn. With a snag of pain in the figurative heart he'd forgotten he possessed, he kissed her awake. "Dixie, it's almost dawn. I can't transmogrify in the light."

Dixie woke in an instant, aware of the weight beside her on the mattress, the strong arm circling her shoulders, and the smile. The smile that swept her into a new reality. Christopher was the answer to every dream she'd ever had and he couldn't stay.

"You have to leave. They mustn't find you.".

"They won't. Not where I'm going."

"Christopher. . . ." she whispered, half-afraid to say his name aloud in case she choked on her worry. "Oh, Christopher. . . ." She wrapped her arms around his waist, pulling him close. He had to go, yes, but she needed one last touch. She rested her cheek against the hard muscle of his chest and inhaled the strange, but now familiar, waxy scent of his skin. She still needed him, but there was no more time.

She jerked herself to a sitting position. Shaking her head to clear the last vestiges of sleep, she glanced across to the triple mirror on the dresser. Her own reflection blinked back at her three times—but she was alone. Only a faint blur, like dampness, showed where Christopher lay beside her. He wasn't mortal. He couldn't be hers. And she'd never even have a photo to remind her of him.

"I'll miss you." She was getting almost British with her understatement. Just saying the words brought stinging tears under her eyelids and a lump as rough as coal to her throat. "You should have left last night. I shouldn't have kept you."

He shook his head, a slow smile curving his lips as his eyes paled and gleamed almost opalescent in the night. "I needed to stay. You needed me. Think what we now have, a memory of love to last us—you, for the rest of your life. Me, well, I'll have eternity to think of you."

"Will I ever see you again?

He shook his head, raw pain searing his eyes. "No, Dixie," he said when he caught his breath. "We're two different kinds. Mortals and immortals don't belong together. Custom, law and common sense preclude it."

"We've not done too badly by each other so far."

"No? You could have bled to death and there's still the risk you'll be linked to me. I've caused enough bother. Tonight was my weakness. My indulgence."

"Seems to me, we're both equally weak—or strong." She wanted to scream at him. Tell him she didn't care about his immortality, that his scruples were nonsense. She didn't. She couldn't deny that staying put him in danger. "You'd better go, or I might just throw you back on the bed and start again." She slid out of bed and reached for her robe.

By the time she'd slipped it over her shoulders and knotted the belt, he was dressed. "How did you do that?"

He grinned. She was slowly falling apart and he grinned. "We vampires work fast when we have to."

He touched her cheek with the back of his hand and stroked the curve of her chin. Tenderness destroyed her resolve. His touch shattered her self-control. Scalding tears ran down her cheeks.

"Dixie. . . ." His voice came hoarse and rough. His arm steadied her shaking shoulders as his other hand smoothed her hair. "I'd forgotten about human grief. I came to satisfy my needs and stayed out of selfishness. Forgive me."

She jerked her head up, wrinkling her brows as she met his still-pale eye. "Yeah, right. Remember how you had to beg me to let you stay? And how you had to twist my arm to get in my bed?"

"You're the finest woman I've ever known, Dixie."

"And you're a better lover than any other man I've known."

"I'm not a man, Dixie."

And that was the crux of the matter. "Is there nothing you can do about that?"

His eye went dark and hard as if frozen by disbelief at her question. "I'm a vampire, Dixie. This isn't a romance novel. You can't make up a magical potion and change me back, and if you could, I'd be dead. Remember?"

She did. She just had a hard time reconciling her lover to the mysterious figure that had fascinated her during English Lit 201.

But she wasn't giving up yet. "But what about me? You've taken my blood. Can't I turn vampire?"

"I've tasted you. Your blood strengthens me. All my feeding does to you is make you lightheaded. We'd have to mingle our blood. You'd have to take mine to become one of us."

"Then come back tonight, or rest in the basement, and make me a vampire. There'd be no problem then." She held her breath, not even believing what she'd asked. Her mind skittered over the possibilities of his "yes."

He shook his head. "Just a very major one. To do that, I'd have to kill you."

Now her head did spin. Somewhere in the last couple of sentences she'd lost him. "Isn't that the whole point? I thought . . ."

"You have read too many novels," he interrupted. "We have rules. One is to never kill a mortal. That's why Tom insisted on Justin giving you blood. If you'd died on my account, I'd have been censured."

"But how did you—and Tom?"

"I died from a knife thrust. Tom never recovered from the rack. Justin was hit by a Brigantine arrow. We died. Then we became vampires." He wiped her damp cheeks with the pads of his fingers. "Don't get any drastic ideas."

She might be brokenhearted and miserable for the rest of her born days, but she wasn't ready to end it all on his account. "You've got to go. After all this, you have to promise to live for eternity."

"I won't just live. I'll love you forever. Never forget me, Dixie."

Before she could reply, before she could even think of replying, he was perched on the window ledge. A dark blur shot though the open window and faded chintz curtains blew inward in the night air.

Dixie set the kettle on the Aga. The hollow thud suited her mood. She sincerely doubted caffeine would heal a broken heart, but it was something to do. If she kept busy, maybe she could pretend it didn't hurt.

Mail arrived as she poured her second cup. Among the offers of credit cards, villa holidays, and a seed catalog addressed to her aunts was a postcard from Stanley Collins reminding her this was the weekend he needed the car. Would she mind dropping it off first thing on Friday? That she'd do, and maybe spend the day in Guildford. She needed to check flights. She'd promised Christopher. Was she really ready to go? But why stay?

The stone flags chilled her feet through her light slippers. She shivered. Was it really that cold? This was June, for heaven's sake. Had she lost more blood than she thought last night? Or did heartbreak cause hypothermia?

Physical activity would warm her up. She had nothing left to polish. Gardening? Cleaning closets? The sealed cupboard caught her eye. She'd been meaning to open it for weeks. Ten minutes with a screwdriver or chisel would warm her up and unstick the door.

It took over an hour.

Some deranged Philistine had actually painted the door shut. Dixie poised the chisel in the groove between door and frame, and hammered. She cracked about two inches of thick paint. Slowly she worked her way round, inch by inch. She let her coffee get cold as she soldiered. It had become a

personal thing between her and the door. Ridiculous, when
all she'd probably find was a collection of antique mops or
perhaps a disused entrance to the basement. But it beat mop-
ing for a love that had, literally, flown away.

She finished at last, at the cost of several broken nails and
a gouge in the back of her hand from when the chisel slipped.
A few good taps with the hammer and the iron latch lifted. A
bit of pressure and the old hinges grated as Dixie forced the
door open. A smell of stale, damp air came at her like a de-
caying breeze.

She stared into the dank space too large for a closet, and
saw steep, dusty stairs. Another basement entrance? No, they
didn't lead down, they rose up to the dark.

Dixie took a step up and fumbled for a light switch. Her
fingers tangled with cobwebs and something scrunched un-
derfoot. Unwilling to climb stairs in the dark, Dixie grabbed
the flashlight from the windowsill. The beam lit up the steep,
narrow stairs. A carpet of dust covered the treads, and the
curled body of a long-dead mouse reminded Dixie to look
before she trod.

She counted eleven steps straight up from the turn at the
bottom. The roof rose to a peak overhead and dark roof beams
protruded through the flaking plaster. The flashlight lit up an
old table, a couple of chairs and several dust-covered boxes
covered with faded marbled paper. Sneezing from the dust,
Dixie pulled one open. Yellowed pages and dog-eared manila
folders smelled of damp and age. Old file boxes? Was this
what the intruder had been after? Why? Whatever they were,
her aunts had concealed them well. What was in them that
had been worth the trouble of painting up the door?

A naked bulb and socket was stuck sideways in one of the
beams. Dixie pulled the attached string. The harsh, unfil-
tered light accentuated the general squalor. Dust and mouse
droppings did nothing to improve the ambiance.

A second room led off the first—a small laboratory. Shelves

filled with glass jars lined two walls and across the room, near the sink, stood a retort and a series of tubes and various glass vessels that Dixie recognized as a makeshift still. Surrey moonshine? Hardly likely. Or was it? She studied the yellowed labels on the dusty jars; "Heartsease," "Henbane" and "Horehound," sounded like ingredients of a magic spell. Dark curled petals in the "Marigold" jars resembled the flowers Gran had grown in her garden, but the dark, twisted roots labeled "Mandrake" looked like something growing in a science fiction story.

This was a witch's kitchen for mixing spells and simples. And the other room? Dixie pulled a rickety chair over to the desk, brushed the dust off the ancient filing cabinet, opened the drawer marked "Current and Possible," and flicked through the files.

The name "Caughleigh, Sebastian" caught her eyes. She pulled out the manila folder and spread it open on the ink-stained surface. Could this possibly be true? Had he fathered three children? Lists of dates, letters and a couple of birth certificates implied that he had. A copy of an agreement to pay a monthly sum for eighteen years to a woman in Guildford looked like hard proof.

This beat the tabloids at the grocery store checkouts. The vicar's wife had an arrest for possession of marijuana during her student days, and a certain Juliet Bleigh had a history of shoplifting. A bundle of faded letters documented a thirty-year-old affair between a Mary Cox and a John Reade. Dixie stared at the spread pages in horror. Some of these documents had to be illegally obtained. She didn't know much about the laws in England, but surely court records were confidential? And private correspondence; how had that found its way here? Why? Should she call Sergeant Grace and tell him about this? Or was the fire the best place for it?

Then she found the black ledgers on the shelf over the desk. Her aunts, and their father before them, had generated a steady income from blackmailing half the county. From 1/6d, whatever that was, from a parlor maid who dallied with a married milkman, to several thousand pounds from a "Mr. Wyatt of Fetcham" in exchange for "photographs." The same Mr. Wyatt paid another sum for "negatives" not six months later.

It sickened Dixie. This little collection was enough to kill for. Her heart slowed and quickened. Kill for! How had her aunts died? Sebastian's explanations of a heart attack and a stroke seemed feasible at first telling. Hope's stroke had happened at the rectory front door. Had she gone there for help? And how had Faith died? There was a killer in the village, that much she knew already. Vernon had died. Had her great-aunts been the first victims? How she wished she had Christopher to talk to.

"We're going to be late," Sally snapped. "You said you'd be ready."

"We can wait ten minutes," Emma soothed. "It won't take Dixie long to get ready."

It didn't. Dixie toweled her hair dry and slipped on her sandals. She'd spent longer than intended reading her great-aunts' record books, and barely had time to wash off the grime and dust before Sally drove up, agitated, and anxious to be off. What was wrong? Sally seemed stressed to the limit, just as she had the night of the Whist drive.

Emma tried calming her, and gave up to chatter. "Have you heard the latest about Dial Cottage? The body in the bedroom wasn't Christopher's. The police think it was Vernon from the Barley Mow. Seems there was an orgy or something going on and it got out of hand."

"Doesn't that sound a bit far-fetched?" Dixie asked. Anything to unsully Christopher's reputation.

Emma turned around. "When you've lived here as long as

I have, you'll know nothing's far-fetched. Mother worried about my going off to college. I never had the heart to tell her I'd seen it all in Bringham. Mind you, I would like to know what really went on. That place was burned to a shell."

"Can't they figure out what happened?" Dixie didn't believe it. That detective she'd met was no fool.

"It seems the last time anyone saw Christopher alive was the Parish Whist Drive. What a headline that would make in the *Mirror*! 'Man Leaves Parish Social for Sex Orgy.'"

"Oh, please! I can't see Christopher being like that."

A slow grin curled up the corners of Emma's mouth. "You've got a soft spot for him!"

Soft in the heart and tender everywhere. "What makes you think that?"

"He was eying you at the Whytes' as if he were a wasp and you were a nice ripe plum."

"Please, Emma."

"Of course you fancy him. We all do. He's been voted the most bedworthy man in the village. That mysterious eye patch and his one, smoldering eye. He must have all sorts of deep, dark, secrets."

If only Emma knew. Dixie held back a smile.

"Get your tenses right, Emma. He's dead," Sally said.

"What makes you so sure? The body they found isn't his. Maybe he's lurking somewhere. You would tell us if he came knocking on your door asking for refuge, wouldn't you, Dixie?"

"I promise you, he hasn't knocked on my door." That much was true. Now for the lie. "The last time I saw him, he was helping Sally out with her flat tire."

As she spoke, the car wobbled close to a hedge until the wheels bounced off the bank at the side of the road. Sally muttered under her breath as she righted the car.

"What's this, Sal?" Emma asked. "Sexy Christopher help you out with a puncture?"

"Yes," Dixie said. "Right after the Whist drive. Sebastian took me home and Christopher stayed to change her flat."

"Ah, ha." Emma gave a deep throaty chuckle. "So *you* were the last one to see him alive. Did you run off with him?"

"Emma, you talk a lot of rot!"

The vehemence in Sally's words shocked Dixie. It didn't faze Emma. "Maybe. But you are the last known person to have seen him alive.

After a pub lunch and long day scouring antiques shops in a half-dozen villages that had Dixie wishing she'd brought a camera, they stopped for a watercress tea in an old water mill in Gomshall. Sally insisted. "We don't have to get home yet. Our kids are taken care of and Dixie is footloose and fancy free."

Was she? Would she ever be again? The peppery tang of watercress reminded her of the taste of Christopher's kisses. The creamy butter was as smooth as his skin against her tongue, and the tea as hot as his touch in the night.

At this rate, she was heading for a long, lonely rest of her life.

"Everything's set." Sebastian watched James's reaction. "Our friend will fix the—er—necessary this afternoon. Sally will keep her gone for at least four hours. He needs two. It will be undetectable, but when Miss Dixie starts the engine . . ." He smiled at the prospect.

James's head jerked up. "You're going too far. Nicking her wallet is one thing, even going through the house, but killing—"

"You had no problem with Marlowe or Vernon."

"Marlowe wasn't human and Vernon was a cripple."

"Too late to get squeamish. Besides, if you'd done your job properly, this wouldn't be necessary."

"I tried everything I could."

"I'm sure you did your best, but your seduction was as successful as your housebreaking."

Glass in hand, James scowled from the leather sofa. "You did no better."

Sebastian turned to the French windows. Outside, the sun shone on the herbaceous borders. He hadn't turned to admire the garden; he'd no wish to let James know he'd scored a hit. Missing getting his leg over Dixie still rankled. He'd wanted so much to hear her squeal as he kneaded her breasts. Her bounce and confidence needed flattening, but that would soon happen. Permanently. This "expert" hadn't come cheaply, but Sebastian saw it as a capital investment.

Christopher sensed everything: the worms burrowing in the earth around him, the screech of the gulls as they dipped spread wings towards the cliff, and every wave that slapped the rocks below. And now Justin. Why?

"Come to check I arrived?" he asked as soon as Justin transmogrified.

"I knew you would, eventually," Justin replied as he smoothed the wrinkles out of his sleeves. "I came to help you rest. You must, you know. Even though you think you can't."

Christopher turned. "Easy for you to say. Every time I shut my eyes, I see her. I smell her, I taste her."

"And every hour you lie awake delays your restoration."

"Damn restoration! What use will it be? The only reason I agreed to hide was to protect Dixie. I'm a conduit for disaster. If I'd stayed, they'd have found me and destroyed her too."

Christopher made to sit up but Justin's hand held his shoulder down. He was weak. That last flight had almost finished him. "Don't let her generosity be in vain. She gave her blood to save you. Never forget that."

"As if I could forget!"

"Do you want to forget?" Justin spoke softly, a whisper that seemed to echo in the earthen vault and the deep recesses of Kit Marlowe's heart.

"Never!"

"Then rest, so you remember."

"Justin, you'd win an argument with a Jesuit!"

Justin smoothed his cuffs. "I have, several times. You must rest, Kit. You don't realize how drained you are."

"I do, damn you! I'm weaker than a fledgling. Almost as weak as when I was mortal. But I can't rest until I know she's left. Someone has to make sure she gets on that plane."

"Well then, Kit, you rest and I will go to our friend Dixie."

"You?" Christopher turned to face Justin. "After all your lectures about detachment and non-involvement with humans?"

Justin shrugged. "I owe a friend's existence to this human. And I agree with you, she must leave."

Christopher lay back on the soft earth. He was too weak even to sit for long. "Justin, if you can do that . . ."

"I know, you will owe me your eternal friendship." He paused. "And I always thought I'd earned that in Deptford."

"You'll go now? Be sure she's safe?"

"Soon. I'm staying out of sight for a couple of hours. The Abbey isn't empty as I expected it would be. I transmogrified without looking around and shocked a couple of campers. One fell off the cliff." He raised a hand as Christopher sat up in horror. "Not to worry. I swooped down and carried him to the base of the cliff. Luckily, he'd consumed a sufficiency of Boddingtons to have no idea what happened.

"Lucky for him I was looking outward. I could just as easily have entered without looking his way. Turned out alright. His pal was running for the nearest phone as I came back up. It's high tide; I imagine the cliffs and beach are swarming with rescue teams and lifeboats just now. I'll stay put for a few hours. No point in causing talk."

Dixie pulled a sweatshirt over her blue jeans, but nothing could really warm her. Yesterday, she'd had passion and Christopher's touch. Today she was alone. The company of her new friends yesterday only served to underscore her solitary state—her *permanent* solitary state. She'd given Christopher her heart as surely as she'd given her blood.

Trouble was, she'd had a Technicolor life the past few weeks. The quiet getaway in the English countryside turned out to be a mad whirl through fantasyland, peppered with passion, murder, blackmail, arson, and a few vampires thrown in for good measure. If she'd wanted peace and quiet, she should have gone to New York and jogged in Central Park after dark.

But she was here and while she was, she'd go through those diaries and notebooks and piece together as much of Gran's youth as she could. She had the whole weekend ahead of her. She'd read after breakfast, take a break to run the car over to Stanley's at lunchtime and pick up some groceries on the way back, and read the rest of the weekend. Then she would call the airline.

Deep in Faith's account book, Dixie lost herself in sales of potions and elixirs and powders to half the county. The old ink had faded to brown over the past sixty years but it was still legible.

In May of 1932, Mrs. Brown of Gordon Farm came for Solomon's Seal for terrible bruises on her face. The next week a name she couldn't read bought a potion of rue and vinegar "to quiet her husband."

In the same month, Mrs. Waite wanted a potion of ergot. Dixie knew ergot wasn't just used to treat migraines. If her great-aunts had dispensed aborticides, they certainly had a hold over desperate women. She pulled open the drawer marked S-Z and fingered through the Ws. There were several Waites. But Tom, F. J., and Earnest seemed less likely than Enid. Yes! Enid received "Ergot. 15/- on May 6, 1933" and paid a total of £500 between July that year and September 1953—when she'd presumably died or ceased to care about what people knew about her.

Dixie flicked back and forth from filing cabinet to account books. Her nasty aunts had a system that would appeal to Al Capone. If they couldn't find dirt, they made it by supplying potions and simples and then charging for their "discretion." The whole stash belonged on the bonfire.

The doorbell interrupted her studies. It was Stanley.

"Hope you don't mind. I was passing and thought I'd switch cars. Save you the trouble." He shook his head at her offer of tea. "Best be going. Can't thank you enough for obliging over this. Hope you like the Fiat."

"Let me move the car."

"No need. I left the new one in the lane. You bring that in after I move the Metro out." He handed her the new keys on a leather tag. "Cheers."

Dixie hoped the Fiat would do as well as the Metro she'd learned to enjoy. It seemed like a nice little car. She liked the dark green, but the dashboard had a dozen unfamiliar switches. She'd have to read the manual to figure it out. Oh well, it was only for the weekend. She'd have the Metro back by Tuesday.

She was bent down, trying to figure out which way to fit the key into the ignition, when the blast came. Sheltered as she was behind a seven-foot wall, she missed the core of the explosion.

"Stanley!" she screamed, wrenching open the door and rushing toward the gate, the acrid, gray smoke billowing over the ivy-covered wall. She never reached the gate. A stray fragment of hot metal struck her on the temple and she fell backwards.

Chapter Eleven

Whirling dervishes spun and droned in her head. Light faded and brightened in shaky waves. Something warm and damp trickled down the side of her face. She could smell her own blood and something else. That smell came in wafts that choked. An arm curled around her shoulders. Someone called her name repeatedly.

Dixie opened her eyes only to shut them again. It felt better that way. But she'd recognized the face bent over her. "Emma, why are you here? It's dangerous."

"Alright now, love," said a deep masculine voice. "Here put another blanket round you. We'll get you in the ambulance in a minute."

"No." It hurt to crease her forehead, but she couldn't help frowning. She couldn't remember why, but she knew she couldn't go to a hospital. "I'll be okay." She struggled to sit up.

"We'll see about that," the voice replied from the shadows. "You took a nasty bash on the head." A hand came into her line of vision and wiped something damp and soothing over the spot that hurt the most. "You'll need stitches there."

She'd had more stitches in the last week than in her entire life. Must be the company she kept! She started to giggle, shaking and sobbing as Emma's arm tightened around her.

Male hands shook her. Not too gently. "Come on now, no need for that!" A more distant voice said, "Someone needs to fix her some tea."

"I've got tea," Dixie said, feeling like she was talking to the air. "I made a pot just before Stanley came."

"I'll make you a nice, fresh one," Emma said.

Two burly ambulance men hoisted Dixie up in a fireman's seat and carried her round to the lane. It seemed half the police force of the county was milling around her house as yet another police car pulled up, blue lights flashing and siren wailing. As they passed the iron gates, Dixie saw two blue-uniformed policemen bailing out blue and white tape around a twisted, metal heap. But what made her stomach clench and roil was a bloody hand in the rose bush.

They deposited her in the rocking chair by the stove and wrapped blankets around her. When she protested, one of them insisted, "You need the warmth. Sooner or later you'll go into shock." He looked up. "Now, where's that tea?"

Dixie wrapped her hands around a still-steaming mug. She took a sip. "Please, Emma, no sugar. I thought you knew that."

"You need it," she replied. "I don't know why, but you always have sweetened tea for shock. If you want to argue, take it up with my mother."

Feeling shakier than ever, Dixie sipped the hot brew. A tear rolled down the side of her nose. As she brushed it away, she slopped tea on to her hand. She barely felt the burn. Would she ever feel anything again? "Stanley's dead, isn't he? He has to be."

Everyone treated the question as rhetorical. The sound of someone vomiting in the bathroom by the back door was enough confirmation. She shut her eyes, held the cup close to warm her chest as well as her hands, and tried to piece together the events of the past few minutes.

"If she's in there, I need a word with her."

Dixie's eyes snapped open at the familiar voice. "Sergeant Wyatt?"

"Morning, Miss LePage. Wondered if you could tell us what happened." He rested his hip against the table and looked down at her. "Nasty business. Wouldn't know anything about it would you?"

"I know a nice, harmless, kind man is in pieces in my front yard. Isn't it your job to find out why?"

"We plan to, Miss LePage. We plan to."

"When you do, I hope you lock him up in The Tower for twenty years."

"We'll put Fred in Pentonville when we get him. You can help by telling us what you remember. Inspector Jones will be along soon. . . . What is it?" He turned as a uniformed constable coughed at his elbow.

"Someone here who insists on coming in. Thought you'd better talk to him, sir."

"Can't you cope with reporters, Mason? We'll offer them a press release soon."

"It's not a reporter. It's . . ."

"I'm a doctor and I believe you need my services."

"Justin!" Dixie stood up, grabbing the arm of the chair for support as the room swayed around her.

"Sit down," Justin said. "I'll take care of things."

Justin wasn't Christopher, but under the circumstances, he was the next best thing. He'd make sure they didn't haul her off to the hospital.

"Excuse me, but who might you be, sir?" Wyatt asked with plastic politeness.

"I'm Dr. Corvus, Dr. Justin Corvus. I'm a friend of Miss LePage's."

"Very convenient, arriving like this."

Dixie suppressed a grin as Wyatt seemed to shrink a couple of inches under Justin's gaze. "Actually, I'm afraid I was rather tardy. But now I'm here. . . ."

"Yes, sir, you're here and that's very nice for both of you. But I need to speak to Miss LePage."

"First, she needs medical attention." Justin deposited a large, black leather bag on the kitchen table. "As you can see, Sergeant, she needs stitches. Let me take care of her and I'm sure she'll be ready by the time your inspector arrives."

Wyatt withdrew and Justin took rolled packets and small, plastic cases out of his bag. "I'll manage," he said with a nod to the two ambulance men. There wasn't much they could say to that.

As the door closed behind them, Justin turned to Emma, who was standing by the sink, looking as if he'd need Semtex to move her.

"I'm Dixie's friend," she said. "I heard the explosion and dialed 999. She never mentioned your coming."

"It's okay, Emma, really it is." Emma looked unconvinced. "What about your kids?"

"Lord! They're probably wrecking the house."

"Go take care of them."

It didn't take much urging.

The door had barely closed behind her when Justin said, "I think I'd better stitch you up before the next visitor arrives." He unrolled his instruments on the scrubbed pine table. "Sit on a firm chair. I'd just as soon you didn't rock as I put in the sutures." She moved to one of the pine Windsor chairs as he scrubbed up in the kitchen sink.

"Alright, my dear, lean back." She brushed her hair away and closed her eyes as he swabbed cold liquid over the cut. She caught her breath as the local anesthetic stung, but relaxed as the numbness set in. "Justin, we've got to stop meeting like this," she said, as much to cheer herself as anything else.

"Must be the company you keep."

"I came to England for a break, for a few weeks in the peace and quiet of a nice, English village." She felt the pressure of the first stitch. "Well, if nothing else, it hasn't been boring."

The thread pulled but didn't hurt. She tried to relax. She didn't have much luck. "Nice is not the word to describe Bringham, after what they did to Kit," Justin said as his wrist moved and pulled another suture.

"There's more. Much more. . . ." She felt lightheaded, and the effort of talking overwhelmed her.

"Later," said Justin as he snipped the last thread. "You can tell me later. The police need to talk to you." He placed gauze over the wound and dabbed with a long cotton stick. She should be used to this by now.

There was a knock at the door and a strong voice called, "Miss LePage? It's Inspector Jones." Jones strolled in with the air of a conquering hero. He must get a charge out of death and destruction. "We meet again, Miss LePage." He sat down without waiting to be invited.

"Unfortunately, yes, Inspector." He could take that any way he wanted, but she forced herself to breathe deeply and hide her irritation. This man was her best chance of justice for Christopher and Vernon and Stanley.

"Got yourself taken care of, I see." Jones looked Justin over. "And you are?"

"Dr. Justin Corvus." Jones nodded. "Dixie needed medical attention. A flying fragment. Fortunately, I was here."

"Very fortunate, I'd say," Inspector Jones said. "Not a local practitioner, are you, Dr. Corvus?"

"No, I have a small practice in London and an interest in Havering Clinic in Yorkshire." That was news to Dixie, but then she knew precious little about him.

"Very nice for you, I'm sure. But right now I need to talk to your patient."

Justin turned his eyes to Dixie's. Dark eyes that had seen

the rise and fall of several empires filled her with calm and confidence. "Not too many questions, Inspector," Justin said. "She's suffered a severe shock."

Justin left, closing the door to the dining room behind him, and Dixie was alone with Inspector Jones, the man who believed Christopher was a murderer.

"Dr. Corvus staying here, Miss LePage? Very convenient."

"He came down this morning. Just after the . . ." She paused. "The . . ." She gave up. What could she call it?

"The detonation," Jones supplied.

She nodded. "What really happened?"

"How about you tell me, Miss LePage."

It wasn't that much, but she told him—everything from Stanley's knock on the door until the arrival of Justin. Jones listened carefully, making notes as she went.

"When did you agree to exchange cars for the weekend?"

"Back when I first rented it. He had a prior booking and someone wanted this particular car this weekend."

"Anyone else know about this?"

"I don't think so."

"When did you last drive the car?"

"Yesterday. No, Wednesday."

He scribbled on his pad. "Where do you keep it?"

"In the drive. Exactly where it was when . . ."

"Quite," he said, frowning a little. "And you were in the house all day yesterday and never took the car out?"

"I didn't take it out but I was gone yesterday."

His eyebrows shot up like black caterpillars. "Gone?"

"I went into Guildford with some friends. We had lunch and went shopping." It was a lifetime ago. Stanley's life ago.

"Friends. I see. Their phone numbers?" He wrote them down. "So you went out, left the car parked here all afternoon, behind a seven-foot wall, next to an empty house." He made it sound like vehicular neglect.

"Inspector, forgive my impatience, but poor Stanley Collins

is blown to bits. Why not find out who booby-trapped my car?"

"Don't worry, we will. Once our bomb boys get on the job, we'll know."

A cold chunk jammed in her throat. "You have assassins and terrorists wandering around and you know who they are?"

"Not exactly. If we did, they'd be in maximum security. But there aren't that many people who do this sort of work, and they all have their own touch. They can match remains up with other jobs. We may not know who he is, but we'll know what else he's done. Sooner or later we'll find him and pin the record on him. It takes time, but we'll get him."

"I'm glad to hear it."

Inspector Jones leaned over her chair. "We'll get him or *her*. Must be PC these days." He paused. "Just one last question, Miss LePage. Who wants to kill you?"

Dixie gasped. Had he said that to shock her? If so, it worked. "All I thought about was the noise and the light and the smoke, and the fact that poor Stanley was dead. It never occurred to me it was supposed to have been me."

"Why not? Someone placed an explosive device in *your* car, parked outside *your* house, with every expectation that *you'd* be the one to turn the key. Who do you think they were after? The Queen Mother?" He paused. "I'll repeat my question. Who wants to kill you?"

She shook her head, as much to clear the confusion inside as to deny something she couldn't say. "I don't know." She had to say more. Much more—enough to satisfy him. "I just don't know. There have been odd things. The break-ins I reported to Sergeant Grace." She looked up and met his steel-dark eyes. He nodded. "They stopped when I moved in. I put on new locks. Good ones. Then the trouble up at Dial Cottage. And Vernon."

"Yes, the nasty business at Dial Cottage. You knew Mr. Marlowe very well, I gather?"

That was her fault. She'd opened her big mouth. "I met him. We spent some time together. We became friends."

Jones said nothing, just waited. Wasn't this an interrogation technique? To say nothing and wait until the suspect spilled her guts? She needed hers.

"Canadian or American, Miss LePage?"

"What?"

"Your nationality?"

Talk about change of tack. "I'm American."

"Mind if I see your passport?"

She did, but figured she couldn't refuse. He flicked through it. "So you entered at Gatwick the beginning of May. Permission for three months. Had half your stay. Planning on extending it? Not thinking of getting a job, are you?"

What was he after? "I'm not too sure what I'm doing. When I came, I didn't really intend on staying this long."

"Why did you?"

"I like it here. I've met some nice people. It's a great place for a holiday."

"In spite of the odd things?"

"Yes." It came out like a hiss. She wanted to snatch back her passport, but he continued to flick the pages as if searching for a secret, a clue to explain why someone had just failed to blow her to smithereens.

"Charleston, South Carolina," he read. "Why come here? Bringham isn't exactly on the tourist route."

"I inherited this house and my great-aunts' money. Anyone in the village would tell you that."

"So you just left your job and came over here for an indeterminate stay? You must have an understanding employer."

"I quit my job."

"Just like that?"

"What has this got to do with poor old Stanley Collins getting blown up?"

"I'm trying to find out, Miss LePage. How about you tell me?"

"Tell you what?"

"Why you threw up a presumably steady job, came hotfooting it over here, established yourself in the community—without legal residence, I might add—and what you've done to make someone want to kill you."

"As to the latter, I'll repeat. I don't know and I wish you'd find out. As to quitting my job, I'll tell you. In the space of a few months, my grandmother, who'd raised me, died, and I was on the receiving end of a broken engagement. My life was a mess. I inherited a house and money. It seemed a heaven-sent opportunity to escape."

Jones nodded. "So you left brokenhearted, came here, and fell into Mr. Marlowe's arms."

Dixie wondered how many years of jail time you got for slapping a policeman. "Not exactly. I'm an adult, Inspector. So is Christopher. What we do is our business."

"As long as you don't break the law." He looked straight at her. "I noticed you still use the present tense when talking about Mr. Marlowe. Wouldn't know where he is, would you?"

That she could answer truthfully. "No, I wouldn't."

"And the last time you saw him?"

"At the Whist Drive on Saturday." The lie came easy.

"Half the village saw him then, it seems. And no one on earth has seen him since. Must have been quite a party."

"Do you have any idea where he is?"

"Can't say I do, Miss LePage." He slid her passport across the table. "Keep it handy, Miss LePage. Oh, by the way, it's our practice after an incident like this to keep the area under surveillance for forty-eight to seventy-two hours. Just in case. So don't let police cars parked in the lane worry you."

"You mean I'm being watched?"

"We wouldn't want anyone to take a second go at you."

"But I can leave?" Or was this British-style house arrest? The question amused him. "Lord, yes. Don't let them stop you doing anything. Of course, if you plan on going any distance let us know, and don't leave the country." And on that, he left, followed by Wyatt.

Justin made her fresh tea, even sweeter than Emma's. "You should lie down. Someone's coming to fix the broken windows. And . . . much as I share your distaste for Inspector Jones, he has a point. Someone went to a great deal of trouble and expense to kill you. Any ideas?"

Dixie swallowed. Twice. "I'm not exactly sure. I can't help thinking it's the same person who tried to incinerate Christopher and undoubtedly did kill Vernon."

"Who's Vernon?"

Dixie explained as best she could, and for good measure added everything she'd learned about her great-aunts and Sebastian. "Sebastian seems to turn up everywhere. I can't help suspecting he was involved with trying to kill Christopher. Christopher never said so. He just insisted I would be safe once he left the neighborhood." She paused, her mouth twisted in a wry grin. "It seems he was wrong."

Justin listened and thought for a while as if mulling over the convoluted information he'd just heard. "I think," he finally said, "there's more than one issue here. What do you know about a coven of witches?"

"Witches?" Dixie repeated, her voice rising with surprise. "Surely you don't believe . . . I get it. I didn't believe in vampires. Once. So there are witches, too? Gran used to say her sisters were witches. I thought it was a figure of speech." Her mind all but scrambled as she tried to piece it all together. What did Faith and Hope have to do with this? They were dead, weren't they? Or did witches come back like vampires?

"What else did she tell you?" Justin asked.

"Not much. I know her family disapproved of her marrying Gramps. When I talked of visiting here, she told me I'd be better off staying away. I took her word for it. I couldn't afford it anyway." She looked across the table to Justin. "You think they really were witches?"

He shrugged. "There's more than one sort of witch. Your aunts sound like experts of herb lore, and they used their skills as a two-edged income. Some witches follow the old religion—the pre-Christian practices that I encountered when I first arrived, and others . . ." He paused. "They practice the black arts."

"You think it was witches who tried to incinerate Christopher?" He shook his head. In denial of knowledge or refusal to tell? "Considering everything, I think I ought to know."

He hesitated, as if trying to decide what to tell. "The knife used was a Druid one. It must have been preserved and handed down. But the practice of slaying us for our powers, that stems from the black arts."

Talk about information overload! "We're dealing with hybrid witches?" Had her notion of normality changed these past couple of days!

"I think we're dealing with an ancient Druid coven that has now embraced the black arts."

"They're dangerous."

He actually smiled. "Is the sun warm? Did Hitler cause trouble? Was the Black Death a problem?"

She got the point. "What's to be done?"

"Kit told you."

Cold settled in her midriff. "I'm not leaving. Not until something's resolved."

"Waiting for a second bomb? Who is the next one going to kill?" That was a low blow. "Think about it," he said, rising. "And while you're thinking, would you let me see your great-aunts' record books?"

They spent the day up in the little attic. Justin read at a rapid speed. Getting through college would be a breeze for a vampire. After reading, he agreed that most papers should be destroyed, and promised to help burn them—after the police left. It took a couple of hours to burn the lot in the living room fireplace, after dark so no one noticed the smoke, but Dixie felt she'd sanitized the village. Those papers couldn't harm anyone now.

Dixie held back the journals. "Taking them back with you?" Justin asked.

"I think so."

"Fair enough. Now, how about you get packed? We'll spend tonight at Tom's. In the morning we'll have a chat with your Inspector Jones, and have him agree to let you leave."

"Okay, but I want to stay here tonight. I should be safe enough with you here."

Morning found them facing Jones behind his gray steel desk.

"Sorry, Miss LePage, you can't leave. Not yet. Maybe in a couple of weeks." He shook his head to underscore his refusal.

"Inspector," Justin said, his voice quiet but penetrating in the badly lit room, "you cannot continue to give protection. You can't discount the possibility of a second attempt on her life." He took a slow breath, then continued, "Under the circumstances, it would serve everyone's best interest to permit Miss LePage to return home. You can see no objection."

Inspector Jones blinked his pale eyes. Twice. He yawned, as if daydreaming. "In the circumstances, it would serve everyone's best interest to permit Miss LePage to return home. I see no objection."

"Thank you, Inspector." Justin offered his hand as they all rose and he threw Dixie a look that silenced her comments. At least until she shut the car door.

"What exactly went on there? Some sort of Svengali act?"

"No," he replied, changing gears and watching for a lull in the traffic to pull out of the side road.

"What did you do, then?"

"I changed his mind." He eased the car out into the traffic and headed for the town center.

"Do it a lot, do you?" She forced her voice to stay calm. But her mind hop-scotched around the implications.

"When necessary."

"You did it on Friday. That's how you got past all the policemen."

"They couldn't prevent me. I promised Christopher you'd be safe." His voiced sounded like concrete.

"So, you changed his mind, but it wasn't a Svengali act?"

He glanced her way, then gave his attention back to the traffic. "Svengali hypnotized. I just let Jones choose an option he'd rejected earlier."

He could twist the police to his will and she hoped to defy him? Damn him, she would. She wasn't sliding offstage the way he wanted. Not after all she'd read and learned last night.

She insisted on a last stop at the Barley Mow. She wanted everyone in the village to know she was going.

"Bon voyage and all that," Alf said as they left. "Good luck. Sorry to see you go. Thinking of retiring myself. It's just not the same around here. You going. Poor old Vernon done for. Marlowe. And now Stanley Collins. I still can't believe *that*." He shook his head as if to ward off tears.

Dixie felt the salt-sting behind her own eyelids as a bitter taste rose from her throat. "It'll work out, Alf," she said as she wrapped her arms around his broad shoulders.

"I hope so. I want them to find that bastard Marlowe. Pity they did away with hanging."

Dixie's soul froze in her throat. Cold oozed out of her spine. "He's innocent until proven guilty."

Alf shook his head. "Sorry to say it, I know he was a friend of yours. But what else are we to think? Burned to death in that man's bed?" He paused. "Terrible way to say goodbye on, isn't it?"

She agreed.

"Someone needs to clear Christopher's name," she said as they walked home.

"Don't get ideas, Dixie," Justin warned. "You're getting on that plane tomorrow. If you and Kit are both safe and out of the way, maybe the rest of us can delve for the truth."

"By the 'rest' you mean you and Tom?" She took a breath. "There are more of you." Of course, there had to be, maybe a whole army of vampires. "I could help."

"Forget it, Dixie. No amateur detective antics. Solving mysteries belongs in Agatha Christie. This is reality, and I promised Kit you'd be safe. You get on that plane tomorrow, agreed?"

She agreed. With fingers crossed behind her back.

"I feel so guilty about Stanley's family. If I'd started the car . . ."

"You'd be dead." They were driving south on the M26 towards Gatwick. Justin never took his eyes off the traffic. "Would that be Stanley Collins's fault? It's the fault of whoever planted the bomb, and the person who hired them."

"But if I'd never come here . . ."

"The evil in Bringham existed long before you came. It was your misfortune to arouse it."

"And now I'm running away."

"In my army days, they called it strategic withdrawal."

"How long ago was that? The Crusades?"

"Much earlier. Remember, I came with the Ninth Hispania. Posted to Eburacum to replace a surgeon who drank himself to death to keep out the cold and damp. I marched out with them the last time and got a black-tipped Brigantine arrow through my throat."

"And then someone turned you into a vampire." What an incredible conversation while they sped down a five-lane highway through the Surrey countryside.

"The healer named Gwyltha. We had formed a tentative friendship the winter before during a typhoid outbreak. She changed me."

There wasn't much to say to that. She had a hundred questions, but suspected she wouldn't get answers. Besides, she needed quiet time to think. She leaned back on the leather upholstery, shut her eyes and plotted.

"Just drop me. Don't park," she said as they took the airport exit.

"No trouble. I'll carry your things."

"I hate goodbyes. I'd rather you just went. Please. You've got all the other stuff to take care of. I'll get a porter or one of those carts. It's easier this way."

She got her way. The black Daimler purred away and Dixie pushed a luggage cart with a squeaky wheel into the confusion of the terminal.

Chapter Twelve

"You're serious. She's really going, saying goodbye?"

"That's what she said last night," Emily insisted from the other end of the phone. "I was in the conservatory at the back. She never saw me but I heard it plain as day. There she was with some man. Doesn't miss a chance, that one. She replaced Marlowe easily enough."

Sebastian tapped his nails against the desktop. "We scared her. She's gone. That's something, but for what we paid, she should be dead. Bomb expert! Pah!" He scowled. A big pity he'd paid for that in advance. "If she goes, she can't screw any of us for money but she could make a small fortune with what she's sitting on. Maybe she's waiting it out."

"Of course she's scared! I was! I heard the blast across the Green. You went too far on that, Sebby. Someone got killed."

"The wrong bloody person. You know the flight she's taking?"

"You can't blow up a plane!"

"Squeal louder, Emily. That way the whole street can hear."

"Sebby. . . ." The whisper became a whine.

"Still watching her bank account for me, are you, Emily?"

"I can't. That one time was one thing, but I can't keep on—"

"I need to know every check she writes. Every deposit, every credit card charge. That way, we'll know if she really gets on that plane or just holes up somewhere."

"Sebby, I can't. . . ."

"You can, Emily. Don't let me down." He hung up and cut off her protests about risks to her silly job. He wasn't interested. He had work to do, and now Valerie was poking her head around the door and blithering on about someone wanting to see him.

"Without an appointment? Tell him to come back tomorrow," Sebastian snapped, keeping his eyes on the papers littered over his desk. He had too much on his mind to take on clients who just strolled in on the off chance he'd be available.

"It's the doctor who's been staying with LePage." His head snapped up. "Dr. Corvus," she said, placing a pristine white business card on the heap of papers, "wants to discuss Miss LePage's affairs."

"He can take a running jump off a . . ." Sebastian broke off, staring at the man behind Valerie's shoulder.

"Forgive the intrusion; I thought your secretary might not understand. I'd best explain myself." The quiet voice wouldn't be denied.

"I can't give you much time." Sebastian waved his hands over the desk. The chaos didn't suggest a thriving practice, even to Sebastian.

"Ten minutes," the man suggested, drawing up a chair without invitation. "I know we won't need to detain your secretary. We can settle things between us."

Valerie disappeared at Sebastian's nod. He picked up the card in one hand, read it slowly and then tapped his fingers against the smooth card. Expensive. "How can I help you, Dr. Corvus?"

"Very easily. I'm an old friend of Dixie LePage. She went home and asked me to watch over her affairs." He smiled. No, the man smirked.

"I can't possibly discuss a client's affairs." Sebastian rose, placing his palms flat on the desk in front of him. "I'm sorry, I can't help you."

A folded document appeared on the desk between his fingers. "My power of attorney."

He unfolded the paper then sat down as he read it. Dated Monday and issued by a firm with a Curzon Street address, it gave Dr. Justin Corvus limited powers of attorney, but enough to control her money, her investments and the sale of the house.

"If you care to contact my solicitors . . ."

Damn the man, he'd like to see him choke on his smug courtesy. "I think I will. I'm sure you understand."

He inclined his head. "Dixie would appreciate your caution over her affairs."

Like hell. She'd probably done this on purpose as a parting shot. He dialed directory enquiries, not entirely trusting the printed paper. *Why the hell isn't Valerie doing this?* he thought, as he connected to the London number and got put on hold while the system played melodies from fifties musicals. At last a law clerk took the call. A clerk!

"Hello," a thin reedy female voice said. "You had a question about one of our powers of attorney?" She made it sound like an impertinence on his part.

"I just wanted to check. My client has quite considerable holdings."

"I know," the voice continued, "she mentioned them on Monday. Rest assured they're in good hands with Dr. Corvus. His investments are impressive. I wish he'd take care of mine," she added as an unprofessional afterthought.

"It seems in order," Sebastian said, looking up at Corvus and wishing him on the dark side of the moon.

He smiled, amusement lightening his dark eyes. "Good. If you would get together the necessary documents, I'll be back in a few minutes after I stop by the bank to see Mark Flynn. Dixie said he is the manager."

He left, leaving the door open and Sebastian struggling to make sense of his collapsing plans.

"Where to then?" the taxi driver asked, glancing at Dixie in the rearview mirror as he pulled out into the traffic.

"I need to get to York-shire."

"Yorkshire?" he repeated, giving the "shur" sound to the "ire." Would she ever master the knack of swallowing second syllables the way the English did? "That's way out of the area. You said London."

"I mean London. I need a train to Yorkshire."

"You need Kings Cross," he muttered.

Dixie fancied she caught a "crazy American" under his breath. He was probably right. But she was certain about Yorkshire. Certain enough to lay her credit card on the line for a first class rail ticket. She just wasn't sure what to do when she got there.

Last night she'd slept as little as Justin. While he hunted, she scoured the book room and pieced snippets of information together. A tattered road atlas showed Havering to be a village on the North Yorkshire moors, a few miles from Whitby, a seaside resort and fishing port on the Yorkshire coast. Aside from the fishing industry and historical connections with Captain Cook, Whitby once had a thriving jet mining industry, and jet jewelry was still produced on a small scale. Dixie's fingers closed over the chain she always wore. Bingo! Whitby, where the Demeter brought Dracula from Varna. Was the connection between Whitby, Dracula,

Justin, her jet pendant, and Christopher a coincidence? She thought not.

The 1924 encyclopedia had a long entry on Druids, mentioned strong resistance to the Romans, particularly in the North of England, and placed a Roman signal station in what was now the modern port of Whitby. She read about the last mission of the Ninth Hispania and how an entire legion disappeared with scarce a trace. She also discovered that Eburacum was the Roman York—county town of Yorkshire and the largest English county. Just her luck to pick the largest, but then, how large could a county be? She wasn't talking Texas here. It was in the north of England and Christopher had flown due north.

There were just too many connections to be ignored.

Dixie vowed to scour Whitby and the surrounding countryside. Part of her told her to get on that plane as Justin and Christopher had urged, and try to forget. But reading her great-aunts' journal changed that. If Faith's words were to be believed, the pair of them had been scared to death—by Sebastian. She wondered why they hadn't just found another solicitor, confronted him, or reported him to the law but they were Gran's much older sisters. They'd been well into their nineties by the time they died.

If Sebastian had killed twice, was he responsible for Vernon and the attempt on Christopher? She darned well wanted to know. Was this why Christopher and Justin wanted her gone? Why Christopher had warned her off Sebastian? She wanted some answers and a bit of justice thrown in.

She had to talk it over with someone and Justin had refused to discuss anything but her immediate departure. She just *knew* Christopher had the answers, and she'd have more chance of learning the truth from him than Justin.

She couldn't do much in a village where someone wanted to kill her, but going north, she figured she was safe. The whole world thought her on her way to South Carolina. All she needed were a few hours with Christopher. Besides, if you had vampire friends, it made sense to use them over mere mortals.

Getting out of York was like changing planets. Used to the fast patter of southern England, the slow, Yorkshire speech, with its unaccustomed vowels, demanded concentration. And then the girl in the car rental place commented on Dixie's accent! Dixie choked back a sharp reply. She was the visitor, even if the speech around her was as hard to follow as Low Country Gullah.

Armed with a map, directions, and a rental car, Dixie set off, and nearly got sideswiped by a behemoth of a bus as she pulled out of the station. She thought Bringham High Street congested, but York traffic at 5:30 made Charleston rush hour seem like a Sunday drive. The road circled the city and skirted a wall that Justin probably saw built. Caught in the wrong lane, Dixie found herself heading for the city center down a narrow street intended for farm carts, not two lanes of fast moving traffic. As she approached a roundabout that reassembled Hyde Park Corner, she was tempted to shut her eyes and scream but she gripped the steering wheel and reminded herself she'd survived a bomb and consorted with vampires—she could drive in rush hour traffic.

She did. She also found a shopping center an hour later, bought herself a backpack, walking shoes and a few essentials, and took the Whitby road. She slipped a new tape into the player and let Vivaldi relax her as her rented car sped northeast. The sunset behind her, Christopher was ahead, towards the sea.

"Why the hell would she go there?" Sebastian was snapping and didn't care. He was sick of Emily's panicky phone calls. "What's in York?"

"The Minster, the Shambles, and there's the Viking thing, Jorvik or something they call it."

He didn't want a shopping list of tourist attractions. "Stow it, Emily. I can't think over your babbling."

Now he had her heavy breathing to contend with. Why York? He wasn't surprised to find Dixie's "departure" a fabrication—she had too much to gain by staying around. But Emily's anxious call, telling of a ticket charged at Kings Cross and a car rental in York, didn't make sense. It would by the time he'd finished.

"Wait, wait!" she said. "There's another. Just came up."

"What?" It wasn't hard to imagine her pale eyes goggling at the moving lines on her monitor as her fat fingers punched the keys.

"She's bought something. Two hundred eighty-seven pounds at a Friendlymart in Clifton Moor."

He saw no reason to keep the swearing under his breath. "Keep watching, Emily. Anything else comes up, use my mobile. And call at once."

"I can't stay here all night."

"Tell them the tills don't balance, that you suspect a cashier of monkey business. Say anything. Just keep watching. I need to know exactly where she is. Sooner or later she has to stop for the night."

He didn't stop to pack, just grabbed his emergency fund from the safe and left, stopping only to fill up his car. Road works on the M25 had him cursing every car on the road, but he got through. At Watford, he joined the M1 and headed north. This time there would be no misses or mistakes. He'd take care of her himself.

Dixie made Whitby just before dark and now she faced another maze of narrow streets. Country lanes seemed easy by comparison—they were at least half-empty. It was getting late; she'd traveled the length of England on a hunch, and she didn't have a bed to sleep in tonight. Was she crazy? No. Somewhere in this town Christopher slept. She'd find him.

Driving into the fog was like hitting a white wall. She slowed to a crawl as her headlights barely pierced the mist. She took a left turn, for no other reason than she could see that curb, and nearly hit a parked car.

She'd be lucky if she didn't drive into the harbor, but she seemed to be going uphill and figured the sea lay in the opposite direction. In a gap in the fog, her headlights caught a hanging board that read "Bed and Breakfast." Taking this as a sign from heaven, Dixie turned. The gravel scrunched under her tires and she crawled the few yards to the big brick house, parked beside a battered Range Rover and little compact even smaller than hers, and walked up to the front door.

"A single room? Yes. We weren't expecting anyone this late. It's not quite the season yet, you know."

Mrs. Thirlwood led Dixie up a wide staircase to a pretty room that had, or so Mrs. Thirlwood claimed, a nice view of East Cliff and the Abbey. Dixie took the view on faith, and the room for its soft-looking bed.

A quick wash, a clean blouse, a cup of instant coffee from the supplies provided, and Dixie found herself casting longing glances at the pink roses on the pillows and duvet cover. But it was barely eight and she'd eaten nothing but a sandwich on the train. She needed something to eat and might as well scout out the town. She'd come to find Christopher, and how else could she spend the evening? Watching TV and snipping price tags off her new clothes?

"Going out?" Mrs. Thirlwood asked as Dixie came down to the wide hall with its polished brass and dark paneling.

"If I can see to drive. The fog was thick as mashed potatoes when I came in."

"That wasn't fog, just a fret come in."

"A what?" If that wasn't fog, she didn't have ten toes.

"A fret. We get them often this time of year. All times of year, really. They rise off the sea. Come in quick and leave faster. You get used to them. You have to be careful walking on the cliffs, but other than that, well, look out the door. It's clearing already." Dixie could see the roofs and upper windows of the houses opposite and the streetlights halfway down to the corner.

Dixie frowned at the now-thinning fret. If this was June, she didn't want to visit in November. She retraced the road downhill, and followed now-visible street signs down to the harbor. The full moon gleamed on the inky-black water that lapped around the hulls of a score or more boats. She then headed uphill, towards what she guessed was the main part of town. She drove slowly, searching for a parking place and a likely restaurant.

Halfway down on the left, a lighted shop front shone halfway across the road. The smell of frying wafted down to greet her, and over the open doorway, a neon sign offered "Fish and Chips." Dixie parked on a double yellow line, trusting to luck that traffic wardens had better things to do than harass hungry visitors.

"Cod, skate or rock salmon, love?" the bald man behind the counter asked. Except he pronounced it "luv."

"Cod," Dixie replied. She'd *heard* of cod. Taking the numbered purple plastic marker, she joined the waiting crowd.

A gray-haired man who'd preceded her offered her a seat. Dixie hesitated—he was three times her age and looked wobbly on his legs—but to refuse seemed churlish. "Thank you very much," she said with a smile, and having said that much, she answered the inevitable questions: Yes, she was American. No, she didn't live near Disney World. Yes, she had hoped for better weather.

She tried to follow the conversation, but broad Yorkshire, after a long drive and a sleepless night, taxed her concentration. She smiled, nodded, and studied her surroundings.

Judging by the customers and the terraced houses outside, she'd wandered into a poorer, older neighborhood. Could Christopher be holed up somewhere here? It didn't match the comfort of Dial Cottage or Tom's elegant house in London, but if he only used it to rest . . .

". . . vampire, he said it was."

Dixie caught the last words from a leather-jacketed young man. "What?" she asked. "What did you say about a vampire?"

"There you are!" a fat woman in a purple raincoat said. "All your talk. Scaring the visitors, you are."

"It's true," the young man replied. "It was in the paper."

"Can't believe everything what you read in the paper," a short man said.

"What happened?" Dixie asked, trying for the appearance of idle curiosity. "Did someone see a vampire? I know about Dracula and Whitby, and all that but surely . . ."

"Just a couple of drunks. Had a few too many Whitby Wobbles if you ask me," the fat woman said.

"Oh?" Dixie said, looking at the young man. She smiled at him and prayed he wouldn't take it as a come-on, but he seemed the most inclined to talk.

He was. "Two blokes camping out, up on the cliff. Just last week it was. Settling down for the night, and what happens? One of them sees this shape come out of the sky. Then, just as it gets close, it turns into a man. Only it's not a man. It's all fangs dripping blood, chalky skin and a big, black cape and a fancy dinner jacket—just like the movies. Scares the knobs off him, it does, and he trips off the edge of the cliff."

The old man chuckled. "More like wandered too close to the edge and the path gave way."

"Where was this? Up on the cliffs?" Dixie tried very hard not to shout.

"Up near the Abbey. Wouldn't go there after dark if I was you," Leather Jacket advised.

Dixie attributed the theatrical details to imagination, alcohol, and fear, but she had no trouble believing the rest.

"Twenty-nine, ready, luv," the bald man called.

Dixie had twenty-nine. She took the warm bundle of newspaper and went out to the car. Now all she had to do was follow signs to the Abbey.

She nibbled chips as she drove, breaking off chunks of batter-covered fish between times. It was too hot and burned her tongue, but she munched on. Nervous eating? Definitely. By the time she parked, her heart raced like a hummingbird's and half-chewed fish and chips congealed in her stomach.

This was it.

She locked the car and walked up to the Abbey—or as close as she could get, what with a high fence and locked gates. The fret had lifted. Stars and a gibbous moon filled the dark sky, and a breeze off the sea cooled her flushed cheeks. Moonlight cast shadows over the ruins, and the swell of waves at the base of the cliffs was the only sound. There were no campers. They'd fled for safer pitches.

She was alone. Or was she?

Christopher, are you here? Her mind reached out as if fumbling through mist. *Christopher!* It was no use. *Christopher!*

Then it happened, like a spark on a pile of tinder. *Dixie! Here?*

Warmth, joy, excitement. Wonders! She wanted to whoop, shriek, laugh and cry. She had to find him. Follow her senses to his resting place.

But how?

Cold wrapped her like a used shroud. The air went silent. Nothing. No answering warmth. No reply. Just the silence of the sky and the slap of distant waves on the rocks below.

Christopher! Her soul shrieked through desperation and loneliness.

The hush of centuries replied with silence.

* * *

Justin arrived a few hours before dawn. "She's safe, my friend," he said as Christopher stirred.

"How is she safe?"

"I persuaded where you could not. She agreed to go home. I can't claim all the credit. Something happened."

"What?" Christopher grabbed his friend's shoulders. "What happened? She's hurt?"

"No!" Justin shook him off. "She's not hurt. Thank Abel! But . . ."

Dry ice crystals formed in Christopher's heart as Justin recounted the events of Friday. So much for no revenge. He vowed a million revenges. An eternity of retaliation. "They tried to kill her. They'll all die. Every last one."

"No! Revenge is beneath us, Kit. You know our tenets. And besides, Dixie is safe. By now she's back in Charleston."

They probably heard his laugh across the coast in Robin Hood's Bay. Christopher didn't care. Nothing mattered now. "Safe, you say? Back in South Carolina? Old friend, you are wrong. She's here."

For the first time in centuries, he'd rendered Justin Corvus speechless. For a few moments. "She can't be. I took her to the airport, luggage and all."

"She can. She was. This very night. Just hours ago."

"She found you?"

Christopher ran both hands through his hair, letting his nails scrape his scalp. Anything to ease the torment of losing Dixie. "Her mind met mine, as I lay half-awake. We joined and then I blocked her out. She couldn't penetrate the wall I built. She stayed more than an hour, crying, her mind searching for me, and I let her drown in misery while I burned with loneliness."

"You kept her safe."

"Safe? What sort of safety is that? Only chance saved her

there. They'll be after her, you know that. If they harm her, forget our code! I'll exact a life for every fingernail she chips."

Justin paced between the resting places. "This changes everything. If only I'd waited. I should have seen her go through customs. I never dreamed—"

"She outsmarted you, old friend, and outwitted Caughleigh, by the sound of things—at least for now. She has to be kept safe and only I can ensure that."

"No. You can't risk seeing her again."

"I need her. And she needs protection. It's that simple."

"And what protection can you offer? A wanted man. A murder suspect. Your description is in every police computer in Britain, and no doubt they lifted fingerprints from somewhere."

Kit Marlowe smiled. "But not my photo." He paced the packed earth floor. "Listen well. I've decided I'll rest today. It's too close to dawn. But tonight, I'm rising. To find Dixie. She crossed the length of England for me. We're meant to be together."

Justin's eyes paled in the gloom. "You'll pay the price? For a mortal?"

"You did."

"It's a heavy price. Banishment from the colony for her lifetime."

"Not as heavy as eternity without her."

"You'll have to watch her age, sicken, get frail. Time is cruel to mortals."

"So is loneliness."

Justin sank to the earthen floor, his head cast back against a stone slab. "Tom and I will miss you. Ours has been an old friendship."

"And will be again. We have eternity."

Justin nodded. "Rest. You'll need the strength. If you're still of the same mind at sunset, we'll part. Tom and I will watch Dixie tomorrow. When you've rested, we'll help you disappear—throw some false trails to confuse the police and the others."

Christopher clasped his old friend to him. "For this, I thank you, Justin. One day . . ."

"One day is all we have."

Sebastian arrived at York just after dawn. Driving through the night wasn't his idea of fun. Damn Dixie! She'd been nothing but trouble from the day he got her first letter. He found a car park near the station and dozed. He had his story for the rental office, whenever they opened. A cricked neck and crumpled clothes could only add color.

". . . so you see, she must have hired a car and gone on by herself. She probably thought I'd stood her up."

The booking clerk wavered between customer confidentiality and thwarted love. Romance won. "I shouldn't be telling you this, but," she lowered her voice, glancing over her shoulder, "a Miss LePage did rent a car yesterday."

Success. "Can you give me the model and number?"

Scruples surfaced. She preferred continued employment to aiding a desperate man. "I wish I could—that I'd get sacked for. But . . ."

Reining in his irritation, he smiled and turned on his full charm. "Can you at least tell me where she went? Did she ask directions?"

"Oh, yes. She wanted to go shopping. I marked a shopping center on her map."

Very helpful! He already knew where she'd bought her toothbrush. He tried a leading question, "Did she say anything about driving to er . . . Beverly?" He recalled a name from a signpost last night.

"No. I'd remember if she had, my old aunt lives in Beverly."

Sebastian hoped her old aunt had arthritis, brittle bone disease and something fatal thrown in for good measure. Where in Hades was Dixie? She could be halfway to Scotland. But he knew she wasn't. She'd come to Yorkshire. Why?

He needed a shave, a shower, breakfast, and some idea of where to go next. He found the first three in the station hotel, and the last during breakfast. His portable phone bleeped as he chewed his bacon.

"Sebby, I've found her. I came in early. I know where she is." Emily almost hyperventilated down the phone line. "She's in Whitby. Last night she bought petrol in Lewisham and later charged something at a Linden House Private Hotel in Whitby."

He had her. Just a short drive away. She'd gone to Whitby and wasn't coming back.

Against all odds, Dixie woke refreshed. She pulled back the chintz curtains and admired the promised view, the ruined Abbey and the cliffs bright in the June sunshine. Christopher was there and chose to shut her out. Was she crazy? Racing across England to find a vampire? No. She smiled at her reflection. Not crazy, just in love. And wasn't that supposed to make fools of everyone?

"Any special plans for today?" Mrs. Thirlwood asked as she cleared Dixie's plate away. "Nice day for a walk on the cliffs."

"I thought about seeing the Abbey. I noticed the ruins last night."

"Haven't been there myself, but all my guests seem to like it. Ancient, it is."

"Yes. Was it ruined in the Dissolution or the Civil War?" She'd learned Henry Vlll and Oliver Cromwell had caused most of the ruins in England.

"The Jerries mostly." Mrs. Thirlwood smiled. "During the war, they shelled it."

Not quite as fascinating as earlier history, but there she was. It wasn't the *history* of the Abbey that interested her. "Can you walk along the cliffs?"

"Oh yes, love. Have to watch for weak places, you do. Erosion, you know. Parts have collapsed—one did just last week—but it's a nice walk on a day like this. You can go all the way to Robin Hood's Bay. It's a lovely walk. So peaceful."

Chapter Thirteen

Sebastian smiled at the gray-haired woman who opened the door. Shouldn't be too hard to bamboozle this old biddy. "My name's Caughleigh, Sebastian Caughleigh. I'm looking for Dixie LePage. She's staying here, right?"

The cold cow gave a grunt that could mean yes or know. What matter? He knew the answer. "Dixie and I were engaged until two days ago. We had a terrible fight. It was all my fault. I'm what you might call bearing an olive branch." The cellophane crinkled as he shifted the sheaf of red roses. "Could I put them in her room? Sort of a peace offering, you know."

"I'll take them."

He wanted to snatch them back from the old crone's grasping hands, but he smiled. "Could I wait until she gets back? You have a bar?"

"Were not open during the day off-season."

He'd like to ram each stalk down her scraggy throat. "Please. I must talk to her."

She folded her arms over her chest. "I'll give her the

flowers and deliver your message. If you want to see her, come back tonight. She's gone for the day."

"Where?" He'd asked that too fast. The old biddy looked down her nose at him. He wanted to smash it but he smiled. "Sorry, I must seem rude. I've been such an ass."

She nodded as if agreeing. The old hag! "She'll be back tonight."

He put a hand on the jamb and smiled, daring her to close the door on him. "Could I maybe find her in the town? I have to see her. I'm getting desperate." The last wasn't a lie.

She unbent a little. It was enough. "She spoke of seeing the Abbey and then walking to Robin Hood's Bay. Maybe she did. Can't say."

A start at least. He left the flowers, hoping the old bat scratched herself on them. A few yards down the road, he pulled out the maps he'd bought. A nice, twisting cliff path led from the Abbey to Robin Hood's Bay. What could be better?

"Curly reddish hair. I'm sure she was here. You must have seen her," Sebastian insisted. He'd used sister rather than fiancée with the old dodderer at the Abbey gate, but it didn't help.

"I sell tickets. I don't watch everyone who comes here. The place was packed this morning. Ruddy school party." The attendant sniffed and went back to counting coins.

Sebastian shared his distaste for schoolboys. One had pinged his car with a tennis ball as he parked. "I'm certain she came. We agreed to meet here. I got delayed."

"Teach you to be on time then, squire, won't it?" The man offered a toothless grin and turned back to his twenty-pence pieces. Sebastian wanted to stuff one in each of the man's hairy ears.

"I say, excuse me." Sebastian turned. The master who inadequately chaperoned the brats smiled at him. "Excuse me," he repeated, "but I heard you ask about a young woman. She wouldn't be an American, by any chance?"

By every chance. How many others could there be in this godforsaken dot on the northern shores? "Yes, my sister. I was supposed to meet her here. You've seen her?"

"Yes. My bunch of hooligans almost trampled her to death. Very nice about it, she was. We're from St. Dunstan's in York. Supposed to have left for Scarborough Castle by now, but one of my little Turks dropped his watch somewhere and we're trying to find it." He nodded towards the knot of boys scouring the grass and ruins. "If they don't trample on it first."

They could have come from the moon for all he cared, and the fate of some urchin's watch ranked right up there with the fate of mosquitoes. But he smiled the smile reserved for his wealthiest clients. "You saw Dixie? Wonderful! I'm sure she gave me up for lost."

"She didn't wait long. Set off along the cliff path before we had lunch even. Haven't seen her come back. She might have, of course."

But he'd bet she hadn't. That old biddy was right. "That's the path to Robin Hood's Bay?"

"Right. Nice walk. We did it one year, but one of the squirts fell off and we had to call out the rescue people. Headmaster has vetoed it ever since."

Opportunity was sweet. Sebastian sang a silent Hallelujah chorus. Soon there would be another fall, but he wouldn't bother the rescue teams.

"Sir!"

"Here it is. We found Jenkin's watch, sir!"

"Binns found it, sir!"

Half a dozen of them came running up, followed by the rest of the tribe as they started shouting and calling and jostling Binns as he pushed forward with his find. The now-muddy watch restored to its owner, the master called the group together. "Right, now, that's everyone, I hope. Let's get on the bus and if anyone else loses anything, we'll donate it to the gulls."

The bus pulled out. Sebastian squashed the memories of his own miserable school days, but spared a fleeting thought for Jenkins who'd be ribbed all the way to Scarborough for losing his watch. Would he get his head sat on in the back of the bus while the master smoked at the front, oblivious to the torture behind? Or have his shoelaces removed and used to tie his thumbs together behind his back?

Sebastian was long past boyhood terrors, with a job to do before he slept. He unlocked his trunk and rummaged under the spare for a pair of binoculars. He wished he'd brought trainers but his wingtips would have to do. After this, he'd treat himself to a new pair. He'd watch that near-deserted path, then go to meet her.

He looked up from locking the car, the binoculars heavy around his neck, to see a puffin perched on a telephone pole. The squat-bodied creature that seemed to be watching him. They were strange-looking birds. This one swiveled his head as if to follow Sebastian's movements. Then, as if thinking better of it, soared overhead and disappeared towards the southeast.

On a happier day and with an easier frame of mind, Dixie would have enjoyed herself. The cliffs offered views on the coast that bordered on the magnificent. The sunshine warmed her back through her tee shirt. The breeze ruffled her hair into tangles and freshened her cheeks, and the scents of fresh-cut grass, sea air, and wild honeysuckle would have stirred a heart that wasn't knotted with anxiety.

In Robin Hood's Bay, she stopped for tea, and beans on toast in a small, dark tearoom festooned with fishing nets and glass floats. A glance at her watch had her gulping down her last cup. She'd better get going. She wanted to return at dusk, but negotiating the narrow cliff paths in the dark was another matter.

Dixie stopped to rest on a handy stile and eased off her

now-weighty pack. She was dog-tired, her legs ached, and the path was narrow. Remembering the walk here, there had been quite a few places where the path sunk or even disappeared completely. She didn't fancy the drop to the rocks below. Turning her face to the sea, she inhaled deeply and felt the breeze freshen her heated face. Why was she standing here, miles from anywhere, probably on a wild goose chase? No. That wasn't true. Christopher was in the ruined Abbey as sure as butter melted on grits.

A loud swoosh broke into her thoughts. Flapping wings crossed the corner of her vision. As she turned, a large bird alit on the fence, not yards from her. A queer bird indeed: squat and broad, like something out of a cartoon. It folded its wide wings against its back and watched her, looking her straight in the eye. That was her imagination. No wild creature met a human's eye without taking flight or freezing; this bird just fluffed its chest feathers, met her eyes once again, preened itself for a few minutes, and then took off in the direction of Whitby as if pursued by the furies. She watched it disappear to a black dot on the horizon and then noticed the mist coming from the sea. A fret!

She didn't have time to go back. She'd press on and walk through it. If only she'd tucked a raincoat or a parka in the backpack. It didn't help that the fret seemed to hasten dusk—she'd reckoned on a couple more hours of daylight.

"Kit! Wake up! Kit!"

Justin's voice sifted through his deep rest. The urgency cutting through his drowsiness. His eyes flickered open as he willed his comatose body to move. If Justin said "Wake," he'd wake. His legs felt leaden, but he sat up, flexing his hands and arms. "Old friend, what is it?" He tried to move his toes but that needed more time.

"Rouse yourself. Dixie—"

"What?" Feeling returned to his arms as he clutched Justin's arm. He cast his still-drowsy mind abroad, but found no trace of her. "What do you mean? She's not here anymore."

"I know that! She's walking back along the cliffs and Caughleigh is here."

Strength returned to his legs in a rush of cold panic. "What has he done?"

"Nothing, as yet. I believe three of us can foil him."

"Three?"

"Tom's here, too."

Kit stood, still a little wobbly, but his old friend made a good prop. "Damn this. If I'd known, I'd never had taken deep rest, but I wanted as much strength as possible for tonight."

"You'll be glad of it before we're through," Justin replied.

"Where is the bastard?"

"In the car park, the last I saw him. Peering through binoculars at the cliff path with a particularly nasty look in his eyes. Watching for Dixie, I imagine. I doubt he's planning on meeting her for a drink."

"He's going to kill her! The bomb failed, so this time he's doing the job himself!"

"Correction," Justin said, his voice quiet but insistent as sunlight. "He's *planning* to kill her. If three vampires can't thwart one puny mortal . . ."

"We might as well stake ourselves out in the sunrise!"

Even in the gloom, Christopher saw Justin wince. With good reason, he knew. He'd never forget the smell of his own frying flesh. Caughleigh owed him and tonight he'd collect. "Chiropterans?" he asked.

Justin shook his head. "Bats will be too conspicuous. It's not yet dusk. You needn't worry about the sun, a thick fret covers most of the coast. I've managed nicely as a puffin."

Christopher nodded. Not what he'd have chosen, but he'd defer to Justin's twelve-hundred-year advantage.

* * *

Sebastian tossed his jacket and tie in the trunk, rolled up his sleeves and unbuttoned his collar. Hardly rambling wear, but what the heck? This was business, after all. Consigning his hand-sewn shoes to destruction, he set off along the cliff path.

He stopped every so often to scan the path ahead with his binoculars. He sighted cows, sea birds and the occasional human, but no Dixie. He began to suspect "Sir" of prevarication. And what about the old biddy in the hotel? What did she know? If he ruined a good pair of shoes for nothing . . .

A couple in khaki shorts and hiking boots came into view. They wore backpacks, carried hiking poles, and had sweaters knotted round their waists. "Afternoon," they said as they approached,

"Excuse me," Sebastian said, "I'm looking for my wife. She set off along this path this morning and I hope to catch up with her. I wondered if you saw her."

They listened with attentive smiles as he described his putative wife. "Eh, I think we saw the lass. Has an American accent, does she?" the woman asked.

Pay dirt! "Yes, that would be her." His heart sped up at the prospect. They'd seen her. They had to have.

"We met her arriving just as we left, oh about ten, fifteen minutes out of Robin Hood's Bay. She's a little while behind us," the man added.

Sebastian faced a long hike. Spurred on by the prospect of success, he tramped on, detouring round brambles and scraping his shoes on rocks. Crossing a stile, he stepped without looking, then swore as he pulled his foot out of a cow pancake. He'd get new shoes and socks after this little venture.

Sebastian ran out of profanities. He tried inventing a few. It helped, but didn't raise visibility or ease the damp that clung under his shirt and plastered his hair to his head. Now he knew why he'd never been to Yorkshire before. The bloody weather. But he only needed a couple more hours and he'd be out of this godforsaken backwater never to return. He trudged on, staying close to the fence on his right, where there was one, dreading the drop to the left. He lost track of time, even debated dumping the binoculars that hung like a lead albatross about his neck. But if the mist cleared . . .

Then a dark silhouette appeared through the mist. Hope rose. This might be his big chance.

Dixie veered to her left as much as she could, preferring cow pats and brambles to thin air. Fret was a darn good name because that's exactly what you did when stuck in one. The next stile she reached, she'd just sit on until the fret cleared . . . but instead of clearing, it thickened. She brushed damp hair off her face, shifted her backpack to ease the pull, and trudged on. So much for Mrs. Thirlwood's lovely walk! Dixie grunted in disgust. Lovely walk, indeed. This was murder. She noticed a dark shape approaching through the fret.

"Hello," she called, raising her voice to penetrate the fog. No reply. He or she mustn't have heard. Fog did muffle sound, after all. She shouted. "Hi! Terrible, isn't it? I'm not sure how much farther I have to go."

The dark silhouette cleared the mist. Dixie registered horror, then panic, but stood rooted for three endless seconds while Sebastian said, "Not much farther at all," and grabbed both her arms just below the shoulder.

The pain of his fingers pressing into her flesh, and a glance at those eyes etched with hate broke her trance. She screamed, only to hear her yells echo back to her in the fog. She jerked and kicked as his hands closed tighter and her feet slid towards the edge.

"Sorry you can't stay," he hissed at her.

Was it mist or spittle that hit her face? She didn't give a

damn. Not now. Twisting, she raised her right knee at his groin, but he moved faster. His right leg caught hers and swept her left one so she lost her balance. As she fell backwards, he swung her towards the edge. Gorse and brambles scratched her ankles. Her feet dangled in the air as she raised her forearms to claw his face, scratch his eyes. Her heart raced and sweat poured down her face.

She kicked out, trying to get his shins, his knees, solid earth, anything. One toe caught a root, a trunk, something firm. A flash of hope burst, then quickly died as the other foot reached out to space. He tipped her backwards. The weight of her backpack dragged her shoulders down. Her neck snapped back. Her legs swung up as dark shapes twisted and turned in her swirling line of vision and cold rose to greet her.

She screamed, but the force of rising air choked her as she dropped. The cliff face came to meet her and she bounced off. Pain in her hip and leg wrenched another scream. This one echoed up as she fell. The fret cleared, waves soared and crashed against wet, dark rocks. Salt spray stung her eyes.

Death waited among the rocks and sea spray.

Christopher heard the scream echoing off the cliffs and dived, his wings widespread. His eyes, better suited to sighting fish in the waves than falling humans in the mist, scoured the water and the rocks. The scream stopped and misty silence suffocated his hopes. He plunged, ready to fight rocks and waves to find her. With Justin at his tail, they scoured the coast, darting into each cove and inlet. She had to be close. Sounds carried little distance in the fret.

There she was, splayed on the slippery rocks like a broken doll, her limbs twisted, her skin scored by the rocks, and her auburn hair plastered over the off-center nose. Without realizing it, he resumed human form, his eyes blinded from spray and tears as he gathered her in his arms. Against all odds, she still breathed. Shallow breaths rasped behind broken ribs and her weakened pulse flickered like the embers of a dying fire. Her lifeblood drained like the dying strains of a symphony, but still her stubborn heart pumped.

On the gray fringes of his consciousness, he heard screams—violent, anguished cries—and imagined them the echoes of his tortured heart. He'd blocked her out last night after she'd crossed the country to find him, and now he'd come to her too late.

Justin alit by his shoulder. He still retained his puffin shape but their minds melded. "I'll go and find a phone box to summon the lifeboat. Wait with her," Justin paused. "If she dies, she's yours."

Light, warmth, and hope rose in his heart and crashed in his mind. The true torture of immortality snared him, crushing hope as surely as the serpent crushed its prey. He possessed the key to immortality but custom forbade its use, unless she died first. He had to watch the woman he loved suffer and bleed. Would he pray for her rescue and recovery so she could live? Or wish for her death so he'd possess her? Would she welcome the dark gift? She'd spoken of transformation, but lightly. She had no notion of the reality.

He'd woken in shock from his own transformation, in Justin's arms, to find he'd defied death. It had taken him years to come to terms with twilight and shadows before he gained enough strength to face the sunlight. Dixie was a child of sunshine, born in the Southern warmth. Could she live in the world of darkness? And if she lived, would she welcome him into her world? He'd gladly have abandoned his friends, his culture and his world for her, but did she want their life?

Sebastian waited, a satisfied smile curling his mouth as the screams died. He'd done it! Taken care of LePage. Sooner or later the tide would wash her up. He wondered how long it would take until that Corvus chap would contact him about settling the estate. He might just do it at cut rates.

Then something attacked. Flailing wings echoed in his ears and claws raked the back of his neck. His arms lashed out in pain, trying to dislodge the creature. It evaded his arms, then reattacked, this time diving at him like a demented kamikaze pilot. From the corner of a half-closed eye, he recognized it as a bat. What in the name of hell? Bats avoided humans. This one had him singled out. He lashed out at it with his binoculars, the only weapon at hand. For a few moments he succeeded, then they slipped from his grasp and claws raked his face as leathery wings batted his eyes and nose.

He screamed, raising his hands to protect his face, so his fingers and palms took the punishment and blood ran down his wrists. He tripped on a tuffet of grass and fell on his face. He stopped screaming after he realized his winged assailant had gone. He was facedown on rough grass and he smelled blood. His own.

Remembering the sheer drop just feet away, he staggered inland. The mist cleared. He staggered across the fields towards the road, reaching it minutes ahead of a milk tanker. Sebastian stood in its path, waving his arms and shouting, his voice hoarse with panic and exhaustion.

"Trouble, mate?" the driver asked. His jaw dropped as he looked Sebastian up and down. "Been in a fight, then?"

Sebastian gasped for breath. His chest ached from running. Pain rose from his diaphragm. "I was attacked. By a bat."

The man chuckled. "Thought it was aliens at the very least." But he jumped down from his cab and hauled Sebastian up, first covering the seat with a blanket and then wrapping another round Sebastian. "Might be in shock. Get you to hospital then, mate." He picked up his radio.

Sebastian leaned back against the seat, glad of the rough blankets after the chill air. In the failing light, his hands and arms welled blood from deep scratches. His soiled and ripped shirt hung from his shoulders and at some time, he'd landed on his knees in a cow pancake. On reflection, he decided the price had been cheap.

Tom coasted to a rock just inches away, still in bat form. "She's gone?" his mind asked.

"Not yet."

"I wish I'd thought to assume another form. I took care of her assailant, but if I'd planned better, I'd be a buzzard or kite and scar him permanently. These wings and claws lack real strength, but I marked him. Better than that Hitchcock film. He'll fear bats for the rest of his life."

"She's dying, Tom." Acid tore into his heart at the thought.

"Then you must watch until she does and transform her."

Tom was right, but his vestiges of humanity made him pray for recovery. Who could wish death on the one they loved?

They watched together, as they'd shared pots of ale in the taverns of Southwark, intoxicated this time with despair, not ale and politics. Christopher fancied her breathing slowed, but still her indomitable heart refused to quit. She never opened her eyes. How he longed to see the sparkle in the green again, but all his will and power couldn't open her cold, blue lids.

Justin returned. "Help's coming. Just yards away. The lifeboat from Whitby. I followed it, directing the helmsman. He'll never know how he set his course. There's a rescue helicopter not far behind."

Now the mortal world would reclaim her. Maybe.

"Kit, you have to leave her, for now. We'll watch together then follow her."

They watched, clinging to the cliffs like the wild creatures they were. A helicopter arrived, its rotors cutting the fret that now threatened to clear and leave them exposed to sight. Christopher marveled as mere mortals defied the rocks and the waves to strap his love to a board and hoist her up to the helicopter and safety. The emergency crew never noticed the winged escort that accompanied them to the landing pad at the hospital.

"Well, lad, what happened to you?" The duty sister in Emergency eyed Sebastian, her eyes wide in her dark face. "Had an argument with someone, did you then?"

"A bat," he replied, wincing as he spoke.

"A bat? That must have been some game. Your team lose then? And what else did he use? A sharp knife?"

"Not a cricket bat. A ruddy flying bat. The demented animal went for me on the cliffs."

Cool fingers touched his forehead. "The eye looks nasty, better clean you up and see what we have."

Back in a small curtained alcove, a nurse disposed of his tattered clothes and sponged off the blood with antiseptic that felt like it had just come out of the refrigerator.

She tucked a pair of rough blankets around him. "I'll try to find you a cup of tea," she said. "You've got a long wait, I'm afraid. Your injuries might be painful but aren't serious, and we had an emergency come in a little while ago. A young woman fell off the cliffs near Whitby. She's in a bad way. Doesn't look as if she'll make it." She paused to smooth the blankets and settle a couple of pillows under his head. "Must have been somewhere near where you got hurt."

Sebastian smiled through his pain. He'd gladly wait until dawn for a doctor. Dixie's demise was a worthy cause. He just hoped they wouldn't try too hard.

The tea wasn't exactly Earl Grey, but it was warm and wet. The dregs were long cold before the nurse came back. "Doctor will be in to see you soon," she said. "Sorry about the wait. It's been rough." She paused, her dark eyes tired. "She didn't make it, the young woman, I mean."

The nurse turned, probably to hide her tears. It saved him the problem of concealing his glee.

Chapter Fourteen

"She's gone." The pink-faced doctor shook his head at the tired-looking nurses. "Unhook her. I'll see to the paperwork before morning. They may want an inquest."

Christopher waited until the door closed behind them, then planted one leg over the sill and pulled himself into the darkened room. He was at Dixie's bedside before Tom and Justin followed, three night creatures on a mission of salvation. Christopher turned to Justin for guidance.

"Concentrate," Justin told him. "You've done this before and your bond is already half-forged, but you must concentrate. There is no time for bungling."

"Bungling!" He'd done more than enough of that, and each time Dixie had paid. He hadn't been this scared in Newgate Gaol. But the very existence of the woman he loved hadn't hung in the balance then.

Justin's hand grasped his shoulder. "Now." Christopher nodded. He owed her this.

Justin turned to Tom. "Hold the door, against everything and everyone. I don't care if it's an earthquake or tornado."

"In Yorkshire?" Tom asked with a twist of his mouth.

"Seal it!"

Tom nodded. "Will do! Good luck, Kit." The door locked.

Christopher's hand shook as he pulled back the sheet. How different from the night he'd lain with her between the sheets in the moonlight. If he succeeded, they'd have moonlight for eternity, and if he failed . . . He wouldn't fail. He couldn't. At the sight of her bruised face, he hissed. Livid marks and blood streaked down her face and neck. The scar on her breast, a thin red streak, seemed lost among the contusions and cuts. "Sweet heaven," he muttered, "I'll kill him for this."

"Forget him!" Justin soothed. "She's been dead ten minutes. Don't waste any more time. Open her neck."

Christopher stroked the cooling flesh to find a vein. She'd have the cleanest, neatest bite that he knew how to give. Sliding an arm under her shoulders, he raised her off the pillows until her head lolled back and her neck stretched to its fullest, offering sweet white skin. He glanced at Justin. A smile and a nod encouraged him. He bent his head to her neck.

Out of the corner of his eye, he saw Justin's hand rest below her left breast. "Put your spare hand next to mine to measure the pressure as her blood flows through her heart."

His fingers rested beside Justin's. Last time, her breast molded warm under his fingers. Now cooling flesh greeted his embrace, but soon . . . His fangs rose and pierced her skin. The sweet metallic taste of human blood filled his mouth and bathed his throat. He sucked and gulped, remembering Justin's warnings about time. As the cooling blood flowed into him, his fingers measured the pump of her stilled heart. He paused after a few minutes, bloated and swollen.

"A little more, old friend," Justin urged. "You must drain deeper."

Deeper! His feet and ankles were swollen and his hands

looked like bunches of bananas. Every cell in his body felt sodden, but if Dixie needed more taken, so be it.

The last few draughts left him giddy and woozy but her heart stilled under his hand. She was drained of life and blood.

Justin smiled. "And now . . ." and handed him a small scalpel.

The curved blade shone wicked in the dull light. Hesitating no longer, Christopher slid his arm under her neck and raised her head. Grasping the scalpel, he slashed his chest. Blood gushed, soaking her neck and staining the sheet. He swore under his breath, but bent down and pulled her closer until a steady stream of lifeblood flowed between her open lips.

Her lips moved, just a quiver at first. Little enough to be imagined. Then again, and this time she gulped, her throat undulating in gentle waves, swallowing the eternity he offered. Her mouth opened and her lips rooted and sought his sustenance until they fixed on his skin and suckled. Like an infant's reflex, her lips moved, drawing on survival. A wordless cry of thanks rushed through his bloated veins. He had succeeded. He felt the blood flowing into her. She was his. His to love. His to teach. His to share eternity.

Slowly his body returned to normal. Still she sucked, but slower, less frantically, and she opened her lids. Myriad emotions flicked across those green eyes—astonishment, confusion, surprise, and shock. "Christopher?" Her white brow wrinkled. "Where? The cliff. What happened? Sebastian?"

"Hush, love, you're safe. You fell off the cliff."

"I did not! He pushed me." She sat up, bewildered eyes trying to make sense of the gloom and the antiseptic room. "Where am I?" She caught sight of Justin and Tom, and grabbed the sheets to cover herself. "Will someone please tell me what's going on?"

"May I explain?" Justin offered.

Dixie gave him her librarian glare. "I wish you would."

"You fell—or were pushed—off the cliff. The rescue copter recovered you and brought you here. We followed." He paused, as if giving her time to brace herself for the new reality. "You died about thirty, thirty-five minutes ago."

Christopher watched the confusion on her face and remembered, as if it were yesterday, his feeling when he woke in the room behind Eleanor Bull's kitchen. Added to that, he'd just turned a lifelong vegetarian into a blood drinker. Would she hate him now?

She looked at all three of them with calculated calm. "Let me get this straight . . ."

The door rattled. Three pairs of eyes joined Tom's in watching the door. It held. "Must be locked," a voice said. "Does Sister have the key?"

"That's the room where the American girl died. Maybe the police locked it. We'll check." In the night silence, the words came clear, then efficient heels clicked down the hallway until they faded into the night.

"If I'm dead," Dixie asked the room at large, "then how am . . ." Her eyes popped as she answered her own question. "Tell me what happened. Please tell me what happened." Her voice rose in panic.

"Dixie," Justin said in the quiet, clear voice that had stilled the Druids and the legions, "I don't want you going into shock. You died about thirty-five minutes ago from injuries incurred in your fall. Kit revived you. We came to help him."

Her shoulders tensed under the rough cotton of the hospital sheet. Her jaw clenched as her eyes widened and scanned the room again, resting longer on Christopher than the others. She turned back to Justin, eyebrows raised like croquet hoops. "By 'revived' I assume you don't mean CPR." Justin nodded. "You mean I'm—like the three of you."

Christopher remembered his own shock at waking up

dead. There was no easy way to grasp the transformation. "You're a fledgling vampiress," he said, "under the protection of the three of us."

She turned, green eyes clouded with confusion, but a spark still remained. "You people haven't gone politically correct then." She sagged back against the slatted bed head. "I think going into shock might be a good idea." She didn't even glance Christopher's way. Justin got every bit of her attention.

"Our ways are old. In time, you will understand how old. Christopher made the first choice for you. The next ones lie in your hands, but first we have to get you out of here."

"What do I do? Transmogrify and soar off with you into the wide blue yonder?"

Justin shook his head. "That you have to learn. Much later. Now we have . . ."

The door rattled again. It almost budged. Tom's attention had wandered to the scene by the bed. "I didn't authorize its locking," a sharp voice insisted. "Check with Bradbury, maybe he locked it. We have to get it open. She's got to go down to the mortuary."

"Not on your sweet life," Dixie snapped at the sealed door. She turned back to Justin. "How do I get out of here if I can't fly like the rest of you?"

"With us, but we need to come in by the front door first."

"This is your idea of a joke, right? I just get wheeled down to the morgue or whatever you call it here, and freeze my butt off until you knock on the front door?"

Christopher put his arm round her shoulders. She didn't pull back. Good. "Listen to Justin. He has it all planned out."

"I'm relieved to hear it." She was too worn to argue as she rested against his shoulder and looked at Justin. "Shoot," she said.

"You have the job of convincing the authorities you are alive. You'll enjoy that, I imagine. They'll need to set your hip and arm. It's important they get set properly. They'll mend in thirty-six hours or less. That's why I'm getting you away. Your resurrection will be enough shock for this establishment for one century. Instant healing will garner too much attention. You take care of things here. I'll be back in the morning."

"How come I don't feel it if my hip's broken? Shouldn't I be in pain?"

"With the immense feeding Christopher gave you, no. They'll give you painkillers and anesthetics, but it won't make much difference. Just play along."

"What about heart rates and pulse? If I'm breathing but have no pulse, won't that raise suspicions?"

"Your heart will continue to pump the new blood for about twenty-four hours. By then we'll have you away. You won't be here long enough for them to discover the truth."

"And if they did, they wouldn't believe it anyway, right?" She looked down at her hands, turning them palms up and flexing her long fingers. "I'm not sure *I* do."

Christopher gathered the shaking fingers into his grasp. "Dixie, hold on until morning. You'll manage. Justin will be here. Then we have forever."

A white tooth bit into her lip. "That will take some getting used to."

"I'll be there."

"Yes." She swallowed. A nervous pink tongue traced her full lips. "I believe you. But what about the daylight, and food, and drinking, and all that?"

"Don't worry. The worst will be a blinding headache. They'll think that's post-operative shock. Small quantities of food or liquid you can take. It's several hours before the transformation is complete. I hate to leave you, my love, but we couldn't come up with a better way. Not in this century. A hundred years ago we could have carried you off and they'd blame body snatchers. We couldn't get away with it nowadays."

She smiled. She'd play her part. He just wished he could stay to enjoy it. He pulled her close. Lip to lip. Breast to breast. Tongue to tongue and gave her a fleeting taste of the passion they'd soon share.

She blinked, shook her head and gulped in the night air, her eyes large as a rajah's emeralds. "Am I just weak from shock or was that a vampire kiss?"

"Weak you'll never be again," he promised. "Next time will be even better. We won't have an interested audience."

"Yeah, right," she whispered. "We need to talk."

"We have eternity."

"Come, come," Justin interrupted. "The sooner we leave, the sooner Dixie can set the hospital on its ear." He moved to the window. Tom followed. Christopher gave her one last look.

"Bye," she said, with a jaunty wave. "See you later."

The night air doused like a cold shower, but nothing could chill the sweet warmth in his heart.

Dixie sat up, bracing herself on her arms and took stock of her new self. Her throat felt dryer than cotton fields in August. Her arms and legs were covered with cuts and bruises, but she felt no pain at all. Justin was right about her heart. It still pumped—in fact, it threatened to pound through her ribs. Men! Just mosey in there, unsettle every given in life as she knew it, then flit out on the breeze, assuring her she'd "handle" things. She wanted to kick the lot of them, but she had a broken hip, a fractured arm, had just been declared dead, and looked as if she'd taken a bath in blood.

The only thing she felt certain of was no one, but no one, was laying her out on a marble slab. Not while she lived and breathed, and that would last—how long? Twenty-four hours. She'd better get busy. If Justin let her down . . . He wouldn't. Nor would Tom or Christopher.

She flicked on the night-light over the bed and reached for the buzzer to summon the nurse. Walking with a broken pelvis might be too much, even for a fledgling vampiress. After counting to twenty, she pressed the buzzer again. This time she held it down. After all, they might not expect to answer calls from a corpse.

The door opened. A girl in a crisp, gray dress blinked in surprise. And stared.

"I need help," Dixie said.

The blinking eyes widened, the young face paled to ashen and with a faint gasp, she dropped to the polished floor. Just what she needed, nurses fainting on her. She was supposed to be the patient. Giving up on the buzzer, Dixie yelled. That got attention.

Two nurses filled the doorway. "Betsy!" they gasped. Looking up from their crumpled companion on the floor, they gaped at Dixie perched on the hospital bed. Faced with their neat uniforms, she felt disheveled. This pair didn't faint but speech seemed a bit much for them, and the way they clutched the door frame suggested weak knees.

"I think that young woman needs some help," Dixie told them, fighting to keep her voice steady. "And I'm feeling pretty rough myself."

They exchanged startled glances, like a pair of horrified parlor maids who'd just discovered a corpse—which, in a way, they had. "I'll c-c-call Sister," the one on the right stuttered, then disappeared like the wind down the corridor.

Sister wore a crisp blue dress, the stiffest white apron Dixie had ever seen, and a confident bossiness that completely failed to conceal her shock at a resurrection occurring on *her* shift. But she did possess the authority to shake her subordinates into action. Even crumpled Betsy got herself to her feet with a bit of help, but she looked ready to do a repeat performance any minute.

"I'm sorry to cause all this disturbance, but I'd like to know where I am. I remember falling off the cliff, and then I woke up, aching all over, with a sheet over my head. What's going on? I need a shower and I'm dying to pee." Justin had been right. Bodily functions did continue.

Sister rose to the occasion. "Fetch a bedpan, Anna," she said and the nurse on the left scuttled away. "Lights, Mary." The room was flooded with harsh, fluorescent light. A thermometer in the mouth and cool, efficient fingers on her wrist reminded Dixie she was alone and injured, at least temporarily, in a foreign hospital. A pulse didn't seem enough to convince Sister to contradict a doctor's declaration of death. "You're in shock. I think you'd better rest until we can get a doctor up here."

"I think I'm bearing up better than she is." Dixie looked across at Betsy sitting limp and shaking in a metal chair. "And I'm dying to wash my hair." It was stiff with blood and as she ran her hand through it, fragments of chalk and weed came off in her fingers.

"You'll have to wait until the doctor gets here, but we'll do what we can."

"What we can" entailed a perch on a bedpan, a quick sponge bath and an ironed cotton gown with the expected rear ventilation.

Betsy recovered enough to get Dixie a brush and comb. "You gave me a turn," she said. "They said you were dead."

"I was," Dixie replied. "I just came back to life."

"That's not funny," Betsy replied. "You've got Sister all upset. She's in a right mood. She isn't used to having Americans on the ward." And Betsy marched off to fetch bed socks.

"Don't mind her. She doesn't mean it," Anna said as Betsy's footsteps faded down the corridor. "She only started two weeks ago and she's scared stiff of Sister, and finding you gave her a nasty turn."

Three doctors arrived, and after extensive prodding and poking and long frowns at a chart on a clipboard, decided Dixie was alive after all.

She came down from the operating room as the orderlies

passed around trays smelling of bacon and clattering vast pots of dark tea. She found herself the next best thing to a celebrity. Too weary to care much about the sensation she caused, Dixie dozed until Justin arrived.

"I feel I've been rescued."

"Almost," Justin replied. "I practically perjured myself. As it is, they think you're a difficult, rich American who wants the luxury of a private hospital."

"I can live with that. Another day of bacon sandwiches and eager nurses trying to spoon chicken noodle soup in me, and I would have *become* an obnoxious American. In spades."

"The ambulance arrives at six. The police want to talk to you before you leave." He paused. "What are you telling them?"

"The truth! That Sebastian pushed me off that cliff."

"Is that impartial truth, or vindictiveness?"

"*Vindictiveness?*" Her own shriek resounded in her ears. "He pushed me off the cliff to my death. I don't doubt he was behind the car bomb, which means he tried to kill me and took poor Stanley out instead. Reading their journal, I believe he hastened my great-aunts' ends. Given all that, I'd put money on his involvement in the attempt to kill Christopher, which means he killed Vernon in the bargain. And you talk about vindictiveness."

Eyes that had seen everything met hers. His hand steadied her shoulder. "Listen to me," he said in a soft, insistent voice. "Think about it. . . . Justice lasts longer than revenge. You accuse Caughleigh and his nephew, and let's say, for the sake of argument, the authorities believe you. It's only a matter of time before he produces an alibi."

A cold lump settled inside her. "So, I'm supposed to just let him get away with it?"

"Oh, no. No one ever gets clean away. Justice always waits."

"I'd like something swifter than the mills of God."

"Remember, you have eternity. He doesn't. Let the police think you fell. The cliff paths are dangerous. Erosion has been a concern for years. You've caused enough turmoil in the hospital. Don't start an attempted-murder investigation. You'll be on the front page of the *News of the World* if you do."

"So, he gets away with murder?"

"No, he won't. . . ." A Machiavellian smile twisted one side of Justin's mouth. "Say as little as you can. They know you're in shock and won't probe. And then I'll get you out of here before anyone needs to check your blood pressure again."

Much to her chagrin, she was wheeled out on a gurney, like a trussed turkey on a butcher's slab. The ambulance didn't help. It looked like a cross between a small school bus and a paddy wagon. Tom waited, dressed in orderly's clothes, and looking every inch the eager medic. They hoisted her up into the behemoth and reconnected all the bags and tubes. The back doors slammed. The engine started and they were off.

"Will you unhook all these contraptions now?" she asked Justin at her elbow.

"Wait until we leave the car park. Someone may come running after us with a last prescription." They didn't, and five minutes later Justin disconnected her wiring and propped her up on pillows. "Don't move too much," he cautioned, "you're halfway healed. Be patient. By tomorrow night, I'll have the cast off."

She couldn't wait. If nothing else, she'd found one advantage to being a vampiress. She sensed there were a whole lot more. "Christopher?" She sensed him near. She smelled him.

Up front, driving this tank.

You're here! she thought, a slow thrill tingling her heart.

Thought I'd leave you to this lot, my love? We're one now. Wait until later and I'll . . .

"Hey, watch it you two!" Tom interrupted. "You'll shock us single guys."

"Shock you! After that wench Molly from Fleet? I remember if you don't! Better behave yourself, Kyd. One stray look at my woman and I'll . . ."

Heat flooded her cheeks. "You know what I'm thinking?" Cold horror stung her. What sort of life would this be, with every thought and feeling broadcast to others?

Don't fret, Justin said, his voice soothing like aloe after a burn. *You're linked to us by the blood bond. Right now you cannot hide your thoughts. You'll learn.*

I'll teach you. Christopher again. Thoughts didn't have separate voices; they all sounded the same in her mind but she knew the source of each one. She knew each one's smell. She could hear the gas in the tank under the ambulance. Taste the blankets covering her and feel the tires skimming the gravel as they turned off the main road. A thousand sensations bombarded her—smells, tastes, and sounds she'd never known. Shuddering racked her worn body.

"Dixie! Focus!" Christopher called aloud, but her mind whirled, tugged by the myriad sensations. Justin's strong hands grasped her shoulders. His will strengthened her. Slowly she surfaced from the whirlpool of feelings and gasped for air as if rescued from drowning.

"What happened?"

Sensory overload, Christopher told her. *You're scaring her to death.*

"I thought that was something I didn't have to worry about."

"Getting cheeky on us, are you, fledgling?" Justin smiled. "We can perish but it takes a lot to destroy us."

"No sunlight, garlic, fire, holy water, crucifixes, and wooden stakes."

"Old wives tales most of them."

"But, Christopher . . . in the sunlight!"

"I was weakened close to the time of my borning, pierced by a Druid blade, and I was naked."

Yes, he had been, his beautiful, lean body writhing against the bonds of human hair. Witch's hair, as Justin had explained. And the stench of combusting flesh. She shuddered, forcing the memory away. Far better to think of the weight of his beautiful body on hers, of the scent of his aroused flesh, the touch of his fingertips on her nipples.

Watch it, Dixie! Now you're shocking us!

She'd have barfed if her body still could. How could she cope knowing they knew every thought, shared each sensation?

"You'll learn to block," Justin promised, as the ambulance began to climb up an uneven road. "For now, lie down. We're almost there and my staff is mortal. They expect postoperative patients to be weak and groggy."

They also expected them to sleep on real linen, in wallpapered rooms with mahogany built-ins and bone china on the tea tray, and roses in every shade of pink and yellow in a silver bowl on the bedside table.

"Lovely, aren't they?" a soft-voiced nurse said. "They came earlier. Someone knew you were coming." After she tucked Dixie into a bed as tight as an envelope, she handed her the card. "Later and forever, Kit." Forever was the scary bit.

She couldn't sleep. That much was certain. As twilight settled over the moors outside, energy flooded her body, and by the time night fell, she felt able to grapple cliffs—even with a plastered arm and a plastic body cast. The door opened and her three men walked in.

Her three vampires might be more accurate.

Justin, still in a crisp, white jacket came first, with Tom somewhere behind. She barely noticed them.

Christopher.

Hello, Dixie. The mattress sagged under his weight and he'd planted a gentle kiss on her cheek before she realized neither had spoken a word.

"This will drive me crazy. I'm not sure I want you seeing into my mind."

"Don't get your knickers in a twist!" His smile suggested what he would like to do to her knickers. "We're here to help."

"I'm glad of some company. I thought I'd be tired. I *should* be, after everything, but I'm wide awake."

"It's night."

"Oh! This will take getting used to."

"You will. Just let your body take over. By dawn, you'll be sleeping the sleep of the undead. Does that scare you?"

"I don't think I know enough to be scared."

A rough, cool palm covered her hand as strong fingers twined between hers. "When you get the hang of things you'll realize not much scares us."

"And how long does it take to get the hang of things?"

His mouth twitched. "A couple of centuries or so." He smiled and warmth spread to her fingertips—and the rest of her.

"Enough, Kit!" Justin pulled a chair up to the side of the bed. "We didn't come to watch you seduce a fledgling."

"Why assume he'd be doing the seducing? This isn't the sixteenth century anymore." She forgave herself for smugness as Tom's eyebrows rose towards his hairline and a dry chuckle became a burst of laughter.

Christopher's hand tightened. She grinned up at him, thrilling at the heat in his eyes and the slow smile that warmed the cockles of her heart. "It's not often you hear Tom Kyd laugh, and Justin's not that easy to shock either."

"But I will be if you keep ogling her like that. We came to teach Dixie mind blocking, not watch the pair of you ogle each other."

Justin snapped the seal on a deck of cards and handed them to Christopher. "You shuffle, then let Dixie cut." As she took the deck, Justin said, "Look at the card when you cut."

"Seven of clubs!" She almost dropped it in shock. She'd barely glanced at it but Christopher knew it.

"Try again." She did.

Tom said, "Knave of Diamonds," before she'd even looked up.

"So that's how you beat Sebastian at Whist. I'll remember not to play poker with you lot. Any of you been to Las Vegas?"

"No, but Tom made a respectable fortune in the gaming hells a century or so ago."

"You haven't done too badly yourself, Kit. I remember one game with John Sandwich when you—"

"Dixie doesn't want to hear tales of your misspent pasts."

On the contrary, she was fascinated, but she decided to get the details from Christopher later. "What's the point of all this? It must be more than parlor tricks or card sharping."

"Survival. Knowing what others think and shielding our own thoughts gives us a great advantage," Christopher said.

"And it goes even deeper than that." Dixie turned to Tom in surprise. He'd said little but now he'd taken the lead. She listened intently. "We share a blood bond, but we still want privacy. I don't need or want to know everything that passes between you and Kit. Nor am I about to share my private life with everyone.

"You've only just met us. Not all undead are as civilized as we are. Vampires are drawn from humanity, ergo you get 'all sorts' as the saying goes. Some congregations initiate just about anyone." He sounded a bit like a dowager lamenting the decline of polite society.

"Another thing," Christopher added, "there are mortals who are psychics, clairvoyants, mind readers. They possess limited abilities but can invade our thoughts. A little power is dangerous. We have to protect ourselves. Hence, we learn to read others and hide ourselves." He took the deck from Justin and cut it. "What am I holding?"

How on earth could she guess?

"Concentrate," Justin said, leaning forward. "Focus your mind on Kit's."

It was impossible.

It's not, Christopher replied without words. *Just aim your mind at mine.* He reached across the white spread and closed his hand over hers. "Focus!" he said aloud.

A deep breath might have helped. If she still had the knack of breathing. She looked up at his face, at the worried cast in his eye and the furrow between his brows. It mattered a lot to him that she succeed. She focused on the dark, leather triangle of his eye patch. One day she'd make him tell her the *true* story of that afternoon in Deptford.

"Not now." He grinned.

This was going to take getting used to. "Concentrate," he said.

This time she did. Her entire mind, being, and reason focused on the man behind the eye patch. She glimpsed a twisted gnarl of proud flesh she recognized as his ancient scar, then a mass of moving shadows and shapes where she glimpsed herself like a trace of happiness. And she saw. "Ten of Diamonds."

"Stay focused." Whether Christopher spoke or thought it, she never knew. He reached for another card.

"Seven of clubs. King of hearts. Two of spades." He drew cards in rapid succession and she saw every one.

"Now watch."

He held the five of hearts. That she knew the second he glanced down at his hand. Then nothing. She was focused as well as ever, better maybe, but faced a dark blank. For a second or two she saw it again, the five red pips as clear as the stars in the sky before facing the impenetrable wall of nothing. "I'm closing my mind to you. You'll learn, too."

"Try with me." She concentrated this time while Justin drew cards, and watched as he opened and closed his mind. It had been easier with Christopher. Repeating with Tom was even harder.

"Why?"

"The blood bond is much closer with Kit," Justin replied.

"Now, you practice it." Christopher squeezed her hand. "Find something that works. I use a slammed door. Tom stays in the theater and drops the curtain. Justin builds a wall as only a Roman could. Pick your image. Close your mind to me."

She remembered Gran's linen shades pulled down against the hot South Carolina sun and smiled. Slowly, with the weight of her mind behind her, she pulled the shade. With each turn of the wooden roller, she closed off her mind until she was safe, shut in and protected. She'd have bounced on the bed if she wasn't weighted down with the strapping and cast.

"It's getting near daybreak," Christopher said. She knew it. She smelled the coming dawn.

"Rest. You're safe here," Justin assured her.

"See you at sunset," said Tom.

And they left her alone with Christopher.

"I'll stay with you, love," he promised. "You've nothing to fear. Justin has this room protected and surrounded." He crossed to the window and drew down a thick, black shade and pulled the chintz curtains together. "The lassitude comes quickly. In time, you'll learn to recognize and prepare." He adjusted her pillow, tucked something flat and square under the edge of the mattress, and then she felt the bed sag as he sat beside her. His cool lips touched her forehead. "Rest, Dixie, until night."

She sensed his closeness, smelled the roses beside her bed, heard the rattle of a trolley outside her door, and sank into the peaceful and deep repose of the undead.

When she woke, she smelled the coming night through the dusk. Christopher was no longer beside her and she heard the whine of an electric saw.

Chapter Fifteen

"What are you doing?"

"Don't worry," Justin replied, "we're all set to get you out of here."

"Where to? Where's Christopher?"

"Bringing the car around. He'll be here in a minute, but first we'll get that cast off."

She struggled up to half-sitting. "I've only had it on two days." Not even that.

"The last one you'll ever need. If you break anything now, just strap it up with sticking plaster, and let a day's rest heal it."

"This Wonder Woman lifestyle will take some getting used to."

She shocked him. "Please, Dixie, we're not cartoon characters. Living with popular fiction is bad enough." He placed a thick pad on the side of the bed. "Rest your arm on that."

She faced a surgical saw-wielding vampire and she hadn't even had breakfast. Would *never* eat breakfast again. That thought faded under the ear-scraping whine and a fine mist of white dust.

"There." He pulled the two halves apart with a minicrowbar and eased them off her arm.

Flexing her fingers and stretching her forearm, she smiled up at Justin. "It didn't feel this good after I broke it playing softball. You were right about instant healing."

"You were mortal then."

Yeah! Life, or rather death, had changed everything. She had a very different future now. As Christopher pushed open the door, a spate of warmth, longing and need roared up from her heart to flood her mind. She wished the others gone, on the far side of the moon if possible, but first she wanted the darn body cast off so she could wrap herself around him, feel his arms tight across her shoulders, and taste his lips, sweet and warm as a hot Southern night.

He crossed the room. "I brought your things," he said. "That woman was a suspicious soul. Had to have her call here to verify you were a patient before she let me have as much as a pair of knickers. You had a bunch of rather garish red roses, apparently delivered in person by your estranged fiancé. He fitted Caughleigh's description. I told Mrs. Thirlwood to keep them."

She couldn't suppress a grin. "Why would I want them? I've got yours—definitely more tasteful."

"You're tasteful yourself. Very tasty, in fact." The heat in his eye made her wriggle, or as best she could in a body cast.

Justin interrupted. "Now you're back, you can help. Stop ogling her. She needs to be lifted out of the cast."

It took all of three minutes to release Velcro and shift the plastic panels that held her no longer broken pelvis in place. Lord, she was ready to fly. "Would you both disappear so I can take a shower and get dressed?" She swung her legs over the side of the bed and willed them to make a gracious exit.

"It's not that simple." Christopher loomed over her, his

hands on her shoulders, keeping her on the bed. "There's a difficulty."

"Don't tell me the running water stories are true or that vampires don't shower. I've got to wash my hair." It felt stiff with salt, dirt and blood, and smelled like seaweed and other less savory things.

"We shower but you'll have problems trying to."

Dixie glared. "What's this? Some male thing?"

He shook his head. "Not male-female. More like a Brit-Yank thing."

At that, her shoulders went back and her chin up. "I'll have you know we fought the Yankees."

"Great move," Justin said from across the room where he tidied up the instruments. "Stop confusing the poor woman and tell her straight, Kit."

Dixie folded her arms. "Right! Tell me straight—Kit."

"The problem now is native soil. We need it for sustenance. We weaken and eventually die without it. We're standing on ours."

And she was four thousand miles from hers. "What am I going to do? How am I managing now?"

"You're on it now." Christopher reached under the mattress and plonked a Ziploc bag on her lap filled with dark, dry powder. . . . Dirt.

"My native earth?"

Justin smiled. "Thank Tom for it. He fetched it while you were in hospital."

"From the States?" Being a vampire was even more impressive than she thought.

"He just went south to Runnymeade. There's an acre of American territory there, donated in memory of Kennedy. The tourists will never miss a couple of cardboard boxes of the stuff. We've enough for a mattress pad and a couple of pairs of shoes. Get used to wearing platform shoes. You'll need a good inch of American soil between you and the ground."

She shook her head to clear her confusion. "What about lining my coffin and all that?"

Christopher's hand crept over hers like a slow promise. "You won't need a coffin, I've got a soft bed ready." A slow blush crept up from under her breasts. She could no more stop it than hold back the tides. He had the sexiest laugh in creation. Add his long, tapered fingers and the possessive gleam in his eye and Justin had better get out of here. Fast.

Christopher leaned close. "Mask your thoughts," he whispered with a throaty growl. "You treated him to a free porno flick."

That did it. She stood up, all the better to glare head-on. "I'm going to wash my hair." She pushed past him and strode across the room, ignoring the draught as her hospital gown swung open. She slammed the shower shut behind her and then clutched the rail as anger and giddiness swirled her senses. Okay, she needed to grab both rails and press her forehead against the cold tiles. She'd take deep breaths, if she still could. Another wave of dizziness shook her. At this rate, she'd be lucky to turn on the water.

Her head jerked up as the door clicked open. "You'll need these." A pair of rubber flip-flops slapped onto the cold tile. "I taped bags of your soil to them. Wear them. You'll crash to the floor if you don't."

That she didn't doubt. Sliding her feet into the slippers, she let go of the granny rails and turned the spigots. By the time she'd adjusted the water, the giddiness faded and she stood upright, face tilted into the warm stream.

The shampoo lather streamed down her shoulders to pool around her rubber sandals. Her fingertips massaged her scalp, as if washing away the terror of the past days. She rinsed the past down the plughole. Now to face eternity, and a vampire playwright with an Elizabethan sense of macho, who'd just brought her back from the dead.

She smoothed back her hair to keep the drips out of her eyes. With a sharp turn of her wrist, she turned off the spigot, and heard a metallic grate. They'd mentioned something about learning her own strength. . . . The water running off her hair cooled as it trickled down her spine. Not that she need worry about catching cold. Not now. Not ever again.

The door snapped open and Christopher eyed her over the collar of the white toweling robe he held out with both hands. "Turn around." Her mouth half-opened to protest his giving orders, but she slid her arms into the sleeves. He settled the soft terry robe over her shoulders and she pulled it closed across her chest, knotting the belt tightly before she turned to face him.

He pulled a fluffy white towel off the heated rack and draped it over her damp hair. "I do know how you feel," he said, his fingers rubbing her curls through the thick towel. "I was terrified when I realized Justin had transformed me."

His hands moved in gentle rhythm over her scalp, easing the tension. "The change is always hard on a fledgling. Tom cussed Justin and me out when he woke. I think you Americans call it culture shock."

"At least you didn't call me a Yankee that time!"

He inclined his head, half-smiling as his hands rubbed faster and pulled her head towards him. "Listen, fledgling, like it or not, I made you. You are mine. I drained you. Our blood mingled. You drew from me. Our bond is closer than husband and wife, or mother and child. It's vampire." That last word resounded in her mind. Still only half-understanding, she turned her head to the white-framed mirror over the washbasin.

Mist still covered the top but in the clear area, she saw a half-fogged reflection of the still-open shower door, the towel rails and the steamy white tiles, and—nothing else.

"I think that's what's unnerving me," she whispered. "I'm not human anymore."

"You're as human as ever. You're just no longer mortal." He eased the towel off her head and pulled it gently across her shoulders to draw her to him.

She pressed herself against him, needing his closeness, wanting her breasts flattened against the weight of him, scared of the unknown that faced her. His hand eased up the back of her neck, stroking her as if calming a frightened animal. "You've just shed one existence. You need to learn to survive in the new one. I'll teach you, don't worry. I won't leave you until you learn how to live our way."

At that, her head snapped up. "But you'll leave me then?"

"Hush," he whispered, pressing her head back to the security of his shoulder. "We'll not talk of leaving now. Later, you'll decide whether to stay with me or go. *You* decide."

This was getting too much. "Go where?"

"I'll explain later. We have time. Now, get dressed. Want me to leave?"

"I think you've seen everything already. Where are we going?"

"A safe place, not far from here. Just the two of us, the moors and a few sheep among the heather."

She nodded, her throat too dry to whisper. Slowly, like moonlight creeping across the fields, he pushed aside the soft cotton of the robe, easing the fabric away from her neck. Dixie let her lids drop as her body sagged, warm and limp between the wall of his chest and the circle of his arm. His fingertips burned a trail of sensation from the curve of chin to the swell of her breasts and back across her shoulders. At the base of her neck he stopped, letting the pads of two fingers press a gentle circle where her pulse once beat. The need, the memory, the ache stirred like a fire kindled in a warm breeze, until every nerve ending burned with need.

"Christopher," she muttered. "Please." Now her arms

locked around his back, wanting him close, closer than even before, needing him in her, starving for his strength. "Oh, please," she begged. "I need . . ."

His lips cut her off. All speech and thought blocked as his mouth covered hers and her brain shorted out. She knew his lips, his tongue and his taste, and the rest of creation faded to a beige mist. She tightened her arms, holding him close until she felt him press against the length of her, hard where she was soft.

She sighed. He groaned.

They drew apart. Suffused in heat and need, she smiled up at him, wanting, needing more, aching for him to continue. "Dixie, you don't know your own strength. One more squeeze and you'll crack half my ribs."

She released him, moving her arms faster than ever before. "Have I hurt you?"

He shook his head. "Not to worry. At the worst, a few bruises."

He might smile about it. She wouldn't. "I had no idea. If I'd hurt you!"

"Before we're through, you'll give me more than a few bruises."

"What do you mean?"

He stroked her cheek with the back of his hand. "Don't look so worried. It's quite normal—for us. Vampire sex is unrestrained and uninhibited."

"I see."

"You don't really, my love, but you will soon! Get dressed." He pushed her gently away.

Dixie glanced at the high hospital bed. "Why wait?" Heaven help her, she'd lost all restraint! She yearned for him to toss her on the hard mattress and go at her like a wild thing for some—what did he call it? Unrestrained and uninhibited vampire sex.

"I have a wide double bed with satin sheets. Beats an iron

hospital bed with envelope corners." His hand warmed the back of her neck, fingertips smoothed the curls at her hairline and worked a caress up to the crown of her head. He tilted her head back and dropped a gentle kiss on her mouth—gentle, but alive with wild promises. "Besides, the staff here is used to face-lifts and liposuction. Vampire mating would throw them off."

What was it going to do to her?

"Show you how much I love you." He grinned at her, enjoying her embarrassment, damn him! "I warned you to veil your thoughts." Easier said than done, with major distractions like him, and immortality, to consider.

"I'm getting dressed." Suiting action to words, she snapped open the case he'd brought in earlier and yanked out a pair of jeans and a tee shirt.

"Want me to leave?" he offered, leaning against the wall like a permanent fixture.

"No need," she replied slowly. "You're making me wait. You might as well, too." She shuffled in her suitcase searching for underclothes, chuckled as she found a black lace bra, and then ruffled through everything to find matching panties. She slid off the toweling robe and slowly stepped into the lace panties, pulling them up and smoothing them over her hips. Then she slipped on the black bra, grinning to herself as she hooked it behind. She reached for her jeans.

"You made your point!"

Dixie turned, jeans in hand and stared. She didn't need to looked down to know he was as aroused as she. She pulled on the jeans, balancing from foot to foot, careful always to keep one in contact with the now-slippery bags of dirt. Tucking her tee shirt in and zipping up her jeans, she turned back to Christopher. He looked like a lean, hungry wolf. "I think I'm ready." She snapped the case shut. "What about these flip-flops? If I walk out in them, I'll leave a wet trail behind me."

"We'll take you out in a chair."

As if on cue, Tom came in trundling a wheelchair. "Hop in."

Feeling foolish, she let him settle her in with a blanket over her lap. "Do something with those bloody slippers," he fussed at Christopher. "We'll have half the ward about our ears if we leave a wet snail trail behind us."

"I've got them." Christopher held them at arm's length.

"No! I need them!" she cried. Without them, she'd be trapped like a jellyfish cast up on the beach.

"Don't worry." Christopher grabbed a towel from the bathroom and rolled up the flip-flops before tucking them on her lap, under the blanket.

"Right, let's get this show on the road." Tom swiveled the chair on its back wheels, but before he reached the door, Christopher pushed him aside.

"Thanks a lot, old chap. I'll take her. She's mine, after all."

He claimed her. The others acknowledged his ownership, but what about her? The thought of being owned, possessed, alternately thrilled and terrified her.

She tensed as if fighting resistance when he picked her up to place her in the passenger seat. As he fastened the seat belt, she half-smiled at him. They left the stone gates posts behind them and turned left on a road bordered by dry stone walls. She pulled off the bed socks and slipped back on the rubber flip-flops.

"Feel better?" he asked.

She nodded. "I feel anchored."

"You are. Without your native soil, you're rootless. You'll have shoes by the time you wake tomorrow. I'll take you across the moors by moonlight. We'll watch the stars come out."

He felt her relax, just a smidgen, and remembered his own shock and fear facing eternity for the first time. She didn't have Francis Walsingham to worry about, but she had her own horrors—especially Caughleigh. No matter. He'd keep Dixie by him until she had skill enough to survive among mortals.

The cool softness of her palm smoothed across his left hand as it rested on the steering wheel. He glanced down at the slim, white fingers that rested over his. "You're worrying about me," she said.

"And I thought I'd masked my thoughts."

"I'll be all right. Once I get used to the idea of living forever." She paused. "It just seems such a long time."

"Forget about time as you knew it. We don't age or change. Think of eternity as a permanent *now*."

"Better pick the right 'now.'"

He couldn't help smiling. Even terrified, she had a ready answer. With full powers and confidence, she could take on the world. "When Justin transformed me, I was furious with him. Furious and frightened and confused. He'd snatched my corpse from the coroner's shed and replaced it with a dead beggar."

"That explains the inconsistencies in the evidence and the contradictions about the inquest."

"You studied them?"

"The last few weeks, I've read everything about you I could lay my hands on. I scoured the library in Leatherhead and then went to the University in Guildford. There's been a lot written about you."

"What did they say?"

She chuckled. "Just about everything and they all seem to disagree. Your politics, your religion—or lack of, your involvement or not in the secret service, your sexual orientation. . . ." She paused. "I could put them straight on that."

So could the lower half of his body, right now. Her fear fading, she smelled of woman. Vampire woman. Unaware of her effect on him, she went on, "Whether you did or did not write Shakespeare, or whether he wrote you. I've always wondered about that. Did you?"

"Use your sense! It's hard enough writing your own work. Why would anyone in his right senses take on anyone else's?"

"Ghostwriters do."

"We didn't. I wrote mine, Tom wrote his, and Will Shakespeare wrote his own—but he wasn't above swiping ideas. He stole from me, and Rob Green swore he stole from Pandosto."

"I read that somewhere." She paused. "I just read *The Jew*. I've never seen it though."

"I'll put that one right. They're putting it on in August at the Barbican. Come with me. Afterwards, we'll climb the dome of St. Paul's together and watch the lights of London."

Her fingers meshed with his. "I'd like that. How about standing on the top of Tower Bridge while we're at it?"

"If we hold hands, we could probably jump it—across from St. Paul's to the Mansion House, then take another leap to the Monument and just a hop over to the Tower. And if it's too far, there are lots of buildings to hold on to."

"Hmmm." She sounded thoughtful. "There are obviously some distinct advantages in being a vampire."

"I'll show you them all, starting in about five minutes." He took a sharp right up the rough track that led to the cottage.

"Starting where?"

He couldn't resist the challenge in her voice. "How about right here?" He tightened his hands on the steering wheel and thought his way up from her toes, squeezing the sensitive spots on either side of her knee, and then wishing his way up her soft thigh, ruffling the short curls between her legs and reaching into the soft, hidden warmth.

"Christopher!" She jerked and turned to him, her eyes wide with fury but pale with desire. "What are you doing?"

"It's called foreplay."

"Any more tricks like that and you may wait longer."

He willed his mind over her tight, hard nipples. "I don't think you can."

"How much farther is it?" She couldn't hide the need in her voice or the heat rising from her skin.

"Almost there." They bumped over a cattle grid, around a corner and pulled up in front of a gray stone cottage.

"Wait here while I get the place open. The rough ground will rip those bags. Can't risk spilling the little bit of soil you do have."

She smiled up at him as he swept her up out of the seat and turned up the narrow path of crazy paving. "I think I could walk," she said.

"Save your energies," he said and his mind stroked between her breasts.

Her hips jerked in response. "More foreplay?" A slow, almost teasing smile curled her wide lips. "I see." She relaxed against his chest. He took two paces towards the door, then felt her touch between his legs, smooth, gentle and insistent until he hardened and gasped. "Two can play that game."

Lord, she learned fast. He put her on her feet, after sliding her down his body inch by teasing inch. Lifting the latch, he unlocked the door and pushed it open. "Go on in. I'll get our bags."

"Suitcases can wait. Why should I have to?"

He didn't need her touch. His body worked on its own now. With both hands he held her hips tight against him, let her know what she was doing to him. What they'd soon be doing to each other. "Impatient hussy, aren't you?"

"Not really." She pressed her soft belly against his arousal. If he were still mortal, he'd be out of his mind by now. "I've had a rough couple of days. I had to sneak around and deceive Justin, which I hated doing. I traveled the length of England on an off-chance that I'd find you. Climbed over ancient ruins, been shoved off a cliff, broke bones, died, and then woke up a vampire. You could say," she tilted her head and grinned up at him, "you owe me for my inconvenience."

"Darling," the word rasped out, need burning his soul. "I'm about to pay you back in full."

"With interest?" She pulled back against his arms, her eyes wide as if to swallow his soul. He wanted to bury himself in her, to lose himself in her warmth, to taste her until sated, to drown in the perfume of her arousal.

He hadn't veiled those last thoughts. He'd broadcast them. He watched the goose bumps rise up her arms, her neck arch and her breasts rise toward him. Her lips parted and her chest rose and fell as her hands grasped the back of his head. As she stood on tiptoe and reached for him, he tilted his head down to meet hers.

Her mouth opened even before their lips touched, warm and sweet as honey, rich as clotted cream and heady as aged mead. He sucked her need into him, not to ease his, but to inflame hers higher. She sighed and pressed her tongue into his mouth, tasting him, draining him and firing him with need and power. She groaned as he tilted her head back and angled her body into his, meeting him touch for tremor as his tongue invaded her. Time stopped and senses roared as she glued her shaking, heated body to his.

"Christopher," she sighed, shaking and clinging close.

"My love," he whispered, licking her ear as she spoke. "Shall we finish this here on the carpet, or would you prefer the bed I promised?"

Her eyes gleamed pale iridescence. He'd roused her, sure enough. "A four poster with satin sheets?"

Clasping her hand he kicked the door shut, turned the lock with his mind, and led her five steps across to the wide, dark oak staircase. "Let's try something," he said, bending his elbow to draw her close. "There's a bend in the stair. One jump up there and one to the top. It's quicker than walking."

"Jump?" she asked, looking up at the bend in the staircase.

"Yes, jump. You have to duck your head, or you'll smash it. You can do things like this now."

"I'll take your word for it." She didn't sound convinced. How he'll enjoy watching her discover her powers

"Stand right by me, when I say 'jump,' jump." She nodded. "One, two, three, jump!"

A split second after him, she leapt and they landed together on the bend in the stair. Not giving her time to think, he repeated the count and she leapt again. Her faith and trust shivered him to the heart. She'd leap off rooftops if he asked.

"That was some jump! I can't believe I did that!" She looked back down, wide-eyed.

"Believe it, darling. Now comes the unbelievable." He whirled her off her feet and through the open door, across the room and tumbled her on the crochet bedspread.

Her eyes smiled invitation, her mouth quivered at the corners as her lips parted. The rosy tip of her tongue moistened her lips and her auburn curls framed her face like a fiery halo. She could drive him crazy or haul him to the heavens while she scrambled his wits. "Stay there!" he whispered. "You're not leaving this bed for any reason."

"Oh yeah? Says who?" Her chin tipped up in challenge.

He could meet that anytime she asked. He loomed over her, pressing a hand flat on the mattress on either side of her shoulders. "Says me," he whispered. "I've waited quite a while for this."

"I've waited as long as you have. Besides, it's not polite for a gentleman to keep a lady waiting."

"Darling, I'm no Southern gentleman. I'm one randy vampire who wants your clothes off."

She grinned, chuckled, then laughed, a deep earthy sound from deep in her belly. A laugh of delight, excitement and need. She tried to sit up, but he bore down on her, latching his mouth on hers and molding a hand over each soft breast. The mattress creaked under their combined weight as she wriggled and shifted to accommodate his weight. She shifted her legs apart until he settled himself in the vee between them. He kissed her until the sweet scent of her pitched his senses into overdrive. He pressed himself against her until she squirmed upwards, moaning as he rubbed against her. She was ready and heated and willing.

"I love you," she moaned, arching her pelvis against him.

"That makes two of us," he whispered back into her mouth.

"I thought you were going to take my clothes off." She almost whimpered the words as her nails dug into his back.

"I am." He rolled sideways off her, slipped his arm under her shoulders until she half-sat, half-lay beside him and in one swift movement raised her tee shirt over her head. "I remember that black bra. Used it to tease me. Not anymore. It's coming off."

It did. And he made short work of her jeans and underwear.

"Don't go anywhere," he said, slowly unbuttoning his shirt. Lord, was she beautiful, pale and smooth in the twilight. And she was his creation.

She blinked and sat up as he shed the rest of his clothes quickly. "How do you do that?" she asked as she stared at him, open-mouthed, her breasts swaying as she moved.

"Old vampire trick."

"Oh," she whispered, in a voice so innocent as to be impossible. "Sort of like this." She mind-pinched his nipple.

"Sort of," he agreed and thought-touched his fingers up and down her neck until she sighed. "It's fun when we both do it."

Her intense concentration amused and amazed him. She put all her mind to her new skill, except when he roused her to distraction. "Christopher," she muttered, her voice hoarse with wanting. "This is fun but I what more."

So did he, but he had to go slowly, help her learn her new strength without lessening her passion. "When we touch, nothing you do can ever hurt me. You're strong, stronger than you can imagine, but not yet as strong as I am."

"I suppose that will take me four hundred years."

"Nah, only a century, or so." He couldn't tell her growth and strength depended on the frequency of feeding. Not yet. He'd explain that later. Much later.

Her breasts were full and golden as Guernsey cream, as smooth as polished ivory, and as sweet as her heart. He cupped then gently squeezed each warm globe, increasing pressure and force until he kneaded and teased and her nipples rose like proud peaks and her breasts gleamed rosy in the twilight. He squeezed hard. Hard enough to bruise a mortal. She moaned and bucked. "More, harder," she whispered. At her words, his hands moved at lightning speed, caressing, covering, pinching and tweaking until she arched and cried, wanting, begging for more with every move and sigh. Then she turned to him.

She became the aggressor, touching, kneading and biting. A wild dance of heat and passion rose between them, and steamed as they rolled and bounced and shook the bed beneath them. Time stopped as they mated with fierce primeval passion. Wrapped in a need more vast than any mortal want, they joined in a frenzied coupling. Her guttural cries echoed off the rafters as he brought her with him in ecstasy and they soared to the heavens together, collapsing on the rumpled sheets—contented but insatiate.

"I never dreamed," she sighed, her eyes misty with contentment, "of loving like that. I thought, the other time, that you were wonderful. But this . . ."

"I know. Beyond mortal imagination."

She cocked an eyebrow at him. "Don't get carried away."

"Why not? What else do you have planned for the next week?"

"Not much point in my planning anything. You seem to have it all organized."

"Yes," he replied and rolled her back on the pillow.

Before he could nuzzle her neck and tickle her as he planned, she pushed herself upright, her hand on his chest and her eyes wide in horror. "You're bleeding!" Her hands traced the nips and scratches on his chest, then she turned his shoulders and gasped at the sight of the lines she'd raked across his back. "I did that?" she whispered, her voice rising with shock.

"Not to worry, you have some too—though I tried not to mark you this time."

She glanced down at the scratches on her breasts. "Why didn't you warn me? But they don't hurt."

Resting a hand on each shoulder, he drew her close. "They won't, and they're healing even now. Watch." Her jaw dropped as she watched the scratches fade and the grazes heal. "Vampires mend fast. A broken bone overnight. A cut in minutes. A scratch in seconds. I told you, you couldn't hurt me. Remember that night James hit me with the car? I had a broken leg. It hurt to walk on, but I strapped it up when I got home and by morning, it had healed."

"Then why did that stone knife nearly kill you?"

The wound ached, even as she mentioned it. "That was different. It was a witch blade. The Druids revered them as ancient knives—some even claim they're extraterrestrial. It drained my strength, but even that couldn't kill me. The addition of sunlight on my weakened state added insult to injury. It'll never happen again."

"What if there's a hidden arsenal of witch blades somewhere?"

He'd have to stop this line of questioning. They'd be discussing Caughleigh next, and one thing he vowed: he wasn't sharing his bed and Dixie with Sebastian Caughleigh in any way, shape, or form. "Let me show you something." He gathered her in his arms, and carried her, naked as starlight, to the window and threw wide both casements. "Night. The dark that rejuvenates. Night eases any hurt or injury. Learn to love the nighttime."

"It's a full moon." She turned in his arms, the light casting silver shadows on the contours of her face and the lush curves of her body.

"Most auspicious."

"What for?" As she asked, she met his eye and read his answer. "Already?" she whispered, excitement raw and rough under the quiet tone.

He carried her over to the sheepskin rug by the empty fireplace. "We'll try the floor now," he growled as he raised her ankles to his shoulders and she moaned with anticipation.

Hours later, he carried her back to bed.

"Let me walk," she said as he scooped her up in his arms.

"Without those shoes, my love, you know what happens." She frowned. He kissed between her eyebrows. "Be patient. You'll have shoes when you wake."

He smelled sunrise coming and sensed the drowsiness behind her eyes. He tucked the pad of earth under the mattress where she lay, and pulled the covers up to her waist.

She still smiled, dazed with passion, and drugged by the scents of love. She had to be sore—heaven knew he ached. "Sleep, my love," he whispered, drawing the sheets up over her shoulders. He closed the windows, pulling down the blackout blind to protect her from stray sunbeams and light shards.

She lay comatose in the darkened room. He should leave, but couldn't. He drew up the armchair, glorying in the sight of his love. She was his. His creation. His possession. The love of his life. His love for eternity.

If he could only keep her.

Chapter Sixteen

Dixie woke with the sunset with no fatigue, no grogginess—coming from sleep to wakefulness in a moment—and saw Christopher watching her from the chair by the window. "Have you been there all day?" When he smiled like that, she knew she could fly.

"Not yet. Learn to run before you fly."

Time to veil her mind—better still, close it like a steel shutter. "Were you here all day?"

"Most of the time. I brought your things in from the car. Watched the news and saw Tom when he brought up your shoes." He dropped the package on the crochet spread. There were two pairs of shoes: black leather sneakers and a pair of patent leather sling backs with a wedge heel. Both had inch-thick platform soles.

"They'll be heavy to walk in." On second thoughts, they wouldn't. Not now. Unlikely that vampires suffered blisters or sore feet.

"Try them out. Want a moonlight run across the moors?"

"Shouldn't I get dressed first?"

He leered at that. "You decide. We'll move too fast for anyone to see us."

She decided on clothes. She was raised in the South, after all.

The night smelled of honeysuckle, rain clouds and freshly turned earth. She stood by the open door, Christopher's arm around her waist, the wide arc of night sky beckoning. Stars gleamed like a thousand hopes as she stepped out the back door. She brushed past lavender and scented geraniums, walking down the stone path. They faced the open moor. A dry stone wall was the only barrier before the vast openness of North Yorkshire.

"When I say 'go,' start running," Christopher said. "When I say 'jump,' jump. It's that easy."

Was it? The wall was three, maybe four, feet high, looked as solid as the house behind them, and hard enough to break bones. But now, that would only be an inconvenience.

She stood firmly on the ground, anchored by the soil beneath her feet, and began running at his signal. Five strides and a jump. Clear the wall? She could have cleared a shed with space to spare. The jump carried her twelve feet from the wall to land on soft, sheep-cropped turf.

"Study the stars. That's how we get home. The Plough. The North Star. In open country we don't have many landmarks and, as fast as we go, we miss most of them."

They weren't the positions she knew from home but he was right. The North Star stayed put.

"See that outcrop?" He pointed to a jagged silhouette on the horizon. "It's called Boggles' Roost. We're going there."

"You're kidding! Nothing is called 'Boggles' Roost.' Besides, boggle is a verb."

"Nay, luv, din fret tha'sel." He did a lousy Yorkshire accent. Even she could tell that much. "Th'art in Yorkshur noo."

"And?"

He gave up on the Yorkshire. "They have boggles here. Or did. There's a boggle hole not far from where you had your tumble."

"And what exactly is a boggle?"

"The local dialect for hobbit."

"Oh, please!" On the other hand, why not? She personally knew vampires. She *was* a vampire! Why not hobbits, goblins and elves too?

Christopher stepped close to her in the moonlight and brushed the hair from her forehead before dropping a kiss like heated velvet. "Let's go. I'll hold your hand until you find your stride. Then we'll race. Last one there has to kiss the other."

"It's a deal."

"Now!"

A split second behind him, she ran, grasping his hand. Chest forward, legs pumping, her face raised to the wind as they raced like comets. She'd skied downhill, galloped across open fields on horseback, and water-skied. Nothing equaled the thrill, the exhilaration of racing across an open moor at sixty miles an hour.

Christopher dropped her hand and sped ahead. So, he'd win would he? Not without a fight! Her legs pumped like weightless pistons. No breath to catch, no heart to pound, her body moved to her will, no mortal limitations—but she still couldn't beat Christopher. He had a four-hundred-year advantage.

He caught her as she reached the base of the outcrop. His hands tightened around her waist as her momentum flung her against his chest. "I win." His lips tickled her ear, his hands slid up to her breasts and she stepped back, not ready to concede.

"Catch me first!" Thrilled with her newfound speed, she raced around the mound. Glancing over her shoulder at

Christopher, just paces behind, she raced on, rounding the curve of the rock, and slammed into him.

This time he held her against him like a vise. "You lose!"

She didn't think so! Not with his thighs taut against hers, her ribs clenched between his arms and her breasts flattened against the muscled wall of his chest.

His kiss wasn't just a kiss. It was a branding. A stamp of ownership. A mark of possession. If she still breathed, she'd probably be fainting. But she was now vampire and could mark as surely as he did. She'd saved him from the sunrise and now she claimed him.

"Well, fledgling, how does the vampire life suit?"

"Fine, so far. What next?"

He pointed up at the dark outcrop, "We're going up."

A sheer climb? In the dark? He had to be kidding. "Just like that?"

"It's easy."

It was. He showed her how to curl her fingers and use her nails for purchase. He had her molding her body to the uneven rock face. They climbed side by side, Christopher showing her handholds and adjusting her feet until she mastered the knack of moving up the rock face. It was as easy as jumping the wall. Easier, because now she didn't doubt her own strength.

"Like it?" His gesture took in the wide moors on all sides. "I love this spot. Few breathers ever come here, not even in daylight."

Standing beside him, she realized the power of her night vision and the range of her sight. "What's that?" She nodded to the cluster of lights to the southwest.

"York."

"And that's Whitby?" She turned to the east.

"Yes, Whitby, Scarborough, Bridlington, and the distant one is Hull."

The towns clung to the coastline like a string of diamonds, and had to be fifty, sixty miles away. This vampire life was something else, like the view from Boggles' Roost. "Are there really hobbits?"

"I've never seen one, but who are we to doubt the existence of reclusive little people who shun humans and choose to hide in holes in the ground?"

He had a point. "I can't quite separate the fiction from the reality."

"Let's talk about it." He settled his back against a ledge and patted the smooth rock beside him. "What's the matter? Must be more than hobbits." They held hands, but only for a moment. She wanted his touch but needed space to think. "What's bothering you?"

"Not knowing everything."

"Have patience. I don't know everything. I doubt even Justin does. Why not start with specifics."

She stared up at the canopy of stars overhead. A plane droned and flashed red lights towards the south, and her man sat beside her, ready to share vampiric mysteries. "I know about mirrors. I noticed that the day you came to the door to see my books."

"Mirrors, plate glass, and cameras. You need to avoid them all. No reflection, no images."

"What if you need a passport photo?"

"Used to be a problem but Tom worked out a way with digital cameras. He's great with things like that."

"This sunlight/daylight confuses me. You go out. I can't. I can't even stay awake during the day."

"You will. Give it six months, you'll have no trouble. In three or four weeks, you can go out some. Daylight won't hurt you. Direct sunlight will. Our strength and power increase with age. I can take ten, fifteen minutes of direct sunlight, Justin several hours if we're dressed. Naked, it's another matter."

"No more sunbathing. I used to be quite a sun worshiper once."

"You'll learn to love clouds. That's why most of us live in the north. Whatever fiction claims, very few of us live in the Deep South or around the Mediterranean and forget Africa or Australia."

"You mean I couldn't go home?" She hadn't even considered it before.

"To South Carolina? It would be hard. You'd have to be almost nocturnal during the summer months for several years."

What was "several years" when they had eternity? "I guess I'll just stay here. For now, we've still got Orchard House."

"No, we don't."

"Why not?"

"Dixie, think! What will happen to me or you, if I appear in Bringham or anywhere for that matter? Why was I hiding in Whitby Abbey?"

"Oh!" Sebastian, Vernon, and the whole coil had faded to the back of her mind. Now they burst to the front like a rocket in the night sky. "They'll arrest you." If the police found him, she'd lose him forever.

"They won't find me or take me. Even if they did, I could transmogrify and escape, but adding jail breaking to everything else would complicate things. Better go to ground. We've done this before. We have to. Perpetual youth attracts attention, so every thirty years or so, we take on new identities. We have a network set up. I was planning to sleep for several years while Justin got things ready."

"And I messed things up."

"I wouldn't say that. We've just changed our plans. Meanwhile I stay hidden. We're safe here."

"But you drove. They'll know your registration."

He wrapped his arm around her shoulders, pulling her closer. "New number plates. We have a system."

"How?" She doubted you bought number plates by the dozen, even in a country inhabited by immortals, myths and legends.

"Later." His fingertip traced her lips. "That will keep until tomorrow. Right now, I going to love you until you scream to the stars." He unbuttoned his black linen shirt.

She screamed three times. Christopher blessed the remoteness of the moors and thanked heaven for his good fortune, as she lay weak and drowsy in his arms. They had hours until dawn. He'd let her rest, then teach her how to climb headfirst down the roost. She was still so helpless, more than she'd ever admit. Still half-believing the myths around her, the twisted truths of popular fiction, the superstitions of unknowing peasants, and a few urban legends thrown in for good measure. But she was his, at least for now, and he'd use every hour to teach Dixie to survive. She had so much to learn before she faced the world of breathers.

Two nights later, he took her into York. After climbing Boggles' Roost twice and running farther and harder each time, she had speed enough to make it to York and back.

"It doesn't seem like only four nights ago that I came on a wild-goose chase to find you."

They'd stopped to rest on the city walls, above the night traffic and the sounds of horns and engines and the petrol fumes. "If you hadn't, you'd still be alive."

She paused, considering her reply. He waited, half-dreading her answer. Were vampire sex and immortality enough to replace what she'd lost? "I don't feel any less alive. More, in fact."

"But you could be safe at home instead of prowling at night with a murder suspect."

"Considering it was my big mouth that got you on the suspect list, I can't complain."

They sat in silence, far above the night hum of traffic. In a tree across the village green, an owl hooted. Dixie nestled against him, her hair brushing his chin and her arm across his waist. "That night I crashed into you in the lane, I heard an owl then—a pair of them. I'd never heard a live one before."

"I terrified you that time."

He sensed her thinking in the silence. "Scared me, yes. I didn't expect anyone there. You made me mad when you grabbed me among the shrubs, but I never thought you'd hurt me."

"What if I'd grabbed you and said, 'I'm a vampire!'?"

"I'd assume you had a few too many pints at the Barley Mow."

She made him smile—hell, she made him laugh and feel in ways he'd long forgotten. Justin was right. Women like her came once every few centuries. "Did I ever scare you? I never meant to."

"I wasn't too sure of you that first time, but figured anyone who chased off James was a potential friend." She paused. "Was that mind control? Like Justin did with Inspector Jones? That *would* be handy."

And dangerous, but she didn't need to know that yet. "You'll learn it in time. It takes practice. And yes, I did suggest he leave. He isn't a very nice person."

"I figured that out on my own. In fact, that village is full of odd people and I've got to include blood relatives in that."

"I'm a blood relative now."

She cuddled even closer, her shoulders quivering. "Gives new meaning to the term kissing cousins." She looked up, her eyes bright in the night, her face glowing up at him. "Christopher, I do love you."

He could die happy after that. Or better still, live forever. He had eternity. Did *they*? How could he doubt her? She'd rescued him, raced across England for him. Hell, she'd even defied Justin for him. She held back nothing. Offered everything. "I love you too, Dixie."

He let the night silence wrap around them while he fought the temptation to exercise his mind control. He could force her to stay. No, he couldn't. Hers wasn't a will to bend. She'd come freely and she'd stay no other way.

"I still think Sebastian is owed his comeuppance."

She looked ready to deliver it there and then. "He'll get it. Be patient. Someone stronger than you will do it."

She pulled away, frowning like an angry lioness. "Really?" She packed a power of fury in that one word. Fury that could blow up on her.

"Don't get ideas, fledgling." Her eyes told him she had plenty already.

"Why not? He pushed me off a cliff. I owe him for that."

"He'll have scars for life to remind him." He explained the part of the incident she'd missed. "Listen, Dixie. Mindless revenge won't help anything."

"There's more to it than that." In a few clipped sentences, she told him about the secret rooms, her aunts' files and the journals. "They were undoubtedly old witches of some sort or another but they didn't deserve to be scared to death. I'm certain Sebastian did it, and knowing him, he did it to get their files. They just hid them too well. For what he's done, to you, Stanley, Vernon and everyone, he deserves to fry."

"We abolished the death penalty before you were born."

"There's got to be something we can do."

"You're thinking like a mortal. We outlive revenge."

"I'd just like to go to the police."

"And tell them what? I'm a vampire and he tried to kill me? That he scared your great-aunts to death? That he killed you but now you're a vampire? If you could get that Mrs. Thirlwood to testify and prove he was in Whitby that day, and that he pushed you off the edge, then what? Can you explain why you're walking around with a smashed pelvis? We survive by being inconspicuous. And, Dixie, I want to survive. With you."

He'd gotten through to her. Barely. "I just hate the thought that he gets away with all this."

"My love, a disadvantage of immortality is that we witness much more injustice, see more wrongs, and face more trouble than mortals."

They made it back an hour or so before dawn. She ran in silence beside him. Was she tired? Angry? He'd give his right hand to know, but she'd shuttered her mind. Maybe he'd taught her too well . . . but what choice did he have? She had to learn to survive in a hostile world, to manage without him, if he had any hope of keeping her forever.

"A little notice would have been nice," Dixie complained a couple of days later.

"I agree, but Justin only told me an hour ago. Heaven help us, Dixie, is it so unreasonable to meet a few friends?"

No, not when friends were mortal. But vampires en masse, that she wasn't so sure of. She looked Christopher square in the eye. "How many?"

"Half a dozen or so, plus Tom and Justin. Look, it's no big deal. They're just dropping by for an hour or so."

Okay for him to say. He didn't have twenty-odd years of Southern upbringing behind him. "Shouldn't we do something?"

"Something?" He shook his head. "Dixie, these are vampires. They have no use for hors d'oeuvres or peanuts."

She'd figured that much out. Her concern was more along the lines of serving the plastic bags of blood she'd noticed in the refrigerator. How did you serve blood bags? On a doily or a plate? It hardly mattered. The kitchen had neither.

"Just a glass of port to drink your health." He was amused. All right for him.

"Don't get your knickers in a twist, love. Just think of it as friends dropping by for drinks."

She hadn't realized he meant that literally.

There were a half-dozen stars out in the sky. Dixie just finished counting them when the first guest arrived. He soared from the south, landed on the drive in front of the house and walked towards her. "You must be Dixie," he said, holding out his hand.

His hand felt cold. She was used to that by now. She smiled, looking into eyes that warmed and chilled at the same time. "Yes, I'm Dixie LePage."

"And this is Vlad Tepes." Christopher had been upstairs a minute ago. Now he stood beside her, a firm hand on her shoulder.

"How do you do?" Who next? Where did reality begin and end?

His dark eyes glanced at Christopher and then smiled at her. "What slander has Christopher spread about me?"

"Not a word. Should he have? You do have instant name recognition."

Vlad still held her hand. Christopher stepped close enough to press his hip against the curve of her waist. "She's mine, Vlad."

Vlad backed a half-pace and raised his hands, palms up. "You misjudge me. For all my crimes, supposed and other-wise, I respect your ways."

"Why do you say 'your ways'? You're vampire, too, right?" Three months ago, his ashen face and hard, deep eyes would have flickered her nerves. Not now. Vampires don't scare when you've seen one naked.

"Oh, yes." He had a thin voice and thinner lips. "I'm vampire but not of the same colony as you. Justin Corvus and I are old acquaintances."

"How old?"

"Seven hundred years. I met him about fifty years after my transformation."

She didn't turn a hair. Her perception of normal certainly was changing. "So, you and Justin will be the senior vampires here."

"No. Gwyltha out-ages us all." His sharp eyes scanned her face. "You haven't met Gwyltha?"

"She will tonight." Christopher hadn't budged a millimeter from her side.

"Oh, surely . . ." Vlad never finished.

Three dark figures dropped from the sky behind him. One thing was for certain, you could host a vampire party in the city and never worry about parking problems. One she recognized as Justin. She'd know his broad shoulders anywhere. The other two were women. She quashed her surprise, chiding herself for sexism. Of course, she wouldn't be the only vampiress in the world. Why think so?

The shorter woman stepped forward. Or maybe the others stepped back. Instinctively, Dixie walked to meet her, half aware that Christopher stood behind her. She was tiny, dark-haired and plain. A little woman, with a power that hung over her like an aura.

Dixie held out her hand. "I'm Dixie . . ."

"Yes." Eyes that had lived met Dixie's. With eye contact like hers, she'd have it made in education or law enforcement. "I know. You're Dixie LePage. I'm Gwyltha." Dixie felt like a slide under a microscope. No, more like a specimen under the pathologist's probe. "So you're Christopher's addition to the colony. What will your contribution be?"

"I'm good at removing witch blades and rescuing dying vampires."

She felt Christopher's tension behind her, and watched Gwyltha's eyes widen as her neck stiffened. "It's not much, I know, but it's a beginning."

Gwyltha nodded. A slow smile curled her mouth and softened her eyes. "A better beginning than most of us can boast." She took Dixie's hand between hers. "So, you saved what you didn't believe existed. Quite an accomplishment."

"It's called a leap of faith."

Gwyltha laughed. "And you, Kit Marlowe, think to hold her to you." She gathered Dixie to her in a hug that threatened to crack ribs. "Welcome," she whispered. "In this lonely world, we need all the intelligent companions we can find." Stepping back but still smiling, she looked around, and Dixie noticed four or five dark figures waiting in a semi-circle behind Gwyltha. "Since Justin's host, I'll let him do the honors."

Justin stepped forward. His eyes met Gwyltha's and Dixie almost gawked. Furnace blast might describe the heat between them. Justin tensed like a stalking panther.

Gwyltha's smile uncurled. Her back stiff as an oak beam, her slim hand clenched among the folds of her black silk skirt, she inclined her head. "Introduce her, Justin. Everyone's waiting."

Dixie watched Justin hesitate, just long enough to tense his shoulders, flex his fingers, and smile. "I think not." Justin's reply drew a sharp stare from Gwyltha. "She's Christopher's. He'll introduce her."

They both stepped back, like combatants returning to their corners. Dixie and Christopher stood alone inside the circle of dark figures in the twilight. "Take it easy." Christopher smiled at her. "They're just old friends."

That adjective took on new meaning in a gathering like this.

Vampire introductions involved shaking hands, smiling and remembering names—just like mortal introductions. She did better on the first two. Some names she remembered—the second woman, Antonia, had said, "Call me Toni," but most of the men merged into each other. Quiet figures in black don't stand out too well. Maybe that was their intent.

One man's voice, deep and gravelly, she thought she recognized from the radio. Then Christopher introduced him as Rod McLean. "Of Midnight Spin?" she said.

"You listen?" He grinned like a pleased child at her recognition.

"I used to. Just haven't the past few nights."

"So, Christopher's depleting my audience. Can't have you doing that, old man."

"She's too busy listening to me," Christopher replied.

She missed the next two names, thinking how she hadn't listened to the radio, seen the TV or a newspaper since she'd been isolated. She *was* getting out of touch. Or was it in touch with a different world?

Simon someone or other's name she caught, a short, bald man with twinkling eyes and a slow smile, and Toby Wise, very tall, very black, and with an accent that Dixie, by now, recognized as pure Oxbridge. An immense man with the build of a stevedore answered to John Littlewood. "Call me Little John. Everyone else does."

Introductions over, everyone wandered indoors, drank Dixie's health with a ruby port they sipped from Waterford glasses, and then settled into groups around the house. It reminded Dixie of a high school reunion, everyone watching each other—the only difference being they also watched her.

"It's nice to welcome a compatriot to the colony."

Dixie knew she was staring at Toby, but a line like that excused it. "You're an American?"

"Technically. I left in 1863. At the time, I wasn't afforded protection of citizenship."

He wouldn't have been. "You took a risk leaving then."

"I thought staying a greater one. I stowed away on a blockade runner in Charleston harbor and ended up in Liverpool."

"What did you do about soil?" The things you talk about with vampires.

"I wasn't transformed for another 20 years. Then my mentor stole dirt from the Chancery garden in Victoria Street. I don't think Ambassador Page ever missed it."

"Pilfering seems to be a way of survival. Mine filched earth from Runnymeade."

"We all do—in an emergency. Every so often you'll see letters in *The Times* lamenting vandalism at the monument."

"We?"

He nodded. "There are half a dozen of us. When Kit lets you off the leash, I'll introduce you."

She wasn't on anybody's leash. "I'll come any time you invite me."

He smiled. Halfway. "In that case, if . . ."

"Not yet, Toby." Polite as a courtier, Christopher smiled. His eyes suggested dismemberment or castration. His hand slipped round Dixie's waist.

Dixie stepped sideways. "I'd love to meet them," she said to Toby and then turned to cross the room. The front door stood open. Evening air might cool her temper.

Vlad and Gwyltha stood away from the front door. They weren't discussing poetry. Gwyltha pulled herself from Vlad's arms. "Hello, fledgling. Come out to say goodbye?"

"I didn't know you were leaving. I needed fresh air."

Vlad nodded. "Our young friend stays close."

"He's not that much younger than you!" Gwyltha said.

"But he still possesses youth's illusions, whereas I am a cynical old bloodsucker." He smiled at Gwyltha. "Lady, let's say goodbye to the fledgling and go feed."

"Oh!" Dixie's throat clamped shut at the thought of their dinner.

Vlad smiled. Slowly. "We are traditionalists. Are you?"

She'd tell him, if she understood the question.

"She's not fed yet." Gwyltha said.

Vlad stared from one to the other. Surprise shone in his eyes as he shook his head. "And she's met so many of us. Before you're sure of her?"

"We're sure of her," Gwyltha replied. Dixie wished she could follow this conversation. "We're confusing you, fledgling. Not to worry, Kit has a lot of explaining still to do."

She could say that again.

Gwyltha hugged her with the same fervor she'd shown earlier. "Welcome again, Dixie. We'll meet soon."

Vlad offered his hand. "If I embraced you, Kit Marlowe would throw fire in my direction."

"I love Christopher, but he doesn't own me." What would it take to convince the lot of them that in this day and age women stood on their own two feet?

Gwyltha took both her hands and clasped them. "You'll understand, in time. You are his. Nothing will ever change that."

With a sharp whoosh, like wind through an open door, they took off. Dixie's skirts flapped around her legs in the back draft as she watched them disappear high into the heavens.

Justin waited by the open door, jaw clenched and brows meeting. "They left?" he growled. Dark eyes stared up at the night sky. "I love her, Dixie. She loved me once. That's why she transformed me after the arrow took me down. I wanted to keep her close. Make her mine. Own her soul. But she left me."

"She probably needed breathing room. Women get antsy over possessiveness and jealousy." Had he even heard her? Without another word, he launched himself into the sky. At least he went east. If he met the other two, they'd probably start a thunderstorm.

She heard a whoosh from the back door as she came back in. Another departure. Only Tom and Toby remained with Christopher and Antonia, the other woman. She was as short as Gwyltha, but prettier, and where Gwyltha exuded power,

Antonia's eyes gleamed with intelligence and curiosity. Dixie wished she'd had more time to get to know her, perhaps later. She could hardly suggest lunch!

They stood in the open doorway. Antonia waved. "Welcome again, Dixie! We'll meet soon, I hope!" she called and shot off into the night. With a nod, Toby and Tom followed.

"I wish I could do that," Dixie said, not turning around.

"You will." Christopher came up behind her. "In time. It takes considerable reserves of strength."

"And strength comes from feeding?" she asked, then paused. "Why haven't I, and what will happen if I don't?"

"Vlad," he hissed the name. "I knew Justin shouldn't have asked him. What did he say?"

"It was more Gwyltha than Vlad, I think. You haven't told me everything."

"We've had four nights. Hardly time enough to share all our secrets." Fair enough, but surely feeding was rather fundamental.

He shut the door, crossed to the front door to pull that to, and then started to close windows.

"Christopher. I want to talk."

He stopped, hand on the latch, without turning around. "Can't it wait until we're upstairs?"

No, because once they were in bed, all she'd think about was his body and what it did to her. "Now. You owe me some answers."

Chapter Seventeen

Christopher turned, his eyes dark with an emotion she couldn't quite read. "You want answers, fire away."

She clenched, then consciously unclenched, her hands, and looked him square in his troubled eye. "I'd like you to explain about feeding."

His shoulders relaxed. "That's all?" He smiled.

Dixie bit back a scream. He thought it trivial? "It's the first thing."

Wariness creased a double furrow between his eyes. "The first, eh?" He ran his hand through his hair and then shook his head as if clearing his mind. "If that's where you want to begin . . ." She did. "You know how we feed—popular fiction has that right. We drink blood—human mostly, mammal for preference and, as you guessed, any animal serves in a pinch. Fresh blood gives the most strength, and many prefer the taste."

She suppressed a shudder. There had to be another way.

"Some of us have ideological problems with live feeding and feed off animals, or use blood bags exclusively, others use them occasionally for convenience." He glanced at her, his brow wrinkled with worry. "You've noticed the supply in the kitchen." She had. The dark, wobbly bags gave her the creeps, and when they squished under her hand she wanted to barf. "I stocked up so I don't have to leave you to hunt. One way or the other, we need blood. Regularly. Once, maybe twice a week. If we don't feed, we weaken."

"And die?"

"Not that easily. A full-blooded vampire can starve for several years but we lose strength. Get slower. Become hypersensitive to light and lose our abilities to fly and transmogrify."

"Yes. Transmogrify. What *is* that, exactly?"

"Changing shape. Becoming the bats and other animals that populate horror stories."

She *wasn't* having this conversation. She *hadn't* spent the evening with a houseful of vampires. Any minute she'd wake up and find herself in her brass bed, looking at the hairline cracks in the ceiling, the faded violets in the wallpaper, and the sunlight dancing off the mirror of her mahogany dresser. *Except she was vampire and would never see her reflection again.* She choked back dry heaves rising deep inside. Her shoulders shook and her stomach clenched as she fought the rising nausea and the dizziness that swirled around.

"Dixie!" Christopher's voice came faint, muffled as if by fog or distance. His arms wrapped comfort around her as she battled the nightmare images. "It's okay," he whispered into her hair. It was while he held her, but she couldn't spend the rest of eternity in his arms.

One arm held her securely against the comfort of his chest. "Don't let it bother you," he whispered into her hair. She looked up at the brown eye, soft with worry . . . for her. "You don't have to worry about that. Yet."

Yet. Hadn't he said vampires could starve themselves for years without worry? His arms met around her, clasping her tightly as she pressed herself against him, wanting, needing just some of his strength. His power seeped into her heart and mind. She felt his will behind the warmth and courage that filled her. The love in the fingers that stroked and slid through her hair. The heat of his body pressed against hers. But she didn't have all her answers. Yet.

Half a step backwards and his arms still held. Tight. She loved Kit Marlowe and wanted eternity with him. Even if she had to drink blood. She'd worry about that later. Much later. "You said vampires, we, can starve for years. Right?"

"Fully-blooded vampires can."

She didn't completely understand, but knew it wasn't good news. "I'm not fully-blooded?"

"You're a fledgling, darling."

That term again. She'd heard it often enough the past few days and thought it meant something like "pledge" for a sorority. "What does that mean?" Did she really want to know? She had to.

He hesitated. "What does 'fledgling' mean in the way you've always known it?"

"A young bird, too young to leave the nest, that's still fed by its parents." Was she going to have to feed from him?

"Lord, no, Dixie." He looked more horrified that she felt. That was progress. "We don't feed off each other."

Back to square one. "You're saying I have to feed, but a full-blooded vampire doesn't need to." He nodded. "Why haven't I fed then?"

"You did. When I transformed you, you had a very deep feeding. I practically drained your body and then replaced everything with our mingled blood. I gave you extra, hence my need for the blood supply in the fridge to replenish my own body. Most times we feed, we take a pint or so. Not enough to weaken or harm the subject. No more than a blood donor gives. Your deep feed will last quite a while."

"How long?"

"Two or three weeks, depending on how you use or conserve your strength."

She pulled from the circle of his arms and walked to the still-open door. The cool night air on her face did nothing to soothe the raging cancer of panic erupting inside. She had to feed. Sooner or later there was no escaping the fact. How long since Christopher fed her? Five, six days. At best, she had two weeks before she had to suck blood. She fought the spiraling. She had to. Or did she? "What happens if I *don't* feed after three weeks?"

"The same as any other fledgling vampire." She waited, silent, knowing in her heart he'd tell her, no matter how much he didn't want to hurt her. "After two and a half, three weeks, you'll weaken, lose your speed and your vampire senses over several days, and slip into a deep rest, that's sometimes been misidentified as drug-induced coma. After twenty-four hours or so, the fledgling returns to their previous state minus, all memory of their temporary transformation."

"I see." She did, with horrifying clarity. She'd be dead.

"Many colonies transform living mortals. We don't. I'm afraid it knocks out that choice for us."

Scents of night stocks wafted from outside, along with the honeysuckle that grew beyond the stone wall. Out on the moor, night creatures stirred in the heather, and miles away along the main road, engines hummed as trucks and cars traveled to and from York. If she concentrated enough, maybe she'd hear the surf on Whitby beach. She sighed at the thought of the powers open to her if she fed. "There's always a choice," she said, speaking slowly. "The alternative may be impossible, unthinkable, or irrational, but there's always an option."

The kitchen got quieter than the night outside. "If I had to set you in a tomb, Dixie, I'd bury my heart, too."

How could she even think it? With a sob, she stepped toward him and let his strong arms and broad shoulders lock out the choice she dreaded making.

"Don't let it worry you." His words soothed as he stroked the top of her head. "It's not as bad as you fear. Trust me. I'll be with you when you're ready to feed, I'll explain what to do." She didn't even want to think about it. At least not now. "I told Justin it was too soon to introduce you to the others, that you needed more time. He wouldn't listen."

"Don't blame him. This way I have longer to get used to the idea, to decide."

"Let me take you to bed. I want to love your anxiety away."

She couldn't, not in this frame of mind. "Later. First I want to walk on the moors."

"Want to run to Boggles' Roost?"

"Walk. Not run. I want to try to remember what it was like to be mortal."

"You can never be mortal again."

"I know." Her throat tightened. "I just want to remember."

They walked all night. Dixie lost herself in the darkness and the choice ahead, until Christopher insisted she turn back. "Dawn is only a couple of hours away," he said as they stood on a ridge, watching two dormice courting. "We must go back."

"Race you."

They ran, leaping over stone walls, jumping streams and racing over the rough ground. They arrived at the back door, neck and neck. "You could have won," she said, turning to him as she stepped over the threshold.

"You dislike being my second. If I'd let you win, I'd have insulted you. Together and equal seemed best." If only they were! "We have eternity, Dixie. One day you'll be my equal in strength and speed."

But could she pay the price of eternity? She didn't want to know. Not yet. She took his hand and led him upstairs to the pitch-roofed bedroom and the four-poster bed. They made gentle, slow love until dawn overtook them, and she slipped into deep rest, nestled in his arms.

She woke to an evening of torrential rain that beat on the roof, poured down the windowpanes, and washed over the gutters. Not a night for strolling the moors. She understood now why old-time builders put in foot-thick walls.

A fire glowed in the stone fireplace in the old parlor. "Come sit by me," Christopher said. The dented cushions on the sofa and an open book showed how he'd spent the afternoon.

"It's a great night for reading, watching the fire and sipping hot chocolate with lots of marshmallows," she said. Except she had no need of the hot chocolate. Or the marshmallows.

"Roasted chestnuts come to mind for me." He settled back down on the sofa and patted the seat beside him. "Sit by me, let's imagine the scents and tastes of chestnuts and chocolate with marshmallows. I've smelled chocolate but never tasted it. What is it like?"

Never tasted chocolate? "You missed something. I love it! Loved it." She amended. She loved it and would never taste it again. "Have you really never eaten it?"

He shook his head. "It didn't arrive in London until the late 1650s. I'd been a vampire almost sixty years by then."

Dixie took the offered seat while she pondered the fact that she loved a man from pre-chocolate times. It made one pause. She spent a lot of time pausing these days.

"Pick something to read."

She had enough choices. Books filled every room but she knew what she wanted to read. Back upstairs, she pulled her aunts' last journals from her bag and settled back next to Christopher for a long night's read.

She hadn't appreciated reading at vampire speed. She got through it in a couple hours and half-wished she hadn't.

Blackmail, finagling and double-dealing aside, her great-aunts weren't ancestors to be proud of, but neither did they deserve the ends their journals implied.

What could she do? Quite a heap considering she could run as fast as a small car and, okay, bullets didn't bounce off her, but they wouldn't kill her, even in her fledgling state. Deliberately, she shielded her mind, tucked her nose back into the book and thought. Everything snagged back to Sebastian. She'd take care of him. She owed him one for Christopher, Stanley, and Vernon and in all probability her aunts and Lord knew what else. And now she had her chance.

True, she might end up another of his victims but what did she have to lose? Her days were numbered unless she decided plasma snacking was her style, and all of Christopher's assurances couldn't ease the instinctive disgust over feeding. It seemed right and fitting to settle the score before her final end. Sebastian believed her dead? Did she have news for him.

"A penny for them." Startled, she blinked at Christopher. "Your thoughts, a penny for them." With a smile like that, he could open her soul. She clamped her mind shut.

"I've been thinking, Christopher. I need some time alone." She ignored the shock on his face. "I want to go back to Orchard House for a while."

He looked like a drowning man robbed of a life jacket. "You'd leave me?"

The hurt in his eyes slashed into her heart and ripped her conscience into shreds. She missed not being able to take a deep breath. "Last night threw me for a loop. Discovering you have two weeks to choose between immortality or oblivion is . . . unsettling. I need a couple of days to sort things out."

He smiled as relief lit his face. "Two or three days?"

She felt like scum for lying. Well, not exactly lying. She'd told the truth. Just not all of it. "Yup." It shouldn't take that long. "Can I get a night train at York?"

"It won't work. You'll end up in London in broad daylight. I'll take you."

No, he wouldn't! She didn't want him anywhere near. "What about the police?"

"We drive at night. I'll drop you a few miles away. You run the last leg of the trip. Just make sure you're safe inside at least an hour before dawn." He ran his hand through his dark hair. "I'll wait at Tom's. When you need me, send me a mind message. I'll be there."

He bought it all. Even offered to help. Now she felt like something on the sole of a shoe. "I don't want you in any danger."

"If push comes to shove, we can both outrun the police." He glanced at his watch. "It's too late to start tonight. If we got held up in traffic, we'd never make it by sunrise. You could survive in the trunk with a bag of soil, but upstairs is better."

Upstairs was better. But the sofa came a close second. They tried them both. Slow and gentle on the sofa, then he carried her upstairs for a wild, crazed coupling that left her sated but tormented with conscience stabs. She felt worse the next evening.

"Here you are." He stopped at an exit of the M24, just north of Leatherhead. "Make for the station, then go out Randalls Road. You'll have a straight shot across country. Come into Bringham from the west, across the common."

"You sound as though you've done it a few times."

"I have." He grinned. "The first few times, there wasn't a railway."

She didn't have time to think about that. She had to hurry.

"Thanks for bringing me. Please be careful." If the police got him, what would she do?

"I'll be fine, Dixie. You hurry. I want you inside, at rest, long before dawn."

"I will be." She blew him a kiss and stepped out. Even at this hour, a steady stream of traffic surged both south and north. Bending her knees, she took one leap over all six lanes and took off running.

Christopher watched her disappear, drove through the deserted town and took the Guildford road. Dixie should be home in fifteen minutes. His drive took thirty. He parked in a gypsy clearing on the common. Hidden behind the high growth of summer, he had a better than even chance of going unnoticed a couple of days. And if push came to shove, he'd abandon the car. He had other hiding places.

"Dixie, I have to talk to you. About Stanley. And you. I know who tried to kill you. He killed my Stanley. Phone me. I'm still at Monica's." Ida's shaky voice crackled on the answering machine. How long had the message sat there?

Dixie had come to plan revenge and to think about her future, to decide if she even wanted one at the price. Ida's desperate appeal offered a chance at her first goal. Ida could help; she'd gladly forgo peace of mind for a little home-brewed justice. It was too late to see her now, dawn was coming. But once the sun set, she'd visit.

A shadowy smile half-welcomed Dixie. Monica, Stanley's widow, held the door wide open. What about the ban on entering human habitations? It worked. A force like steel blocked her entry. "Come on in." The block dissolved and Dixie passed into the small hall filled with bicycles and roller skates and a soccer ball squeezed between the newel post and the banister. From somewhere in the back of the house came the sound of TV and young male voices.

Ida sat beside the empty fireplace, a ball of yarn and a cylinder of gray knitting on her lap. The TV hummed in the background, the flickering white light bathing the room in a eerie glow. Ida looked years older than the day Dixie met her.

"I got your message, Ida."

"I left that days ago. Then I heard you'd gone home, left without seeing anyone. What happened?"

"I did plan on going home but something came up. I'm just back in Bringham for a very short time. You said there were things I needed to know?"

Ida nodded and stared. A toothpaste ad jingle intruded on the silence and Dixie noticed a strange, sweet smell. Potpourri?

"How about I fix us a cup of tea?" Monica suggested. "You and Mother could sit out back and talk."

Talk, yes. Tea, no. "Not for me."

"I want a drink. We're going to the Bell. Can't talk here with the telly." Ida stood up, her legs a little shaky but her voice determined.

They walked to the Bell. With great concentration, Dixie slowed her pace to Ida's walk. The fresh night air came welcome after the stuffiness of the Collins's house. But the Bell was another matter; the same sweet smell filled the main bar, not unpleasant, but cloying. Some new room freshener?

Ida let Dixie buy her a gin and tonic. For herself, she bought a glass of port. Good thing it wasn't the Barley Mow. Alf would have drawn her usual Guinness and wondered about her change in drinking habits.

"Cheers." Ida raised her glass.

"Why did you phone me, Ida?"

The old eyes came straight at her. "Let's make a deal."

Dixie's brain slowed to mortal pace. "What sort of a deal?"

"Information. I tell what I know and you promise me revenge."

"Why not settle for justice?" Lord, she sounded like Justin. But maybe she should.

"I don't care what it is as long as he suffers for killing Stanley. He murdered my son, left my grandsons orphaned and Monica a widow at twenty-eight. For that he should suffer. Long and hard."

"Who should?"

"Sebastian Caughleigh."

Dixie forced a dozen questions still. "You have proof?"

"I don't need it. He killed Stanley. He meant to get you."

Her suspicions had been dead-on, but why did he want her dead? Okay, he *was* a bit peeved she hadn't fallen for his charms, but murder was going a bit far. "You think Sebastian set the bomb?" Imagining Sebastian under a car wasn't easy.

"He paid for it to be done."

A little more believable. And the professional job failing, he'd gone for do-it-yourself. But again, why? "Why do I frighten him? Why does he want me dead?" An idea dawned. "My money? Something to do with my house and my money?"

"Not money." Ida shook her head. "Knowledge. For the coven."

"What coven?" At this rate she would be here all night. Why not? She wasn't sleeping until daybreak.

Ida drew herself up. Straight-backed, she took a deep breath. "An ancient coven that once boasted great herbalists—your aunts and others. If we had stayed faithful to the Old Religion . . ." She shook her head as if shaking off cobwebs and regrets.

"A coven of witches?"

"You don't believe in witches?"

"Yes, I do." Two weeks ago she hadn't believed in vampires and look what happened. "I just don't understand how the bomb in the car and my aunts all link up. Why me?"

"Lust. Lust for power. Sebastian hungers for power. That's why he joined the coven. For your aunts' knowledge." She paused. "*All* of it."

So that was it! The nasty files. With those, Sebastian could set himself up for life. "He won't get it."

"That's why he's trying to kill you." Barely above a whisper, Ida's words cut across the space between them. "He wants what you have and if he can't have it, he won't let you use it. He's dangerous. Mad, even. He fought your aunts for power but they died and hid their secrets. Then you came."

"When he couldn't prevent me from coming, he tried persuading me to leave."

Ida nodded. "You drove him crazy! Few people oppose him. Even fewer succeed. You did."

"About time someone did!"

A shadow of a smile glimmered on Ida's mouth. "He threw a wobbly over you. I'm not sure whether being foiled by a woman or bested by an American irked more."

"Nice to know I managed something. Let me get this straight, you think Sebastian had the bomb planted."

"I know. Emily told me."

"How did she know?"

Ida drained the gin. A mangled slice of lemon lay on the two melting ice cubes. "I need another."

"Tell me about Emily and Sebastian and the bomb, and I'll buy you a bottle."

"Emily is Sebastian's mistress. Has been for years. Thinks no one knows. She keeps all his secrets and toadies for him. But now, she's after his hide. Wanted me to go to the police with the information. I told her they'd laugh at me."

"And they won't at me? If you've no proof . . ."

"Listen!" Her bony hands clutched Dixie's. She almost drew back at the warmth. Was this how mortals felt to touch? "Sebastian wanted your aunts' papers. First you got in the way, then you started blackmailing Marlowe. That's when they decided to eliminate you."

"What made them think I was blackmailing Christopher?"

Scorn crossed Ida's dark eyes. "He paid you. Emily works for the bank."

The check for the books! And Sebastian thought it was hush money. "Handy place for Sebastian's toady to work."

Ida ignored that. "The bomb killed my Stanley instead of you. Sebastian told Emily he'd killed you up in Yorkshire. Insisted you were dead." Her old shoulders sagged. "You don't believe me."

"But I do. I believe every word."

"You'll go to the police?"

Probably not. "Maybe. One thing I don't understand: Why did Emily tell you this?"

"Emily caught Sebastian in flagrante delicto with his secretary."

Dixie couldn't help grinning at the image of immaculate Valerie tumbled on Sebastian's carpet. Why not? What's a little infidelity after murder? "How did my aunts fit in all this?"

"They were part of the coven and old in wisdom. They taught me. But when Sebastian joined, he wanted to use the black arts. He also wanted their papers shared among the coven. They disagreed—but they were old . . ."

"And easy to scare and hound to death?"

Ida's eyes darkened. "Don't waste too much sympathy on them. They'd driven a few to their deaths already. Little Jennie Waite drowned herself when they threatened to tell her husband the real father of her child, and old Doctor Miles overdosed on sleeping pills two nights after they invited him to tea. They were evil."

She wouldn't disagree. "Their mischief is over and I hope Sebastian's is, too."

Ida's face lit with hope. "You'll go to the police!"

"I'll take care of it." Soon. She needed fresh air. Her head ached from the stuffiness of the bar and her gums itched. Maybe the port hadn't been a good idea. Ida tapped her empty glass. Dixie took the hint.

Dixie came back with another gin and an unopened bottle. "I pay my debts."

Ida gaped. "What will Monica say when I come home with that?"

"Tell her a crazy American gave it to you."

James couldn't believe his eyes. He wasn't *that* drunk. Hell, he couldn't be drunk. He'd only had two scotches. And that's all he'd get, unless he conned someone else into buying. But sober, drunk or pie-eyed, he'd know that head of auburn hair anywhere. So much for Sebastian's assurance. Miss Dixie still walked and breathed.

Dear Uncle claimed Dixie's elimination. Did he have news for him. Better still, a chance to best Dear Uncle at his own game. He might not have cliffs in Surrey, but there were a lot of lonely lanes between the Bell and Orchard House. He drained his glass and pushed away from the bar, his fingers closing over the knife in his trouser pocket.

She was with someone, Ida Collins. The old bat! What he wouldn't give to know what they'd been yammering about.

Dixie followed Ida out into the evening. If she still breathed, she'd gulp the fresh, night air. After the closeness of the crowded bar, the evening breeze felt like spring water.

She left Ida at her gate and set off, at mortal pace, down the lane towards Bringham. She needed time and quiet to plan her next step. She couldn't just go to Inspector Jones with "an old lady I know thinks" or "Stanley's mother said . . ." What she really wanted was Sebastian Caughleigh's confession. But she'd always wanted the impossible.

Walking between hawthorn hedges, in and out of the shadows, Dixie thought back to the night she found Christopher in her yard. The night they saw lights in the book room and disturbed the intruder. The night he held her close among the shrubbery and she'd noticed his vampire scent and thought it aftershave. She wanted him. Close. But not yet. Not before she came to terms with her self, her past, eternity, and her need to drink blood.

She'd come back here for peace and contemplation and lunged back into turmoil. Should she just walk away as Justin advised? No! She wanted Christopher exonerated. She just wasn't sure how to do it. Might as well want world peace, the end of prejudice, and equal rights for all humanity while she was at it. Night scents bombarded her: honeysuckle in the hedges, turned earth, and cow pats in the fields. And sounds—rustling in the hedges, the hum of car engines on the main road to the east, the cry of a night bird.

Footsteps.

Dixie swiveled around to see the dark figure ten yards behind. Poised mid-step, he froze, moonlight glinting off his hand.

"Bitch!" he called and ran at her full tilt. The glint in his hand became a knife. As the blade arced towards her, she grabbed both his wrists, wrenching them up to steer the blade away from her face.

There was a sound like tinder snapping and a scream that echoed in the night. He fell back, his head smashing against the metaled road with a splat like falling bricks. Dixie straddled him, fear and anger rising in her gorge as she saw his face in the moonlight. James! Not Sebastian, but the next best thing—*"thing"* being the operative word.

He might bellow like a rutting elephant, but he looked more like a broken puppet against the dark road. "You broke my arms! Fuck you!"

"In your dreams, Jimbo!" Sweat rose in silver beads

across his forehead. He sneered. Or it could be a grimace of pain. "Beats what you had planned for me, right?"

His eyes flashed pale in the moonlight, pure venom animating his glare. "You couldn't guess what's planned. They'll get you in the end. Don't you understand?"

"The coven, I presume?"

"Start worrying." Something like venom rose with his words. "You'll not be so cocky then. You'll bleat like Marlowe did but they won't even need to stake you out."

Pure acid anger boiled inside. "You were there?"

"Sweet on him weren't you? Thought so. We took care of him. Did you a favor. He wasn't a nice English gentleman after all. Nasty bloodsucker, he was. We took care of him. Cooked him out in the morning sun."

Acid vaporized behind her eyes. Fury boiled at his boast. Her mouth ached. Her gums itched like crazy. She opened her mouth as if to breathe but yawned wide enough to swallow the world. He screamed, again and again, as if calling for heaven's succor. Terror lightened his eyes as he twitched away from her but her legs pinned him steady.

Unfamiliar instincts drove her. The terror in his eyes passed as in a dream. His blood pressure rose in a roar. His heartbeat pounded until it echoed in the night. He twisted and writhed, straining to evade her. Without thought or reason, she bent over and bit into the vein that stood out in his neck.

She drank. She supped. She gorged. Sweet warmth filled her mouth, triggered her taste buds and coursed down her throat. She savored the living taste, as her teeth gripped, ignoring his weakening moans. The taste, the scent, and the warmth intoxicated as his lifeblood became hers. She lost all track of time. A minute? Five? An hour? He resisted at first, but her hands held his shoulders firm and his struggles lessened until he collapsed. Sated, she lifted her mouth, drunk on the strength and richness she'd imbibed.

And then she recognized the scent she'd noticed at the Collins's and in the pub. The sweet, cloying smell, not unpleasant but unusual, and still unfamiliar to her, the scent of human blood.

She was kneeling in the middle of the lane, in the moonlight, with James Chadwick supine between her legs. She jumped up, looking both ways, half expecting a tractor or a midnight herd of cows. Nothing coming, at least not yet. Horror clutched her. What if she'd killed him? But no. She crouched down and noticed a weak pulse. She smiled. He'd live long enough to face justice.

If he didn't get run over first.

She gathered up his limp body as easily as she'd heft a bag of groceries and jumped over the hedge, dumping him on the ground. He groaned and she noticed, with some satisfaction, that he'd landed in a cow pat. He should feel quite at home.

She stepped back and stretched her arms.

The rush hit her. Energy, life, like a shot of adrenaline to the bloodstream. She could climb mountains, leap over rooftops or swing from the St. Michael's steeple. She settled for running home, vaulting gates, broad-jumping roads and speeding over fields, until she reached Orchard House and slipped through her own front door. And looked in the gilt-framed mirror and saw nothing but the faded striped wallpaper and the open sitting room door behind her.

She was vampire! She'd crossed the final line. Taken the last step she'd feared and dreaded and wanted.

She sat at the bottom of the stairs, knees drawn up to her chest, pondering Ida's information and wondering how on earth she'd prove it. And remembered the pleasure of feeding. Would she dare again? Yes! Yes! Yes! *That* thought both horrified and thrilled her.

She had the key to the whole nasty business at her fingertips. All she had to do was figure out how to deal with it.

Confront Sebastian? Intimidate James until he sang like a canary? Insist Ida and Emily go to the police?

She was alone, unsure and confused. "Christopher, I need your help," she said, closing her eyes and resting her forehead on her knees.

"Right, love, what do you need?"

He stood three feet away, smiling and eyes twinkling like the stars outside. She could have hit him. Lucky she hadn't dropped with shock to his feet. The look on his face suggested he'd enjoy that. "Where did you come from?"

He pulled a neatly folded linen handkerchief from his pants pocket. "Wipe your mouth."

"What?" Half understanding, she took the handkerchief and felt her stomach drop as she saw blood smeared on snowy linen.

"It's considered etiquette to wipe your mouth after feeding," he said, refolding the handkerchief and sitting beside her on the stairs. "Plus, leaving your mouth bloody tends to bother breathers. If they see blood-stained lips and fangs, they tend to think about wooden stakes and garlic." Vampire wit! Right. "You need to retract your canines, too."

"What?" Her tongue investigated. Her eyeteeth felt twice as long as usual. "How do I do that?"

"Just think them back."

It worked, on the second try. "I'm still not used to what my mind can do."

"Thirty years a mortal really limits your intellect."

That he wouldn't get away with. "You had twenty-nine."

He ignored that but reached out and tucked her hand over his. Their fingers twined. How she'd missed him, just this one day. "I thought you were coming back if you decided to join us. We were to feed together. I could have helped out. We have certain conventions."

"It happened."

His shoulder and arm stiffened. An eye hard and dark with worry met hers. "*What* happened?"

She told him, side by side on the threadbare carpet, starting with the red light flashing on her answering machine. He listened in silence and left Dixie wondering if she'd committed a score of vampire solecisms.

"Did you kill him?" he asked when she finished.

She shook her head. "He had a pulse when I left him."

"At least you thought to check." That irked. "Did you obliterate the memory?"

"What memory?"

He spoke slowly as if to a child, or a foreigner. "The memory of seeing you and being your evening tasty." He didn't wait for her answer. "You didn't."

"How could I if I didn't know I was supposed to?"

His hand tightened over hers. "That's why we should have fed together." He looked so worried. What else had she done wrong? This vampire life was all too new. "We'd better find him and anyone else who saw you."

"That means Ida, Monica, and the children. And everyone in the Bell."

"Just anyone who recognized you. We shouldn't need to worry about most of them." He squeezed her hand. "We'd better get going."

"But didn't I tell you? We have to do something about Sebastian."

"First things first. You don't want word spreading around the village that Dixie LePage is back and drinking blood. Around here, too many people believe in us. Come on." He stood up and offered his hand. She reached out and closed her palm over his.

*   *   *

"You pick your places, don't you?" James hadn't moved. "The whole damn field and you drop him in a country pancake."

"Like belongs with like."

"We don't need pettiness, Dixie. We have power. Just take the memory out and let's go." Great! How exactly was she supposed to "get it out?" "You just have to concentrate."

Dixie frowned at Kit. Would she ever get used to his reading her thoughts? "If it's so easy, why don't you do it?"

"Because, my love, he doesn't remember me tonight. Touch his forehead, concentrate on his thoughts until you find the one you need. Then filch it."

He made it sound like picking daisies. "Nothing is ever as easy as it sounds."

"It will be if you stop thinking like a mortal."

Would she ever? "Here goes," she whispered, half to herself, and knelt beside James, being careful to kneel on grass. Her fingers touched his brow. Was it a trick of the moonlight that left him white as sour milk?

"Concentrate," Kit urged.

She did, and almost screamed. She'd never imagined such thoughts. Touching dry ice with bare skin couldn't burn worse than delving into the murk of James Chadwick's mind.

"Easy," Christopher whispered, "you're going too deep. Float to the surface, to the recent memory and skim off the traces of you."

She did just that and stepped back, ducking as if to avoid a noxious cloud. Christopher's arm wrapped around her waist. She needed him. She hadn't realized vampires got the shakes.

"Got it?" he said. She managed to nod and then he ran with her, lifting her over the hedge, the lane and racing across the fields, only stopping when they reached the corner behind the Collins's house "Doing alright now?" he asked, his hand smoothing her hair.

"That was gross!"

"He is a rather nasty individual, I admit." His lips touched cool on her forehead where he'd brushed back her hair. "Not what I'd have suggested for your first time, but it's done now. These," he glanced up at the open windows in the darkened house, "will be so much easier. But be careful! Only remove the memory of you tonight. Human brains are easily scrambled—especially elderly ones. Don't take too much."

"You mean I could cause brain damage?" The cold horror of the thought grabbed her throat.

"Not all blackouts come from alcohol or drugs."

That was an encouraging thought to take with her! But despite, or maybe because of his warning, it was easy. Two minutes in the boys' room where they slept in bunks, surrounded by model airplanes and posters of Manchester United, then Monica, alone and lonely, stirring in the big, front bedroom, and Ida, sleeping on the rollaway in Monica's sewing room. Anger threatened to shatter Dixie's concentration as she stood on the landing. If she did nothing else, she'd incriminate the killers who had shattered this family's peace.

Outside, Christopher waited. Dear Christopher, her Christopher, how had she ever thought to be without him? "Done?"

"Yes. Now I need to take care of Sebastian." Righteous indignation fermented into a fervor for retribution.

"Soon."

"Now! He caused all this. He had that bomb put there. He harried my aunts to their death. He tried to kill you—James boasted about it—and that means he did kill Vernon. He can't get away with it."

"What do you think you can do?"

Disparaging wasn't the word for his tone. "I planned on asking for your help. We can control his mind, right? I saw Justin do it to Inspector Jones. You did it to James, that first evening in the pub. We'll use that and shock tactics. He thinks he killed you and believes I died. If we both appear, unannounced in his bedroom, he'll be surprised, to say the least. Then we exert mind control and get him to confess. We can do that can't we?"

He said nothing for a good minute. What was wrong? Had she misunderstood what she'd seen with Justin? "Won't it work? If I don't have the power to turn his mind, can't we call Justin to help?"

He shook his head. "Dixie, it's a good enough plan, except for one snag."

Only one? That should be easy enough to overcome.

"How do you propose we get *into* his house?"

"What?" She remembered the barrier that blocked her entry to the Collins's house before Monica offered the invitation to enter.

"You're one of us now, my love. We can't enter a breather's habitation without invitation, and do you think Caughleigh would let either of us over the threshold?"

Chapter Eighteen

"There has to be a way." They argued the point all the way back, and continued while sitting at the bottom of the curving staircase. Dixie wasn't stopping now. Not this close. She wrapped her hand around the banister until she noticed the old wood splintering. Releasing her grasp, she swore under her breath—to have all this strength and be stymied by a front door.

Christopher's hands closed over hers. "Why are you so set on revenge?"

"I don't want revenge. I want justice. For Stanley, his family, you, Vernon—even my old aunts. He shouldn't get away scott-free. We've got to think of something. Surely Justin can. . . ."

"Can what, dear lady?" Justin stood an arm's length from her, one immaculately polished shoe covering a pastel rose on the rug.

"I know I'll get used to this. One day."

"You're used to it already. You're one of us now. We can't call you fledgling any longer." How the hell did he know?

What she'd give to wipe the satisfaction off both their faces. "It's written all over you, Dixie. You can't hide it from us."

She frowned at Christopher. "What does he mean?"

"Your skin has a bloom from fresh feeding. Your body is completing the last stage of transformation. You'll increase in strength, and soon your skin will have a vampire scent."

She didn't want to think of body scents right now. Change of tack needed. "Where's the third musketeer?" She shot at Christopher what she hoped was a glare.

"Outside." Justin turned his head to the front door. "He can't come in without your invitation. One of the immutable laws of our nature."

And the one that was causing an impasse in her plans. Maybe Tom had an inspiration. "Let him in."

Justin opened the door. Tom stepped into the hall and looked at the three of them. "I told Justin this was a bad idea," he said. "I warned him you wouldn't want a committee."

"Bad idea or not, you're in it too. Might as well join the party."

"She fed," Tom said to Christopher. "I didn't realize . . ."

"She fed before I arrived."

"Alone? But surely—"

"Never mind." She snapped but forgave herself. Stress wasn't the word for the last few hours. "Since you're all here and obviously concerned about my welfare, you can help me."

"She's got a crazy idea about revenge."

"No, I haven't, Christopher. I want . . ." She looked at the trio of skeptical faces. She had her work cut out before she even left home. "Come into the kitchen and I'll explain what I want."

They sat round the old pine table as Dixie told them everything. From the beginning, when Sebastian stalled her possession of the house, right through to her discoveries of the files, and the contents of her great-aunts' journals. "He killed, or *had* Vernon, the bartender, killed. He tried to kill Christopher. He hounded both my aunts to their deaths to get their papers. He tried to kill me, twice. And as far as he's concerned, he succeeded the second time. The bomb meant for me got poor Stanley, and if that isn't enough, he planned on taking over my aunts' blackmailing business. And I'm not even starting on the nasty things he probably got into with the coven."

"You don't want to," whispered Christopher.

She took his word for it. She had quite enough on her plate as it was. "Murderers shouldn't get away with it."

"We don't go after revenge," Justin said. "We tend to out-live our enemies."

"I explained all that to her," Christopher said. "She wouldn't listen."

"I listened. I'm not after revenge either. I just want him to confess to the police. The courts can take over then." That got their attention. She suppressed the urge to smile. This was serious. Deadly serious.

"Go on," Justin said.

She looked at Tom. He nodded. Christopher smiled. She plowed on. "Justin, that afternoon in the police station you got Inspector Jones to agree to let me leave. That wasn't his first choice, but the idea had been in his mind, right?" Justin nodded. "So, if I get Sebastian to admit his guilt, one of you can fix the idea in his mind to confess."

"You'll never get him to do it." Christopher shook his head. Thanks a lot, Kit Marlowe! She could have used a vote of confidence. She'd get it before she was through.

"But if I did?"

"If you did, his mind could be controlled and he could be made to confess," Christopher said.

"I'll get him to confess. You help me out on the mind con-trol, and the law will do the rest."

Justin flexed his fingers. "Just like that. He'll confess?"

"I'll scare it out of him. According to Ida, he thinks I'm dead. I'm a ghost back for retribution. As superstitious as he is, he's bound to believe. Christopher could come in on it too. Enter second ghost."

"That was Will Shakespeare's ploy. I never went in for ghosts."

"Cut it out, Kit. She's got a point," Tom said. "But it won't swing. You can only move around at night and he'll never let you into his house."

"*He* doesn't have to."

"Dixie . . ." Christopher began.

"All I need is *someone* to let me into the house. Like Justin let Tom in."

"And who's going to let you into Caughleigh's house at," Justin glanced a his watch, "one o'clock in the morning?"

She grinned. Ida had given her that key. "That's easy—Emily."

"Who's Emily?" Tom and Justin spoke in chorus.

Christopher beat Dixie to the answer. "She's Caughleigh's inamorata. But she'll never do it, Dixie. She's besotted with him."

"Not anymore she isn't. She's the one who told Ida about the bomb set in my car. Both of them want his blood and will do anything to get it. They'd go to the police but are scared of implicating themselves. Emily will let me in and offer to knot the noose."

"Why this sudden change? The woman did everything but lick his feet," Christopher asked.

"She found Sebastian celebrating my supposed demise with Miss Valerie Fortune over the desk."

"A woman scorned," Tom whispered.

"Not just that." They might as well hear it all. Now was her chance to find out if vampires shocked easily. "She knew he had other women—that she learned to live with. What upset her was seeing Sebastian with his head between Valerie's legs. He'd always refused to do that for her."

"Ida told you this?" Christopher was shocked.

So was Tom. "Women talk about this sort of thing?"

"Yes, Tom. When we're not exchanging knitting patterns."

"Enough." Justin had a thousand year start on them. "You think this woman, this Emily, will invite you into his house?"

"Watch me make it happen." Dixie picked up the phone from the hall table. "Emily, it's Dixie. . . . I know it's late. . . . I'm not, but he *tried* to kill me. . . . I have to talk to you. . . . I'm on my way over."

"That easy?" Admiration bloomed from Christopher's eyes.

"Stage one, I'm going over to her house. Stage two is at Sebastian's. If I get him to confess, y'all back me up with the mind control?"

"Dixie, you have him confessing, I'll summon the entire colony."

"You're all I need, Christopher."

She had to run. Emily was waiting and if she stood here much longer looking at Christopher, she'd drag him upstairs. If fact, she had to get something upstairs. Now. She shoved two pairs of panty hose in her jeans pockets and switched her white tee shirt for a dark one.

"Wise woman," Tom said as she came back downstairs. "That white shirt stood out like a truce flag."

"Don't need it. This is war."

"Let us come with you. "

"Not yet. Please wait here. Emily expects me. She'll probably have a cow if she sees three of you. Especially since she believes Christopher is dead. One resurrection a night is enough for any woman."

Emily opened the door in a long flannel gown and robe, looking like an illustration from Beatrix Potter. "He said you were dead."

"He lied!"

Emily closed the door behind her. "He wants you dead. He's scared of you."

"With good reason. I get snippy when people try to push me off cliffs and put bombs in my car."

Emily sank down on the deacon's bench in the hall. "That was terrible, killing Stanley like that. Poor Ida. He was her only child. I told her we had to do something. He shouldn't be allowed to get away with it."

"He won't."

"What are you going to do?" Nervous hands fiddled with the ribbon ties at her neck. Sneaky eyes wanted to know more.

"The less you know, the less you need to worry about. I just need to get in there without breaking in. You can do that for me."

"How?" she almost whined. "He never lets me in his house. We always meet at his office."

Another reason to take care of Sebastian Caughleigh. "You want revenge for Valerie, right? Get me in there. Tell him something."

"What?"

"Tell him . . ." What would get his interest without fail? "Tell him you think you saw Christopher Marlowe in the village this evening and you want to know what to do."

"Tssk," she hissed with scorn. "That won't work. The police are still looking for him, but Sebastian knows he's dead."

"Oh, really?"

Emily looked down at her hands. Her index finger twisted in and out of a buttonhole. "You may not believe this, being American and modern and all. But Christopher was vermin, a vampire. We destroyed him for the good of the village."

Choking Emily wouldn't help her to get to Sebastian—besides, that was old toast. "Tell him you saw me. No, that might warn him. Tell him the police just came by, asking a lot of questions about his movements last week." That should worry him nicely.

"I don't know. Maybe in the morning. If I call him now, he won't be happy."

Let him start unhappy. By the time she finished, he'd miserable. "Remember Valerie on his desk."

"It was her desk," Emily hissed and picked up the receiver.

Emily was wasted in the bank. She should have been on the stage. She sounded suitably panic-stricken and wound up, but maybe the latter was anger. "I've got to come. . . . Now. . . . No, I'm *not* staying the night and wouldn't if you asked . . . . I just need to know what to do if the police come again. . . . Yes, I know it's after midnight. That didn't stop them." And it wouldn't stop her. Not now. She slammed the receiver down and grinned at Dixie. "That good enough for you?"

Good enough for an Oscar, or a Sebastian.

"I should never have let her go. Why didn't one of us stop her?" Christopher paced hard and long enough to wear a faint trail in the rug.

Justin looked up from peering at the marble clock on the mantelpiece. "French, this, a very nice piece. My friend, stop fretting. She wouldn't have been stopped, for one thing, and for another, she's strong enough to do this. Let her win her spurs."

Dixie didn't need spurs, she needed to be safe. "She shouldn't have gone. Why the hell couldn't she just stay in Yorkshire until things cooled down?" Because that wasn't her way. Because his woman made her own justice and drove him crazy with worry while she did it.

"The only way you'll keep her is by letting her go. She's like quicksilver, Kit. Grasp her and she'll trickle out your fingers. Cup her in your hand and you'll hold her. I know." He should. Gwyltha, Annette during the Civil War, the governess in Brussels in 1815, Justin had lost them all.

Christopher shuddered. If he lost Dixie . . .

"She's just crossed the village green." Tom stood up and looked out the window over the night garden. "She'll be back any minute."

It took three and she was there, cheeks rosy from racing through the night air and eyes bright with excitement. "All systems go!" She almost bounced. "We must hurry. She thinks I'm driving. I told her I'd wait ten minutes. She's opening the back door for me."

"And then?" Christopher wished he'd beaten Justin to the question.

"And then, I get his confession and call you three in. If need be, I'll call in Christopher first. The scare might do Sebastian good."

"Give him a heart attack, more like. Remember, dead men can't confess."

"He'll be alive, don't you worry." She paused as if beset by sudden doubt. "You'll be with me, right?"

"Forever, my love," Kit said. Not stopping himself, he kissed her full on her gorgeous lips.

Her eyes widened to emerald orbs. She swallowed, hard, as if smoothing a lump in her throat. She had to be nervous. Lord, he was, and she was the one going in alone. He shouldn't let her. No, he should. Justin was right. This was her chance to prove herself. If he loved her, he had to bite his tongue, clench his fists and let her go ahead. "I'm right behind you. Just lead the way and the rest of us will follow."

* * *

The door opened. "You there, Dixie?" Emily's heart raced with fear. Even her skin smelled scared. Why not? She *was* in the same house as a multiple murderer.

"Here."

"Come on in, I can't stand here all night. He thinks I'm in the loo."

That's all it took. A simple invitation and a step over the threshold. If only the rest went as smoothly. "Leave, Emily. Go."

She shook her head. "No. I'm staying to see him get his comeuppance."

And three seconds ago she'd thought it was going well. She grasped Emily's shoulder. "Go, Emily." She felt the other woman's will waver, her resistance fade.

"Alright."

Power like this was scary. As Emily stepped out the door, Dixie reached out to her mind and filched the memory of the past half hour. A dazed Emily tottered down the path. Dixie trusted the others to see that she got in the car safely.

It took a moment to get her bearings. Three closed doors led off the front hall. Where was he? She paused a moment, and knew. She smelled human blood behind the nearest door. He sat with his back to her, wearing a dark green dressing gown and reclining in his desk chair like an emperor on a swivel throne. "You took your time." He didn't even turn his head. "Come on, on your knees, Emily."

"Hello, Sebastian."

He turned. The bruises had faded but livid scars criss-crossed his face and neck. He gaped and with great effort hissed out the single syllable, "You!"

"Me," agreed Dixie and smiled, just to get his dander up. Faster than he could reply, she grabbed his shoulders. "Please don't get up."

He winced. "What the hell do you want? And how . . . ?" He paled to the color of sour milk. "You should be dead. The damn nurse said you were."

"That's socialized medicine for you."

His eyes blinked, fast, as if trying to figure it all out. "You fell. I saw you drop." She bet he'd watched, gloating. She shifted his shoulders, letting the chair turn him, and grabbed his hands behind his back. "What in the name of blazes?"

"Just getting you settled." She had a pair of panty hose twined through the chair slats and twisted around his wrists before he figured out what was happening. "That'll do nicely."

He made a few nasty comments about her qualities as a woman. "I'm a client. You shouldn't talk to me like that. I pay your bills."

"You? Pay? You've cost me a small fortune."

"I'd like to talk about that."

He didn't talk, but his eyes widened as she ripped the other pair of panty hose in half. He kicked and twisted as she bound each leg to the chair, speaking unkindly about her father.

"Now that you're not going anywhere, we can cut to the chase." A portable tape recorder on his desk caught her eyes, but she realized she didn't need it and drew up an armchair opposite him.

"I like Bringham. Love my house, and I've had a really great time finding out about my ancestors. Did you know they kept journals?"

"Journals?" he snapped. "They won't stand up in court."

She ignored him. "Quite detailed ones. And records. File drawers full. Gran's sisters were nasty old ladies. Crime paid for them and you. Your file is a couple of inches thick."

"Maundering and imaginings of a pair of senile old ladies." He gave her a glare.

She smirked, remembering how kids used to drive her

crazy with an inane smile. "Uh-uh." She shook her head. "They've got a twenty-five-year dossier on you, starting with buying exam papers in school and photography commissions for my aunts. They taught you a lot, and you repaid them by killing them—and a few others, including me." Let him take the hint.

He missed it. "You've got nothing. Your aunts died of old age. The bomb came from a random terrorist act. The police are still looking for Marlowe for Vernon's death and you can't prove I was in Yorkshire."

"Maybe I won't have to." That time she grinned. "Let's start with my aunts. Faith fell downstairs, just after you'd spent the evening there." Eyes as cold as obsidian stared through her. She went on. "And Hope, the ditsy one, something scared her enough to run out of the house in the middle of a February night. Noises in the chimney? Rocks thrown against the house? Lights that flashed on and off?"

Those eyes now stared from a face like putty. "What if I did kill the old bats? You can't prove anything."

"No problem." She reached over for the desk lamp. "Now we get to Vernon." She flicked the lamp switch on and off.

"Trying the searchlight torture? Halogen lights to the retina?"

"Not that." She noticed his feet, bound to the chair legs, didn't touch the floor. Better fix that. "Must get you nicely settled. Can't have you uncomfortable." She lowered the seat three notches, until his knees bent slightly, his feet flat against the floor, and picked up the lamp and unscrewed the bulb. "All set. Now, first tell me all about the bomb in my car."

"You'll have to try harder than that."

"Okay."

His scream echoed long after she took the empty socket off his finger. His eyes bulged and he babbled a string of curses as his breathing settled. He gasped for breath between

profanities. "You can't prove anything. And if you're record-
ing this, it was made illegally, under duress. I can take legal
action against you for this."

"My car, Stanley," she repeated and moved the lamp a
half inch from his finger.

"James arranged it and you'll never prove I had anything
to do with it."

Yeah, right. Her heart might not beat, but her stomach
still clenched in horror at his callous complacency. No matter. She had to get answers. "Why?"

"What?" He actually looked perplexed.

"Why kill me? What had I ever done to you—other than
turn you down?" His eyes flashed dark, like smoldering vol-
canic rock. He spat at her. The sputum hit cold on her arm.
"Tell me or I'll need to use the lamp again—on a more sensitive protuberance."

The sheen on his forehead turned to beads of sweat. He
wrenched uselessly against his bonds. Brits made good
panty hose. "You're in the way and still are. Think you'll get
away with this little game? I have the law on my side and
forces more powerful than you can imagine. The only creature that could help you against me is dead. Frizzled up."

Time to contradict *that* later. "So you wanted my aunts'
papers, their recipe books, and negatives and all that nasty
stuff. Too bad, Sebastian, I burned it all."

"Fool," he hissed.

She watched his snarling mouth and blazing eyes and realized she was sharing the room with a madman. Thank
heavens the others were close. "Now, Vernon." She made a
point of smiling. Just to irritate him more.

"You're really worried about a crippled half-wit?"

Dixie moved the lamp towards his crotch. Her other hand
went towards his belt buckle.

Sebastian spat at her but he talked. "James had breakfast
with him and slipped something in his coffee. The rest was

easy." He looked up at her; even now a sneer came easily to him. "We tied him up with gauze bandages, so as not to leave marks on the skin, and left him on Marlowe's bed. We had a timed incendiary device in the house. It took care of itself."

Easy for whom? She shuddered, thinking about Vernon lying for hours in Christopher's house, until finally burning to death.

"Getting sentimental?" He smiled on one side of his face. "Marlowe was dead by then. He burned too, you know?"

"Of course Christopher is dead." They stared at each other in the silent room. "Christopher is dead," she repeated and forgave herself a gloating smirk, "and so am I."

He gulped as if swallowing a toad. Whole. His eyes popped like a Pekingese. He sucked in air so hard, his gut clenched. The sheen of sweat glistening on his forehead trickled down his cheeks. Dixie smiled sweetly at him and walked across the room and threw up the wide sash. "Come in," she said and stood aside as three irate vampires stepped onto the Aubusson rug.

Sebastian now looked as if he had an alligator jammed in his innards. Justin and Tom stayed by the window, out of Sebastian's line of vision. Christopher didn't. Swinging a fine Sheraton chair in one hand, he planted it inches from Sebastian's knees and then straddled the seat, resting his forearms on the curved satinwood back. He could have reached out his laced fingers and touched Sebastian's face. Dixie sensed he made a conscious effort not to.

"Evening, Caughleigh. Or should I say good morning?" A glimmer of a wry smile fluttered on Christopher's lips. "Not exactly good for you either way, is it? Time to settle accounts."

"Monster! Fiend!" The words hissed out like spent bullets.

And had as much effect. "Too late, Caughleigh. It's my

turn." Under Christopher's acid gaze, Sebastian wilted like a jellyfish in the sun. "No time to waste. You have a job to do. You're going to call our friend, Inspector Jones, and tell him the truth."

A mocking laugh strangled halfway up Sebastian's throat. He shook his head, turning away from Christopher's implacable eyes and mewling from between quivering lips.

Sebastian jerked as if shocked again, sweat trickling down his face as Dixie joined, by instinct, in a bombardment to twist Sebastian's will.

"You'll tell him the truth," Christopher said. No demand, not even a question, just a statement of fact.

Sebastian sagged, his slack face matching the droop of his shoulders. "I'll tell him the truth."

"Grab the phone, Dixie. There's a love. I think the Inspector will gladly lose a bit of sleep to hear what Caughleigh has to say."

She grabbed the phone and dialed 9-9-9. "This isn't an emergency," she said, "but I do have to speak to Inspector Jones right way, about the murder and arson in Bringham." She stayed on the line as requested and soon heard the *brrr-brrr* tone at the other end. She crossed over to Sebastian and obligingly held the receiver to his ear.

"What is it?"

Secure under vampire sway, Sebastian never faltered. "Inspector, this is Sebastian Caughleigh. I apologize for disturbing you, but I have some information for you about the recent events here in Bringham. I've been quite involved."

Jones's interest vibrated down the phone. "I'll be over with a sergeant and a squad car."

"No. I'd prefer to meet you at the station."

"I'll be there in twenty minutes." The line went dead and Sebastian stared at the phone as if dazed.

Christopher broke the bonds round Sebastian's ankles and wrists. "Hit the road, Caughleigh. Wouldn't do to keep the good inspector waiting. Grab your keys and go." He pulled Sebastian to his feet and shoved him towards the door.

Pausing only to grab his keys from the desk drawer, Sebastian walked out of the room and across the hall to where his car waited by the front door. As he drove off, Dixie noticed a dark shape on the trunk and realized only three of them stood on the gravel drive.

"Tom's going to keep Caughleigh safe," Christopher replied to her unspoken question. "Wouldn't do to have him hit by a lorry. Not on the way there."

"Shouldn't we lock up the house?" Dixie was only too aware of the open door behind her.

"Just a minute." Justin disappeared into the house and re-turned in an instant with a handful of tattered panty hose. "Wouldn't do to leave this for the law," he said. "Come. He'll be there before us if we dawdle much longer."

"Hold my hand, love," Christopher said. "You have to concentrate."

"What on?"

"Flying."

"Ready to learn, young one?" Justin asked.

She'd progressed beyond fledgling—that was something. "Anywhere in particular?"

"The police station," Christopher replied.

Their old strength flowed through her. Stretching her neck, she looked up at the moon between the trees. "Focus your mind. Think with us." Whether Christopher spoke, or Justin, or both, she never quite figured out. One minute she had two feet squarely on the crunching gravel and the next . . .

She felt wind in her hair, air under her feet and the cool of night rushing past her as she shot through the darkness to-ward Leatherhead. They'd dropped hands. She sliced the air like a missile, just dimly aware of a dark shape on each side of her. They passed the church steeple below them to the left and dark shapes of village buildings on the ground. Open fields, lanes of houses, and the watercress beds by the river. Passing over the train station, Justin and Christopher descended and she followed just a beat behind them. The tiled roof of the police station came towards them as they slowed, circled and alit on the ridge.

She still had hands. And legs. And a face. Her hair had to be a mess. No point in looking in a mirror to see what it looked like. Come to that, how was she going to get her hair done?

"Dixie!" Christopher's call brought her back to the present. Just in time to see Justin disappearing headfirst off the roof.

Toes on the gutter, Dixie crouched beside Christopher as Justin climbed down the building and hoped she wasn't expected to follow. Playing around in the middle of the moors was one thing, but courting detection on the side of a police station was another. Justin crawled sideways, then disappeared around the corner of the building to reappear ten minutes later on the other side. He was stopping at each window. Listening.

He climbed back up and perched beside them on the edge of the roof. "Not here yet, but expected. Jones called in from his car a little while ago." He glanced at Dixie. "Get her safe. I'll let you know what happens."

"I'm not going anywhere. I want to be in on the kill. I got him to confess." She folded her arms on her chest and glared.

She might have broken the will of a venal solicitor. She couldn't intimidate a seventeen-hundred-year-old vampire. He just curled one side of his mouth. "Dawn comes in less than an hour."

"So what? How long did it take us to fly here? Five minutes? Ten?"

Christopher's arm eased around her shoulders. "You can't

risk staying there. What if the police get a search warrant because of your aunts? You can't have them finding you resting."

She wanted to push the pair of them off the roof for being so darn right. "I can't get back to Yorkshire. Not in an hour, even if I fly."

"We'll stay at Tom's."

"How come I get the feeling you cooked this up between you?"

"Why not?" Justin said. "We had to do something to take our minds off things will you were threatening to emasculate Caughleigh with a desk lamp. I'll listen to every word that's said. If he prevaricates, Tom and I have enough will to redirect him."

Christopher stood up and took her hand. "Come on, Dixie."

They launched together, streaking through the night sky. The countryside gave way to suburbs with straight lines of street lamps, then closely packed houses and thousands of car lights that crawled into central London. The night air burned her cheeks and hands, and the wind against her breasts made her thankful she wore blue jeans and not a dress. On they flew, over the slow, sluggish river, skimming the fairy-tale lights of Albert Bridge and along the Embankment.

Now they flew lower, just above the rooftops. Her shoulders ached from the air pressure and her eyes stung. She dropped lower, barely missing chimney pots and TV antennas. Christopher grabbed her arm. "Aim for the park."

The dark, unlit mass of Hyde Park loomed ahead like a massive black island in the sea of light. She dipped and sank, fighting to stay aloft as her body shook and her legs dropped below her waist. Treetops rushed up to meet her, she smelled some night perfume from the flowerbeds, then swished by a painted bench as the mown grass came up to meet her. Christopher landed a split second before her and caught her before she smashed into the ground.

She felt his vampire arms around her. "What happened?" She could barely think through her dizziness. "It's not light yet."

"You're used up. That session with Caughleigh took more than we realized. I'll carry you the rest of the way."

She sank against this broad chest and rested her head on his shoulder. Lost in the comfort of his arms, she heard engine noise and smelled traffic fumes as if on the fringes of a dream as he ran with her, jumping over locked gates and leaping over the six lanes of Park Lane. On Christopher ran, up a few steps, and then they were inside Tom's house, away from the noise and the bustle. A gray fog enveloped her. "Hang on love. We'll get you upstairs and you can rest until night."

She joggled against him as he climbed the stairs to the softness of a cool pillow under her head, the crackle of earth in plastic, and freshly ironed sheets drawn up to her chin. Cool lips pressed her forehead as sleep closed over her.

Chapter Nineteen

Dixie woke to night, the hum of traffic, cool air wafting through the open window, and the sure knowledge that Christopher waited downstairs. A rustle got her attention as she swung her legs to the floor and she picked up the evening paper. "New Developments in Surrey Arson Death." Some headline! But as she scanned the page, her excitement plummeted in seconds. Apart from the coy statement that a man was "helping the police with their enquiries," the story just rehashed the old details, except for mentioning possible "further victims."

"You're disappointed," Christopher said a little while later as she walked into Tom's study to find the three of them seated by the open French windows.

How could she stay angry with her love standing beside her and the scent of night stocks filling the room? "I wanted him hung, drawn and quartered, or at the very least an hour or so on the rack."

"Don't wish that on anyone," Tom said.

Who could ignore the spasm of pain that twisted his face

as he looked out into the dark and the past? "Sorry, Tom. I suppose what I want is swift, precise justice."

"I think we have it," Justin said. "It's just a matter of waiting."

She had to adjust her notions of time. No point in giving into impatience when one faced eternity. She sat down in the empty seat when she realized they were all standing, and would as long as she did. "I'll wait for the mills of justice to grind him down."

The ten o'clock news lifted her spirits, with news of Sebastian's arrest. "Let's celebrate," Christopher said. "I promised you we'd climb the dome of St. Paul's."

They soared over the stuccoed mansions of Mayfair, the crowded West End and the silent streets of the city to alight on the rim at the bottom of the dome.

Dixie's throat tightened as she stared up at the vast curve of the dome. "We should have brought ropes and climbing gear."

"No need."

"This isn't Boggles' Roost."

"And you are no longer a fledgling." True! She'd bested James and broken Sebastian, and drunk blood from a mortal, and the man she loved offered her a climb of St. Paul's dome as entertainment after a rough twenty-four hours. "Use your knees and elbows for purchase. Press into the curve and hold on. Take your time and if you slip, fly."

Following his lead, she spread her arms and legs, pressed her hips into the lead casing and scaled the dome. It wasn't climbing stairs. If flying yesterday hadn't impressed on her the extent of her newfound strength, this did. The vast size of the dome surpassed her imagination. The quiet so high above the streets with nothing but sky overhead seemed uncanny, like a strange, small planet in a lonely universe. Up she went, just paces behind Christopher, until they stood on the peak beside the great gilded cross that crowned the lantern atop the cupola. She looked up at the crosspiece way above their heads.

"Want to climb up there?" Christopher asked.

"Why not?"

He let her lead until they sat on either side of the great crosspiece, three hundred and sixty plus feet above the ground. Balanced up here against the stars, the air clear and free from the traffic fumes below and her love beside her, Dixie was halfway to heaven. When they got home, she knew he'd take her the rest of the way.

"Soon," he promised. "First you need to feed."

She never imagined a vampire's mouth went dry with fear. "I thought you said only every week or two." She figured on at least a week to get used to the idea. She hadn't made her initial decision in the calm reasoned way she'd envisioned. She needed time to accustom herself to the idea, let alone the actual doing.

"Normally, yes."

"Normally?" What in heaven's name was normal for a vampire?

"You need to learn the right way. You can't go around overpowering mortals by force. That sort of thing gives us a bad name." That rebuke stung, even if his eye gleamed softer than his words.

"Look here, I didn't ask to be a vampire. It happened. It's something I'm trying to get used to."

"*I'm* still getting used to it. Maybe together it'll be easier." He mind-touched her cheek and lips a second before he reached over and kissed her. Anger, irritation, peevishness all evaporated under the caress of his lips and the soft touch of his tongue.

"You've been here lots of times." She wanted to ask whom else he'd taken up Wren's dome.

He nodded, his faced turned away towards the shiny black river. "I was here the night after they set this cross. I've come here often, but always alone. There's peace up here above the crowds and the chaos. That's why I brought you here."

"To find peace?"

"To help you realize what you are."

If her heart still beat, his quiet words would have caused cardiac arrest. What she was. The who and the what jangled together. Dixie LePage, school librarian, media specialist, daughter of the late Mr. and Mrs. Robert LePage, and vampire. How would that look in her high school reunion credits? As if it mattered! She'd just climbed the dome of St. Paul's, she could fly, and she was loved by Christopher Marlowe.

She'd skip the reunion.

"I've got eternity to figure that out, and if I get messed up, I'm sure you or Tom and Justin will straighten me out."

Christopher's eyes glowed translucent. His mind touched her throat, a soft, feathery caress that drifted over her shoulders and down her arms. "Come." This time when he spoke, his voice was husky with need. "You need to feed."

"Show me how." She'd said it. Agreed. Committed herself to him and his life forever.

He looked back over the river. "See there?" She nodded. "We'll fly to the top walk of Tower Bridge and then across the river."

They hit ground just beyond Blackfriars Bridge and his mind met hers. "No talking. Come with me and watch."

She walked beside him, holding hands, down a couple of side streets—narrow streets that resembled the set of a World War II movie. Christopher's presence reassured, until it struck her that she could handle anyone who lurked in the dark alleyways. Anything more removed from Tom's elegant house, she couldn't imagine, and they were just a bus ride away. Christopher stopped, dropped her hand and then took a couple of steps forward, his arm held stiff and his hand palm down.

Dixie waited. He didn't need to signal, speak or think to her. Two huddled shapes filled a dark doorway. She swallowed hard, fighting the tangle of emotions at the misery of homelessness and the prospect of her part in the next few minutes.

Christopher stood over the two unmoving sleepers, reached over each human heap for a second and beckoned her over. She stepped off the curb and was halfway across the street before she realized she hadn't looked either right or left.

She stood close enough to feel Christopher's thigh against her calf. He glanced up, and signaled for her to kneel beside him. "Watch." The message came clear, just as she realized these were old women.

"Christopher." She felt the panic rise as she thought her doubts to him.

"Trust me, Dixie, we won't harm them. I've put a glamour on them. They won't wake for several minutes." With a strange tenderness, he slipped his arm under the old shoulders, lifting her just enough to let her head fall back, exposing her neck. As he bit and drank, the tired mouth smiled. He set the woman back down after drinking only a minute or so, then looked over his shoulder. "You see? Just a little. No gorging."

Seeing the contented smile on the lined face and remembering the panic-stricken, wide-open eyes on James, Dixie understood. Following Christopher's example, she reached for the second woman.

Dixie counted sixty seconds, the thrill came swift and wild, and she drew away, satisfied and content. How right he'd been. She felt every bit as nourished as from her hideous gluttony over James. She settled the old woman back as comfortably as could be on cracked cement.

"Here, wipe your mouth." She took the linen handkerchief he offered. When she handed it back, he pushed a roll of bills in her hand. "Tuck it in a pocket somewhere. It'll feed her for a week or two." The notes rustled as Dixie tucked them into the pocket of the shapeless coat.

They took the tube back to Bond Street Station at Dixie's insistence. "I've been here two months and never ridden it. It's something I've dreamed about." It was also a vain attempt to feel mortal for a short time. It didn't work. An invisible barrier separated her from the theatergoers and teenagers out on the town.

The walk down Duke Street and across the Square brought her back to the familiar world of South Audley Street and the black front door flanked by bay trees and sporting a polished lion doorknocker. She hadn't expected the reception in the living room with the dark velvet curtains and the long windows overlooking the street.

Tom poured four glasses from his last bottle of pre-phylloxera. With one arm on her shoulders, Christopher raised the Bohemian crystal glass that had toasted the success of Wellington's army, and proposed her health before leading her to the bedroom overlooking the garden.

Later, as they lay in a tangle of warm limbs and crumpled sheets, Dixie sensed the coming dawn. She nestled in the crook of Christopher's arm, her cheek pressed against the four-hundred-year-old muscles of his chest, and let the stillness of rest overtake her. She was safe with her man, her vampire lover and her future, a very long future, lay ahead like a great adventure.

Four weeks later her nice, safe future cracked apart.

Back at Tom's after three weeks in Yorkshire, Dixie woke one evening and pulled on the black jeans she'd started to wear despite Christopher's teasing. Okay, so he liked linen pants and silk shirts; she'd been raised on comfort and blue jeans. Now that she wasn't getting up each morning for school she'd make the most of life without panty hose.

She ran her fingers through the short haircut Toni had given her one evening. She'd been right, it was easy to wear, could be kept neat without a mirror, would never now need trimming, and wouldn't mess up while flying. Not that Dixie had flown since her ascent of St. Paul's. "Now you know you can, you don't need to," Christopher had said, "unless there's urgency." So she'd settled for riding beside him in his black Mercedes.

But tonight she'd barely zipped her jeans when the door opened. Even before she turned to smile at Christopher, her shoulders and spine stiffened as she sensed the anxiety that hung over him like a fog. "What's wrong?"

"We've got a bit of a problem."

She'd been in England long enough to know that probably meant the terrorists had bombed Grosvenor Square. "What happened?" He crossed the room in a moment. He held her hands, then grabbed her tight, holding her against him as his lips brushed her hair, her forehead and her eyes before meeting hers in a kiss that both thrilled and scared her. Scared her because she'd never sensed such desperation or panic seething in his mind. "What is it?"

He ignored her question, looking down at her with his eye so brilliant and a face so taut that his panic became hers. "Whatever happens, I want you with me. Know that. If you can't face it, I'll understand. I love you, Dixie. You're mine."

Talk about mixed assurances. "How about speaking English so I can understand?"

"Come downstairs."

Downstairs, Tom and Justin waited. With Gwyltha. That was a surprise. Not five days ago, she'd told Dixie she seldom left the North. A miasma of worry hung over the room. A sea of spread newspapers covered the table and half the floor, and Tom and Justin looked as worn and hungover as a pair of fraternity brothers on Sunday morning.

Gwyltha looked up as Dixie entered, her eyes as hard as dark marble in her drawn, ancient face.

"You didn't tell her!" she said and then hissed, "Coward! You made her; you're responsible for her. You're no longer a rake-hell youth."

Justin intervened. "Let him be, Gwyltha. He . . ."

"I will tell her. And take care of her. Give her a chance to wake up," Christopher interrupted.

"Would someone please tell me what in the hell is going on?" That stopped the bickering. It could have been the "hell" or her stop-the-eighth-grade-dead tone but all four of them gaped. It takes something to awe four vampires at once. She doubted she'd get the opportunity very often.

"Sit down and I'll tell you."

She took the chair Christopher offered. He drew another close enough so that their knees touched. Across the table, Tom and Justin sat but didn't relax. Gwyltha held herself stiff as a standing stone on the moor. Even the moth outside the windowpane battered its wings in a cold panic.

"It's about Sebastian, isn't it?" She picked up that much from the walled minds around her. "What?"

Christopher took her hands, as if to reassure her, but his shook so much she clasped them to comfort him. "The papers," he nodded towards the scatter on the table. "We've been reading them all day. Following everything."

"And?"

"Caughleigh isn't going to trial."

"What!" After all their efforts, she didn't want to believe this. "They're letting him off?"

"No. He's been found unfit to plea. He's going to Broadmoor," Christopher said. "It's a prison for the criminally insane."

Sebastian belonged there all right. "He'll serve his sentence there then?" But how could he if he wasn't tried?

"He'll probably be there for life."

That suited her fine. Locked up he couldn't do any more harm. "That's taken care of then. So what's the problem?"

"The problem, my love, is you . . . we were too successful. He told *everything*."

"No wonder they called him insane." The goose bumps on her arms felt like pebbles. "There's more," she said after a long silence. There had to be. Otherwise they'd be celebrating Sebastian's incarceration with Tom's vintage port.

"The press took what they'd been told and ran with it. Bringham made the front page of all the world's papers today." She felt her eyes widen to popping point as she read the *Daily Mirror* that Christopher pushed onto her lap. She did remember to close her mouth.

She hadn't made the front page. Sebastian filled that with the headline "Manson of the Manor House: Stockbroker Belt Svengali." But they'd blown up her awful passport photo to fill a double column with the caption, "Transatlantic Vampire or Innocent Victim?" Just above a photo of the shell of Dial Cottage ran the heading, "House of Horror."

Reading large print and short sentences didn't take long. They'd written to capture attention and succeeded. Sebastian was depicted as the crazed leader of a village cult. It seemed Ida, Emily, and—this surprised Dixie—Sally were accused as accessories, along with James and a couple of names that meant nothing to her. Between the deaths of her aunts, and Christopher and Vernon's killings—both established, despite one missing body—talk of a witches' coven and confusion about her own role in the whole fiasco, the press was having a field day. Even *The Times* talked of "Cult Murder and Ritual Slaying in the Home Counties."

And she'd worried about Christopher being implicated in

Vernon's death! What if she got recognized and reporters started trying to take photos and got prints of no one? She couldn't risk that. She daren't show her nose outside the door.

"I'm not sure 'successful' is the right word," she said. Her voice faded. "What's going to happen?" A fierce desperation strangled her spirits as she clenched Christopher's hands, seeking the support she'd offered him minutes earlier.

"It'll be alright, Dixie. Trust me. We'll be together."

How could they not? He'd given her back her life.

"This has happened before," Justin said. "Don't worry, my dear, Tom had a similar problem back in 1820. We all do from time to time. Things get too public, mortals pry and suspect too much. Christopher planned a long rest when they suspected him of Vernon's murder. We disappear until they forget us."

"What do you mean?" She was afraid she already knew.

"Justin's suggesting you take a long rest, several years, until everyone connected with this is too old or too dead to care. I'll rest with you, so you won't wake alone." Christopher's strong hands smoothed hers as he spoke, as if trying to calm her rising panic.

It didn't work. "You're telling me I need to sleep for forty, fifty years and then wake to a changed, different world."

"We'll see those changes anyway."

"Yes, but a year at a time seems less of a shock."

Tom leaned across the table. "This way you'll be safe. When you wake, we'll all still be around. I slept through most of the Industrial Revolution."

"There has to be another way. A better way." She walked across the room and through Tom's study to stare out across the night garden. How things had changed since she'd first come here, driving through the night with a fading vampire she'd scarcely believed in. She hadn't expected anything like that when she'd left Charleston for a—that was it!

She fairly raced back into the dining room, bursting through the doorway so they all stared. Tom and Justin stood slowly.

Christopher moved to her side. "Dixie," he started.

She didn't wait for him to finish. "Listen. We can't stay awake here in England in this year, right? Justin's suggesting we stay in England and wait for another era. Why not stay in this time but go to another place? We could go home. My home. The U.S. We can fly under our own steam. I've got money, so have you. Let Justin take care of all that." She paused, willing Christopher to agree. They could make a good life in Charleston. And the thought of running into a certain lawyer with Christopher at her side caused most uncharitable and satisfying thoughts.

"Will you come with me?" she asked. "To South Carolina, the land of yellow jasmine, palmetto trees and grits?"

"I'll go with you anywhere, Dixie, but . . ."

"But what?" She'd come up with the best solution so far.

"The climate. The sun," Tom spoke quietly. "You'll be trapped indoors for most of the next few years. Even in winter the sunlight could be fatal that far south."

"Well, let's go to Seattle then. I've heard the sun never shines up there."

"Not Seattle. Nowhere in Washington State!" Justin frowned.

"We could arrange . . ." Gwyltha began.

"Never!" Justin's interruption shocked Dixie.

Justin and Gwyltha's eyes met, like granite and obsidian.

"What am I missing?" Dixie demanded.

Justin raised both hands in the air. "I'll ask no favors of Vlad. Not for any of my making."

Tom answered Dixie's unspoken question. "Vlad Tepes has a large colony in the Midwest that spreads out to the coast. We try to avoid each other's territory."

Dixie's mind boggled. "You mean there are vampires all

over the States?" Living in South Carolina *had* kept her out of the swing. That amused them all enough to ease their tension. It only increased Dixie's.

Christopher tightened his hold on her hand. "Thousands maybe. Many left Europe during the eighteenth and nineteenth centuries."

American History 101 missed that little snippet. "Any space left for us? Out of the other forty-nine is there anywhere that doesn't belong to Vlad?"

"We'll find you somewhere—if Christopher's in agreement to leaving the country." Everyone looked at Gwyltha. It never occurred to Dixie to doubt her. Gwyltha carried a couple of thousand years' authority.

"I'll go with Dixie. Anywhere," Christopher replied.

"There is that house in Columbus, that Dylan had to abandon last year. It's still empty. You could go there. Ohio doesn't have too much sun," Justin said.

"Ohio?" Dixie asked. No LePage had ever lived above the Mason-Dixon line. But no LePage had ever become a vampire. At least as far as she knew. . . .

"What about leaving your native soil, Kit?" asked Tom.

"He can wear platform shoes and sleep on plastic bags. I do now."

Gwyltha chuckled. "I warned you women have changed." She turned from Tom to Christopher. "It's quite a proposition. What do you think?"

"I think Walter Raleigh is looking down and laughing. He always told me I should see the New World."

As his arms wrapped around her, Dixie felt herself in a haze of happiness. She didn't give a hoot for audience or company. She wanted him to kiss her to oblivion and he obliged.

Try these other great titles in Rosemary's vampire series!

LOVE ME FOREVER

Does This Come In My Size?

Justin Corvus. That was the name of the gorgeous, dark-eyed charmer holding her hand in a sensual clasp, turning her knees into jelly. All struggling, single mother Stella Schwartz meant to do was let her son, Sam, browse through books at Dixie's Vampire Emporium. She hadn't counted on the shop assistant being a stylish super-hunk with the kind of Hugh Grant accent that makes a woman's thoughts wander through a neighborhood called Take Me Now, Please. And to top it off, the man's a sweetheart. The way he picked up on the fact that she didn't have two red cents for the Halloween costume Sam wanted but made it happen anyway? Total head-over-heels time. When Justin smiles at her, it's as if he's known her forever . . . and when he asks for her phone number—to let her know when the costume is ready, of course—Stella can't help wanting this feeling to go on forever. There's something very different about Justin Corvus . . . different and irresistible . . .

BE MINE FOREVER

Just For The Thrall Of It . . .

Six months ago Angela Ryan woke up from a mysterious attack with no memory, no ID, and no idea why what had once been girlish about her suddenly seemed . . . ghoulish. Being rescued by a clan of vampires is strange enough, but nothing compared to the fact that one of them is the kind of man she's always fantasized about. Tom Kyd has smoldering eyes, a sculpted body, and supernatural staying power. True, Tom is sure he knows best about everything, including how to figure out who she was before her life turned into an episode of *Dark Shadows*. But when his kisses are so dark, so sinful, and so damn good, Angela is tempted to say yes to whatever he wants . . .

KEEP ME FOREVER

Some Guys Are Real Animals . . .

Antonia Stonewright isn't about to change her views on love. A sexy mortal companion is fine every now and then, but a soul mate? A partner for life? Please. She was burned once, and hundreds of years haven't healed the wounds. But reclusive potter Michael Langton is . . . different. His gorgeous wares are perfect for her new art gallery—and his gorgeous body is perfect for her. She can't get enough of his toned muscles or his amazing, dark eyes. Their nights together make them both purr with pleasure—except in Michael's case, purring comes naturally. So much for finding a regular boyfriend. Antonia has a truly sexy beast on her hands . . .

MIDNIGHT LOVER

There Are Beings Worse Than Vampires . . .

Vampire Toby Wise knows there is a spy in his organization.
He thinks Laura Fox, the beautiful nurse who looks after the
invalid founder of Connor Corp., is one. But Laura is no
mere spy—she's a reporter out for a hot story. So when Toby
receives a call for aid from a witch, Toby reluctantly in-
volves Laura. There are sinister goings-on in Dark Falls,
Oregon. A bloodthirsty beast of the night has been plaguing
the town. As Toby struggles with his feelings for the irresistible
Laura, she struggles to accept the alluring yet perilous world
of the vampires. And as their attraction grows, so does the
danger. For the prey they are hunting will prove to be a more
deadly predator than either can imagine . . .

And if you're in the mood for a romantic snack,
try one of Rosemary's novellas
in these great Brava anthologies!

TEXAS BAD BOYS

These bad boys can deliver passion and pleasure with their boots on—and they're more than happy to let a woman mess with Texas . . .

"In Bad with Someone" by Rosemary Laurey

Rod Carter was supposed to end up running the Ragged Rooster. Instead, Old Man Maddox gave the bar to his grand-daughter, some prissy Brit art gallery owner right off the boat from London. Miss Juliet Ffrench—yeah, two "f's"—knows jack-all about beer, winning friends, and running tabs, but she's got a killer smile. All the lady needs is some-one to give her an education in Texas hospitality, up close and personal . . .

"Run of Bad Luck" by Karen Kelley

Nina Harris loves photographing naked, sexy men. But when she inherits her grandfather's ranch in Texas, and meets fore-man Lance Colby, she thinks she may have met her match. Lance is pretty sure real cowboys don't drop trou for national magazines. Still, as a Texas gentleman, he'd be more than happy to give Nina a private showing . . .

"Come to a Bad End" by Dianne Castell

Silver Gulch Sheriff John Snow thinks women have their place—in his kitchen or his bed. He would certainly never go for some women's libber businesswoman like Lillie June. The men in town want him to close down her fancy new spa, and he's happy to oblige. But once he meets Lillie, soothing massages, personal pampering, and one-on-one body wraps don't seem like such a bad thing at all . . .

THE MORGUE THE MERRIER

Take one town devoted to Christmas. Add a mysterious morgue-turned-hotel, a wonderland snowstorm, star-crossed lovers, determined spirits, and three of today's hottest romance authors, and you've got a sizzling treasury of hot and haunted Christmas tales . . .

In Christmastown it's always a special time of year. Just ask Annette. While visiting for the holidays, she discovers her Big Mistake from high school is in town and hotter than ever. A few Christmas spirits later, she finds out what she's been missing all these years. Or Sydney, the songwriter on sabbatical—until a ghostly Elvis impersonator gives her a hunk, a hunk of Christmas cheer. And is it the weather or a meddling ghost that forces Holly's ex-husband to land his plane right down in the middle of a steamy, delicious reunion?

Romantic, sexy, funny, and spirited, time to unwrap your gifts from . . .

Rosemary Laurey
Karen Kelley
Dianne Castell

. . . includes special holiday bonus story!

GREAT BOOKS, GREAT SAVINGS!

When You Visit Our Website:
www.kensingtonbooks.com

You Can Save Money Off The Retail Price
Of Any Book You Purchase!

- **All Your Favorite Kensington Authors**
- **New Releases & Timeless Classics**
- **Overnight Shipping Available**
- **eBooks Available For Many Titles**
- **All Major Credit Cards Accepted**

Visit Us Today To Start Saving!
www.kensingtonbooks.com